TORQUERE

MW01712166

Achilles' Other Heel by Tulsa Brown • Bareback by Chris Owen
Blasphemy edited by M. Rode • Broken Sword by Emily Veinglory
Bus Stories and Other Tales by Sean Michael
Caged by Sean Michael • Catching a Second Wind by Sean Michael
The Center of Earth and Sky by Sean Michael
Chance Encounters edited by M. Rode
Cowboy Up edited by Rob Knight • Date Night by Kathleen Dale
Don't Ask, Don't Tell by Sean Michael
Dust and Violets by Mike Shade
Farr Anderson Lane by Kathleen Dale
Fine as Frog Hair by Sean Michael
Fresh Starts edited by Rob Knight • Gemini by Chris Owen
A Gentleman of Substance by Julia Talbot
Gods and Monsters by Sean Michael
The Happy Campers by Gale Chester Whittington
Honor Bound by Wheeler Scott • In the Strangest Places by Willa Okati
Jumping Into Things by Julia Talbot • Lassoed by BA Tortuga
Latigo by BA Tortuga • The Long Road Home by BA Tortuga Manners and Means by Julia Talbot • Monsters edited by Rob Knight Mysterious Ways by Julia Talbot • Myths edited by Rob Knight Naughty edited by M. Rode • Need by Sean Michael
Night's Kiss by Catherine Lundoff
One Degree of Separation by Fiona Glass
Out of the Closet by Sean Michael
The Peacock and the Firebird by Julia Talbot • Perfect by Julia Talbot
Playing with Fire by Sean Michael • Post Obsession by Julia Talbot
Rain and Whiskey by BA Tortuga • Second Sight by Sean Michael
Shifting and Shifting Too edited by Rob Knight
The Sound of Your Voice by David Sullivan
The Stallion and the Rabbit by Mike Shade
Stress Relief by BA Tortuga • Tempering by Sean Michael
Three Day Passes by Sean Michael • Tripwire by Sean Michael Wheel of Fortune by Julia Talbot
Where Flows the Water by Sean Michael
Winning Hand by Sean Michael

Tempering

Sean Michael

Torquere Press

This is a work of fiction. Names, characters, places, and incidents either are the product of the author's imagination or are used fictitiously. Any resemblance to actual events, locales, organizations, or persons, living or dead, is entirely coincidental and beyond the intent of either the author or the publisher.

TOP SHELF
An imprint of Torquere Press Publishers
PO Box 4351
Grand Junction, Colorado 81502

Cover illustration by Jessamy Falcon
Published with permission
ISBN: 1-933389-42-7
www.torquerepress.com

First Torquere Press Printing: December 2005
Printed in the USA

Chapter One

Lance Corporal Richard Main.

The name on the envelope didn't seem like his, although Dick knew it was. He wasn't used to the new rank yet and nobody called him Richard these days. He was Dick at home and to his friends. Still, the Corps called him Lance Corporal Richard Main and so that's who the letter was addressed to. He opened the envelope, grinning. It was the results of his yearly health exam and he'd passed everything with flying colors. Not that he'd expected any different, but they had a little tradition going since that first time his blood tests had come back all clear and he wasn't going to miss out on it this year.

He figured he'd find Rock and Rig in the front room and sure enough, there they were, Rock watching the news, Rig trying to talk the big guy into playing instead, the blond head close to the dark one, Rig whispering into Rock's ear. Rock was playing stoic, probably waiting for Rig to get out the big guns and go for the blow job.

He watched for a minute, loving the way they played and teased and loved, the world of medicine and marines left outside the door where it belonged. In here they weren't Nurse Roberts or Gunney Sergeant South or Lance Corporal Main. In here they were Rig and Rock and Dick, where fucking was more important than fighting. Hell, in here fucking was more important than anything.

He cleared his throat as Rig started to nibble his way along Rock's neck. "I got my health exam results back."

Two pairs of warm eyes -- one clear blue, the other grey -- turned on him and he got two slow, wicked smiles.

"Yeah? Tell us, now. Are you a healthy little marine?" God,

Rig's drawl was pure sex, just heavy with want.

His cock started to fill and he handed the paper over to Rock. "I am."

The big guy took the paper and looked it over as carefully as he had that first time. "Yep. He is." Blue eyes twinkled up at him. "So what are you going to do with your condom fund?"

"Lube," he answered immediately. "Lots and lots of lube."

"Mmm... Good answer." Rig reached up and pulled him down, drawing him into a long, deep kiss that curled his toes. Their own personal Texan had a mouth that simply wouldn't quit, tongue fucking his lips, making promises he knew Rig would keep.

"What do you want to do first, kid?" Rock asked him, hands sliding up under his shirt to warm his skin.

He was slightly breathless by the time the kiss ended. "Um... everything?"

Rock chuckled. "Greedy."

"Uh-huh."

"Spoiled rotten." Rig started on his clothes, periodically stopping to lick at his lips.

He wouldn't deny it -- how could he? He had two of the hottest men in the world as his lovers. Instead he returned the favor, stripping off Rig's clothes. Once they were both naked, they turned to the big guy, tugging and tearing at Rock's clothes to get at that hard fucking body. It went pretty quick, his hands only got sidetracked by Rig's tight little cowboy butt once or twice or so. Then they were all rubbing together, hard muscles and hot skin and hotter cocks sliding over each other. Rock's big hands guided their movements, keeping them focused.

"Who's going to fuck my ass and who's going to fuck my mouth?" he asked, letting them know exactly what he wanted.

Rig took a hard kiss, hand wrapped around his prick and teasing. "I want your mouth."

He moaned, nodding.

"That leaves me with your ass, kid." Rock's voice was growly and thick. "You ready for a piece of the Rocketman?"

"Oh, yeah. I'm ready for both of you."

Rig shifted to one end of the sofa, settling him up on hands and knees, long hands sliding over his skin. He looked up into the soft grey eyes, smiling and eager, before turning to lick and suck at the tip of Rig's cock, taking his time. Rock's hands slid over his ass and then a thick, slick finger pushed at his entrance and he rocked back, groaning as he took it in.

"Mmm..." Rig's hands kept moving, kept stroking. "Such a sweet ass. Hot little mouth, too."

"Yeah, I think we'll keep him."

He grinned, moaned as Rock slid another finger into him and then jerked and gasped as it slid across his gland.

"Oh... He liked that. Do it again." Rig wiggled those lean hips, cock sliding and rubbing his tongue.

Rock did, fingers sliding over his gland again and again, making him shiver and moan and clamp his lips down hard on Rig's prick.

"Oh. Oh, Rock. Fuck." Rig arched, shifting and pushing into his mouth.

Rock chuckled. "No, that's Dick who's sucking you, Rig. I'm getting ready to fuck him."

"Uh-huh..." Rig bit into that full bottom lip, grey eyes rolling. Rock's fingers disappeared and blunt, hard heat pressed against his hole, making him whimper and suck harder, hands digging into the couch cushions. Solid and sure, Rock pushed into him. So fucking huge and hot and good. "Oh, sweet fuck. Feels good. Fuck him, Rock. Makes him... oh... makes him hungry."

He moaned and groaned, making noises around Rig's cock, working it hard as Rock started to thrust, to make him fly with that fat cock. Rig's hand landed on his head, palm burning against his scalp as his mouth was taken, Rig matching Rock's rhythm. He moved between them, rocking back and forth, caught between two hot, hard cocks. There was nothing on earth like it, nothing at all.

The pleasure rode him hard, making him arch, mouth and ass tightening.

His lovers leaned in, kissing each other, low sounds filling the air. The sound was wet and sexy and full of love and he lost it, crying out around Rig's prick as he came. Rig groaned, hand gripping his neck as that hard cock pushed deep, matching the desperation of Rock's motions. He sucked harder and licked the tip, ass working Rock's cock. Rig's cry came first, sharp and needy as come filled Dick's lips, their cowboy arching and flushed.

"That's it," muttered Rock, thrusting a few more times before filling him with heat. He swallowed Rig's come down, holding Rock tight inside him.

They all panted together, breath slowly easing into something normal. Then Rig slid out of his mouth, settling down beside him, hand petting. "Congrats, kid."

Rock sat at the other end of the couch, helping him lie down with his head in Rig's lap, his feet in Rock's.

"Thanks, Rig." He groaned suddenly and shifted.

"What?" asked Rock. "You can't be up again already."

"I'm in the fucking wet spot."

Rig chuckled and grabbed his T-shirt and shoved it under him. "Thank God for Scotchguard..."

***

Fuck, Rig was freezing.

Twenty goddamned, motherfucking degrees.

Twenty goddamned, motherfucking degrees and the fucking heater in his jeep was dead.

Twenty goddamned, motherfucking degrees and the fucking heater in his jeep was dead and it was fucking icing and why the fuck did he leave Texas again?

Rigger pulled into the driveway, shivers rocking him deep, looking at the Christmas lights still blinking through the window. He was going to have to take those things down eventually. He killed the engine, slip-sliding across the icy grass, heading for the door. He pushed inside, shuddering and waiting for the heat to hit him. "Hey. Home."

It smelled like a mix of Christmas and summer inside, cocoa butter battling with pine for dominance.

"Hey, Rig," Dick called out. Rock just grunted, the big marine's blue-blue eyes smiling up at him from the floor.

"H...hey." He moved to the thermostat, turning the heater up to eighty and standing in front of the vent, shivering as he slowly defrosted.

Rock and Dick were oiling their military issue leather gloves, which explained the cocoa butter. Both of them were at the stage where they were rubbing their gloves together, working the butter in, Dick's dark head making Rock's brown hair almost blond. Rock frowned at him and stood, coming slowly over. "You're cold."

"F...fucking freezing. Goddamned weather. Goddamned winter."

"Why didn't you turn on your car heater?" Dick asked.

Rock just kept on coming, wrapping him in strong arms. "Jesus, you're like a fucking ice cube."

"Oh, fuck. Good, Rock. Yeah." He pushed against Rock's heat, groaning. "Heater's broke and I haven't had the cash to fix it yet. Not with Christmas just gone by."

"You should have said something," Rock growled, gloved hands sliding up and down his arms.

"No big deal. It'll keep." He closed his eyes, burying his cold nose in his Rock's throat. One of Rock's hands slid up to the back of his head, holding him close, the other slid beneath his jacket and his T-shirt, rubbing small circles into the small of his back, the leather of Rock's gloves soft and slick against his skin. He was purring, nestling into Rock's body. So warm and right, the feel of the leather supple, the scent of cocoa butter reminding him of summers at Padre, soaking in the rays and avoiding jellyfish.

Dick chuckled. "You're looking warmer."

"Yeah." He wrapped his arms around Rock's waist. "Better."

Rock chuckled. "Some of you's warm."

He slid his cold fingers under Rock's sweatshirt. "Is it?"

Rock yelped. "Not your hands!"

Dick laughed and joined them, sliding gloved hands under Rig's T-shirt and stroking his belly. "Why don't we take him to bed and warm him up good and proper, Rock?"

"Like how the kid thinks, Rock."

"Yep. We've trained him right."

He finally lifted his face for a kiss, smiling as Rock's lips covered his, Dick's tongue joining in short order. Oh, yeah, better. Much better. Rock and Dick both pressed up close to him, Rock pulling off his jacket and letting it drop on the floor. They kept him warm, were starting to make him hot. He slid his hands up Rock's back, turning them, warming them back and front. Rock was chuckling into their kiss, hands tickling over his ribs in warning. He grinned, letting his warming, but still cold fingers, slide under Rock's fucking hot arms.

"Asshole." It was all the warning he got before Rock hefted him up, carrying him down the hall. "Come on, kid. We need to get this good ol' boy warm and then teach him not to mess with marines."

"Rock! Put me down!" He was holding on, laughing. The icy, evil weather was forgotten, only his very own marines on his mind.

"Hell, no. I can't think of a quicker way to get you in my bed."

Dick was following, laughing.

"Neanderthal." The insult was fond, warm, amused and happy. This was why he'd left Texas.

"Neanderwhat? Now you know it isn't fair when you start using those six syllable words around me."

Dick was bent almost double, looked like he was gonna bust a gut laughing at them.

Rig chuckled, wrapping his legs around Rock's waist. "How about caveman? Stud muffin? Hard ass sexy motherfucker? Those better?"

"Yep. I'm partial to that last one." Rock dumped him on the bed, coming down with him.

"Are you now... sweet cheeks?"

"Sweet cheeks!" Dick was leaning against the door now, wheezing.

"Sweet cheeks?" Rock was looking at him like he couldn't decide whether to kiss him into silence or beat it out of him.

"Sugar dumplin'?" God, he loved playing with these boys. Dick managed to fling himself onto the bed. The kid was going to seriously hurt something if he didn't take a breath soon. Rock just looked shocked. Rig leaned up and kissed Rock hard. "Sex on a fucking stick, hard-bodied stud who rocks my world and you know it."

"You better believe it." Rock kissed him back, stealing his breath, pushing him into the mattress. He moaned, happy and warm, pushing up against Rock, rubbing. "Besides," Rock murmured into his mouth, "there's only room for one sugar britches in this house."

"Mm... hey, gotta love the kid, don't we?"

"He meant you, asshole." Dick's gloved hand slid across his cheek in a soft leather and cocoa butter caress.

"Soft." Rig smiled, rubbing his cheek against Dick's hand. "Smells like summer."

"Yeah? You like that?" Dick's hand trailed down to stroke his neck.

"Yeah. Almost slick. Warm. Feels good." With every few words he shared another kiss with his Blue.

Rock chuckled. "Slut."

Blue shifted off him, just enough for him and Dick to work on getting him naked. With the gloves on, they were just the tiniest bit clumsy, not nearly as efficient as usual at getting him undressed.

"You, too." Rig tugged at Rock's sweatshirt, Dick's sweater, wanting skin. Rock and Dick reached for each other, laughing as their hands tangled, until they were finally naked from the waist up.

He leaned up, licking Rock's throat before turning to kiss Dick's shoulder. His hands pushed Rock's sweats down over the muscles of that sweet ass. Dick was making his happy fucking porno noises and Rock was rumbling the way he did when he was happy and they were helping him pull down their pants now and in no time there was a pile of naked flesh on the bed.

Well, nearly naked as Rock and Dick had both opted to keep their gloves on. "Y'all can't feel with those things on, can you?"

Rock shrugged. "You said it felt good."

Rock ran his hand from the middle of Rig's chest, down to his prick, leather sliding easily around his flesh.

"Oh..." His head fell back against the pillows. The dark leather was hot, butter-slick, looked fucking sexy and then to add Rock and Dick's strong hands... "Oh, Christ. That's nice."

Dick laughed and bent to kiss the tip of his cock, hands starting to move over him, random, sliding touches. Rock just kept on lazily pumping Rig's cock, free hand sliding along his thighs, cupping his balls. Rig spread his legs, humming softly. He was turned on, but in that relaxed, laid back, oh, fuck that's nice sort of way. The way that meant it was Friday and they had all fucking weekend to play and God, it was good and warm in bed with his men.

Bending, Dick started to suck on one of his nipples, gloved fingers tugging at the other one. Meanwhile, Rock was searching for his hole, taking his own sweet time doing it. He held Dick's head, stroking over the stubble, then down over the broad shoulders. "Oh, fuck. Y'all are something else."

"Nah, he's still the kid and I'm still your Rocketman. We're just wearing gloves so we aren't leaving grubby fingerprints on ya."

Rig chuckled, smiling up into those blue eyes. "Leaving no evidence?"

Rock grinned and winked. "I think we'll manage to leave a little bit of physical evidence."

"I'm fucking counting on it, Rocketman." His words ended on a moan as Dick's teeth closed on his flesh and nipped. "Oh, fuck..."

"That's the idea," Rock told him, sliding a leather-clad thumb into him.

He gasped, arching up into Dick's mouth before pressing down against Rock's hand.

Dick raised his head for a moment, grinning over at Rock. "Oh, he likes that."

Rock just nodded and pressed his other thumb in as well.

"Oh, yeah. Yeah. Just like that." He bent his knees, hips moving up and down on the hot leather inside him. "Good."

"Slut." Rock's voice was husky, turned on.

"Yes. You love it." He twisted, riding a bit faster, mellow heat turning into something needier.

"Fuck, yes." Rock stretched him with those thumbs, spreading him wide and teasing him with the heat of that fat prick. Dick kept working his titties, free hand sliding over his stomach and curls.

"Oh, fuck. More Rock. Want more." Even as he spoke he tugged Dick's hips over close enough so that he could wrap his lips around that long, sweet prick.

"Fuck!" The kid jerked, cock sliding in deep.

Rock spread him wider with his thumbs. "More of this, Rig?"

That heat teased at his hole again. He groaned, sucking hard at the flesh in his mouth, hips jerking and riding. His cock was throbbing hard, balls tight and hot. Rock kept teasing him, thumbs keeping him open, cock head there and then not.

The kid's hips started to move, pushing into his mouth with soft movements. Dick's groans vibrated against his nipple. Rig whimpered, moaning against Dick's cock. He was hot now, burning up, sweating slightly as Rock teased and pulled and stretched.

Dick gasped. "Oh, fuck, Rig!"

The kid came, hips jerking Dick's cock deep. He dropped one hand down to his cock, pumping hard as Dick's spunk filled his mouth. Fuck, he wanted to come. Wanted that pressure at his ass to go on for fucking ever.

Dick's mouth slid down his belly, taking the head of his cock in. A gloved hand pushed his own hand off his cock, the kid starting to suck and pump. Still Rock teased his hole, never giving him what he wanted.

"Oh, fuck. Please. More, Rock. Dick. Need more."

"Go on, kid, suck him right." Dick did, taking him in all the way and sucking hard, gloved hands playing with his balls and rubbing his stomach. Rock, that fucking asshole, kept teasing.

He groaned, pushing up hard, wanting to find a solid rhythm and fucking come, but that bastard he lived with wouldn't let him settle into one, kept him off-balance and needing. "Rock..."

Rock chuckled. "Sorry, let me..."

With that Rock's thumbs and his cock disappeared and the asshole shoved his fucking pinky in, fucking him fast with the small leather covered finger.

"Bastard." He focused on Dick's mouth, pushing his cock into that beautiful, talented, sweet-as-fuck mouth, with that wicked, playful, hot tongue.

Rock chuckled, still fucking him with that one finger. "I'm just waiting until it's less crowded down there."

"You're teasing. You know it." Dick swallowed around the tip of his cock and he groaned, shoulders rolling up. "Oh, fuck, kid. Yeah!"

"You don't seem to be complaining... much."

He would have made a smart-assed comment, but Dick swallowed again. The last thought that crossed his mind before he came was that the kid was getting the first blow job every fucking morning for a week.

Dick was still working his cock, pulling sweet aftershocks out of him, when Rock's thumbs came back, sliding into his hole and stretching him open for that fucking teasing cock again. Rig stretched, humming, relaxing into Rock's touch now that the edge was off, and enjoying it.

"You think you can take my cock and my thumbs, Rig?" Rock asked, pressing the head of his cock in a little harder now, the tease becoming more serious.

"Oh, fuck." He spread his legs with a moan, heat washing over him again. Maybe Rock'd get one blow job first... "Yeah, Rock. Yeah."

"Yeah, I think so, too." Rock pushed in, just enough that the head of his cock pushed past the top of his thumbs, then pulled back out again. Then he did it again.

"Oh..." He stretched out, arching his back as Rock played his ass. "Fuck, Rock. Hot."

"You're a fucking dream, Rig. I can do anything I want to your ass and you just beg for more." Rock pushed in a little further now, back and forth, getting him used to the burn and stretch of fingers and wide, thick cock.

"Everybody's got to have a... oh..." He lifted his knees, whimpering and pushing onto Rock, wanting more. "...a talent."

Rock gave him a little more, pushing in and out. His Rocketman was still teasing, but there was a promise to it now -- he was going to get fucked. Hard. Any minute now. He closed his eyes, going with the sensations, moaning low. He forced himself not to tense, to let Rock take them where they needed to go. Fuck, he was full, stretched. Hungry.

Dick was licking lazily at his belly, occasionally tonguing his slit. The kid's leather-clad hands were sliding over his skin in wide, random sweeps. It gave him another sensation to focus on, something else to feel alongside the maddeningly slow progress Rock was making. His toes curled and he reached down, petting Dick's head for a minute before reaching down to touch where Rock was holding him open, to touch the thick cock.

Rock groaned. "You are one sexy fucker, Rig."

"Mm..." He shivered, touching Rock as he slid in and out of his body. Oh, Rock didn't know what the fuck he was talking about. That fat cock fucking him, those blue eyes, the kid's tongue and sounds -- pure fucking sex.

Rock teased him a moment or two longer and then whispered, "Shit," and pushed into him all the way, those big thumbs still inside him, keeping him open.

"Rock! Fuck, yes! Yes!" He reached up, grabbed Rock's shoulders and held on tight, fucking flying.

Dick's hand wrapped around his cock, the leather warm, but not hot like a hand would be, and smoother than Dick's hand, too. The kid found Rock's rhythm easily, pulling in time with the long, hard thrusts. He just let them take him higher and higher, working his body between hand and cock, grunting and moaning with each motion. Oh, fuck, it was good. Better than anything, fucking these men, getting fucked by these men. Rock was grunting now, panting with effort, pushing hard and harder, nailing his prostate with every thrust.

"Gonna come, Rock. Shit." He groaned, eyes closing, grinding down onto Rock's hands and cock before pushing up into Dick's fingers.

"Yeah, do it, Rig. Come on my cock. Make me come."

Rig keened, slamming onto Rock again and again until he shot, come hitting his belly and chest, clenching so fucking tight around leather and skin.

"Fuck! Fuck! Fuck!" Rock shouted and came, filling him with pulse after pulse of hot spunk.

"Oh, shit, yeah. Yeah, Rock. Yeah." He shook, sinking back into the pillows again. Rock's thumbs slid out of his body, followed by the big cock and then his Blue collapsed onto him, Dick somehow managing to get out of the way just in time. He wrapped his arms around Rock, holding tight. "Good."

"Yep." Rock kissed his neck.

Dick cuddled up next to them and one of Rock's arms slid around him. He settled, warm and happy, too boneless to move and utterly fucked into goo.

"Warm enough, Rig?" Rock asked, gloved hand sliding lazily over his belly.

"Yeah. Never leaving this bed again. Happy right here."

Rock chuckled. "Dick -- go lock the front door and turn down the fucking heat."

Rig hummed low. "Not too low. Wouldn't want to get cold, you know."

"Oh, I don't know; it seemed to work out pretty good this time."

"Be good or I won't cook chili tomorrow." His threat was lazy; he was already half-napping and hoping someone would order pizza later for tonight.

"I better not turn it too low," Dick called back to Rock as he left the room. "Don't like pizza two nights in a row."

Rock just grunted, his breath slowing, growing loud and heavy.

"Good kid." Rig pulled the blanket over them both. Rock would kick it away in short order, but Dick'd be back by then and adding his heat to the mix, so it worked.

Rock was snoring before the kid slipped back into bed next to him. Dick chuckled. "He wore himself out, worrying about you."

"About me?" He blinked, hand immediately sliding over his Blue's skin.

"Yeah, kept muttering. Was worried you'd be cold." Dick curled in closer. "Guess he was right. But he knew how to warm you right back up."

"He always has." Rig leaned over and gave Dick a long, lazy kiss. "Y'all set me back to right."

Dick grinned sleepily. "We'll set you back to right again after a little nap, 'kay? Make you so hot you explode."

"Good plan." He slid his hand down Dick's arm, holding on and nuzzled into Blue's heat. So warm. So good.

Sometimes twenty fucking degrees wasn't so bad. It all depended on where you were sitting. Or lying. Whatever.

It wasn't Texas, but from his vantage point? It was home.

Chapter Two

"Thanks, Ranson."

Dick grinned at his friend and closed the truck door. He gave a wave as Ranson drove off, shouldered his pack and headed in. Almost midnight, but he had a three day pass ahead of him and he knew that both Rig and Rock had the time off as well. He'd been looking forward to this all week long.

He took the stairs two at a time and pushed open the door, laughing as the dogs almost brought him down. "Hey girl, hey Grimmy, you guys miss me?"

"Hey, kid! Rock, someone remembered the way home! Go figure!" Rig was cuddled up in the chair, reading some dime-store novel, while Rock was stretched out on the couch, wearing nothing but sweatpants.

Rock waved a lazy hand in his direction and grunted. Laughing Dick dropped a kiss on him, Rock's hand sliding around his neck and holding him in place, deepening the kiss when he would have ended it. It was nice to be missed.

Rig chuckled, grey eyes watching lazily, finger still holding his place in the novel. "When you come up for breath, kid, there's a plate of fried chicken and potatoes in the fridge for your sweet, sexy ass."

He wriggled said ass in Rig's general direction, making a soft noise as Rock's tongue went deep.

"Mm... what a show." The book hit the coffee table about ten seconds before Rig's hands slid over his ass, squeezing.

Rock let him up for air and he gasped, pushing his ass back into Rig's hands. "Fuck, I've missed you guys."

Then Rock was kissing him again, making sure knew the feeling was most definitely mutual. One of Rig's hands slid between his legs, cupping his balls, warming them through. The other pushed up his BDU jacket, his T-shirt, exposing skin for the touch of those hot, open lips. A shudder went through him and he pushed a keening noise into Rock's mouth, legs spreading wide. Fuck, it had been almost a week. Too fucking long.

Rig's fingers started moving, rolling his nuts, teeth just scraping over his lower back, making him fly. One of Rock's hands found their way up the front of his T-shirt, tugging at his nipples. Shit, they were going to make him cream in his pants.

"Fuck, you're hot. You been missing us, kid?" The words were chuckled against his back, tongue hot and wet.

He made another noise and then another, body twisting, trying to arch into each touch at the same time. Rig pushed his clothes higher, short nails teasing his skin. His balls ached, his skin rippled, he whimpered. Rock tugged, Rig touched and licked, he whimpered. Then he was coming, making noises that Rock's mouth just swallowed up, shaking with pleasure.

"Mm... welcome home, Dick." Rig kissed and licked his back until the shudders stopped, then backed away. "We missed you, too."

Rock's mouth let his go, the big hand behind his neck sliding away as Rock grinned up at him. "Ditto."

He dropped a last soft kiss onto Rock's mouth and then straightened and turned, knowing he wouldn't really feel home until he got a kiss from Rig as well. Rig pushed into his arms, humming happily. Those lips were open and hungry, needing him. Wanting him. He made a small noise, sharing control of the kiss with Rig, tongues sliding together in an intimate dance.

Rig was dressed in a heavy sweater, sweatpants, cuddling into his arms with a moan. Oh, it would be a snuggling night, he could tell. He tugged gently on Rig's lower lip as the kiss ended.

"I've got to go shower, got a bit of a mess inside my pants." He grinned and took another quick, hard kiss. "Anyone want to join me?"

"Hot shower?" Rig's eyes twinkled, fingers tickling up his belly.

He laughed, diving back for another kiss. "I've had enough cold ones this week to last me a month of Sundays, so unless you tell me you and Rock just used up all the hot..."

"Nope. Been waiting on you. The old man keeps it fucking bitter in here and I avoid getting wet and freezing to death." The good old boy moved like a shot, avoiding Rock's hands like a master.

He laughed as Rock's swat landed on his own ass.

Damn, it was good to be home.

***

Rig stretched out along the sofa, some old movie just barely up loud enough to hear on the television. Dick had come home worn down to the bone, and Rig had shuffled him through the shower and into the bed to let the kid sleep. Rock had come home in the same condition about four hours before Dick had, so Rig had spent the day puttering and relaxing and napping and being quiet.

Now dinner was in the oven, the house was quiet and he was... well, pretty fucking bored, but not bored enough to bother his marines.

A half-asleep rumble came from the doorway and he looked over to find Rock standing there naked, hand rubbing over his stubbled head. "What time is it?"

"Mm... almost eight. I didn't figure y'all'd wake up 'til midnight at least." He shifted over, offering Blue some space. "How you feeling?"

"Like I got run over by a semi. Which is actually an improvement." Rock slid in behind him, one arm coming around to pull him tight against that hard body. "Feels like morning," murmured Rock, rubbing heat against his ass.

Rig chuckled, leaning back against Rock's strength. "Does it? You trying to get me to make a pot of coffee, Blue?"

He grinned up into those blue eyes, knowing full fucking well what Rock was trying to get -- hell, what Rock was fixing to get. Didn't hurt to play a little first. Rock chuckled down at him, the sound half growl. "I don't want any coffee, Rig."

"No?" He turned, kissing Rock's jaw. "Toast?"

"Is that what you're calling it now?"

Rig laughed and took a kiss, fingers sliding down Rock's side to circle the fat prick beginning to stiffen for him. "Does it matter what the fuck I call it, so long as we do it?"

"Nope." Rock's mouth covered his, giving him a long, slow kiss that made his toes curl. "You call it anything you want."

"Fucking good." He nipped Rock's bottom lip, sliding down to lick and nuzzle the hard muscles of Rock's belly, chin brushing the tip of that hard cock. His Blue rumbled for him, muscles rippling beneath his lips.

Rig drew circles around Rock's hips, humming as his lips wrapped around the flared head, tongue teasing the slit. Oh, yeah. Fucking sweet. Didn't matter how often, how familiar -- his Blue was... He just made things right.

The rumbles got louder, one big hand landing on his head, fingers sliding through his hair, palm cupping his head, just touching, deepening the connection. Slow and easy, Rig nestled against Rock's legs, mouth sliding down to wet the shaft. He pulled with no hurry -- they had nowhere to go, no reason to rush. He cupped Rock's heavy, hot balls in his palm. No reason to rush at all.

Rock shifted a little bit, widening his legs, giving Rig better access. "Sweet, Rig. Fucking sweet."

He nodded, cheek brushing against Rock's skin. His tongue slid along the thick veins just under the silken skin, tracing them one after another. Shudders went through Rock's body, his Blue's hips starting to move restlessly. He let his finger slide into his lips alongside Rock's prick, then let it slide out. He reached back, gently pressing inside Rock's body as he swallowed the hard flesh down.

Rock made a noise -- not a whimper, not a choke, but a sound that meant oh, fucking shit that's good. Rig hummed, head bobbing as he searched for Rock's gland, wanting to make his Blue feel fucking good. Rock started to move, pushing into his mouth and then back onto his finger. The hand on his head held him in place.

Rig relaxed, opened wide and let Rock take what he needed, gave him all he asked for. Another of those deep, pleased noises rumbled through Rock's chest and the movements grew longer, sliding more of that thick cock into his mouth. He shifted so he could take it all, swallow his Blue down to the root, nose buried in Rock's groin.

"Fuck, yes, that's it, Rig."

He groaned, pulling harder now, pushing deeper. Loved hearing Rock, feeling that amazing body beneath him when Rock **wanted**.

"Fuck, yes." The words repeated, groans of hunger, his Blue rocking back and forth, breath slowly becoming labored. He added another finger, stretching Rock's hole, and starting fucking that sweet slit with his tongue every time his Blue's cock pulled back. "Holy fuck!"

Rock started making noises. Hungry, needy noises that went straight to Rig's cock as the big body pushed harder, faster, deeper. He started rocking against Rock's leg, groaning around Rock's prick, fingers curling to rub that flat gland. His eyes were closed, his entire focus on his Blue.

"Fucking good," muttered Rock. "Fucking perfect."

Rock shoved hard into his mouth, shooting down his throat. He swallowed, fucking taking it all, drinking his Blue down. Rock held him with his nose buried in the dark curls until the shudders stopped and then he was released with a soft groan.

He relaxed, lips still sucking, being so careful, tongue sliding over the softening shaft. Rock's hands slid over his face, his head, his shoulders, stroking slowly. "Mm... Rig."

He let Rock slide free, nuzzling the warm skin. "Blue. Fucking good."

"Yeah." Rock tugged, pulling him up along the hard muscles and taking his mouth. He groaned, body moving into Rock's, groaning as his sweats got in the way of their skin. Rock's hands were there, sliding them down off his hips. "Slow down, Rig -- we've got all night."

"Easy for you to say. You already got to come," he teased, and grinned, then slowed down, undulating against the strong heat.

Rock chuckled, hands sliding down to cup his ass, guiding his movements. "You'll notice though, that your sexy-as-fuck ass has me up again."

He took one kiss, then another. "You like this skinny Texan ass, do you?"

He rocked up into Rock's touch.

"I surely do. Almost as much as I like this fine Texan mouth."

"Good." Rig snuggled close and settled in for another long, hot kiss, pulling the quilt over the top of them, warming up his back.

"Things not hot enough here for you, Rig? Or have you gone soft, used to being sandwiched?"

Rig arched an eyebrow and grinned. "Look, Yankee, it's your job to keep me warm. Quit bitching and start with the heating."

"Oh, is that how it is?" Without warning, Rock rolled him

onto his back, that hard body pressing him into the couch as Rock's mouth closed over his.

His laughter faded into a moan, his head swimming as Rock kissed him like... Like... Oh, fuck, what did it matter, it was his Blue. Rig melted, lips parting wide. Rock drove their hips together, that thick prick sliding from his balls to his belly, so fucking hot, so fucking hard.

"Thought... thought we had... Oh, shit, Rock, you're so fucking good!" He arched up with a groan, moving with Rock easily. "Thought we had all night."

"So you'll get me up again and I'll take it slow." One of those big hands slid between their bodies to play with his nipple, Rock's knowing look full of lust.

"Blue..." He groaned, leaning up to nip Rock's bottom lip, entire body shuddering. "'s got to be cheating."

"Like you using that mouth for anything, including breathing, isn't cheating?" Rock didn't back off, not for a second.

Rig groaned, pushing up hard. "Gonna fuck me, Blue? After I come? Want your cock."

Rock growled. "Through the fucking floor."

"Good." He came, crying into Rock's mouth, hips jerking furiously. Rock shifted while he was still shaking from it, and slid into him, solid and so fucking hot.

"Oh, fuck, yes." He arched, purring and humming as Blue filled him. "God, that's it. Just what I needed."

"Yeah? Just like this?" Rock thrust, deep and even, dropping into that zone where he could fuck all goddamned night.

"Just... oh, yeah. Just like that." Rig wrapped his arms and legs around Rock, mouth fastening over the salt-warm skin.

Rock rumbled for him. "Nice, really nice."

"Mmhmm." He licked and sucked, nuzzling close. "Good, Blue."

Rock nodded and moved a little faster, pushing into his body at a steady, hard pace. Rig moved beneath Rock with the ease of years. They knew exactly when and where and how to make it last, to make it good and hot. And it was good and hot and it just went on and on and he was fucking floating on the high of it.

Finally Rock grunted. "Soon, Rabbit."

"Yeah, Blue." He lifted his face for a kiss, body tightening as his climax built in his spine. Rock's kiss was wet and hot and just taking his mouth. He let himself go, coming on his own belly with a cry. Rock made a noise and jerked into him a few times before filling him with heat and collapsing onto him.

He wrapped himself around Rock, hands stroking the heated curve of lower back and ass. Loved touching there. Rock purred for him, heavy and happy and right on top of him. He'd need the big guy to move soon enough, but for now, it was just perfect the way they were.

Dinner in the oven, Dick safe and sleeping, Blue sated and warm, everybody home and happy -- oh, yeah, perfect.

Chapter Three

It had been the longest three weeks of his life.

They'd been doing some training, practicing drawing blood, putting in IVs, haz-mat shit, when Reed had come in with a look of sheer fucking horror in his eyes and said the words none of them ever wanted to hear. "Colonel says this shit's been contaminated. Everybody get to the showers and report upstairs."

He'd been inoculated and tested for every fucking bug known to man. Kept in the hospital for five days. Told not to 'risk their partners' for at least six months.

Six months.

He'd moved into the guest bedroom when he'd made it home.

Then today, almost three weeks to the day, Reed had sent a message down. The contaminated shit had been found.

Untouched.

On the third floor in a storage facility.

He'd called Rock on the cell, left a message, and, as soon as his fucking shift was over, he was heading home to put his fucking pillow back on the goddamned bed where it belonged.

He pulled into the driveway and hit the door running. Only to be stopped in his tracks and slammed up against the wall, Rock's body solid as it followed. His Blue didn't say a word, just devoured his mouth like a man starving. He crawled up Rock's body, hips and tongue moving furiously, so fucking needy. His entire body felt like it was burning, like someone had dipped him in napalm, so fucking hot.

Rock was humping against him, driving him into the wall over and over again, rumbling sounds vibrating the wide chest, feeding into his mouth. Rig didn't fight it, just let Rock's body help him burn. He gripped Rock's shoulders, lips open wide enough to ache, taking all Rock could give.

Rock's hands tore open his shirt and then his pants, leaving the torn scrubs hanging from him. He tried to return the favor, sobbing his frustration into Rock's mouth as the fucking buttons wouldn't work. Rock growled and grabbed his ass, pulling him closer as his Blue carried him into the living room.

He was dumped on the couch, Rock waiting only long enough to pull off his clothes before covering his body again. Rig wrapped around that beautiful, hard, warm, amazing fucking body, groaning as their cocks slid together. "Blue..."

"You know how many times I've been this close to throwing you to the ground and fucking you through the floor?" Rock growled, mouth moving over his skin, teeth nipping at his neck.

"As many times as I wanted to bend over and ask for it?" He bucked up, rubbing hard, toes gripping the leather of the couch. "Couldn't risk my old man." Rock growled again, hips pushing down into him hard, mouth moving to grab one of his nipples and sucking hard. Rig shot with a scream, hips still moving even as he stopped spurting, cock still hard, needing. "More. Got weeks to make up for."

Rock bit his nipple lightly and then looked up at him, blue eyes hot, burning. "You think you're getting vertical again before dawn?"

"It's fucking Friday, Blue. Monday morning. Want to be bowlegged and broken and fucked dry by Monday morning." He smiled at Blue, took a long, almost gentle kiss. "Need your cock, need you."

Rock nodded, his smile slow and sexy. He could feel Rock sliding his hands under the cushions.

"Looking for this?" asked Dick, the kid leaning over Rock's back, waving the lube. "I take it the moratorium is over?"

"False alarm. All clean. Get naked." He reached up, cupped Dick's jaw, rubbing it in greeting.

Dick turned into his palm and kissed him, tongue sliding over his skin. Rock grabbed the lube with another growl and quickly pushed two slick fingers into him. Dick's eyes were dark as he shimmied out of his clothes, BDUs flying across the room with abandon.

He cried out, riding Rock's fingers, shoulders lifting off the sofa as he ground down, thighs parting. Dick's mouth closed over his, swallowing the end of his cry as Rock worked him open, stretched him with hard, sure movements. He moaned into Dick's lips, pushing their kiss hard while trying to tempt Rock into fucking him with that sweet fat cock. Dick's hands slid down over his body, fingers pressing hard into his skin. Shoulders, collarbones, pecs and then his nipples, all were touched, caressed.

Rock slid another finger into him, fucking him hard. Whimpering, he rode the sensations, asshole spread wide, nipples tight as little rocks. The fucking room was spinning, it felt so good.

Dick broke the kiss and popped Rock on the ass. "Hurry the fuck up or I'm going to slip in there ahead of you!"

Rig cackled, tweaking one of Dick's nipples. "Somehow think you'd lose that fight, kid."

Dick groaned, body jerking. "It's just been so long, Rig and he's taking his merry fucking time."

"Got all weekend, kid. And it's been three weeks, gotta make sure he's good and stretched."

"Oh. Right." Dick leaned over and kissed Rock.

Rig groaned, body tightening at the sight of his men. "So fucking good..."

They kissed a moment longer and then turned back to him, two sets of eyes hot and eager and hungry, promising him the weekend of his dreams.

He grinned, giddy and horny and completely at home in his own fucking skin for the first time in weeks. "C'mere marines. Remind me again why I left Texas."

"I thought you left Texas because the scenery here was better," teased Rock. His Blue's cock was hot and hard against his ass, teasing him there as well.

Dick chuckled. "I thought you left Texas because everyone there talked funny."

Rock's hard prick nudged a little harder, not quite penetrating him. "Nah, he left Texas because it was too hot there."

"Nope, it was because their marines are all straight."

Rock winked. "No, I think it was because of this," he said, pushing in.

"Mm... And they told me y'all marines were dumb as posts..." His tease was married to a groan, body arching as he took his Blue in deep.

"Just the ones in Texas," said Rock, voice a growl.

Dick was chuckling, moving to straddle him, blocking his

view of those blue eyes. "In me or me in your mouth?"

"Options, options, options..." Dick's laughter was bright as he tugged that long, thin cock up to his lips, words muffled as he wrapped his lips around the head. The kid's laughter faded into a groan, warm fingers sliding through his hair.

Meanwhile Rock was settling into that rhythm of his, the one that meant his Blue was there for the duration, stroking hard and deep. He fucked, was fucked, by both of his men, moaning as he thrust and shifted, body and lips tight as they worked two hot pricks. The air was full of their sounds, Dick's like a porno soundtrack, Rock's all grunts and growls and hot, needy groans.

God, he was a lucky man. He couldn't balance much, so he just held onto Dick, pulling the kid in deep and then deeper still.

"Oh, fuck, yeah." Dick's hands tightened in his hair and then slid around his scalp, holding him as the kid started fucking his face. Rock just kept plowing into him, steady and good. Rig just closed his eyes, let his body work for what it wanted, what it needed. What he needed.

They moved together like a well-oiled machine, taking and giving pleasure and it had been so fucking long and it was so fucking good.

His lips and ass tightened simultaneously, body shuddering as the pleasure grew sharp, harsh. Dick cried out, jerking and pushing deep, coming down his throat. He drank Dick down, throat working hard, welcoming the splash of heat and salt and *man* on his tongue.

Rock was still working him, thrusts growing harder and faster as Dick slid trembling fingers over his face. Groaning, Rig bucked, hips shifting to find the perfect angle, the right spot for that amazing fucking cock to...

"Oh, fuck! There, Rock! There!"

Dick moved, kneeling next to him to lick at his neck, at his nipples. "I think he wants you to hit that spot again, Rock."

Rock just grunted, nailing his gland over and over again.

"Can't... oh, fuck, Blue -- so sweet, missed your cock... can't get what you want, you don't... Oh... oh, shit. So good... if you don't ask, kid."

Dick chuckled, the sound hot against his nipple. "Harder, Rock -- he's almost coherent."

"Better than alm... oh..." He arched, arms stretching up above his head, electricity shooting through him. Rock didn't stop to banter with them, didn't stop to tease or anything, he just kept pushing, hard and fast and just where Rig needed him to be. Dick began to work his nipple, sucking and biting and just fucking cheating. He caught Rock's gaze with his own, losing himself in the incredible mixture of orgasm and Blue.

When things settled again, Rock was still gazing down at him, that fat prick still pounding into him, steady and true. He reached up, lifting himself, Rock moving until he was in Rock's arms, riding those thighs, able to take one amazing kiss after another. Rock purred into his mouth.

"Gonna stay right here all fucking night, Rig. Right here."

Dick knelt on the couch behind him, chest pressed up close along his back, arms reaching around him and Rock, holding them all tightly together.

"Yes. God, yes. Please." He smiled into those blue eyes, one hand reaching back to cup Dick's ass. "Was a false alarm. 'm okay."

"Might not be next time," murmured Dick. "Don't like that." He could hear a new understanding in the kid's voice, like suddenly Dick got why he was always so hot for them whenever they got back from maneuvers.

"Shh... just c'mere. Touch me." He took one kiss from Blue, another. One more. Dick's mouth was warm and wet on his neck, the kid's hands sliding over his body in random patterns.

Rock rumbled again, moving them together in their very own dance. He closed his eyes, rested his forehead against Rock's strength, breathed his Blue in.

He didn't know how long it went on for -- it didn't matter. All that mattered was that they were together, touching, fucking, loving.

He could do this all fucking night. With any luck they would.

All fucking night and for the rest of their lives.

Chapter Four

He was having a damned fine day. He'd mowed the lawn, trimmed the bushes, fixed the screen door in the back and hung up a hummingbird feeder one of the nieces had sent him. Then he'd pulled the kiddie pool out of the storage building, filled it up with water and soap and rounded up Grimmy and Lucy for their baths.

Now Rigger was up to his armpits in water and suds and wet barking dogs. Grimmy was just slightly less enthusiastic about playing in the water than Lucy was, but much more interested in knocking Rig over and getting him soaked, resulting in laughing curses and multiple violent threats involving skinning ungrateful mutts.

He was in the midst of scrubbing Lucy's back, stripped down to his soaked cut-offs, when Grim ran through the pool again, splashing water everywhere. "I'm going to have you stuffed and mounted, mutt!"

"God fucking damn it!"

He turned at the sound of Dick's voice, the kid glaring at Grim as the mutt finished shaking himself out and trotted off, tongue lolling happily. Dick was wet from head to toe.

"Sorry, kid. He's in rare form today. Pushed me in three times already." He grinned over at Dick, brushing the soapsuds off his nose. "I'm almost done with Lucy here. She's been almost an angel."

"You know I can wash my fucking dog myself. I am capable of at least that goddamned much." The kid was glaring at him, but it looked more like he wanted to cry.

Ah, shit. He hated when his boys were upset. Rig nodded. "Yeah, I know, man. I'd mowed the lawn and Grimmy went rolling and got himself filthy and you know how these hooligans are. Where one goes, the other follows."

He started rinsing Lucy off. "You look like you've had a shit day. Want a beer?"

"You think I can handle getting it out of the fridge without a fucking escort? Hell, are you sure I'm up to the goddamned decision making process? I mean, 'do I want a beer' -- it could be beyond my little private's brain's power to fucking come up with an answer for you."

"A really shit day, huh?" He nodded, glad as fuck he wasn't Rock right now. Even if Rock hadn't done whatever had pissed the kid off, Rock was an NCO and just as guilty by association. "Well, if you decide to get a cold one, I'd appreciate one myself. Hand me the hose? Your girl's just about dying to get to you and she'll be on you soon as I let go of her collar."

Dick glared for a moment longer and then trudged over to the hose, giving it to him. He gave Lucy a grudging pat on the head before heading back inside, screen door slamming behind him.

"Good lord, Lucy love. He's sure got a burr under his saddle, huh?" Rig sprayed her down, shaking his head and murmuring. "Tell you what. You stay out here and out of trouble and I'm going to go love on your daddy and make him smile so that he wants to come out with me and brush y'all later tonight."

She gave him a tongue bath and a couple of woofs in reply before shaking herself just like Grimmy had. He turned over the pool and headed in, reaching for a towel. "I tell you what, Dick. Those two are enough to drive a man crazy. Your Lucy's growing up good, though. She's a smart one alright."

Dick managed a small smile. "She's a sweetheart."

He was handed a beer, Dick putting his empty in the sink.

"Thanks. She is." He dried himself off and stripped off his shorts, tossing them in the washer as he wrapped himself in a towel. "You want to come take a quick shower? I'll scrub your back, make you forget your troubles?"

Dick looked at him for a long moment, pout firmly in place before it twisted into a sigh and a half smile. "Yeah. Best fucking offer I've had all day."

"Cool." He reached out and slid his arm around Dick's waist, offering Dick a kiss. "I like being your best offer."

Dick made a face. "Going by my day that probably wasn't quite the compliment you're taking it as. Meant it as one though. I mean -- ah fuck it." Dick's mouth closed over his, lips hard, tongue pushing into his mouth.

Oh, yeah. This he understood and could answer. Rig opened his lips, humming softly and letting Dick take what he needed. He ran his fingers over Dick's temples, body pressing close.

Dick's arms wrapped around him, pulling him close. "Can't decide if I want to fuck you through the wall, or get fucked by you..."

"Why choose?" Rig started pushing off Dick's damp clothes, mouth sliding over Dick's cheeks. "It's early still."

Dick moaned softly and started to help with the clothes before pulling off Rig's towel. "You first then. Where do you want it?"

"Here. Now." Rig took another deep, hungry kiss, groaning as their skin met, sliding and hot and right. "Fuck, you feel good."

"So do you," Dick said, soft, needy noises coming from him as he rubbed up against Rig.

Rig's fingers moved over the sweet spots at the small of Dick's back, playing and arousing. Whatever happened today, Dick would talk. Dick would need to, but later, after he was well-fucked and clean and relaxed and settled. Home. Dick would talk after Rigger made sure all his pieces were at home.

Dick turned him around and pushed him gently toward the table. "Need you now."

"Yes." He bent over the table, spreading his thighs for Dick, tilting his hips. "I'm all yours."

"Fucking shit!" Two of Dick's fingers slid into him, the kid obviously in a hurry but not willing to skip this step.

He pushed back hard, twice, and then lifted his head. "Your cock, Dick. Fuck me like you need to."

Dick gave him a warm look and made a soft sound and then that long cock was sliding into him, slow and sure, fingers finding a home on his hips.

"Oh, that's it." The burn was sweet, a distant second to the need to dissolve that terrible fucking tension and replace it with pleasure. A low groan came from Dick and another of those soft sounds. Dick started to fuck him, driving the long prick deep over and over. He pushed back, riding the waves of sweet fucking pleasure. Dick's cock could hit him so deep, pushing him farther and higher and making him shiver.

"Oh, fuck, Rig. So good." Dick shifted, finding his gland and nailing it with each new thrust.

"Oh! Shit, Dick! Right there! Oh, fuck. Right there. Right fucking there." He lifted up, grinding back onto Dick's cock, bodies rocking together. A half sob came from Dick, the kid pounding into him with hard, needy thrusts. Rig shuddered, ass clenching on the prick fucking him. He needed to pump his own cock, bring himself over the edge, but he couldn't let go of the fucking table. "Dick, fuck. Please. Touch me. Need you to."

One of Dick's hands let go of their death grip on his hips, circling his cock and pulling roughly. He wailed as hot fucking sparks shot up his spine and he came, convulsing on Dick's cock and spraying the table with his spunk.

"Oh, fuck, yeah. So fucking good." Dick waited until his body loosened and then started thrusting again, moaning and groaning and making such sweet noises. It wasn't long before the kid was crying out, shoving hard into him and filling him with hot come.

"Oh, yeah. Fucking good." They panted together, Dick's chest hot and damp against his back.

Dick dropped a soft kiss on the back of his neck, licking. "Taste good."

"Mm... Flatterer." He chuckled, rubbing against Dick, cheek resting on the electric bill.

Dick's hand began to slide along his cock again. "You ready to do me now, Rig? Want you to fuck me into oblivion."

"Give me a few minutes and a hot shower and I'll fuck you until you can't remember your own goddamned name, kid." Dick's thumb was working the tip, just the way he liked it, making him shiver and twitch. "Or you can keep that up and you're going to get it hard and fast here on the kitchen floor."

"How about both?" Dick asked, fingers still working him, mouth sliding along his spine.

"Because I'm getting old on you? Oh, fuck, that feels nice. Do it again." He bucked as Dick's thumb caught his slit just right. "Shit, Dick! You'd make a dead man hard."

"I'll take that as a yes," Dick chuckled, the sound vibrating against his spine as Dick's thumb slid over the tip of his cock again, slowly, pressing as he passed the slit.

"Sweet Jesus. Dick." Rig shuddered and stood, turning to take Dick's lips in a kiss, pushing hard and fast, backing Dick up against the wall. Dick hit with a thump, moan pushing into his mouth just like those hips pushed against his own. They rubbed together, hips moving faster and stronger, the need building again as their lips played and tongues tasted. He cupped the strong, hot ass, fingers sliding along the crack, promising and teasing all at once.

Strong hands slid around his head, cupping him, holding him, Dick's mouth needy and giving and right. Rig murmured happily into Dick's mouth, looking into those pretty riverstone eyes while their cocks rubbed together.

"So fucking good, Rig." Dick's lips wrapped around his bottom lip, tugging and sucking.

"Mm...yes. Yes." He grinned, the action moving his lip inside Dick's mouth, making them both chuckle. Dick's hands slid down to his back, pulling him even closer. The kid nipped his lip sharply and then soothed the hurt with the tip of his tongue. His upper lip was given the same treatment, Dick's tongue lingering this time.

Rig moaned, leg rubbing along Dick's thigh. He took a kiss, then another, then another, humming as his lips fastened around Dick's tongue and sucked. Dick made a noise that was quite possibly his name -- it was hard to tell, the lean body pushing up hard against him, hands pulling him tight, digging in, wanting him so bad.

"Here or in the bed?" He couldn't fuck Dick face-to-face against the wall and he hated to lose contact with that mouth, those eyes.

"Bed. Need it hard and deep."

"Yes." He stepped back, pulling Dick alongside him. Dick walked down the hall with him, hands and mouth busy, never losing contact.

They made it to the bed, Dick's body bouncing only twice before Rig was crawling over him, cock nudging that sweet, hungry hole. Dick grabbed his knees behind his legs and pulled them back, opening himself wide.

"Yes, fuck, yes." He licked his palm and slicked his cock, pushing in deep. "Tight. Dick. Fuck."

"Yes. Fuck me, Rig." The kid's eyes were huge -- all pupil, dark and full of pleasure.

"Yes." He grabbed Dick's shoulders and began to thrust, pushing hard and deep, fucking that fine ass as hard as he could. Dick started making noises immediately, groans and moans and gasps and whimpers and little sounds that had no name. "Love fucking you, Dick. Love your tight ass. Gonna make you come on my cock. Gonna make you fucking scream."

"Oh, fuck!" Dick made a noise that was halfway there to that scream, writhing, muscles working his cock.

"Yes. Come on, Dick. Want to feel you shoot. Want to feel your ass when I make you come." He leaned close, licking Dick's shoulder.

One of Dick's hands slid over Rig's belly and then down to wrap around his own cock, pumping.

He sobbed, pushing deep, losing his words as the fucking and the need and the heat took over, leaving only him and Dick, moving together. Dick got louder and louder, body growing tight and taut around his cock and finally the kid screamed, prick spurting.

"Fuck! Yes!" He came hard, toes curling as his hips thrust and his balls emptied themselves. Dick's legs slid slowly down, wrapping around the back of his thighs, arms holding him tight. The kid didn't say anything, just murmured and held him close. Rig snuggled down, holding Dick and touching him. This was his secret passion, holding and comforting and feeling skin on skin. Loving his men.

Dick nuzzled against his hair. "Thanks, Rig," the kid said softly.

"Anytime." He dropped a soft kiss on Dick's shoulder. "Anytime at all."

Dick laughed softly, hips pushing up against him gently. "Now?" the kid teased.

Rig stroked the soft tube of flesh still held in his hand, making Dick gasp. "After a nap, Dick."

"Gonna hold you to that," Dick murmured.

"You do that." He settled, wrapping himself around Dick's warmth. "You do that."

He would have asked after Rock, but the kid was relaxed. Easy. Happy. Dick's hand slid down over his back until it curled possessively over the top of his thigh. "You feel good, Rig. Make me feel good, too."

"That's what lovers do. 'S my job."

"Fucking good at it, too." Rock's voice came from the door and Dick stiffened for half a second and then relaxed again.

He looked over at his Blue with a warm smile. "Hey there, Rocketman."

Rock looked tired but good. And muddy. Really muddy. The kid was chuckling.

"Shut up." Rock mock glared at the kid and shook his head. "Fucking CO wouldn't give the kids' ideas a chance and we wind up to our armpits in fucking mud while they get an afternoon off."

"Ugh. Nasty. Bathroom. Shower. Now." He pointed toward the shower. "I'll scrub you down and then y'all can both come nap with me."

"Scrub and nap?" Rock pouted at him while Dick laughed softly.

"Oh, I forgot your blow job, didn't I?" He grinned at his Blue. God, he loved that old man. "I'll guarantee that thick cock one orgasm before your nap."

"Well, that's all right then," Rock told him, returning the grin.

Rock turned to Dick, trailing a finger down the kid's arm. "You okay?"

"Yep."

Rock nodded. "Good." Then those blue eyes were turned back on him. "Meet you in the shower, Rig."

"I'm on my way." He turned to give Dick another kiss. "You coming?"

The kid gave him a long lazy grin. "I just did -- twice." Dick shook his head. "Go blow his ... mind and then come back and snuggle -- I'm still holding you to more fucking after our nap!"

"You got it, Dick." He took one more kiss, making it a promise. "Let me go take care of my other favorite marine and then I'll expect you here waiting to keep me warm."

"Hoo-ya." Dick let a hand slide down his back, the kid blinking sleepily up at him.

He grinned and backed away, leaving one sated lover recovering from a bad day and heading to repeat the favor for the other. He'd had a fabulous day; it was only right to spread the wealth. After all, Momma always said you got what you gave.

Chapter Five

Rig chuckled as he flipped the channels, his head resting on the kid's lap, Rock reading some Hot Stud with Gun and Boobie Chick on the cover magazine in the armchair. Or trying to read, at any rate. Every now and again, when the flipping went too fast, those blue eyes would flash up and Rock would rumble a warning.

It was really pretty fucking fun, honestly, teasing the bear.

Flip.

Flipflip.

Pause.

Flipflip.

Flipflipflip.

He winked up at Dick, who was just grinning and shaking his head.

Flipflip.

Flip.

There was another growled warning and then Rock closed his magazine shut, flinging it on the coffee table. "Rig..."

He shifted, so he could move quickly, Dick's chuckle shaking his shoulder. "Yeah, Rock?"

Flip.

Flippityflip.

Fuck, Rock could move when he wanted to. And silent as shit for someone so big. Not that he really wanted to be anywhere but plastered beneath that big, fucking hot body. "Turn off the fucking television."

Click.

"I was watching that!"

Rock looked up at the kid. "No, you weren't. You were watching Rig's mouth."

"Yeah, well, you're ruining my view of that, too."

Rock just chuckled, hand sliding behind his head to knead at the kid's prick.

He chuckled, stretching out and rubbing against Rock's body, hips pushing their cocks up toward each other. "Y'all could argue over anything, I swear."

"This isn't arguing," Rock informed him.

"That's right," agreed Dick. "We're bonding." The kid groaned as Rock's hand continued to move. "Oh, yeah... bonding. Right there."

Rig arched an eyebrow. "Bonding. I see. Shall I turn on Oprah for you two sensitive guys? Maybe Dr. Phil?"

"You know what's scary?" Rock said conversationally, hand still moving, Dick making all sorts of pretty noises and wriggling beneath his hand. "That you can spout those names off the top of your head."

"Hell, Blue. I bet we even have the Soap Opera channel and Lifetime: Television for Women. Want me to see?" He could tease and taunt with the best of them and Rock wasn't a lightweight, poor Dick was still way out of his league with them.

"Yeah, you'd best check and we'll order it if we don't -- it'll give you something to do next time the kid and I are out on maneuvers."

"You mean when I'm not at work or fixing the transmission in your truck, Stud?"

"That was you? Thanks, man."

Dick groaned. "Shit, Rock, don't stop."

He grinned up into Rock's eyes. Fuck, this was fun. "Yeah, Blue. Cleaned your carburetor, too. Need to get new brake pads, though. Front left is squishy."

Rock shook his head and squeezed Dick hard. "No, Rig, squishy is definitely not what I'd call it."

"No? Is it sticking, then?"

Rock chuckled. "Not at the moment, though I'm sure that could be arranged."

He laughed, leaning up to take a hard, happy kiss. Oh, yeah. Loved this man. "I'm betting you'll find squeaking before you hit sticky, Rocketman."

"I'm counting on it."

He chuckled and winked, head nuzzling back against Rock's hand. "I'm laying on it."

Rock blinked down at him for a moment and then started to laugh.

"Shit, would the two of you just can the sweet talk already and get busy?"

That just made him laugh harder, holding onto Rock's shoulders, hilarity filling him top to bottom. With the two of them laughing, Dick had enough strength to roll them off and onto the ground, Rock's body cradling his. Then Dick was on top of him, trapped cock hard, pressing into his ass.

He pushed up against Dick with a moan. "Somebody's wanting something. Fuck, y'all do feel good."

"Kid's not the only one who wants something." Rock's hands were solid on his hips, pulling him down against a hard cock.

He bent his head, nibbling along Rock's throat, thighs parting so he could move between them both. "No, no he isn't."

Rock rumbled as he and Dick found a rhythm together. Rig just worked on opening Rock's shirt, licking and kissing skin as it was exposed.

"Now there's a plan. Being naked." Rock's words vibrated against him.

"I don't know, it means stopping."

He just let them talk. He was busy, tongue sliding over the fine skin, lips teasing hard little nipples. Rock moved beneath him, their cocks sliding together through too many layers. Purring, he tested Rock's skin with his teeth, tugging at nipples and skin. Rock growled, pushing harder against him.

Dick's hands slid between them, fingers playing over the buttons on their jeans. He sucked in his stomach, helping Dick out. Tiny marks were peppered over Rock's chest, little love bites and bruises. Dick pulled his jeans off first and then Rock's, letting their cocks slide, flesh on flesh. His Blue made a soft noise, not quite a whimper. "Fuck, yeah."

"You're welcome," replied Dick. The kid lay on him, naked and hard.

He rocked back into Dick's heat, down into Rock's strength. He parted his thighs, licking and sucking on Rock's lips. "Fucking *sweet*."

"We do what we can." Rock grinned up at him, blue eyes dark with need.

"Much obliged." He smiled back, taking another hard, hungry kiss after another.

Dick's fingers slid along his crack, slick and warm, teasing. He arched his hips, offering Dick more, open and hungry.

"Want something?" Dick asked, voice teasing.

"Always." He wiggled again, grinning against Rock's lips as their cocks rubbed together. Dick's fingers slid into his ass, two long, sweet fingers that crooked and nailed his gland, just like that.

"Fuck! Again!" He jerked, moaning long and loud. Dick did it again, and then again and again. Rock's hands tightened on his hips, pulling them together as Dick finger-fucked him. He was close, balls tight, cock leaking against Rock's belly, panting as he moved.

"Better make it quick, kid, if you want to ride his ass while he comes." Rock's hands were still hard on his hips, sliding their cocks together, making him so hot. Dick's fingers disappeared and then that long, sweet cock was there, pushing in, going deep. So fucking deep.

"Oh... Oh, fuck..." He groaned, fighting hard not to come, but it was a losing fucking battle, that long cock spearing him, Rock's beautiful fucking body so close. Dick didn't tease or take his time, just filled him and then started to fuck, quick hard thrusts that slid him along Rock's body.

"Yes. God, Dick..." he sobbed, jerking as his spunk sprayed over Rock's belly, ass clenched tight around that sweet cock.

"Yeah, Rig, yeah." Dick pounded into him and Rock pushed up against him. The kid's cry and Rock's growl came together, heat splashing in and against him.

He groaned, stretching out against Rock, loving the heat of Dick's weight above him. He lay sandwiched between them until Grim and Lucy came to check them out. Dick pushed the mutts away and a soft kiss was pressed to the back of his neck and then Dick was helping him and Rock up.

Rock groaned and glared at the two of them. "I'm getting too fucking old for this floor shit."

He grinned and leaned up to lick Rock's lips. "Come to bed and I'll rub your back for you, make you forget your troubles, old man."

"Best offer I've had all night."

"I don't know, Rock, he did offer to fix your brakes."

Rig chuckled, leaning back for Dick's kiss, smiling into riverstone eyes. "Be good, Dick, or you won't get your oil changed until hell freezes."

"Can't have that."

Rock laughed at the kid. "He really does hold all the trump cards, doesn't he?"

"Nah, just that one, but it's the granddaddy of all trump cards." Dick gave him a kiss, hand stroking over his belly. "Come on, before Rock starts complaining about getting too old to be doing this up against the wall, too."

Rock cuffed the kid on the head and Dick swatted Blue's ass, the two of them mock wrestling their way down the hall.

He followed behind with a grin, then ran to tackle them both as they turned toward the bedroom. Oh, yeah. Much more fun than flipping channels.

Chapter Six

Rig had redone the garage himself -- built shelves and a workbench, sawhorses and tables. It was **his** room, as much as Rock had the workout room and Dick had control of the front room with his movies and games. He'd built Grimmy's doghouse, fixed the dining room table, made toys and spice racks for Christmas and rebuilt carburetors. He spent at least one day a week in here.

Hell, the old green couch that used to be Rock's was sitting in one corner, in case his boys wanted to sit and visit.

He was building a little entertainment center for the bedroom. They'd moved the little television into the middle bedroom, but no one ever slept in there and Rig wanted to watch movies in bed every now and again. He'd moved the TV, but then all the fucking electronic paraphernalia had to come with it and it made a mess and that made both him and Rock irritable and, by God, they weren't doing irritable in bed. So he was building a little entertainment center.

He hammered and glued, humming along with the radio and sweating, the big fan drawing the cool air in. By the time the outer walls were clamped and steady, the dogs were aching to get in and play with him, his soda was getting warm, and it was looking like rain.

He was just deciding to pack up and head inside when Rock strolled out, shorts and wife beater wet with sweat, a beer in both hands. A soft kiss was dropped onto his neck as one of the beers was dropped onto the workbench beside him and then Rock sat down onto the couch with a groan.

"Well, aren't you a sight for sore eyes." He grinned and nodded at the beer. "Thanks. Hard workout?"

"Yeah -- they seem to be getting harder and harder."

Rig frowned. "You getting light-headed while you're pumping? Getting shaky?" He held up his hand before the growling could commence. "Don't. I won't lose you to stupidity, Blue. You're not twenty-five anymore."

"I'm fine."

Dick came bounding in, freshly showered, a can of Coke in his hand.

"Hey Rig." He was given another soft kiss and then the kid went and sat next to Rock. "Great workout, Rock -- thanks."

Oh. Right. A lesser man would have pushed -- hell, he would've pushed the point if he didn't know it'd send Blue into a growling, unapproachable funk for days. Not only that, but a few, in private, words with Dick would fix things. The kid wouldn't hurt Rock for the world. So he let it go, giving his boys a wide grin and showing off his woodwork. "What do you think? It's coming together right pretty, isn't it?"

"You or the thing you're making?" asked Dick with a wink.

"Nicer than anything we found in the stores," put in Rock.

"You were looking for men in the stores?" Dick asked, mock horrified.

He stuck his tongue out and rolled his eyes, pleased as punch. "Y'all are something else. If I recall correctly, the last man Rock found up on post."

Dick actually blushed a little, a look he hadn't seen in ages -- he'd forgotten how good it looked on the kid. Rock just laughed and took a long swig of his beer.

He chuckled. It was a damned good find, too. "I think I'm gonna shut the front door and open the back. That'll let the pups in." And keep prying eyes out so he could grab himself a few kisses.

He shut the big front door and slid the back open, just as it began to pour down rain.

"Good timing," grunted Rock. "Nothing worse than the smell of wet dog."

Dick chuckled, throwing his legs over Rock's and scooting close. The kid rested his chin on Rock's shoulder, watching Rig move around the room.

He found one bone each for the pups, Lucy immediately climbing up into the entertainment center, Grimmy pushing beneath Rock's feet. "I tell you what, those dogs sure aren't conflicted about where they belong."

Then he washed off a bit in the sink and went to get his kisses.

Rock was grumbling at the dig, making no effort to dislodge Grim. Dick was smiling up at him though. "Here he comes, Rock, and he's got that look. That I'm a man on a mission look."

"Yeah, that's me. I got my men, together, looking fine and I'm thinking, Rigger? What's missing from this pretty picture? Then it hits me. Tongue. There's not enough tongue." He bent forward, licking Dick's lips, then Rock's collarbone.

Dick chuckled, bending to lick at the shell of his ear. Rock just grunted, hand coming up to stroke through his hair. "You needing help with this tongue issue?"

"Mm... I'm looking for volunteers, yeah."

"A few good men?" Rock asked with a straight face. Dick's soft laugh chuffed air into his ear, making him squirm.

He grinned. "The few, the proud, the well-hung."

"I think I know of a couple of men who fit the bill."

"Oh, good. Somehow I think you'll fit more than the bill..." He chuckled, bringing Rock's lips against his own. Rock's lips opened slowly, tongue slipping out to stroke across the soft skin just inside his own mouth. The kid made a happy sound and slid his legs away, hands going around Rig's waist to tug him down onto them. He went willingly, happily, hands and knees and ass finding their places on hard muscles, holding onto that slow, sweet kiss with all he was worth.

Rock's tongue and lips were making a long, thorough meal of him, spiced with the kid, whose tongue was licking at their cheeks, their lips, not asking for more than a taste of his own, for now.

It was as close to heaven as any one good old boy could ask for -- his men, the smell of wood chips and rain mingling with sweat, all perfect and warm and his. Rig reached up and cupped the kid's jaw, moaned long and hungry into Blue's mouth. He got a happy fucking murmur from the kid, floodgates to those sweet sounds opening and letting them flow out of Dick in soft waves. Rock's hands settled on his hips, just holding him lightly. His Blue shifted, settling in for a good long make-out session.

The long kisses were flavored with beer and soda, sometimes breathless, sometimes shuddering, sometimes full of laughter. Rig ended up held between them, kissing and being kissed, nuzzling and admiring when he got to watch his men kiss each other. Neither Dick nor Rock tried to make it more than that, hands only touching, holding, but the kisses still built, passion growing in each press of lips, each swipe of tongue and each soft sound of pleasure.

His hand was tracing the muscles of Rock's belly, petting and feeling, making them jump -- especially when he dipped down below the hollowed navel. Eventually, Dick's sweet noises were joined by Rock's rumbles, the purring sound vibrating along his lips, against his hand. The next time Rock and Dick kissed, it seemed the easiest thing to lean down, pull the fabric away, kiss and lick those amazing abs, rub his chin against Rock's cock. The rumbles got louder, a hiccup in Dick's breath telling its own story -- Rock's hand planting firmly on the kid's ass.

Rig smiled, licking little patterns, his hand reaching to push Dick's shorts away, let Rock's hand have flesh. Rock's legs spread wide, hips pushing that thick bulge up against his chin. He hummed, leaning down to stroke his cheek against the sweet fucking shaft, rubbing through the cloth, teasing them. Rock's hand slid through his hair, not hurrying or pushing, just touching, fingertips soft and careful, mapping his skull and the way his hair curled just slightly over his ears.

He could hear their kiss going on, Dick's porno noises made soft, muted by Rock's mouth. Their lips came apart with a wet sound, tongues lapping, sucking noises going straight to his own cock.

The wind on his back was cool, but where he was touching his men was warm, good. He placed his lips over Rock's balls and blew, heating that soft skin with his mouth. Rock rewarded him with a groan, more felt than heard and Dick's hand fell to tangle in his hair too, one of the kid's legs coming up to rub against his back.

Oh, fuck, yeah. He moaned, repeating the action as his hands freed Blue's cock. God, he loved this -- surrounded by hard, happy, wanting men, lost in tastes and touches.

Dick moaned loudly and jerked against him, Rock's hand sliding into the kid's shorts and finding the long cock as he got Rock's prick free of his shorts. He rose up a little, licking at the tip of Rock's fat prick, letting Rock's salt and musk fill his mouth, then swallowing it down with a happy hum. Yeah. Loved this. Fucking loved it.

Rock's moan was echoed by Dick, the kid's hand sliding behind his head, almost guiding his movements. Out of the corner of his eye he could see Rock's hand working the kid. He reached out, finding Dick's thigh, moaning and sucking harder as that softer-than-fuck skin slid against his fingers. Dick's hand left his head, insinuating itself between him and Rock and finding one of his nipples through his shirt, stroking softly.

Oh... He shuddered and gave a long moan around Rock. So sweet. Oh, fuck. So fucking sweet.

Rock half-bucked up at his moan and then settled back again, hand sliding over his head in small circles. "Good, Rig. Fucking good."

He nodded, head bobbing over the hot skin, taking Rock deep, sucking hard and steady. Dick was moving, shifting and settling down on the floor. When the kid finally stopped moving, his head was pressed up close to Rig's, the kid's tongue licking at Rock's cock every time Rig pulled up. It made him shudder, the flavor of Dick on Rock's prick, made him pull Dick closer, rub up against that heat.

"You guys taste fucking amazing together," Dick whispered in his ear, hands working on his clothes, tongue still playing between his lips and Rock's cock.

Rock just murmured, "Oh fuck," and started moving his hips, slow pushes into his mouth.

His hands were reaching for Dick's cock, Dick's ass, while his tongue searched along Rock's shaft for Dick's. Dick's hand closed over his cock just as he found Dick's. The kid groaned and pushed into his touch, tongue sliding into his mouth along with Rock's cock. All of a sudden they were *hungry*, arching and moving and calling out. So fucking hot he was going to die and so fucking good he was in heaven already.

Dick curled up so that they could rub their cocks together, mouth still working on Rock along with his own. He was calling out around Rock's cock, eyes fastened on Dick, feeding on his pleasure. Rock started to push up faster, that hard cock getting harder. It wouldn't be long now. Dick felt it, too, the kid pulling on their cocks with stronger strokes, sliding his thumb across both slits.

He buried his nose in Rock's pubes as he shot over Dick's hand, entire body convulsing. Rock's spunk filled his mouth, Dick's cry pushing in with it. Rig swallowed hard and then let Rock's cock go, fastening his lips over Dick's, sharing and tasting and... yeah. Yeah, that was right. Dick's hands slid though his hair, holding him tight against the kid's mouth. The kiss was hot and sweet and right.

They managed to keep the kiss going as they settled back on the couch, snuggling around Rock, bringing him into the kiss. They filled him, his men, filled his mouth with the flavor of themselves and his life with love.

The kisses eased as they relaxed together, watching the rain. Eventually, Lucy hopped down and settled down next to Grimmy and went right back to sleep. Yep. Coming together just fine.

Chapter Seven

He buttoned up his fly, making sure his black shirt was smooth and settled. He fastened his belt, buckle shining almost as bright as his boots, and then settled his good hat on his head.

He was in a dancing mood.

The boys had spent the day lounging and he'd pottered about in the yard and the garage and the house and he finally just pottered out -- now he was showered, cologned, dressed and ready. His wallet in his pocket, keys in hand, Rigger headed out to the front room.

"I'm going out for a couple beers and a couple waltzes, Marines. You need anything while I'm out?"

Dick looked up from his game and whistled. "Wow, looking good, Rig."

Rock's paper rustled and one eyebrow went up. "We've got beer at home."

He grinned, spinning playfully for the kid's benefit, giving his ass a little wiggle. "Not bad for an old cowboy, huh?"

"Not bad at all." Dick had put his game pad down and he leered openly.

Rock's other eyebrow went up. "Bet you can pick up a couple of dances here, too, if you know what I mean."

"After I went and got all dressed up?" Rig leaned up against the wall, hip cocked, a slow heat building in his belly. "I put Stetson on and everything."

"It's like you're all wrapped up for us -- I'm really good at unwrapping things," Dick said, raising his hand as if volunteering.

Rock chuckled. "Ah, Stetson. That explains it."

He tilted his head. "Explains what?"

Rock glanced southward and then grinned over at him. "All the attention you're getting."

"Oh." Rig grinned, eyes following down Rock's body.

Fucking hot. Then he treated himself to a long look over Dick. Oh, yeah. Fucking hot. He widened his stance, stomach clenching under the starched cotton, cock beginning to fill, making tight jeans damned near unbearable.

Rock set his paper aside and spread his legs a little, setting his arms along the back of the couch. Those blue eyes were looking him up and down. Dick just looked from him to Rock and back again and then grinned and pulled off his T-shirt, hands dropping to the tie on his sweats.

"There's a honky-tonk out there waiting for me." He dropped his hand down, thumb caught in his waistband, fingers framing his cock. Fuck, he loved to dance -- whether it was two-stepping or the lead-in to a nice long, hard fuck with his marines.

"Kid," started Rock.

"Way ahead of you." Dick stepped out of his sweats and went over to the stereo, naked ass swaying with each step. The sound of country music filled the air and Rock spread his legs wider, pushing up his hips, the big bulge tenting his sweats.

"Mm..." God, he was fucking hopeless -- that thick cock and ripped belly calling to him. And then Dick's strong, muscled back, those heavy balls, long prick. "I do like this song."

He pulled off his hat and hung it on the coat rack.

"Oh, no, that won't do," said Rock.

Dick turned around and looked at him, grinning. "He's right, you know -- put the hat back on."

"Back on? Pervs." He winked and grinned, settling the Stetson back on and arching an eyebrow. "Better?"

His Blue looked him slowly up and down and then nodded. "Getting there."

Dick just walked up to him and started unbuttoning his shirt, fingers lingering on his skin. "Boots on or off?"

"Off," answered Rock. "And move over a bit so I can see what you're unwrapping."

He reached out, hands sliding down Dick's back, fingers playing lazily at a sensitive lower back. His lips trailed along Dick's jaw, sucking and tasting. "Hey, there."

Dick shivered for him, his long body just sort of rippling with it.

"Hey." The word was softly spoken and husky, the fingers on his belly stuttering with the next button.

Rig pushed into the touches, licking the corner of Dick's

mouth, hips moving with the music. "You feel good." He breathed in deep, shuddering just a little. "Smell good, too."

"Yeah, so do you." Dick was finished with the buttons of his shirt, the kid's hands trailing up over his chest to push the material off his shoulders.

Rock groaned. "Fuck, you two are hot."

The shirt stopped falling at his elbows, his hands too busy stroking Dick's ass to let go. He took soft, sucking little kisses, enjoying himself thoroughly. "You gonna dance with this old boy?"

"Uh-huh." Dick's hands slid over his ass and then around to the front of his jeans, rubbing his prick before working on his button and zipper.

Rock stayed where he was, shoving his sweats down and wrapping his cock in one hand. He pushed himself away from the wall, hips moving into Dick's fingers, tongue sliding into that sweet mouth as he watched his Blue work that sweet cock. Fuck, yeah. Dancing.

Dick's mouth opened wide, tongue sliding along his own, the kid whimpering. Rig groaned and tugged Dick closer, stomachs sliding together, his hands gripping Dick's ass as they swayed. Fuck, the kid could kiss, could make him fucking *melt.*

Dick finally got his pants open, fingers pushing the material down around his hips. Their cocks slid together, heat on heat. Whimpering, Rig rocked, tongue and hips moving in time with the waltz filling the room. So hot; Dick's cock was leaving wet trails over his belly, kissing his skin with heat.

Rock's groan made Dick jerk, Dick pressing him against the wall. He cried out into Dick's mouth, cock throbbing. They started rubbing together furiously, Rig pulling Dick closer and closer, the kiss wild and fierce now. Needy.

Dick grabbed his hips, pulling them tighter together. Rock groaned again. "Fuck yeah, up against the wall."

Rig tried to reach up, grab Dick's neck, but the shirt got stuck. He rumbled, giving the cloth a few hard tugs, crying out in triumph as the cloth split and he could touch his marine. "More. Want you."

"Fuck, yeah." Dick pushed his jeans down further and grabbed his ass.

Oh, yeah. Good. Fucking sweet. He rocked between hands and body, moaning as he watched the colors in those riverstone eyes. So fucking pretty. Dick's mouth made love to him, as did Rock's moans and groans, sweet and hot against his ears.

He just rode the sensations, letting the heat and music and pleasure grow until he couldn't separate them anymore, could just go with them. Go with his men. Go with them right where he fucking belonged.

Rig arched into Dick's heat and came, pulling on Dick's tongue, Dick's ass. Rock called out and the kid shuddered against him, spilling over his belly. Oh, man... The scent of spunk and sweat and cologne mingled, gave him goose bumps. "Better than a fucking honky-tonk any day."

"Bring him over here, kid. He said he wanted 'a couple' of dances."

Dick chuckled and kissed him hard, hands on his ass gathering him close. He laughed, following eagerly. "I'm up for dancing all night, Rocketman."

"I know. That's what we love about you, Rig."

His fond chuckles were captured in Dick's lips as they stumbled across the front room floor. One of Rock's hands slid around his waist and pulled him in, the kid right there along with him. Rock was naked and hard and warm. He lifted his face for his Blue's kiss. "Hey."

Rock chuckled, tongue sliding teasingly across Dick's lips first and then his. "Hey there, cowboy."

"Mm... You looking for a dance partner or two, Marine?"

"Or two."

His lips were twice taken, Dick and Rock sealing them all together. He opened to the kiss, hat finally falling to the floor, hands finding two strong, muscled necks. Oh, yes. It was good to be him.

Chapter Eight

Ringing woke him.

Dick aimed a fist at the alarm clock, but it kept ringing at regular intervals. It finally occurred to him it was the phone and he struggled up, reaching over Rock to grab it. "Wha?"

"Rock?" It was a woman, a crying woman. "Rock? Are you there?"

Shit. "Jus' minute." He shook Rock. "Wake up." Rock rolled and growled at him, even baring his teeth. "Some chick asking for you."

"Chick?"

"She's crying."

Rock was still half-asleep, but Dick was getting more awake by the second. He could still hear the woman crying. He pushed the phone at Rock. Rock grunted into the phone.

He looked around for the clock. Where the fuck was Rigger?

Dick had never seen Rock turn grey before, but he'd seen him bark orders and he'd seen that blank-faced focus in the field. "What happened? How bad? Where? Stop fucking crying, Julie and tell me where." Rock threw the phone on the bed and headed for the closet. "Put some fucking clothes on. We gotta go."

He was halfway dressed, obeying Rock implicitly, before he even thought to ask. "What's wrong?"

"Rig's been hurt. He's in the ER on his way to surgery." Rock threw on a T-shirt and grabbed his boots. "Move it, corporal! I'm not waiting for you."

"Shit!" He grabbed a T-shirt for himself and slid his feet into his tennies, grabbed his wallet and ran after Rock.

He must have opened his mouth a hundred times on the trip to the hospital, wanting to know what happened, wanting Rock to tell him everything was going to be okay, but then he'd get a look at Rock's tight, closed face and he'd look back at the road. The trip to the hospital took a half-hour on a good day. They made it in just under fifteen minutes. He didn't even want to think about how fast Rock had been going.

Julie and Alison were pacing outside the emergency room door, smoking and crying. Dick stopped short as they walked up to the girls. Their jeans were covered in blood and both girls were wearing hospital scrubtops. Then Julie looked up, blond hair flying everywhere. "Rock! Oh, fuck! I'm so sorry!"

"Where is he?" growled Rock, looking like he was going to pound someone into the cement.

Dick bit his lip, wishing to hell that he'd asked Rock what had happened.

Alison grabbed Rock's arm. "He went into surgery ten minutes ago. He... he lost consciousness in the ambulance and was still out when he went in. They said it'd be a couple hours."

"What the fuck happened?" Dick's voice wavered but he didn't care. He was scared now. All that blood and talk of surgery and unconsciousness and he was fucking scared.

"We were at the Tejano, having a couple, you know?" Alison shook her head. "Julie and I were giving Rig shit, playing around. He went off to the bathroom and didn't come back. The bartender went in and found him."

"You're nurses -- give us the straight shit." Rock was still growling, still looking like he wanted to hit someone and not looking too picky about who it was gonna be.

"So far? His left femur is broken in three places. His right wrist's cracked. His stomach and kidneys have been beaten and his testicles took a blow or two." Julie took a deep breath. "They're patching up his lung. He took two hits with a knife and lost a lot of blood."

Julie looked like she was about to start crying again. Dick thought he was going to be sick and Rock was looking grey.

"Who?" Rock asked. He grabbed Julie by the front of her scrubs and picked her up, shaking her. "Who did this to him?"

"He said a bunch of jarheads jumped him. Overheard us teasing him about getting more cock than we did." Julie gasped and shrugged. "We didn't see them."

"Jarheads? Marines did this to him?" Dick didn't understand, didn't want to understand, but Rock seemed to know what was going on, putting two and two together fast as anything.

He still hadn't put Julie down and his voice was menacing. "Who?"

Alison grabbed Rock's arm. She was a fucking Amazon, almost as big as Rig. "Put her down, goddamnit, before the fucking cops come out here! He didn't say who it was and we didn't see them, okay? We don't know!"

Rock put Julie down slowly, glaring at the two girls. "When can I see him?"

"When he's out of surgery. He's got you listed as his next of kin in his wallet." Alison held out a plastic sack. "Here's his wallet, his phone, his ring and watch."

Rock just stared at the bag like he didn't know what it was, so Dick took it from her. "Thanks."

"He's going to be fine, Rock. The doctors said he was strong." Tears started flowing down Julie's cheeks. "I'm sorry, Rock, Dick. I am."

Rock was still just standing there, pale and not entirely steady, not saying a word.

"Thanks," Dick said again. He grabbed Rock's arm and led the big guy through the doors and into the waiting room. The smell of the place hit him and he felt his stomach roll. Suddenly it seemed more real. He pushed the bag into Rock's hands. "I'm gonna go find some coffee. You want one?"

"Yeah. Better call Rig's momma." Rock sighed. "Need to find a fucking doctor and find out where the fuck our Rig is."

"Rig's cell phone's in the bag." He knew he was chickening out, making Rock make the call, but he didn't think he could tell her what Alison had told them. "You want me to stay while you talk to her?"

"No. Find coffee and somebody who knows something. I'll call her." Rock's voice was flat, hard, cold.

He nodded, backing away, telling himself he wasn't abandoning Rock. He just... he couldn't tell Rig's Momma, he couldn't. Shit, he could hardly believe it himself. He wandered through the halls, finally coming across the little alley with gift shops and coffee shops. Most of them were closed this time of night, but the Starbucks was open, hawking their coffee 24/7.

He picked up two larges and headed back to emergency. He'd get rid of the coffees and then find someone to tell them what the fuck was going on. That's what he wanted to know. What the fuck kind of world was it where a man like Rigger...

He turned into the emergency waiting room, searching for Rock.

Rock was pacing the waiting room, still on the phone. "Yeah, Momma. Yeah, you know I'll take care of him. Either me or Dick will pick you up at the airport. Bye." Rock turned off the phone and sighed, shoulders slumping. "Fuck."

Fuck, he wanted to wrap himself around Rock so fucking badly.

"How'd she take it?" he asked, handing over the coffee instead.

"She's flying in tomorrow. She's pissed as hell and these fucking doctors better have him stable before she gets here." Rock reached for the coffee, gulping half of it down without a thought. "We need to find out what's-"

"Is there a James South here?" A fat older man in scrubs looked in, clipboard in his hand. "Mr. South?"

"Shit, Rock, that's you."

Rock gave him a look and stepped up to the man. Dick hovered. "I'm James South. You gonna tell me about Alex Roberts?"

"Yes. I'm Dr. O'Brien. Mr. Roberts is out of surgery and in recovery. I'm sure you've got some questions. Shall we sit?" The man's attitude, professional and quick, made Dick feel better, feel like someone was in charge.

Rock was back to looking intimidating, but he let the doctor lead them back to the chairs.

"When can I see him?" were the first words out of Rock's mouth once they were all settled.

"You can see him now, but only for a minute and he's still really groggy." The doctor held his hand out. "Hold on. Let's talk. He's pretty banged up and he'll go into surgery tomorrow or the next day to fix his leg. We're hoping the internal swelling -- kidneys, testicles -- will ease up on its own."

"Shit." Dick didn't realize he'd said the word out loud until two sets of eyes turned to him. He felt his face color and ducked his head. "Sounds pretty bad."

"Yeah, Doc -- kid's right it does. Just how bad is it?"

The doctor sighed. "He's going to be in a lot of pain. He'll have some fairly extensive recovery time and has some serious contusions, but, if the swelling goes down and infection doesn't settle in? He'll be fine. It will just take time."

"So his chances of that happening are what? Fifty/fifty? Better, worse?"

"Better. He's young, healthy. No reason to expect the worst."

"When can he come home?" Rock was firing questions as quickly as the doctor could answer them.

"Could be a week, could be longer."

"You got anything else you need to tell me before I go see him?"

The doctor stood. "He's been badly beaten. His nose is broken. One ear was badly cut. His face and eyes are swollen. His lung collapsed and has been reinflated. He's not fully conscious and he's hurting badly. One arm is casted and so is one leg. He looks like hell, frankly."

"The cops been in to see him yet?"

"He's not been conscious. They're waiting for him to come out of recovery."

Rock nodded and stood. "I want to see him now."

Dick stood, too. "Can I come? Please?"

The doctor shook his head. "I'm sorry. Mr. South is the next of kin. Mr. Roberts will be in a room within the next few hours and you can see him then."

Dick bit his lip and nodded sitting back down carefully. "Tell him I asked after him, Rock."

Rock nodded. "I want to see him now."

The doctor led Rock out of the waiting room and down the hall. Dick watched them go. Fuck, it was real now. Too fucking real. He was supposed to be at home. Curled up in bed with two of the best men he'd ever known. Instead he was in the fucking hospital, waiting to see if Rigger would live.

It sucked and it wasn't fair.

***

Rock stood in front of the door to the recovery room and took a deep breath. It wasn't that he'd never seen friends hurt before. Being a marine was a dangerous business. He'd seen friends dead and friends dying and blood and guts and...

This was different.

This was Rigger.

He pushed the door open. There was a soft light on in the corner, shining on a lone figure in a bed. Before he could head toward it, a nurse stopped him. "You're-"

"I'm James South; Mr. Roberts has me listed as his next of

kin." He needed to see Rig now; he wasn't going to let anyone stop him from crossing to that bed.

"Five minutes, Mr. South. And then you'll have to wait until they move him to his own room."

He nodded and pushed past her. His steps didn't slow at all and in no time he was right beside Rigger's bed. Rig looked... fuck, he didn't even look like Rigger with his eyes swollen shut and bandages and tubes everywhere. Even the long fingers poking from inside the cast were bruised.

"Rig. Rigger." He repeated it a couple of times, but Rig was out. Jaw clenched, he looked at the wall on the other side of the bed. The light threw strange shaped shadows on it, his own like a hulking monster, ready to pounce.

Reaching out, he let his little finger touch Rigger's. Rig's finger was cool to the touch, but slowly warmed beneath his. He would have stood there all night if they'd have let him. Just stood there and listened to the soft sounds of Rigger breathing, watching the monster that was his shadow lurking at Rigger's bedside.

Rig's finger moved, squeezing his just slightly. "Blue? Hurts."

"Rig? Yeah, I'll bet it does -- you got beat up real bad." He turned his hand, curling his fingers around the tips of Rigger's, looking down at the swollen face.

"Yeah. Wanna g'home, now." One eye was open just enough that Rock could see a flash of grey.

"Yeah, Rig. We want you home." He tried for a smile, but couldn't quite bring himself to lie to Rig. 'Cause that's what he'd be doing. "Doc says it'll be a week if you heal up right."

"Work Monday. Can't stay." Rig shifted and moaned, the sound no more than a whisper. The swollen eye closed, but Rig's finger still held his.

"When you can sign the fucking AMA forms, you can go home, Rig." Fuck, but he wanted to grab Rigger up in his arms and just bring him home. Where he and Dick could hold him and protect him and touch him as much as they needed to.

"Girls okay?"

Fucking shit. "The girls are fucking fine, Rig. You're the one that got bashed."

"'kay." Rig squeezed his fingers. "Good."

Fuck. He took a deep breath and forced himself to calm

down. He squeezed Rig's fingers back, wanting to say something, anything, but everything was caught at the back of his throat.

The nurse held up one finger and he nodded, starting to pull his fingers out of Rig's grip. When he moved, that one grey eye cracked open again and Rig shook his head. "Stay, Blue. Please."

"Sh..." He looked back at the nurse and then leaned down to whisper in Rigger's ear. "If it was you on duty, what would I need to do to get around the five minute rule?"

"You? Be good 'n quiet 'n take me t' dinner." Rig's voice was fading, breaths coming slower as he drifted in and out. "Need t' call Momma 'n Daddy to feed Grimmy and the fish."

It fucking broke his heart. "I took care of it, Roberts. You just get well, okay?"

"'kay, Blue." The fucking beeping and whooshing and dripping was driving him out of his fucking mind. He didn't know how Rig listened to it every fucking day.

The nurse gave him a look and he squeezed Rigger's fingers and put on his best smile as he went over to her.

"Look, there's no one else here. What would you say if I asked to stay awhile longer? I'll just pull up a chair and sit quietly with my friend -- he's awake and a little freaked out to be here all by himself, you know?" He gave her a subtle up and down, like he was thinking of picking her up and let his smile grow. "I'd owe you one."

She looked at him suspiciously for a second and then sighed. "Look, I'm going to give him some more morphine in five so we can move him. It'll knock him out. You can stay until he's asleep -- if no one else shows, okay?"

"Thank you. Thanks a lot." He gave her a nod and hightailed it back to Rigger's bed, hoping he hadn't insulted her with his quick getaway, but he thought he'd heard Rig moaning. He snagged a chair and sat on it, leaning his chin against the rail as his fingers slid over Rig's again. "'S just me."

Rig squeezed his hand, soft pained sounds coming every few breaths. "'s it bad?"

"Yeah. It's bad." He squeezed Rig's hand back. "You could have been killed."

"Too mean t'die." Rig held on tight, slow tears leaking from his closed eye. "Shoulda stayed home."

He reached up and stroked Rigger's head, careful not to jar

him. "Come on, Rigger, you know it wasn't your fault."

"Blue..." The sound was broken, lost. He'd heard Rig call him like that once before, when Rig's dad had died and Rig had just paced and smoked for days until one night he finally came to bed and let Rock touch him. That had been easier than this.

"I'm here, Rabbit. I've got you now."

"'kay." Rig seemed to relax, the tears drying as those bruised fingers held onto Rock.

"There you go." He kept stroking Rigger's head, holding his hand, refusing to fucking cry.

Rig squeezed his hand and he frowned, eyes fighting to focus. "My ring? Blue? Tell me they didn't get my ring."

"You mean this one?" Rock asked, bringing his right hand up where Rigger could see it. He had Rig's ring on it, on his little finger, a plain silver band with a garnet in a simple setting.

"Oh. Oh, good. 's *mine*; you gave it to me." Rig looked at his swollen, twisted right hand. "Save it for me, Blue."

He nodded. "Yep, don't worry about it, Rig. I've got it. You get better and I'll put it back on."

"'kay." Rig blinked, giving a little whimper. "Hurts, Blue. Please."

"Sh. I know. I know." He felt so fucking helpless and he just wanted to hit something so bad, but that wasn't going to stop Rigger from hurting.

The nurse came over and checked Rig. There was a tube coming out of his chest, attached to some machine, another coming out of Rig's dick and... Fucking shit, there wasn't so much as a square inch of unbruised skin from bottom rib to thigh. Rig's nuts were huge and already purpling.

"He's looking really stable. The lung's draining well. Kidneys have some blood in them, but not much." The nurse nodded, satisfied. "Gonna give him some pain meds. He's going to float right away."

"You gonna be on for the rest of the night?"

"'til seven a.m., but he'll get new nurses upstairs and you'll have a more comfortable chair." She injected something into Rig's IV and smoothed a patch onto his chest. "He'll sleep soon."

Rock nodded, holding tight to Rigger's fingers. "You hear that, Rigger? She gave you the good stuff."

"Yeah. Hear you." Rigger was watching him with that one swollen eye. "Take me home soon?"

"Soon as I can, Rabbit. Soon as I can."

"Promise?"

"I do."

"'kay." Rigger's eye watched him for another minute or two, the battered body sinking into the bed as it relaxed. Finally the swollen eyelid closed. Through it all, Rigger held his hand.

Rock dropped his head, eyes closing. Fuck, he wanted this gone. It wasn't right. It shouldn't have happened. Not to his Rig.

He didn't know how long he sat there before a soft hand touched his shoulder. "We're going to move him now and we need your signature on a few things up front. Once he's settled, you'll be able to sit with him again."

"Thanks." He cleared his throat and tried again. "Thanks." He gave Rigger's hand one last squeeze and got up, putting his chair back against the wall. "Are they... uh... gonna let his other friends come and see him? And his Momma's flying up tomorrow -- she's not gonna take no for an answer."

"Should be two at a time round the clock and anybody at visiting hours, so long as they let him rest." She smiled at him, beginning to unhook wires from machines. "He'll be fine. Don't worry."

He nodded and took another look at Rigger, wondering how he was supposed to not worry.

A glance at his watch told him he'd been in with Rig for nearly an hour. The kid was going to be pissing bricks. He took one last look and headed off to find Dick and deal with the paperwork.

Chapter Nine

Fuck, he hurt. He'd floated for a long time and then the pain started and the fucking cops with their fucking questions and now he just hurt. The orthopedic surgeon had come in an hour ago and set his surgery up for Tuesday. The internist said the chest tube should be out by then, catheter out by Thursday. God willing he'd be home and in his own fucking bed by Friday afternoon.

Fuck, he hurt.

His fingers ached. It was fucking cold in here. He hadn't noticed before because the boys had held his hands all night. Dick on one side, Blue on the other. They hadn't left until the cops came.

As if thinking about him had made him come, there was his Blue. He looked upset. No, he looked fucking pissed.

"Hey." He would have arched an eyebrow, except his fucking nose was broken and he was too fucking sore to move.

Rock's face softened. A little. "Hey, Rig. How're you feeling?" Rock's fingers slid across the top of his.

"Mm... like that." Talking was getting easier as his lung drained, although he was pretty sure he wasn't going to be singing karaoke anytime soon. "Feel like hammered shit. Hospitals are for sick people."

Rock nodded. "You are hammered shit. Pretty fucking hammered." The pissed-as-hell frown was back.

"Yeah." He closed his eyes for a second and then took the bull by the horns. Rock wasn't gonna get any less pissed just standing there. "You got a burr under your saddle, Blue?"

"Yeah, I do." Rock grumbled and glared at him hard and then crossed his arms. "Talked to the cops."

"You catch 'em on their way out?" He didn't want to talk about this now. He hurt, damn it, and he didn't want any shit from Rock about this. He knew better than to not pay attention, not keep his eyes open. He knew better and now he was paying for it and he'd be damned if Rock or Dick paid, too.

"Yes, I fucking did. Goddamn it to fucking hell, Rig -- they say you can't give them a description of the guys who did this. They say you can't even fucking confirm whether or not it was marines like the girls said it was."

"Sorry." Fuck, but he didn't want to lie -- not to Blue.

"Sorry? You're fucking sorry? Alison told me you said they were jarheads. Shit, Rig -- they were in your fucking face for how long, beating the shit out of you and you can't remember a single thing about them? What the fuck are you doing?" Rock was half-pacing now, hands clenched into fists at his sides.

"Saving our asses, Rock. Let it go." He didn't want to do this now.

"What the fuck are you talking about?" Rock was back and he looked hurt and confused and so fucking angry. "These guys nearly killed you and you're going to let them get away with it?"

"Let it go." He closed his eyes, hating the tears that he knew were going to come. Fucking drugs.

He heard the scrape of the chair being dragged closer to the bed and then Rock's hand was stroking over the tops of his fingers, so fucking gently. "I can't just let it go, Rig. These guys nearly killed you. I-" Rock took a long, deep breath. "If you won't tell the cops, then tell me. I won't say anything to anybody, I promise."

"And have you get your ass arrested?" He forced himself to focus on Rock, blinking back the tears. "Listen to me, Blue. People aren't stupid. It gets around that you're bunking with the gay nurse and you can kiss your fucking retirement goodbye. You got what? Three years left? Just three. And the kid? He's just starting. He gets drummed out on a dishonorable and his life'll never be the same." Rig shook his head. "Won't do that to you. Won't do it to *us*."

"So we just let them get away with it -- tell them fuck yeah you can beat the shit out of a gay man any time you want?" Rock got up and picked up his chair, throwing it across the room. "Well, I don't think I can fucking *do* that."

"You want the cops back in here?" He was going to be sick, or would, if there was anything his stomach. He couldn't do this. Couldn't.

This whole thing was a fucking nightmare. From the first

blow that smashed his face against the bathroom mirror to the laughing and spitting and fists to the too fucking long ambulance ride -- it didn't seem real.

Felt pretty fucking real.

Rock's muscles worked beneath the tight fabric of his T-shirt, clenching and unclenching and then his Blue made a broken, hurt sound that was trying to be a sob, but wasn't. When Rock turned back, his face was drawn, eyes hooded. His Blue looking fucking old. Without saying a word Rock picked up the broken chair and set it outside the door and then moved to sit in the chair on the other side of the bed.

He should have stayed home last night. He should have stayed in the house and safe and quiet and...

"Jesus Christ, Baby Boy! What the hell happened to you?" His momma's voice poured over him, warm and familiar and right.

"Momma?"

"Yeah, Baby." Warm, soft fingers grabbed his and the round, sweet, wrinkled face of his momma peered at him. "Momma's here."

Rock got up out of the chair. "Here, Momma, you sit here. Dick'll rustle us up another chair."

As his Momma was moving around the bed, Dick came over and slid warm fingers gently over his own, sad blue eyes looking down at him.

"Hey." He squeezed Dick's fingers as tight as the cast would allow. He wanted to be home, in bed, where Dick could hold his hand and Rock's strength could be beside him. He wanted that more than anything.

"What happened to this chair?" The voice belonged to a nurse, who had the seat in her hand, holding it out accusingly.

"It broke," Rock told her.

Momma stood up and held out her hand. "Charlene Roberts. Nice to meet you... Linda. I'm sure we'll be seeing a lot of each other the next few days. We're gonna need two more chairs and I want to speak to his doctors."

Rigger grinned up at Dick, who looked a little stunned. Go Momma.

"You can have a couple more chairs from the waiting room down the hall, but until regular visiting hours I'm going to have to ask you to keep it to just two visitors at a time, please."

Dick squeezed his hand again and gave him a small smile. "I'll go get the chairs."

Rig held on. "Stay."

He heard Momma's snort. "Bullshit. We'll keep it close to two, but sometimes it'll be three. We'll stay out of the way and we'll let him sleep, but family needs family. Richard, dear, go get the chairs and dig in my purse for some change and get us all a Coke, please?"

"Yes, ma'a-- I mean Momma." Dick squeezed his hand again, and the smile he got was a little more genuine before Dick started rummaging through the purse he seemed to have forgotten he was carrying.

"He's such a good boy."

Rigger chuckled and relaxed back against the mattress as Momma started giving the nurse the third degree. It was a familiar, comforting sound and he sort of floated away, dreaming about Daddy and Bobby getting dressed down for leaving live catfish in the washtub.

Momma was still giving the nurse heck when Dick's hand returned, warm and good in his own. He looked over at Rock, at the furious lines of his face. Then he turned to Dick. "Hey. Thanks for fetching Momma."

"No problem." Dick leaned forward and whispered, "She only made me nervous the first three-quarters of the way here."

"You're doing good then. Sissy refuses to be in the same car with her."

"Watch it, Son. You're not too big to turn over my knee." The threat was given and then Momma dove right back into her conversation.

Dick gave him a smile, almost looking normal for a moment. Then the kid sighed. "I have to go back to work tomorrow. Rock called in a few favors, but I haven't exactly got any to call in, you know?"

"'sokay. Somebody has to bring in the dough, right?" He winked and squeezed Dick's fingers. "You'll come when you're off-duty."

"I will Rig, I promise." Then the kid was whispering again. "You look like shit, Rig."

"Feel like it." He wanted to curl up with his boys. Wanted Rock to touch him, say something to him. Wanted his pillow. "Just want to go home."

"Doc says at least a week. Rock said if you didn't have so many tubes in you he'd just throw you over his shoulder and hightail it home..."

"And then I'd kick Jim's butt. Lay still, Baby, and rest." Momma gave the boys her 'listen to me now' look. "I've been chatting with Linda and she says Alexander's gonna be fine. Listen to me now -- she says about half the people with a tube in 'em like my boy's got? They get the pneumonia. And lots of them pass on. I'm having none of that." Momma's face got really pink and her lips pursed. "We're gonna be good and do what the doctors say and take him home whole and right and then we're gonna talk about calling old women in the middle of the night and breaking their hearts. Jim, honey, hand me a tissue?"

"I'm sorry, Momma," Rock said as he passed her the box. "I didn't think you'd want me to wait until morning to make that call."

"Of course not, darling boy. I'm just..." She sniffed and wiped her eyes. "What happened to him, Jim? Who did this to my boy?" Rigger groaned and opened his mouth, only to feel soft, plump fingers brush against his lips. "Hush, Son. You're resting. Jim?"

Rock gave Rigger a hard look. "I can't say ma'am."

"Jim? Richard?" Rigger shored himself up and met his momma's eyes. "Alexander? You gonna talk to me about this?"

"No, ma'am. I got nothing to say about it." He didn't either. He didn't want to talk anymore, didn't want to think or remember or feel. He wanted to go home and drink a beer and watch some stupid fucking movie on HBO.

Momma's eyes got a little hard and then they looked at him again and filled with tears. "We'll just let it sit then, until you heal a bit and feel more settled in your bones. You hurting, Baby Boy?"

"Yeah, Momma."

"Okay, then." She nodded her head and looked over at Rock. "I'm gonna go speak with the nurses and get acquainted, find out how to ease him best. Somebody needs to call his boss and the insurance company. Richard, dear, have you fetched his jeep from wherever and has anybody fed Grimmy today?"

"Insurance company's taken care of, but I didn't think to call his work," said Rock, face softening somewhat. Rock rubbed his hand over his eyes and sighed. "I've got his cell phone, I'll take care of it."

"I'll go with you," said Dick, giving Rigger's fingers another squeeze and leaving him with a last soft smile. "I took care of Grim and Lucy before fetching Momma, but the jeep's still at the fucking bar. Oh, shit - I mean sugar -- Momma, I'm sorry."

Momma laughed. "Richard, I don't imagine there's much language I haven't heard. Y'all get on with what you need to do and then come on back here and we'll chat a bit. I want to get my boy settled."

His marines left, Rock without a backward glance, Dick's lingering.

Momma looked down on him. "How you doing, Baby?"

"Hurting, Momma." He tried to take a deep breath, wincing as his chest screamed. Rock was never gonna forgive him. He should have stayed home.

She squeezed his fingers. "I'd take it from you if I could, Baby." Big tears started sliding down her cheeks, catching in the wrinkles. "Tell your momma how she can make it better, Son."

He let his tears go, trusting Momma not to comment on them. "Find the floor nurse and get me some meds? Find out if I can have some more water? Take care of Rock and Dick for me?"

"It's done, Baby." She stroked his forehead. "I tell you what, you close those baby eyes for me and rest and I'll go hunting, 'kay?"

"'m sorry, Momma."

"Hush. You just get better. Nothing to be sorry for, Son. Sleep."

He let her presence soothe him into sleep.

Chapter Ten

One day over a week after Rigger was beaten, they brought him home. Rock had been quiet, almost aloof the whole time, face set, hard, even in sleep. They were all exhausted, none of them wanting to leave Rigger's side at night and sleeping on those chairs had quickly been declared impossible.

Rigger had steadfastly refused to give any sort of description of his attackers. Rock had steadily grown surlier. Dick had spent his evenings running errands and getting home set up. Clean sheets in the spare bedroom for Momma, clean sheets on the big bed for Rigger. Everything needed to be scrubbed down so that Momma wouldn't feel she had to and, just that morning, he'd been given a great big long list of foodstuff to buy, "fixings for some good solid food for my boys."

The sun was on its way down by the time the paperwork had all been signed. Rigger was snapping and complaining. The man wanted home. Dick couldn't blame him. He didn't know how Rigger was keeping it together -- he felt like he was going to break down and bawl like a baby all the time. Those guys hadn't just broken Rigger's bones; they'd torn apart the relationships he'd started to count on as family.

Dick was scared. The more Rigger and Rock hurt, the more he did and the more the fist in his belly tightened. He was pretty sure the only thing holding them all together was Momma.

Rock had driven Momma in the truck and he'd driven Rig, wedged in the backseat of the jeep, casted leg almost hanging out the window. Rig was wearing a pair of old sweatpants and a T-shirt hanging off him that had been tight on his skinny ass a week ago. Rig slept all the way home.

When he walked around the jeep to start the process of getting Rig out of the car, he found Rig staring, grey eyes filled with tears. "Shit. Rig -- you okay? I'm sorry! I swear, I tried to avoid all the bumps."

"'m okay. Just ready to be home." Rig looked up at him, hideous bruises and swellings starting to ease a bit, their Rig peeking out again. "I'm tired, Dick. I want to be home."

"I know." Dick found his hand and squeezed gently and then leaned forward and kissed the skin near Rigger's ear. "You want me to carry you?" he whispered.

Rigger leaned into him, cheek resting on his shoulder. Nothing was said -- not about hurting, not about Rock helping Momma take in the flowers and assorted medical crap, not even a yes -- but Rig relaxed into his arms and took the care he was offering.

He pressed another kiss to the small patch of unmarked skin and picked Rigger up. He'd carried Rigger before, playing around and stuff. He swore Rigger was twenty pounds lighter, cast and all. Without a word or fanfare he shouldered his way in and carried Rigger to the big bed.

Rigger sank down into the mattress with a soft groan. The doctors had been fucking strict about what Rig couldn't do for the next few weeks. No hard coughing. No intense activity. No lifting. No smoking. No swimming. No dancing. He'd worried that it would be hard for Rig, but as pale and skinny as the good ole boy looked? A few weeks might not be enough.

Dick fussed over him -- it was the first time they'd been alone since it had happened and he was selfish enough to hope Rock and Rigger's Momma would take their time. "Want to me to help you take off your sweats? Or you want to leave them on?"

"I want 'em off, I think. I'll need something to wear when I need to piss. Maybe a pair of shorts." Rig raised his arms and Dick couldn't help but wince at the patchwork of black and purple and green and yellow bruises. The stitches along his shoulder and chest looked obscene -- sort of like spiders.

Dick slowly took off Rigger's clothes, being extra careful not to jostle anything.

"I think the doctor would call that intense activity, not to mention his Momma could walk in any minute."

Dick looked up to find Rock lounging in the doorway. "I'm just helping him get more comfortable."

Rigger grinned over at Rock. "I promise, no acrobatics. Just needed to get a little more naked."

Rock nodded. "I wanted to talk about the sleeping

arrangements actually. With Rig hurt the bed's not really big enough for three."

Dick felt his stomach clench, but he managed his offer with an even enough voice. "Dibs on the couch."

Rig went white, eyes fastened on Rock. Then his chin lifted and he sat up. "No. I'll take the couch. It'll be easier to get off of."

"No!" Dick fussed with the pillows. "You need the bed, Rig. You've been dreaming about sleeping here instead of in that hospital bed for a week now. I don't mind taking the couch. You should have someone nice and warm to snuggle up against."

Rig looked over at Rock, back muscles trembling and jumping. Dick looked from one to the other, feeling miserable. He didn't understand what was going on. He just wanted things back to normal.

"You got a problem with that, Rig?" Rock asked, arms crossed over his chest.

"Yeah, Rock. Come in here and shut the fucking door."

Rock gave Rigger a long look and then looked up at him and for a moment Dick thought the big guy was going to ask him to leave. But Rock didn't. Rock closed the door and sat gingerly on the edge of the bed. Dick stayed where he was, even if he did feel like he was looming over Rigger.

Rig shifted, little tiny, painful movements that hurt Dick's gut, until he could rest his head on Rock's lap. Then Rig's good leg settled in Dick's lap.

"Oh." Rig's sigh was the first truly easy sound Dick had heard in a week.

Dick started to stroke the bare leg, looking up at Rock as he tried not to cry. Rock's eyes fell closed and he started stroking Rigger's hair. Rigger gave a sweet moan, soft, and fuck, but it was good to see the tension ease in those bruised muscles, to hear the quiet sighs that meant Rig wasn't asleep yet, but wasn't awake, and was happy.

Rock sighed loudly. "Rig... What if one of us pushes up to close or rolls against you while we're sleeping? I'm not trying to be an asshole here -- I just don't want you going through anything else."

"Need to be touched. Been so alone. Need you."

Dick just kept stroking Rigger's leg, waiting for Rock's decision.

"All right, Rigger. We'll all sleep here. But the minute you so much as flinch, Dick's on the couch, got it?"

Dick slumped, relief going through him. He hadn't realized how much he'd needed to be here with them. He squeezed Rigger's leg lightly.

"Yeah. Okay." Rig wasn't showing any sign of moving anytime soon. "Missed this."

Rock snorted. "You missed lying in your bed, hurting so bad you can barely move?"

Dick squeezed Rigger's leg again before started up the long smooth strokes of his fingers over the skin.

"Yeah, asshole. I've been waiting for this moment my entire life." Rigger leaned over and bit Rock's thigh with a grin.

There was a knock at the door. "Baby Boy? Jim?"

Dick put Rig's leg carefully back onto the mattress and covered the skinny body up with the sheets. "I'll get it."

Momma was standing there with a tray loaded down with soup and bread and juice. "Food wagon's here to fatten up our favorite skeleton and get him medicated. You boys gonna do the honors so this old woman can get a nice long bubble bath and a nap?"

"I'm fine, Momma. Quit fussing."

"Pshaw. 's my job to fuss." She grinned and handed the tray to Dick. "I want him to eat it all. Don't let him feed it all to that damned mutt of his."

Dick smiled at her as he took the tray. "I won't, Momma. You relax; we'll make sure he follows orders."

"You do that." She patted Dick on the cheek. "Such a good boy."

Rigger snorted and she winked at Dick, shutting the bedroom door behind her.

He couldn't help grinning as he headed back for the bed. "Your Momma likes me, Rig."

Rock rolled his eyes and started fussing, getting Rigger sitting back up against the pillows.

"Told you she did." Rigger groaned as he got settled and looked at the tray. "That's for all three of us, right?"

"Nope, she was pretty clear. It's for you -- along with the meds and she wants you to eat it all." Dick sat down on the edge of the bed closest to Rig and grinned. "And like me or not -- you're her baby boy and I like the number of balls I've got thank you very much so you are going to eat every last bit."

"Rock..." Rig's eyes looked up at the big guy for support and Dick'd be damned if Rock didn't actually grin.

"I like the number of balls I've got, too, Rig. And I think yours are still too sore to risk another go-round. Eat."

Dick dipped his spoon into the soup and held it up to Rigger's mouth. Rig opened, humming at the taste, and, to Dick's surprise, they managed to get half the bowl of soup and a few swallows of juice into Rig before he started complaining. He just kept feeding Rigger though. Every time Rigger would open his mouth to complain, Dick would push in another mouthful of soup.

"You're pretty good at that, kid."

"I've been watching, Rig," Dick answered, giving Rock a wink.

Finally Rigger caught his hand. "No more. Maybe in a minute, but not now." Eyes closed, Rig leaned back against Rock and the pillows. "Room's moving."

Dick nodded. "'kay."

He put the juice and the little plastic cup of meds on the side table and proceeded to finish up the soup. "Don't you dare tell Momma," he warned Rock.

Rig chuckled, reaching out and taking Rock's hand. "God, it's good to be home. I fucking hate being on the patient end of the hospital."

"Which is your warning that he's the world's worst patient," Rock told Dick dryly. The big guy turned to Rig. "Wish I'd known that the year you got the flu."

Rigger actually blushed, the tips of his ears turning bright red. "Are you suggesting I was difficult, Rocketman?"

"Not suggesting it in the least, Roberts. I'm out-and-out saying it."

Dick chuckled. For a moment it almost seemed normal, like the last week had all been a nightmare, and then he looked from Rock to Rigger and it was very real.

Reaching out, Rig took his meds and drank some juice before settling back on the pillows. "Come here, both of you, and keep this old man warm until the meds start working."

Dick smiled and lay down on the bed, curling up against Rigger's good leg, head resting on Rigger's thigh. Rock grunted and shifted closer on the other side of Rigger, hand sliding briefly over Dick's head.

"Oh, God." Rigger's whisper was... Dick didn't know what it was, but it sent shivers up his spine. "Kiss me, Rock?"

He looked up, watching as Rock tilted Rigger's face, big hands cupping the bruised face. The big guy's tongue traced Rigger's lips and then slid between them, Rock's mouth closing lightly over Rigger's. He could see the tears sliding down Rig's face, Rig's thigh relaxing under his head. Rig's good hand stroked Rock's jaw, long fingers trembling.

He slid his arm around Rigger's leg, just holding and lying close. Rock let the kiss go on for awhile and then gently licked at Rig's lips again and ended it.

"You need to rest." Rock's voice was gruff.

"'kay. Stay." Rigger nuzzled into Rock's chest, his hand reaching down for Dick and holding on.

"We can do that," Rock answered for both of them.

Dick just nodded and pressed a kiss into the hand that held his shoulder. He didn't sleep. He just lay there, listening to Rigger breathing, feeling the heat of Rigger's leg against him. He thought he could lie like this for a year or two before he started to take it for granted again.

***

"And you make sure my Baby Boy gets his meds at three and-"

"Momma," Rock interrupted her before she could start up again. "Dick's taking you to the mall and the grocery store. You'll be gone an hour, maybe two. I think we'll stumble through 'til you're back."

"All right, all right. We won't be long."

Dick rolled his eyes behind her back.

"Good luck, kid."

Then he was finally closing the door, sagging against it for a minute. Shit, he was tired. Rigger'd only been home a day and he'd hardly slept all night, worried he or Dick would roll over and open stitches or make Rigger's lungs worse.

Stitches. Broken bones. Bruises. Someone, several someones, had worked Rigger over good. It was time to convince Rigger to spill the beans. He headed for the bedroom, determination in his stride.

Rigger was dozing when he opened the bedroom door, bruises looking so dark against the pale blue sheets. The crazy bastard had thrown the blankets off and Rock could see everything -- every bruise and mark and swelling, the casts and the stitches. It was just wrong. And somebody had to pay.

He went and sat next to Rigger, just watching the man breathe.

Rigger's hand stroked along his arm. The grey eyes watching him were quiet. "Hey. How goes it?"

"I've been better. You?"

"Sore as a boil, but working on it."

"You look like shit."

"Flatterer." Rigger arched an eyebrow at him. "Wasn't ever up for Miss Texas anyway."

He gave Rigger a smile, but his heart wasn't in it. "You're going to make me ask, aren't you? Fine, Rig. I'll ask. What the hell happened?"

"What do you need to hear, Blue?" Rigger moved closer, looking at the wall. "I walked into the bathroom and they followed me. They slammed me face first into the mirror and broke my fucking nose. Once I was dazed, they muscled me into the stall and finished the job. One of 'em had a length of pipe, 'nother had a pocket-knife. The others just used their bodies."

His fingers curled into fists, his entire body clenching. "I need to hear what they looked like, Rig. I need to know that someone is going to take care of them."

"I can't risk it, Blue. I can't risk you." Rig looked at him, slow and serious. "You're my family, Blue. What kind of a man would I be if I put you at risk?"

"And you're my family, Rabbit. What kind of man would I be if I didn't take care of this?"

Rigger took his hand, squeezing hard. Those grey eyes were full again and if he never saw another tear from Rig, he'd still have seen one too many. "Three years, Blue. Three years until you retire. And the kid? They drum him out and his life will never be the same. I... Fuck, you think it's easy for me? They're right fucking here and..."

Rigger sighed, the sound shaky and rough and wrong. "It was bad, Blue, some of it. Real bad."

"I want to kill them. I want to pound them into the ground and kick their heads in. Once for every fucking bruise on your body. I need to hurt them, Rig. Need to do that for you." He wanted to hold Rigger, but he couldn't, he couldn't risk hurting Rig -- he was too angry.

"I know." Simple as that and Rig was close and in his face. "I can't lose you, Rock. I can't let them hurt you, too."

"Rabbit..." His voice broke and he closed his mouth tight on the sob that wanted out. He hated this. Hated it! It wasn't fair. It wasn't right. And there wasn't a fucking thing he could do about it. He, better than anyone, knew how stubborn his easy-going, laid-back cowboy could be when he got his mind set on something.

"Touch me? Please, Blue." Rigger squeezed his hand, the whisper broken, grey eyes on the bed. "Please. Let me feel your hands. I... I need you."

Fuck.

He just wanted to go away and pound something. Hard. He *needed* to hit something. Anything.

He closed his eyes and swallowed tightly and forced his fists to unclench. As gently as he could, and he prayed by God that it was gently enough, he stroked his hand down the front of Rigger's chest.

Rig sighed, watched his hands, relaxing back into the pillows. With his lung weak, Rigger faded quick. "The doctor says I can't go back to work for eight weeks and can't fly on the birds for longer, maybe never, depending on the leg."

"You don't want to be fixing up jarheads after they did this to you anyway, do you?"

Rigger shivered and shook his head. "I don't know what I'd do, Blue, if I had to help one of them."

Bingo. They were jarheads. Fuck, he wished the kid was here while Rigger was still talking but out of it. Subtlety was not his forte.

Rigger shifted under his hand, relaxing. "Feels good. Right."

"Yeah..." He kept the gentle touches up, stroking the abused skin carefully. "How many of them were there anyway?"

"Four, five -- it gets fuzzy, you know, Blue? Like I can see certain parts and then others I can't." Rig's eyes closed and he stretched carefully, the hot skin moving underneath Rock's hand. "The music was really fucking loud -- "Wild Horses" and then "In Another's Eyes" and then a band came on stage and played."

"Guess you're never going to be a fan of that band." Rock

just kept moving his hands gently, wondering how long it was going to be before Rigger fell asleep. "You remember which guy had the knife?"

Rig snorted, the sound angry and lost and sick all at once. "Like I could ever forget. The knife didn't hurt as much as the pipe. Fuck, if that son of a bitch had hit me one more time, I think I'd have lost my fucking mind."

Rock had to fight with everything he had not to tighten up, not to let his own anger show. "What did they look like? The guy with the knife and the one with the pipe?"

Rig's eyes opened. "And if I tell you, Blue? Can you swear to me that if you see one of them on base you'll just walk by? What if one of them's in your unit, Blue? Or your company? What then?"

"I wonder every time I see a fucking marine, Rig. Is he one of them? Did he hurt my Rigger? It's all I can do not to pound each and every one of them into the fucking ground."

"Oh, fuck, Rock. Don't ask me." Those tired eyes were heavy on him, weighed down his heart. "I'm doing this for you, Blue. I'm not letting you throw away twenty years of service because your lover's a stupid fucking redneck. I should have stayed home. I should have kept my fool mouth shut. I should know better."

"You should have known better?" That was it; he couldn't fucking lie there and gently pet Rigger and tell him it was going to be okay. "They were fucking marines, Rig -- the few, the proud? How fucking proud does it make you to gang up on a lone man and beat him near to death?"

He was shouting, getting right up in Rig's face and screaming at him. Shit. He got up, practically shaking he was that pissed off. "That's not what the fucking marines are about, Rigger. Been a fucking fag all my life and in the Corps for twenty fucking years and I've never been ashamed of either before now."

He turned on his heel and high-tailed it out of there, slamming the door behind him. The workout room was just a few steps away and he barreled into it, going straight for the punching bag.

It wasn't long before he was lost in the sound of slamming his fists into the worn leather, feeling each hit up into his shoulders.

***

She was really getting too old for this.

Between Jim's constant pounding in the back room, Richard's nervous wandering through the house and her boy's deepening silence and refusal to eat enough to keep a gopher alive, Charlene figured she'd best start doubling up on her damned blood pressure pills.

The phone had been ringing off the hook, the offers of help and the flowers and the gifts coming constantly. Made her proud, really, given these people weren't southerners and she'd heard they didn't know how to take care of each other. Lots of people loved her boy. She looked over at Richard, pacing between the bookshelves Alexander had built to hold their movies. And her boy loved his fair share of people too, it seemed.

"You know he built his first set of shelves like that when he was thirteen?" She grinned. "He got mad 'cause his daddy wouldn't buy bookshelves at the Wal-Mart and so he stormed out back and built himself some. His daddy was proud enough to bust."

Richard looked startled for a moment and then he smiled and came to sit by her. "Yeah? He doesn't talk about his father much, but when he does... you can tell he loved him a lot."

"Jeremy was a good man. He loved that boy to death. Used to call him his little shadow." She smiled, heart aching a little. She still missed that sweet smile and she could have used one of his hugs right about now. "You'd have liked him, I think. He was a bit like Jim, less military and more cowboy, but they were cut from the same cloth."

"I'm sure I would have, ma'am. I mean Momma." Richard gave her an apologetic smile.

"You know it's gonna be a hard row to hoe, the next little bit, don't you?" She worried about this boy. Alexander loved Jim, and even if they never spoke again, lived in different rooms, they'd love each other and be stubborn and miserable 'til death. But Richard? She didn't know where he fit, didn't understand it, never had, and she worried he'd get lost in the stubborn silence.

"It's been a pretty hard row to hoe all along, Momma, I don't see why I should expect anything to change." The pounding from the back room started up again and Richard looked toward the noise, face full of longing. "I can't do anything. For either of them."

She sighed and shook her head. Men were so damned twitchy. "Before Julia was born, I was working at a dime store on weekends while my momma watched Bobby. One of my husband's kinfolk came in, robbed us, knocked me around a little. I didn't think Jeremy was ever gonna come in from the barn, and it almost broke us -- guilt and anger and hurting are nasty things."

Charlene patted Richard's hand. "Lucky for them, they have you to tempt one out of hiding under the bed and the other out of the barn."

Of course she didn't envy him the job. Good lord and butter, those two were the most stubborn critters known to man.

"I hope so, Momma. I'd hate to see this come between them."

She nodded, wincing as another loud slap sounded. "Just keep praying and trusting in what your heart says, Richard. It'll steer you right. I s'pose I ought to go try talking some sense into Jim while you pick out a movie for us to watch. Something with that Stallone fella. He's got a nice butt."

Richard's mouth dropped open for a moment and his cheeks got a little pink and then he laughed. "Yes, Momma."

She patted his hand and stood. He was such a good boy, no wonder Alexander liked him. "Why don't you make some popcorn and grab a couple of sodas. I'll be back shortly."

She peeked in on her boy on the way to braving the lion in his den. He was sleeping restless, poor baby, skin all bruised and torn. It wasn't right that someone would do this. Alexander was a good man, a decent man. She walked in and straightened his covers, stroking his hair.

He opened his eyes for a second and smiled -- Good Lord save her, that sweet, open smile hadn't changed a bit in thirty years. "Love you, Momma."

"I love you, Baby."

He nodded and those pretty eyes closed and her baby boy was back to dreaming again.

The sound of Jim's pounding on that poor bag got louder and she thought maybe she could hear him grunting with effort now. The man was going to wear himself out before his time if he didn't stop this nonsense. Not to mention her baby boy needed support from everyone he could get, but especially from Jim. She closed Alexander's bedroom door behind her and then knocked on the backroom door. Ninety percent of Jim's trouble was he needed a few beers, a fistfight, a hug and a week's worth of sleep.

The pounding continued for a moment more and then it stopped and the door was yanked open. Jim looked awful. He had large dark circles under his eyes and his color was bad, he'd lost some weight, and he was soaked with sweat. He sighed when he saw her and wiped his face with his sleeve. "Something wrong?"

"Yeah. You look like death walking and you're gonna hurt yourself you don't stop this shit, Jim." She figured she'd best start strong or she'd not even have a shot.

"Momma, you'd best save your concern for Alex -- he's the one who needs it." Jim went to close the door.

"Don't you shut that goddamned door on me, young man. You and I have some talking to do." She pushed inside. By God she'd raised two boys and stayed married to the single most close-mouthed man on the planet, she would not be put off by her son-in-law. "And don't you think for a second that I don't have enough worry for my boy and you and Richard all together, either."

Jim sighed again and went and sat on one of the workout benches.

She followed, sitting in an ugly old yellow chair that Alexander used to have in the front room. "You're gonna hurt yourself, son. You've got to sleep, got to eat. This is eating you up."

"I've tried eating and I've tried sleeping. Didn't have much luck with either. At least when I'm working the bag I can pretend I've got the boys that did that to Rig and beat them into shit."

"I can understand that." Charlene snorted at Jim's look. "What? You don't think I'm not angry? That's my boy in there, Jim, my baby and those sons of bitches damned near killed him, and for what? I want them alone in a room worse than you do."

That surprised a bit of a chuckle out of Jim and he nodded. "I guess you would at that -- and I might just be satisfied with watching."

She nodded and leaned forward, body aching and tired and old -- fuck, being pissed off was hard on the soul. "I doubt it, son. Now, listen to me. Alexander's got a point. You'll not find many friends in this situation. Think on it -- he can name, what? Three songs? Four? It took ten, maybe fifteen minutes and nobody came into the bathroom on a busy Saturday night? Nobody saw anything? Nobody helped him?"

Jim's hands had curled back into fists. "If you're here to piss me off more, you're going about it the right way, Momma."

She shook her head, tears in her eyes. "He's trying to protect you, Jim, you and Richard."

He dropped his head into his hands, rubbing at his eyes. "It isn't right. They shouldn't have done that to him, not Rigger."

"You're right. It isn't." She stood and walked over, hand resting on his shoulder. "But they did and now we have to deal with it -- you and me and Richard. He needs you, Jim. You're the dead center of his whole life. I'll help you anyway I can, Jim, but you're going to have to stand strong."

It wasn't fair, but precious little in life was.

"You're wrong you know. Rig's the strong one. Always has been. Stubborn cuss." He patted her hand awkwardly.

"Yes, mule-headed as anything. He got that from his daddy." She took Jim's hand in her own. "You're a good man, Jim, and dear to me as any of my own. No more hurting yourself. Come out. Shower, eat, sit with me and Richard and watch explosions on the TV. Let your soul rest for a bit."

"All right, Momma, I'll do it for you -- at least there's something I can do."

"Good boy. You want some pork chops and mashed potatoes or beans and cornbread?"

"It doesn't much matter, Momma. Whatever you want."

She patted him gently. "I love you, son. We'll find our way through this. You have faith."

"In *what*?"

"In that man sleeping in your bed." She tilted her head. "He left home without so much as a word from you. He gave up family and friends and never regretted it once. He loves you, Jim. You have faith in that."

"Yes, ma'am. I guess I can do that."

"Good deal. You jump in the shower and I'll fix you up a plate." She sighed and headed back out the door, stopping and looking back. "You ever do find the ones who did this, I expect that you'll ensure they can't ever do it again, you hear me?"

"You can count on it, Momma." Jim's voice was hard, like his eyes, the blue like chips of ice.

She nodded, tears filling her eyes even as she lifted her chin. They hurt her baby boy, her laughing, easy-going, sweet boy, and God forgive her, she wanted them to hurt in kind. Jim nodded back, understanding passing between them. On this they were in perfect agreement.

She turned and let Jim get to his shower, covering Alexander up again on her way to the kitchen.

Chapter Eleven

He was driving faster than he should be, he knew that, but every time he slowed down he'd start fucking thinking about it again and his foot would get heavy. Stupid fucker. Planning a stupid birthday party while this close to death. Rock was headed home and he was going to find Rig and pound him into the fucking ground. Or just hold him and be fucking grateful he could.

You could have knocked him over with a feather when he'd walked into Carol's house and a bunch of his friends yelled surprise. Only fucking Rig would make sure he had a fortieth birthday party with all this other shit going on.

He'd left after almost an hour of meet and greet, making the kid stay behind as a stand-in. Dick had apologized about a hundred times and said Rig insisted. He just bet Rig had.

He pulled into the driveway and took the stairs two at a time. Rig had been alone for almost two hours, what with travel time and the time he'd spent saying hello to everyone. If anything had happened to the stupid idiot...

Rig blinked up from the pile of blankets on the sofa, eyes red-rimmed and swollen, some stupid fucking black and white movie playing on the TV. "Rock? Blue? What's the matter? What are you doing here?"

His anger was stopped in its tracks by how Rig looked. "I should be asking you that -- what's wrong?"

"Huh?" Rig blushed dark, shook his head. "Too many pills make you stupid and silly, you know... Why aren't you with Dick?"

"You mean at the fucking party, Rig? The goddamned *celebration*?"

Rig nodded, settling into the cushions. "You only turn forty once. I planned that party two months ago, didn't want you to miss it. Lots of folks helped me out. Did a good number of people show?"

"I'll say, took me a fucking hour to get out of there. I don't want to party, Rig. Not while you're at home hurting." He gave Rig a good glare. "You think it means anything if you're not there?"

"You deserve a birthday. Not your fault I'm laid up, Blue. You deserved a party." Rig smiled at him, the motion slow and careful. "Did y'all take pictures for me? I wanted to see, but the doc said there was no way with this damned lung."

"You'll have to ask Dick about pictures." Rock sighed and rubbed his face. Fuck, but he was ready for this to be over, ready for this to have been a nightmare, a hallucination. Ready for Rig to be just fine, thank you very much. The only fucking thing he wanted for his birthday, but he had a hunch he wasn't gonna get it.

"I got you something."

He swallowed down his growl and managed a smile for Rig. "Yeah?"

Rig nodded and handed him a little ring box. "Wasn't gonna give it to you at the party anyway. So this part's almost right, almost not fucked up, you know"

"It's not fu..." He looked down at the box and closed his eyes for a moment, taking a deep breath. He wouldn't lie. "Thank you."

Rig nodded. "Happy birthday, Blue."

He popped the box open. It was a gold Corps ring, big as life, just like the one his grandfather had worn until the day he'd died. He took it out of the box, holding it in his hand. It was heavy. A man's ring. "Rig..."

"Do you like it?"

He nodded. He did. It was the one of the nicest things anyone had ever gotten him. He told Rig as much. "It's the nicest thing I've ever been given, Rig."

And he'd never ever wear it. He wouldn't tell Rig that though. Wouldn't tell him that the ring would always remind him of what had happened.

"Good. I saw a picture once of you and your grandpappy and he was wearing one. Figured it was only right you had one, too." Quiet grey eyes met his. "You going back to the party?"

He slid his hand over Rig's, just touching. "I can't."

"Want to sit and watch Humphrey Bogart with me?" Rig

nuzzled into the touch. "The couch is awful fucking big for just one."

"I can do that." He turned to the TV, one hand resting on Rig's, the other clutching the box holding the ring.

Today was his fortieth birthday. So why the hell did he feel like he was pushing fucking eighty?

***

Rock was still up, long after the kid managed to drag Rig off to bed.

Forty fucking years old.

He looked down at the ring Rig had given him. A couple of months ago he'd have worn it with pride, but now... now it would only remind him of what had happened to Rig, that it was marines that had done it. Five fucking assholes who had taken not only from Rig, but from the Corps. He liked to believe a marine was better than that, that a marine had honor. He guessed even an old dog like him still had a lesson or two to learn.

He put the ring back in its box and slid it into the drawer on the telephone stand. Then he picked up a phone and dialed a number he hadn't used in years.

The phone rang and rang, then a rough, familiar voice sounded. "'lo?"

The sound of that one word, a mixture of curiosity and aggravation and impatience, was so familiar that he almost smiled. Almost.

"Hey Sarge. It's South. I need your help." There was no beating around the bush, no small talk. The Corps took care of their own.

Sarge would know he wasn't calling to ask for a fucking date.

"You got it. Talk." He heard a lighter click, heard the puffing as one of those ugly fucking cigars was lit.

"April seventh. The men's room at Tejano's. Five marines. A cowboy who rides bulls. You can do the math. The cowboy's not talking, but dollars to donuts the fucking assholes who don't deserve to wear the uniform are. They need taking care of, Sarge." Needing fucking beating to fucking death. By him. But he'd live with being hands off because it was what that stubborn asshole in his bed wanted.

"Uh-huh. This is personal, then. Not just a slapping on the wrist sort of situation?" The question was heavy, loaded.

"About as personal as it gets," he growled, free hand fisting hard.

"I got your back, South. You don't think on it anymore. It's as good as done. Your cowboy gonna pull through?"

"He is." Or there wouldn't be anything stopping him from tearing those pricks limb from limb with his own bare hands. He'd like to feed them their balls, too. Make them eat them with a bit of hot sauce before he finished the job of choking them on their own cocks. "Thanks. I knew I could count on you."

"You know it. Tell me, now, you boys had a chance to play with the new NVGs that are being issued? Damn, those things are fun." Just like that, they were talking shop, the gravely voice easing his fury.

If Sarge said things would be taken care of? Things would fucking will be taken care of.

They talked shop for awhile and he signed off.

He hung up the phone, feeling better than he had in weeks, knowing those bastards were going to get what was coming to them.

It had been weighing on him -- a man took care of his house.

Now he had.

Chapter Twelve

Rig watched Grim and Lucy run the fence, swinging in the hammock while he caught his breath. He'd been home for damned near two weeks and hadn't been able to play with the pups at all. Momma didn't like dogs in the house and neither of the boys had given Rig the chance to get up and around since she'd gone.

Today though, Dick was working and Rock had to run to the base to deal with some stuff and he was alone. He didn't know whether he was grateful or scared.

He'd woken up to the front door shutting, Rock's note on the bedside table. He'd had a good day of it. Took out his stitches, got himself good and washed, got himself dressed in as close to real clothes as he could, had a beer and gone out to sit with the pups. His face was starting to look right again, the torn ear the ugliest of it. He was thinking of letting his hair grow, maybe keep the moustache and beard for a while. He thought maybe he'd look a little like Alan Jackson then.

Grimmy brought him the yellow ball, dropping it in Rig's lap with a happy bark, Lucy eager and panting behind him. Rigger smiled and threw it, wincing as his healing muscles pulled a little.

"Jeremy Alexander Roberts, what in the hell are you doing?" Rock didn't sound anything like his Momma, but at the same time... for a moment he thought she had come back.

Rig blinked over at Rock and then grinned. "Damn, did Momma give lessons while she was down?"

Rock strode forward, not impressed. "I told them I only needed a couple more days, but if this is what you're going to do when I'm not here, I'll arrange for another couple weeks of leave. Damn it, Rig -- you trying to knock yourself back to last week?"

"Rock, I'm sitting in the hammock. *Sitting*." He looked up at

Blue, one eyebrow arching. "And no, if I can't go back at least a few weeks, I think I'll just sit here, thanks."

"Is that a beer? Are you supposed to have alcohol with your meds? And you got dressed. By yourself. And you're outside. In the fucking hammock. And I saw you throw that thing for the mutts. Saw you wince, too, Rig."

"Shit, Blue! I'm just a little tender from taking the stitches out... Fuck." He looked down at his beer and shut his mouth -- he'd just said that out loud. With Rock already half pissed off. Fuck. Fuck. Fuck.

"Taking the fucking stitches out... Shit. I should have known. I should have gotten Julie to come and stay with you while I was gone." Rock took the beer bottle out of his hand and grabbed Grimmy's ball as it was brought back, tossing it at the other end of the garden. Then Rock picked him up unceremoniously and began to head back inside.

He wrapped his good arm around Rock's neck. "You're going to strain something, picking me up. The stitches were ready to come out. I'm trained to do it, you know?"

"You do it before or after the fucking beer?" Rock did not look assuaged.

"Before. Don't be an asshole, Rock. You know I can fucking deal with it." He shook his head. "I'm not broken, for chrissake."

"You could have fucking fooled me. You were nearly dead, Rig. Looked pretty damn broken to me." Despite Rock's anger, he was put down on the bed with a gentleness that nearly brought tears to his eyes.

"I wasn't going to die. I told you, I'm too mean to die." His fingers trailed along Rock's hands and fingers. "Wouldn't have left."

No matter what those sick motherfuckers had said and done.

"Good," Rock told him roughly. "You don't go first. That's the deal." He got another glare. "And you don't go fucking playing doctor with yourself or drink while you're on your meds or play fucking ball with the goddamned dogs. Don't make me get you a fucking babysitter."

"Rock, I can't just sit in the fucking bed all day. I need to get up and move. I need to get back to living."

"So take a walk to the living room, pee by yourself, shave -- you don't have to fucking climb Mount Everest the first fucking time I turn my back!" Rock's hands curled into fists. "Fuck this.

I'm taking a fucking shower."

"What the fuck are you talking about? I fucking walked to the backyard to see my goddamned dog!" Rig sat up, ignoring the twinge from his chest. Fuck, but he was tired of being weak. "Three weeks ago I was rappelling, Blue! Now they tell me I can't go do my job, that I'll have to prove I can do the work and you're in here bitching because I went outside and... Fuck! I can't even drive my fucking jeep." He was not going to cry.

Not.

"I don't ever want to see you that close to dead again, Rigger -- and if I have to tie you down to make sure you take it slow I fucking will! Baby fucking steps. You may not fucking like it, hell, I fucking hate it -- don't you think I want to watch you playing with your stupid dog? Don't you think I want to wake up in the morning and fuck you into tomorrow? Don't you think I want to chase you around the house and tackle you to the floor and..." Rock made a funny noise and just raised his hands in a gesture of surrender and left.

The shower came on a moment later.

Christ on a crutch! Rig stood up, pushing all the meds off the nightstand with one sweep of his cast. Those motherfuckers just kept taking and taking and taking. He limped toward the bathroom. He wouldn't let them have his Blue.

The door wasn't quite closed and as he went to push it open he could hear a sound. Deep, harsh noises that rattled his soul. His Blue was crying.

Rig stopped, eyes closing.

He turned and went back to their bedroom, taking off his clothes and putting them in the hamper. He picked up his meds, crawled into the bed and took three Vicodens with the last half of the beer Rock had left behind. He covered himself up and closed his eyes. He'd thought the worse of it had passed, he'd thought he'd hurt enough, he'd thought...

Fuck it. It didn't matter what the fuck he thought.

They were going to steal his entire world and get away with it.

***

They were watching the game on TV. Him and Rock and Rigger. He was in the chair, Rock and Rig on the couch. It almost felt normal. Almost.

They'd been sitting there the better part of two hours though, and no one had gotten off. Hell, he didn't even know if Rigger could yet. He wanted to find out. He wanted some of the tension to ease and to enjoy himself and them. "Hey, Rock."

The big guy grunted. "What?"

"You gonna play with what's beside you or are you gonna trade seats with me so I can?"

Now he had Rock's attention, the blue eyes turning on him. "What?"

"When's the last time you saw that sweet cock hard? Felt it? Tasted it? Aren't you fucking horny?"

"In case you'd forgotten, Rigger was beaten to shit."

"Yeah, six fucking weeks ago. Fuck, Rock -- I'm not suggesting we play ride 'em cowboy, but a little hand job or a blow job -- I bet that'll make Rig feel a hell of a lot better than any of those pills."

Rig looked over and gave him a little half smile. He'd refused to shave or cut his hair and it didn't cease to amaze Dick that Rig's white-blond hair was curly.

"Or I could sit in the chair." Rig motioned to his leg with his thin, pale, newly uncasted hand. "This thing's been cramping y'alls style in the bed."

Dick settled more comfortably, turned toward them and resting his head on the back of the chair. He let his hand drop to his package, rubbing at his prick through his sweats. "Cramping your style too, I think. Besides, I'm happy here -- 'specially if you two are gonna give me a show."

Rock made a noise, shifted and looked like he was about to protest again.

"Oh, come on, Rock -- all he has to do is sit there and let you tug -- he can't possibly hurt anything. If he's willing, and you're willing, and I'm willing -- I am willing, by the way -- why the hell can't we all just have a little fun tonight?"

Rig looked over at Rock, skinny frame silent and still. Rock stroked his hand along Rigger's face. "You willing, Rig? You feel up to this? Do you want it?"

"Have I ever not been willing? Ever once?" Rig nuzzled into Rock's hand with a soft sob.

"No, Rig, never once." Rock leaned forward and slowly brought their lips together. Dick didn't think he'd ever seen anything so hot and romantic in... oh, at least six weeks. Rig's entire body shuddered, a sweet, needy sound filling the room as Rock kissed him.

Dick slid his hand into his pants, stroking slowly, just watching as the kiss deepened, as Rock's hands moved oh so slowly and oh so gently over Rigger's body. He hadn't realized how much really he missed this, missed the hunger and the noises and the need. He almost came as Rock went to his knees, slipping between Rigger's legs and carefully pulling down the front of Rigger's sweats. Dick grabbed his balls as Rock moaned, the sound almost a sob. "Shit, Rig. You smell so fucking good."

"Oh, fuck. I want you so much." Rig's hand slid over Rock's head and around to his lips, caressing them. Then Dick heard the soft whisper. "Need you."

"You've got me." Rock turned his head and sucked on Rigger's fingers, blue gaze glued to grey.

It was... it was almost painful to watch and so intimate. Dick almost looked away, but he was a part of this too, and it felt so good, looked so fucking good. It went on for a long time and then Rock slowly let Rigger's fingers slip from his mouth and he leaned forward, burying his face in Rigger's pubes and breathing deeply, Rigger's cock sliding along his cheek.

"Oh..." Rig spread his legs as far as he could, eyes desperate, hips just barely moving. "Fuck, yes."

"You want this?" Rock asked as he brought his head up and started to lap at the tip of Rigger's cock.

"Every... everything you'll fucking give me." Rigger's words were broken by soft gasps and shudders Dick could see through the T-shirt Rig was wearing.

"Everything..." Rock murmured the word and then took Rigger into his mouth, lips slowly swallowing up that hard prick. Dick started to make soft noises, his hand working his own cock as he watched. Rig sobbed, head lolling back on the sofa, body tight and moving toward Rock. Rock's eyes were closed, shut tight, his hands wrapped around Rigger's hips and Dick thought he could hear soft, broken noises.

Rig stretched, leg digging into the sofa as he moved within Rock's hands. Dick could smell Rig, Rock, too. He hadn't even realized the smell of sex had faded in here, but now it was back. Fuck, it felt good to be doing this. Not, oh I'm fucking horny good, but oh I've missed this and it's right good. And shit, who would have thought jacking off would ever make him feel this full, this close to other people?

"Gonna come soon, Rock. So good... so fucking good." Rig was moaning constantly, hands clenched on Rock's shoulders. "So good." Rock made a grunting noise and Dick could see his cheeks hollow as his suction increased. He sped the movement of his hand, hips pushing up into it. Rigger gave a happy cry, body stiffening as Rock's throat worked. "Oh, fuck! Yes."

Dick moaned. How long had it been since they'd heard that sound? He stroked his cock faster, watching as Rock swallowed and then lapped at Rigger's cock like it was a fucking ice cream cone or something. He pulled faster and faster and, as Rigger turned and met his eyes, he came, spunk spraying over his hand. He got a slow, lazy, almost one-hundred percent pure Rigger smile, that one that could melt ice in the middle of a blizzard.

He smiled back, feeling lazy and easy for the first time in weeks.

Rock still had his head in Rigger's lap, licking at Rigger's cock and nuzzling the thin stomach, eyes closed in concentration. Rig ran his hands over Rock's head, soft, pleased sighs sounding. Rig looked debauched, happy, with his sweats at the tops of his thighs and his T-shirt pushed up out of the way.

Dick let himself relax back against the chair, hand still in his lap, too lazy to move. Rock was making these soft noises, exploring Rigger's skin: licking and smelling and loving on Rigger. Rigger leaned up and pulled off his T-shirt, giving Rock more skin to touch. He looked paler and skinnier than normal and there were two still-pink scars, but the bruises were gone and he looked like Rig. Their Rig.

Dick waited as long as he could, watching as Rock reverently explored every little bit of skin, but he was only human. With a small sound, he moved over to the couch, settling next to Rigger and pressing close for a kiss. Rig's lips opened beneath him, tongue soft and hot and welcoming, a quiet hum pushing into his mouth. He searched for Rock with his hand, finding the big guy's shoulder and stroking, closing the loop. Now they were all touching.

He'd missed this. He needed it now, needed the touching and warmth and family and it made him relax inside, knowing it wasn't gone, wasn't dissolved. Rigger tasted good and Rock felt good and the connection between them was solid.

A soft chuckle was pressed into his lips, Rigger pulling away to grin down at Rock. "Tickles."

Rock grinned and sighed, laying his head down on Rigger's good leg. Dick shifted and laid his own head against Rigger's shoulder. Rigger settled, snuggling between them. "'s good."

Rock grunted a soft affirmative. "Yeah, it is."

Dick nodded. It was -- it was very good.

Chapter Thirteen

Dick wiped the sweat off his forehead with the back of his arm. It wasn't that hot out yet, way too early, but mowing was dammed hard work and he'd ditched his shirt about halfway through. Now he was dripping in sweat and damn glad to be putting the mower away.

A cool shower and a nice cold beer sounded like just the thing.

Rig came limping across the yard, beer in one hand, crutch in the other. "Looks good. I'll weed eat next week."

"I don't mind doing it, Rig." He grabbed the beer and downed a few mouthfuls. "Oh, that's good. Thanks."

"You're welcome." Rig held his hand down for the ball Lucy brought him, throwing it across the yard. "Summer's sure on her way in, isn't it?"

"Yeah." He nodded, looking at Rig closely, hating the bags under Rig's eyes and the way he held himself.

Something of what he was thinking must have shown because Rig straightened some and flushed. "Let me get a few weeks of sun and I can run for Miss Texas again."

"I'm sorry," he said softly, reaching for Rig and then letting his arm drop. "I didn't mean..."

"S'okay." Rig gave him a quick flash of smile, a wink. "No stress. I'm making hamburgers for supper -- you want potato salad or French fries?"

Rig started back toward the house, throwing the ball for Grimmy this time.

"The good potato salad, or the quick potato salad?" he asked, trotting up ahead to get the door for Rig.

"The good potato salad. Rock won't eat the other kind; he says the celery's too big." Rig's hand trailed across his waist in thanks as they passed by each other.

His cock jerked at the touch and he surreptitiously gave it a hit. "Potato salad then. I can peel the potatoes for you."

That should be suitably non-horny.

"If you want to. Or you can just stay and visit." Lonely. Rigger sounded lonely. Dick didn't think he'd ever known Rig to be lonely.

He reached out again, this time touching Rig, two fingers gently stroking the gaunt cheek. "You okay?"

"Yeah. Missing y'all. Missing work. I'm not much of a TV watcher, you know." Rig nuzzled into his touch, moaning soft and low.

"Oh..." He stepped closer, wanting so badly, not sure how to ask, not sure if he should.

"You still want... 'cause you don't have to, if you don't want to." That bearded cheek got hot in his hand, Rig looking down toward the floor.

"If I don't want? Fuck, Rig -- only every hour of every day. All it takes is a touch or a look from you and I've got to head off to the bathroom to jerk off."

"Oh." Those grey eyes met his, hungry and bright, wanting. "I want you. Take me to bed."

"You sure?" he asked softly. "I don't want to hurt you..."

"I'm sure. Nothing amazing, just us, together, in a bed. Naked." Rig's lips brushed against his. "Don't make me beg for it."

He moaned softly, tongue tracing Rig's lips. "You won't have to beg, I promise." He managed a little smile, hand going down to take Rig's, to carefully tug his lover down the hall. "That could be fun though."

Rig chuckled. "Yeah? God, you have a pretty ass, kid. Want you."

A shudder went through him, cock going way hard. "Oh, fuck... Please, Rig? In me? It's been so long since it's been you."

"You'll ride me?" Rig groaned, leaned against him.

He moaned again. "Okay."

"Fucking A." Rig pulled their T-shirts off, then sat on the bed and started working off the too-big shorts. He grinned, bouncing on his heels and then shimmied out of his jeans, pulling off his runners and socks. Fuck he was hard. Really, really hard. Rig chuckled and he looked up into a blinding grin. "You look like a kid let loose in a candy shop."

He grinned and nodded. "And you're the big old bin of penny

candy."

"Come get me and I'll let you eat me all up." Rig leaned back, hand slowly working that filling prick.

He groaned, climbing into the bed, straddling Rig. "'m not hurting you, am I?" he asked, mouth hovering over Rig's.

"No. Kiss me like you mean it." Rig's tongue slid into his mouth, hot and sweet.

He was lost. He just had to trust that Rig would say so if he did something wrong. He kissed Rig hard, filling that sweet mouth with moans and whimpers and so much need. Rig just wrapped right around him with a low cry, holding on tight, opening wide. Oh. Oh, yeah. Whimpers and moans and groans, he fed them all into Rig's mouth, shivering, pushing against the too skinny body. Oh, fuck, he wanted this so badly.

"Lube. Wanna watch. Come on, now. I need." The words were low, hungry.

"Oh, fuck...I'm gonna... fuck, you're going to make me come, Rig." He reached under the pillows for the lube, skin sliding against Rig's.

"Fuck, yeah. Gonna make you come all over me, gonna make you come on my cock." Rig's drawl was hot, husky. Pure sex.

"Rig! Oh!" Like a virgin, he came all over Rig's cock and belly, body shuddering. The look on Rig's face was pure bliss, fingers trailing through his spunk so Rig could lick them clean. It made him shudder again, made him stay hard, and he moaned, leaning down to help clean Rig's fingers.

"Oh, yeah. Missed you." So honest, so sure -- those eyes were enough to make a dead man hard. "Missed this."

He nodded hard. Yeah, he had, too. He'd made sure Rock and Rig were touching again, loving again and then he'd left himself out in the cold. He kissed Rig, rocking against him, cock sliding on Rig's skin, slick from his own come.

Rig reached down, fingers wrapping around his hip. "Dick. Fuck. I need."

His nod was jerky and he sat up, straddling Rig's thighs. Leaning back, he pushed two fingers into himself, gasping as he stretched the opening.

"Oh... Oh, so fucking pretty..." Rig's hand wrapped around his cock and started pulling, tugging, thumb working the tip.

"Oh, save that for me." He was blushing just a bit -- he

wasn't pretty.

"Hell, yes. Want to see you on my prick." Rig's eyes were hot, focused, trailing over his body. He moaned, body flushing from his cock all the way to his ears. He shifted, lining Rig's prick up with his hole and then sat slowly down, moans and groans pushed out of him as Rig filled him.

"Oh, sweet fuck... Yes." Rig's hands settled on his hips, thumbs rubbing his shaft. "So tight." He couldn't say anything, could only whimper, hands finding Rig's wrists and holding on. Rig's eyes closed, lips parted. "Oh, fuck. Sweet. C'mon, Dick. Pretty. *Move*."

"'m not," he muttered, but then he started moving and he couldn't remember his own name, let alone what he was protesting. He started moving faster, making all sorts of noise as he rode Rig's hot, hard prick. Rig's noises joined his own, low and desperate, sharp hips pushing up hard beneath him, fucking him. "Oh, fuck. Good. Rig. Oh."

He just kept moving, eyes glued to Rig's, starting to shake as he shifted just enough that that hard cock pushed against his gland, over and over again.

"Yes. Oh, fuck. Gonna make you come again, gonna make you come on my cock." Rig had his hips, was pulling him down over and over.

"Rig!" He shouted, screamed as the pleasure pulsed from him, his ass squeezing hard around Rig's cock. Oh, fuck, it felt so fucking amazing. Like heaven. Just like heaven with grey eyes.

Rig whimpered, pulling him down into a long, desperate kiss as heat filled him, Rig shuddering beneath him. He stroked his hands along Rig's sides, calming them both, their kisses slowly gentling. Rig relaxed under him, eyes closing, breath slowing, a thin coat of sweat sheening the thin face.

He groaned as he lifted off Rig, the sound turning into a sigh as he curled around the long, thin body. "Oh... fuck that was good."

"Mmm... Yeah. Needed that." Rig snuggled, cuddling close. "Needed you."

"Me, too." He buried his face in Rig's neck, feeling silly for having held back, for not wanting to pressure Rig into anything and winding up just depriving them both.

It didn't take long before Rig was asleep, softly snoring in his arms, their cowboy still so easily worn out. He waited a bit longer, just enjoying holding Rig, and then he slipped out of bed, pulled on a pair of sweats and went to start the potatoes for supper.

Chapter Fourteen

Rig pulled up into the driveway, hands trembling on the wheel. He didn't get out much these days and driving had somehow become a stranger to him, something stressful and uncomfortable. Not to mention it made his leg ache like a motherfucker.

He killed the engine, sighing and finishing his cigarette before going around the back and grabbing the various bags and the case of beer, leaving the forty-pounder of dog food and the sodas for trip two. He kicked at the door, hands fumbling around for his house key. "Hey, assholes! Anybody in there?"

The dogs set up to barking and Rock's voice was right behind them. "Shut the fuck up, mutts." The door opened for him and the case grabbed out of his hands. "Shit, Rig, what the hell are you doing carrying this kind of weight. And leave a goddamned fucking note next time or I'm calling the cops to find you. Thought you were dead."

"Sorry, Mom. Had to do some shopping and I had an interview at the hospital. I bought beer and toothpaste." He handed the rest of the bags to Rock and headed back out. He was going to beat this protective streak out of Blue if it killed him. He had bills to pay. He couldn't stay in the house, no matter what anybody wanted.

Rock followed him out. "Excuse me for being fucking worried if I come home to a goddamned empty house. And what the fuck are you doing interviewing at the hospital -- I thought the army was holding your job?"

"I didn't mean to worry you, man. Thought I'd be home before you, is all." He hefted the dog food onto his shoulder with a grunt. Fuck, he was getting old. "I called Reed on Monday and told him I wasn't coming back."

"What the fuck?" Rock grabbed the bag off his shoulder, hefting it like it was nothing. "And don't you dare pick up the soda Rig, or I swear I will beat you myself."

Rigger chuckled and shook his head. "I'm fine, Blue. Best shape of my life." He patted his stomach with a grin. "Hell, I'm down to my fighting weight. I'd been getting fat."

"You're down to fucking skin and bones." Rock shook his head and nodded toward the house as he manhandled the soda out of the back of the truck. "Get your skinny ass inside, Roberts and we'll talk about this quitting crap."

"Pushy bastard." He shook his head and grinned, admiring Blue's chest and belly as they rippled. He went to open the screen door and shove Grimmy and Lucy back in with his foot, wincing as his muscles pulled. Fuck but he wished the jeep wasn't a stick.

"What's the matter?" demanded Rock.

"With what?" Rigger shut the door after them, chuckling as Lucy barked happily at the sight of the dog food. "Damn, but she's a smart little thing."

"With you, asshole -- you winced."

"Oh, leg's a little tender is all. Fucking clutch." He started putting shit away, pulling out the three new sets of scrubs he'd bought to throw in the washer. He'd not had to buy any since nursing school and, given that he was the same size as he'd been then, these would keep him for awhile.

Rock worked slowly with him, putting away the dog food and getting the drinks in the fridge. "So you quit the army hospital. Shit, Rig -- I thought you loved that job."

"Yeah." He cut the tags off the scrubs and threw them in the washing machine. "I... I needed a change. Got a job at County in the ER. Money's great, about $1000 more a month."

He couldn't go back on base. He wouldn't.

He could feel Rock looking at him and then all of a sudden his Blue was wrapping tight arms around him and kissing the top of his head. "Good. Couldn't stand the thought of you being on base."

He pressed back against Blue's heat, relaxing against that strength, nodding. "Can I get you to return my gear? Reed said he'd sign it all back in."

"Yeah, put it together for me and I'll take it on my way in tomorrow." He felt Rock nuzzle the top of his head, his Blue's arms tight around him. "When do you start?"

"Thursday night. Got the shit shift 'cause I'm the new guy.

Seven p.m. to seven a.m. for the first few weeks and then, once I'm up to speed, I can start coming in around ten." He sighed, hands trailing over Blue's arms. He was losing his nights, his weekends, but it was a job and he'd be damned if Rock picked up his fucking car payment again.

"Shit, Rig, that's in less than a week -- are you sure you're up for twelve hour shifts so soon?" Rock all but carried him back to the kitchen table and sat him down. "And night shift? I've already called in most of my favors to get those four weeks off; I'm not going to be able to pull night duty without owing favors myself."

"I know, but it was the only shift they could offer me." He rested his head on his hands. "I'm good at what I do; I should be able to move to a better shift, soon -- six months, a year, tops. I couldn't turn them down, Blue. My saving's account's got twelve bucks in it."

"I wish you'd let me carry you for awhile, Rig. I'd feel better if you were more healed up before you started working long hours."

"I can't keep mooching off you, Rock. I know you're pulling from your savings to float us." He was so tired of feeling weak, feeling useless. "Besides, you promised me a vacation next year, Blue. I don't work, we'll end up grilling burgers in the backyard instead of drinking margaritas in Mexico."

That got a smile out of his Blue. "You looking forward to that, are you, Rig? You, me and a little celebratory action?"

"Fuck yes." He grinned, lifting his eyes to meet Rock's. "Been waiting for years to rub oil into those muscles while the sun bakes you by the pool. Room service, sunshine, coconuts, and hours and hours of fucking. Perfection."

"You figured out yet if the kid's invited or not?"

"Oh, no. You're not leaving that decision to me, you sneaky bastard." He nudged Rock with his shoulder. "Going to be a tough little bit ahead, starting at the bottom of the totem pole again."

"You'll have them all charmed in no time, Rig. Hell, you could sell ice cubes to Eskimos." Rock got up and got himself a beer, grabbing a Coke and passing it over to Rigger.

Rig arched an eyebrow. "You seem to have grabbed the wrong can there, old man."

"And you're still on enough meds to start a pharmacy. Have

the Coke and be happy it's not water."

The front door opened and closed noisily and the dogs started up barking. "Hey Grimmy, hey Lucy, how's my girl? How's my baby -- you miss me?"

Rig popped the top on the soda and sent a prayer to whoever watched over cowboys who had stopped taking their meds a week ago. He'd had to pass the fucking drug test before they offered up the job, so he'd sort of shuffled his meds away, saving the narcotics for when he could use a bit of a break. "Kid loves that dog."

"Yep. You did good. Even if it does mean a second fucking mutt to trip over."

Dick came in, followed by two dogs just a wagging their tails right off. The kid made a beeline for the fridge. "Hey guys, what's up?"

"Hey, kid. This old redneck got himself a job." Rig grinned as Grimmy came up to him, taking a wide berth around Rock. Blue had been very particular about the dogs not jumping on him and Rock was not Grimmy's favorite person in general.

"Congratulations," Dick told him as he took out a beer and joined them. "I thought you had a job."

"I quit. The new one's a lot better money, over at County. Get to stitch up drunks and handle Saturday night boozers."

Dick grinned at him and tapped their cans together. "Congratulations, Rig." Dick downed about half his beer in one shot.

"Thanks, kid." He stole the kid's beer and managed a swallow or two before Rock grabbed it and gave it back to Dick. "Come on, man. A beer won't hurt."

"You're on a hundred and fifty different meds, smartass -- I'll bet a good half of them say do not take with alcohol."

Dick just gave him a sympathetic look and finished the beer.

"You worry too much, Rock." Rig sighed, scratching restlessly at his beard and stretching. "I've got to climb up into the attic and dig out some of my old scrubs. Gonna box up my old uniforms and shit and stick them up there, too. Y'all think you can manage to order yourselves some supper?"

"Dick can order the fucking supper and I'll go find your scrubs and put the box up there once you've got it packed. And I don't want to hear a fucking argument about how you can do it your goddamned self. It's only been two months."

"Ten weeks, Rock." Rig took a deep breath. "How about Dick orders supper and you and me can start packing shit away. Then the three of us can dig out and put up. Maybe share supper and a shower after?"

Rock looked like he was about to argue but Dick kicked him underneath the table. Kid probably thought he was being subtle and he was studiously looking at his beer, but the kick definitely happened, Rigger would swear to it.

"All right," Rock relented. "As long as you don't put a strain on anything."

He leaned down for a quick kiss, missing the freedom of being fucked hard, of running and moving easy, of being at home in his own skin. "Only your patience, asshole. You have my word."

"I'll hold you to it, Rigger." Rock stood up and wound an arm around his waist. "Now where's this box you want for packing?"

"It's on the bed. I started it this morning." He let his Blue lead him into their room, listening to him fuss and telling himself that everything would get back to normal one day.

Chapter Fifteen

Middle of fucking August and it was hotter than hell. Rock was hot and he was tired and his head hurt. He just wanted to get home and have a cold shower and then an even colder beer and maybe the kid would have the energy to call for a pizza.

Rigger had been pulling extra shifts, so they weren't even seeing him nights except on weekends anymore and then he was too tired to do anything but sleep and sleep and fucking sleep some more. Five fucking nights and two weekend day days. Fucking insane.

And what made it worse was a part of him was convinced Rigger was doing it on purpose, doing it to avoid him and the kid. He was getting fucking paranoid in his old age.

The dogs were there but they didn't go nuts when he got home and he figured the kid must have beaten him home for a change. He called out a half-hearted "hey" and headed straight for the shower. He'd managed to get undressed and the water started when something ice cold rolled over his hot skin.

He whirled around to find Rig holding a beer, wearing nothing but an old pair of shorts. "You looked like you could use a beer, Blue. Hot out there?"

"Hot enough to fry eggs." He took a long swig of the beer and gave Rigger a good once over.

All of his injuries were healed now, a couple of fresh scars left behind and if you looked past all that hair you could make out a slightly wonky ear. He didn't like the beard and for a moment was surprised he'd never said anything. Except he didn't see Rigger enough to complain. The good ole boy was tanned and Rock figured he spent most of his off time sleeping out in the hammock. When he wasn't shopping and cleaning. It was like there was a housekeeping fairy in the house -- he'd come home and there'd be clean clothes and clean sheets and dinner in the oven.

But underneath that tan, Rigger looked grey, old and tired. And those sweet grey eyes looked lost.

Out of nowhere Rock felt the anger slam back into him. How fucking dare they. "Thought you had to work."

"Don't I always?" Rig shook his head and chuckled, leaning up against the doorjamb. If Rock wasn't mistaken, Rig was still losing weight, living on a steady diet of cigarettes and adrenaline. "No, I start the new schedule today. Got an extra couple of hours."

"That going to be the usual? We actually going to see you for dinner most nights?" That way he could make sure Rig ate. Even if he had to hold the fucker down and spoon it in himself.

"That's the theory, unless I get called in early or get asked to pick up more hours." Rig closed his eyes for a second and then opened them again. "Keep telling myself I'm padding the old saving account, about three a.m. when I'm thinking I should be home in bed."

"At this rate we're going to be able to upgrade that vacation to a five star hotel. Hell, at this rate, that's the only time I'm going to sleep with you." He tried to keep the fucking whine out of his voice, but he fucking missed his Rabbit. It was like Rigger was fading away right in front of him and all he could do was eat his anger and fuck the kid until he fell into an exhausted stupor.

Rig sighed and straightened up, one hand brushing through his curls. He needed a fucking haircut, too. "Yeah. It's been a long damned summer. Hey, you got Dick still, yeah? Got somebody there."

"And who the fuck looks out for you?" Rock shook his head and stepped back into the lukewarm water, letting it clean away the heat and the grime and hoping some of his anger would go down the drain with the dirt. When he opened his eyes again, Rig was gone. The beer can on the sink was the only proof he had that they'd even been in the same room.

Anger and sorrow caught together at the back of his throat. This slow fading away was almost worse than if Rigger had been killed. Somebody had to fucking pay. He could feel the growl building inside as he turned off the shower and stepped out. Months later and his Rigger was still missing in action. And somebody had to pay.

The growl turned into a roar as he put his hand through the

fucking wall.

Shit. He just stood there, staring at where his hand disappeared into the wall.

"Blue! Christ!" Rigger hit the door at a dead run, naked, scrubs in one hand. "Rock? Fuck! You okay?"

He blinked over at Rigger and then at his hand. "I don't know. Hurts." He tugged gently and made a face. "I think it's fucking stuck."

"Okay, hold on. Don't move, Blue." Rig dropped the scrubs, pulling away pieces of drywall slow and easy, long length of naked body pressed up against him like it hadn't been in too fucking long. Rigger was in full nurse-mode, eyes sharp and focused, so fucking careful.

Shit, he hadn't seen the man this animated in a long time. If this was the only way he was going to get Rigger's full attention, he was gonna have to stock up on polyfiller. Whatever was holding his hand loosened as Rig moved pieces of plaster and between the two of them, they got his hand out. "Let's get you over to the sink. How's it feel? Hurt?"

"Kinda numb." If he wasn't jonesing on the attention, he'd have felt pretty stupid right now. He was starting to get hard. It would be funny if it wasn't so fucking sad.

Rig had his hand under the water, moving his fingers carefully. Fuck, Rig was pressed up tight against him and he smelled antiseptic and tobacco and soap, but beneath that, he smelled his Rabbit. "Tell me if it hurts, Blue."

He fucking ached, but somehow he figured Rigger didn't mean his balls.

"Just a couple of scrapes, probably be bruised. Don't see anything broken." Rig looked up at him, right into his eyes, so fucking close. "You okay, Blue?"

"No." He grabbed Rigger's arms and pushed him back against the wall. "No, I'm not fucking okay."

His mouth closed over Rigger's hard and desperate. Rig was stiff and surprised for a second, maybe two, and then those long arms wrapped around him and Rig's lips opened wide, a needy wail sounding. Their bodies met, Rig pressing tight, skin rubbing on skin.

Oh, fuck, yes. This was what he needed. How long had it been since he'd held Rigger, naked and squirming in his fucking arms? Too fucking long. "Going to fuck you."

"Fuck, yes! Now, Blue. Please!" Rig sobbed, one leg hooked over his hip and pulled them tighter together. "Need your cock. Need you."

He spared half a thought to Rigger's injuries and whether or not this was a good idea, but Rigger's cock was dragging against his own and any thoughts went flying out the window. With a low growl, he grabbed Rigger's other thigh and encouraged it up around his waist with the first. Holding Rigger up against he wall, he let his hands slide around to the tight butt, fingers spreading Rigger's ass cheeks apart. Just a little bit of wriggling and he was there, pressed tight against that tiny little asshole.

Rig leaned forward, mouth pressed to his ear. "Fuck me, Blue. Take me." A shudder rocked the spare body and Rig kissed his temple. "Remind me why I left Texas."

Fuck, yeah, he could do that. He grunted and pushed in hard. "Shit, you're tight."

It didn't stop him though; he just kept pushing in until his entire prick was up Rigger's ass.

"Been... oh, fuck, so good. Been four months, Blue. Four fucking months."

Shit. Four months. He bent and took Rigger's mouth with his own and then he began to fuck Rig hard, shoving him up against the wall with every thrust. Rig met every thrust, body eager and on fucking fire, while that amazing fucking mouth kissed him like there was no tomorrow.

Maybe there wasn't.

Maybe instead of worrying every time Rigger sneezed or coughed or limped, he should have been fucking him blind. He groaned low into Rigger's mouth and fucked him harder.

Rig's eyes caught his, body tight and dancing on his fucking cock. "I miss you."

"Fuck, yeah," he agreed, breathless and needy.

A twist of those hips and Rig's legs squeezed him tight and then Rig was coming hard on his cock, hot spunk splashing on his skin.

"Oh, fuck!" He shoved deep once more and came, Rigger's tight hole milking him dry.

Rig's mouth covered his again, tongue pushing into him with a soft hunger. It was so fucking good. He shifted, wrapping his arms around Rigger's back and carrying him into the bedroom, still buried deep inside that tight hole.

"Again, Rigger? You up for another one?"

"Fuck, yes." Grey eyes laughed for him, glittering. "Hell, you think you can keep it up all night and I'll call in sick."

"It's a deal." He reached for the phone, still hard, still inside his Rabbit.

It felt fucking good when Rig did it, told his boss he was sick, voice low and raw because a hard cock was buried inside him. It felt right and good. Almost as right and good as fucking that sweet, tight hole. He took the phone from Rig and hung it up, eyes never leaving Rigger's. Then he started to move, long slow strokes that he swore he could keep going all night long. Or he was going to die trying.

Rig reached up for him, pulled him down until their lips met and he was breathing Rigger-flavored air -- and goddamn it if he wasn't going to add quit smoking to the list of shit Rig was fucking gonna do or die. Rock groaned as Rig undulated beneath him, tongue sliding along his bottom lip. He was never going to let the sexy son of a bitch die.

It was good and slow and urgent at the same time. Like there was a little voice in the back of his head demanding that he get it all in now in case Rigger disappeared back into 7-7 overnight shift hell and this was his only chance to fuck the man into the mattress. Long, callused hands were sliding over his back, down to his ass, around and up his belly. Again and again, Rigger found every sweet spot, every favored place that hadn't been explored by those fingers in too fucking long.

Shit this was good.

He murmured the words into Rigger's mouth, pushing them in along with his tongue. Rig grunted an agreement, lips closing around his tongue and sucking in time with their thrusts. Time could have stopped, he didn't know, didn't care. All that mattered was the man in his arms, the sweet thrust and slide of their bodies together, the rhythm of their movements.

Rig was smiling against his mouth, giving him long, lazy, breathless fucking kisses that never seemed to end. It was too fucking good to stop, too good to let go, but it was too good to endure and he could feel his balls drawing up to shoot again, the sensation tingling up his spine. He slid a hand between their bodies, wrapping it around Rigger's prick. A sharp, hungry noise was pressed into his mouth, Rig's ass clenching around his prick. Rig was hot and hard in his hand, slick with the pre-come dripping from the slit. He pumped Rigger hard, matching the rhythm to his thrusts.

Rig threw his head back, crying out with short, fierce cries. "Rock! Blue! Fuck! Yes, yes!"

He bent his head to Rigger's throat and bit down on the pale skin, making a mark. Hot. Rig's spunk was hot and wet, pouring over his hand. Tight. Rig's hole was tight and grasping, milking his own orgasm from him. He groaned against the hot skin beneath his lips, still moving, slower now, just small little movements of his hips because he didn't want to lose this, not for one second.

A whimpering moan distracted him, and he turned to find Dick leaning against the door jamb, coming into his hand, eyes fixed on the bed.

Rig followed his look, blinking over at Dick, body still jerking on his cock. "Hey... hey stranger."

Dick smiled at Rigger. "Hey yourself -- what did you do, call in sick?" Rock chuckled as Rigger sort of half-nodded and Dick grinned and then he gave the two of them a long look. "Is there room for one more on that bed?"

Rig held an arm out, reaching for the kid. "Fuck yeah."

The bed dipped as Dick climbed up next to them. He slid one arm down Rock's back and pushed the other beneath Rigger's neck and leaned in for a soft three-way kiss.

Fuck, it had been so fucking long. Too fucking long.

Rigger hummed into the kiss, body slowly starting to rock again. Two hands ran over his back, every now and again sliding together. He couldn't fucking believe he was still hard, but he was. Blind need making him hard and keeping him there.

"Gonna stay right here until the end of fucking time." Rig moaned into their lips, holding on tight.

"Oh, that sounds nice," murmured Dick.

Hell fucking yes. He couldn't agree more.

For the first time in months, things were starting to feel like they just might someday get back to normal.

Meanwhile, he had some lovers to fuck.

***

The girls at work had asked Rig out and he'd -- well, he'd said yes, but couldn't quite manage to walk into the club, could he? So he'd turned around and driven two hours to Wilmington and gone to the beach and walked and watched and stood in the surf with the cool water getting his jeans leg wet.

Felt damned good too -- walking and splashing, smelling the salt in the air. He must have walked for an hour, maybe two, singing his favorite songs, two stepping along the surf, good hat in his hand, boots back at the Jeep.

Rig was tired of two-stepping alone in the basement. He was tired of having his whole life consist of work and school and running errands for his marines. He was tired of being scared of crowds, of his heart speeding up a little whenever a bunch of marines moved together.

Hell, he still couldn't go on post. Still, he wasn't a shut in. He was out here on the beach, in the dark, walking along the surf and not stressing it. Not stressing it at all.

And his thigh was complaining a little, but his lungs felt damned good and his wrist? Just fine, thank you. And he missed Grimmy walking with him, but because he never saw Grimmy anymore to just play and...

Oh, sweet fuck.

Rig looked at his watch and grabbed for his cell phone to call home and tell them where he'd gone. Damnit. And he wouldn't be home for two hours after he figured out where the hell he'd left his jeep...

Chapter Sixteen

It was his birthday in a few days and the guys wanted to take him out for drinks, seeing as he was about to be legal. Dick had told them he probably could, but he'd have to double check, which had brought rounds of teasing about how he was going to be twenty-one and didn't have to ask his mommy if he could go out anymore.

The thing was, that he probably would have been safe just saying yes, because the odds of Rig and Rock having anything planned... well, stuff like that just didn't occur to Rock most of the time and Rig... under normal circumstances there'd be at least a pretty raunchy private celebration, but things weren't normal anymore, now were they?

He'd best ask though. Rig would be hurt if he didn't. And maybe he'd be surprised; maybe those haunted eyes were just an act to throw him off the scent. Well, a guy could hope. He found Rig in the kitchen, making supper, looking tired and wrung out. Dick wondered if he was going to make his shift tonight. "Hey Rig."

"Hey." Rig gave him a tired smile. "How's it hanging, marine?"

"Not bad." He gave Rig a gentle kiss and started washing the dishes in the sink.

"Cool." Rig put the chicken in the oven and starting peeling potatoes. "You going out drinking with your unit Friday night? Doing that turning twenty-one deal?"

"Yeah, they asked. I figured I'd check and make sure there wasn't anything planned at home first, yeah?"

"You should go and play. Rock and me -- we'll be here when you get home." He got a wink, the look almost normal for a heartbeat. "We'll break in our new legal adult right."

He grinned, holding onto that look. "I like the sound of that."

"Yeah?" Oh, that got him another smile, one that echoed in

Rig's eyes.

He nodded, putting the last pot in the rack and drying off his hands. He wanted to hold that smile there, keep it on Rig's face. He brushed their hips together, need filling him, making him ache.

"Mmm..." A potato fell on the counter with a thud. "Do that again?"

"Okay." His voice was husky, his cock hard. He pushed their hips together. Rig moaned softly, put the paring knife down and cuddled right into his arms, lips parting. He made a soft noise and covered Rig's lips, kissing like a man drowning, losing himself in Rig's mouth. Rig gave back as good as he got, arms twining around his neck, one leg wrapping around his hip.

Oh, fuck, he was hungry. So hungry. He pushed Rig back against the counter, rubbing hard.

"Oh. Oh, yes. Dick. I want you." The words were whispered against his lips, those grey eyes hot and bright. "Please."

He nodded. "Fuck yes."

He worked open their jeans, too impatient to take Rig to bed. Maybe after, when his balls didn't ache so badly.

Rig tugged his shirt up, palms hot and good on his spine. "Hurry."

"Uh-huh." It didn't take long at all before he had their jeans open and his hand wrapped around both their cocks. He gasped as they slid together, lightning going up his spine as he started to stroke them off together. Rig took his mouth, tongue pushing deep, matching the rhythm of his hand. God, it felt so good, Rig wanting him, needing him.

It wasn't going to take him long at all and sure enough, his toes curled as Rig's fingers stroked the small of his back and he shot, crying out into Rig's mouth. Rig groaned, skinny hips moving faster, harder, fingers gripping him. He got his free hand between them, tugging on Rig's nipple through his T-shirt, as sweet aftershocks went through him.

"Pretty!" Rig jerked, entire body rippling as he shot, spunk spraying between them.

Whimpering, he brought his hand up to his mouth. It tasted so good, the two of them mixed together. Rig's tongue slid over his hand, stealing a taste, a happy sigh sliding over his skin. He moaned, rubbing their noses together and then resting his forehead against Rig's.

"You taste good." Rig held on, seeming content to just rest with him for a minute.

"You, too," he murmured, just enjoying being with Rig, the afterglow soft, familiar and wanted.

The phone rang and he sighed softly, giving Rig a kiss before going to answer it.

***

Dick opened his eyes as they pulled up to the house. He flashed Ben a wide, lopsided grin and deliberately half-tripped as he got out of the car. Ben was there next to him, looping an arm around him, in a flash.

"I think I can make it to the door from here," he said, speaking slowly and over-enunciating his words.

Ben snorted. "I've seen the gunny sarge you room with -- I am not risking him beating the tar out of me for letting you walk to the door on your own. He's gonna have my hide as it is, you getting into a fight your first night in a bar."

Dick swallowed his smile. Once Rock heard the story he was only going to be mad about missing it himself.

"I don't look too bad, do I?" he asked.

"You don't look as bad as the other guys did." Ben laughed. "Course that's not saying much." Ben rang the bell.

"I can fucking walk in the door on my own, Ben -- I don't need you handing me off like you're some kind of babysitter."

The dogs were going fucking crazy and he could hear Rig's voice, low and firm, sliding beneath Rock's harsher grumbles. The door opened as he reached for the knob, coming face-to-face with Rig's tired grey eyes, which became Rig's worried eyes. "Jesus! What the fuck happened to him! Rock, come here and bring the kid in. I'll get my bag."

"I'm fine."

"He really is, sir -- we just got into a little fight."

"What the fuck?" Rock was roaring and Dick winced.

"You'd better get while you can," Dick whispered to Ben.

"I don't think so." Rock grabbed him and Ben and dragged them both inside.

"He looks worse than he is, sir. And you should have seen the other guys."

"Other guys? Jesus Christ, kid, what the fuck were you

doing?" Rig had him under the light, looking at him closely. Dick gave Ben an apologetic look. He should never have let the guy walk him to the door, not when he could have done it himself without a problem.

"We took Dick out to celebrate him becoming legal and all and I guess we kind of lost track of how many beers we'd had, though I swear Dick didn't have more'n three, but I guess he's not used to 'em so when these jerks sitting at the other end of the bar started ragging on us, he took it personal and the next thing you know we were taking it outside. It was a pretty fair fight, but they were fucking wusses and cowards to boot. Dick looks better'n any of them!"

Rig turned his attention to Ben. "You don't look too bad. You'll want to put some ice on that cheekbone or it'll swell."

"Yes, sir. He really is fine, sir. I'll just go now."

Rock looked like he was going to protest, so Dick spoke up and half-shoved Ben out the door.

"'m fine! Thanks, man!" He faked a hiccup and winked sloppily at Ben, sighing with relief when his friend made it out the door. He turned back to his own personal firing squad and dropped the drunk act, though he couldn't keep the happy-as-shit smile off his face. "I really am fine."

"What the fuck happened?" Rig brought him back over to the light, taping closed the cut over his eyebrow. "You were supposed to be celebrating your birthday!"

"Oh, and I did. I could not have asked for a better fucking birthday gift."

Rigger gave him a hard look and went to sit on the sofa, mouth tight. "Rocketman, you find out what the fuck this lunatic marine is talking about before I dunk his head in the goddamned toilet."

Rock stood in front of him, arms crossed, looking like a fucking mountain. Dick grinned up at him. "Talk."

"Yes, master sergeant." Dick winked and then held up his hands when Rock's look became thunderous. "All right, all right. The guys took me to the bar out near the base and we were having a great time getting drunk -- I only did have three beers and you both know it wasn't enough for me to be drunk, but I was kind of playing that up for the guys.

"Anyway, so we're sitting there and I'm overhearing the conversation of these four guys at the other end of the bar.

They're real drunk. Seems they're shipping out tomorrow morning, well, this morning I guess now, and they were looking for one last night of fun.

"And they started saying as how they wanted to find another faggot like that one at that pussy cowboy bar who they pounded into shit last spring." He grinned as Rock's face changed.

"Yeah, Rock -- it was *them*. The guys that fucked up Rigger." He grinned over at Rig. "I went along with the being too drunk to know what I was doing thing, got one of them to insult me and when I called them out my friends backed me up and we beat the living shit out of them.

"I doubt any of them are gonna head to the hospital -- we didn't kill any of them and the last thing they want is to be stuck in the hospital for fighting when they're supposed to be shipping out. But it'll be a long time before any of them fucks again -- I got some good kicks into their balls. The guys had to peel me off them. They were nothing but cowards and assholes -- as soon as they realized the fight wasn't going to be four on one they were ready to turn tail and run. Assholes."

Rigger was looking at him, stunned, face and eyes completely still.

Rock sat down. "No shit?"

He shook his head. "No shit. It was them -- they gave enough details that it had to be them."

Rock stood again and grabbed his shoulder. "Let's go and finish the job."

Dick shook his head. "Too late, Rocketman -- they're as good as gone. This was my birthday gift. You're just gonna have to be happy knowing they got what they deserved even if it wasn't you who gave it to them."

Rigger stood up, looking more than a little grey. "Need a smoke. 'm glad you're okay, kid."

"Wait a minute! I thought you'd be happy. I got 'em, Rig. The guys that did this to you, now it's over."

"I know. I am. I just..." Rig looked at him and then Rock and then back to him. "Thanks, Dick." Then Rig hit the back door, dogs yipping at his heels.

"Fuck, I didn't mean to upset him." He gave Rock a serious look. "I'd do the same damn thing again though, Rock, if I had it to do over, even knowing he'd react like this."

"He's not pissed off at you, kid."

"I know, but he is upset."

"Yep. I am, too."

"What?"

"You think I don't know you're lying?"

Dick blinked. Well, he hadn't expected that. "You think I got my friends to lie for me? Maybe one of them hit me so it would look like I was in a fight."

"Oh, I think you were in a fight all right, I just know it wasn't with the guys who did this to Rig." Rock's arms folded across his chest, the big guy looking immoveable.

He only thought for about half a second about bluffing his way out of it. "How? How do you know?"

"Because I already took care of it."

"What? How?"

"You don't have to worry about that. Just know that they're not going to hurt anyone ever again." Rock was growling.

He nodded, leaning against the back of the couch, feeling suddenly heavy. "Does Rig know?"

Rock snorted. "What do you think?"

"No."

"Smart boy." Rock's eyes narrowed. "So where did you get the battle scars?"

"A bunch of assholes talking smack about fags." He looked up at Rock. "But it *could* have been them. It could have happened just like I said. And I thought... well, I thought Rig'd be happy to know someone took care of them, you know?"

"And you thought you could be the hero." He gave a sad nod. Rock grunted and then rubbed his head. "Go get a shower, I'm gonna go talk to the good ole boy. Take away his fucking cigarettes anyway."

"Okay." He got up and then turned. "Rock?"

"Yeah, kid?"

"It's going to be okay, right?"

"Yeah, kid. It's going to be okay -- you wait and see."

"Good."

He turned and headed for the shower, thinking maybe, just maybe, they were going to push through this thing.

***

He paced from one end of the backyard to the other, pulling

hard on his smoke. He was going to be sick. No question, he was fucking going to be sick. He hadn't thought about it much -- only every fucking time he closed his eyes and trimmed his beard and tried to drive the jeep and heard Garth Brooks on the fucking radio -- and he just wanted...

He took another drag. He didn't know what he wanted.

Yes, he did. He wanted to go back to April and start again. He had given up a job he loved. He didn't dance anymore. Didn't play. Hadn't even been out for a beer in six months. His entire fucking life was changed and Dick runs into them?

Of course, Dick ran into them and came home with a black eye and a scrape. He'd been a fucking fool and ended up pissed on and dripping blood over a commode.

Funny how things worked out.

He crushed out his butt and lit another one. Come on, Rig old man. Pull yourself together. It was the kid's birthday, for fuck's sake and no one wanted to listen to him bitch and be a wuss.

"It's about time you quit those things, wouldn't you say, Rigger?"

He leaned against the back fence and exhaled. "Told you I wouldn't smoke in the house, Rock. I've been good to my word."

"I want you to quit altogether. I want you to come back to the land of the living. If the best you can do is pretend, then fine -- you fucking pretend that you live here with us." Rock was suddenly in his face. "Those goddamned motherfuckers didn't kill you, so fucking quit playing ghost."

"Back the fuck off. I'm living. I work. I pay the bills. I do fucking live here." He shook his head, trying to calm down, trying to keep the little panicked voice quiet. "I'm no ghost."

"We see you one, maybe two fucking days a week and for a couple of hours when we get to fuck weekday evenings." Rock didn't back off, instead he got right up Rigger's face. "You look like a ghost to me, Rabbit."

"What the fuck do you want from me, Blue?" He was shaking, he was so pissed. What the fuck was this? A ghost? He was working his fucking ass off, keeping shit together. He was doing the best he could.

"I want you back."

"I'm right fucking here!"

"Bullshit! The man in front of me is a scruffy, pale, skinny-assed, smoking fucking imitation of my Rabbit."

"Get the fuck out of my face, Jim." He pushed Rock backwards, fury filling him. "Don't you dare lecture me, you sorry son of a bitch! I have lived out here in this goddamned place without decent iced tea for years. Lived where I couldn't fucking touch you when I wanted to, where I can't even pretend to be your fuckbuddy, much less your lover. Then I'm out with fucking girls so that I could do the one thing I've never once done with you and MARINES jump me because I'm queer!"

Rig threw down his cigarette and crushed it out. "You don't want this scruffy, pale, skinny, smoking fuck? What? Too weak for you, Blue? Didn't just get back on the fucking horse? Didn't heal up good enough to suit? Fine. I've lost everything else. Why the fuck wouldn't you be next?"

He turned and headed for the back gate. Fuck this shit. He was fucking tired.

Before he'd made it four steps he was tackled to the ground, Rock heavy, solid on top of him. "You are not walking out on me, Jeremy Alexander Roberts. Not as long as I have breath in me."

He fought to catch his breath, telling himself that the tears running down his cheek were all adrenaline, not really crying.

"Fucking goddamn it! I need you. *You*. My Rigger. My Rabbit." Rock's voice was thick, words pressed against the back of his neck.

"And if he died in that bathroom, Blue? What then? What do we do if this is all of me that's left?"

"Is that what this is -- a test?"

"No." It was Dick's voice and then Dick himself was bending down in front of them on his haunches. "He's just scared, Rock. Scared that he did die back there and that we won't want him anymore, so he's hiding behind the cigarettes and the job and the beard." Dick's fingers were soft along his face, tracing his features. "Have a little faith in us, Rigger. Have a little faith in yourself."

Dick pushed at Rock. "Come on, get off him and let's get him inside before the neighbors get even more of a show."

Rock grunted and stood and the two of them lifted him up like he was just a kid and walked him between them back into the house.

"Where?" asked Rock.

"Bathroom. We'll strip him down, shave him, cut his hair, give him a shower. Prove to him that no matter what he hides behind we can find him again." Dick was shaking his head. "I can't believe I let this go on so long. I can't believe *you* did."

"Me? Why the fuck is this my fault all of a sudden?" growled Rock

"Because he was the one who was hurt -- you and I should have been here for him instead of licking our own asses."

"Who the fuck are you and what did you do with Dick and don't you even think I'm letting you assholes cut my fucking hair." He would have stormed off, but between pushing Rock and being tackled and not crying, he was too exhausted to fucking fight. "You crushed my smokes, Rock."

"Good, you're quitting anyway, asshole." Rock started to pat him down, confiscating the smashed package when he found it.

Dick shook his head and grabbed the cigarettes, tossing them into the garbage. "Enough. You're both fucking hiding and I've had enough. You guys are the only fucking family I have that I care about and I am not gonna fucking watch you turn into my mother and father, bitter and drinking and smoking and hating each other *and* me."

"What? You were the one in the drunken brawl tonight, marine. I was sitting here." Like he could hate the kid.

"That's right. Here or work -- you don't ever go out anymore. When was the last time you took the dogs to the beach for Frisbee? When was the last time you went dancing? When was the last time you asked me or Rock to do anything with you?"

"I'm busy working." They muscled him into the hallway, both warm and strong on either side of him. He wasn't going out anymore. He should have stayed home then.

"Busy hiding," corrected Dick. "You can kick me out tomorrow if you want, Rigger, but the hiding stops here tonight. I'd rather know you and Rock had put this behind you and not be here than stay and watch everything I care about just crumble slowly apart."

He looked over at Rock, hoping for some help, some assistance, somebody to tell Dick to stop this fucked up emotional shit and go get naked. He didn't want to do this. Not today. Rock was looking about as stunned as he was though and they just continued right down the hall to the bathroom. This was Dick's show.

"Sit him down on the toilet." Dick was going through the cupboards, pulling down shaving cream and his beard trimmer and a razor and a pair of scissors.

"Rock..." He was... oh, fuck, he was scared and pissed off and really, really fucking screwed up.

"Let the kid do what he wants, Rig. We'll kick his ass when he's done."

"Gee thanks."

Rigger rolled his eyes. "Tell the truth, Dick -- this is some fucked up mid-western birthday ritual, right? Good lord, I need a beer. You two yahoos would drive my momma to drinking."

"Speaking of your momma, when was the last time you talked to her?" Dick picked up the scissors in one hand and the beard trimmers in the other. "Hair or beard first?"

"I talk to Momma plenty, smartass. She understands that I've been busy." He glared over at Rock, who was looming over him like a psycho ward nurse. "And you. You're only going along with this because you don't like the beard."

Rock just crossed his arms, refusing to talk, watching him and Dick closely.

"I talked to her just this evening," Dick told him conversationally as he put down the razor and came at his head with the scissors. "She wanted to know when I was going to stop 'pussyfootin' around and bring her baby boy back from no-man's land'. I guess today is that day -- I'm gonna do that or die trying."

"Did she give you hairstyling tips, too?" That was it. He was moving back home to Texas where, if you got your ass kicked in a bar, your psychotic lovers didn't get pissed off because you didn't shave! Momma warned him about taking up with Yankees.

"Nope, but I have a feeling she'd approve." Dick tilted his chin and gave him a kiss. "Don't move now."

That's when Dick started to cut.

He couldn't believe this. He kept trying to figure out what the fuck had happened. Maybe if he'd just applauded Dick's fight and oohed and aahed over being avenged, then they'd both be asleep and he'd be watching some old western on cable. But no. He had to go have a smoke and try to calm the fuck down and now this... this whatever-the-fuck-this-was was going on.

Dick started talking as he cut. "I remember the first night when Rock brought me home. I was terrified you were going to leave me out and just as terrified you were gonna invite me in.

And then I thought I'd just ride it as long as I could. But it's been more than that for a long time. Family. You taught me that, Rigger. You taught me all about family and told me I was a part of yours." Dick stood back and tilted his head. "What do you think, Rock?"

"Don't quit your fucking day job, kid."

He groaned and closed his eyes. Bad enough they were making him pissed off and not listening to him, now Dick was making him ugly. Fucking wonderful.

"Fuck off, Rock. It's not that bad, Rigger -- and I left enough you can get it cut by a stylist in the morning." Dick tilted his head and dropped another kiss on his mouth, this one lingering, tongue sweeping through his mouth.

"Why aren't you at work anyway?" the kid asked as he started up the beard trimmer.

"Sheer fucking stupidity on my part." There was no fucking way now he was admitting to staying home for the kid's birthday. He'd leave the little prick his present to find later.

"You look old with the beard, Rigger," Dick told him as he got rid of most of the length with the trimmer. "And if I thought you had it 'cause you liked it, I might think twice about doing this. But you're hiding behind it, just like you're hiding behind that job. I chatted up a nurse the other day. Found out that you only get the shit shifts for a couple of months, tops. Unless you volunteer for them."

"Somebody has to work them."

Dick snorted. "Doesn't mean it always has to be you."

The shaving cream came out, Dick's fingers sliding over his face lovingly.

He was going to get through this and then he was going to put the dogs in the truck and blow the fucking house up. With both of them in it. The dogs were at least reasonable and didn't bitch so long as you fed them. Then he was going to take the dogs to the beach and drink enough tequila to kill a lesser man. After he hexed Rock and Dick's souls 'til they glowed and then cursed 'em in the dark, that was. Assholes.

Dick shaved him carefully, face close, eyes meeting his implacably every now and then. When Dick was done, he cleaned Rigger's face with a towel and stood back with a smile. "There -- better, Rock?"

Rock just grunted grudgingly. Dick nodded and then stood

back. "All right. I've just got one more thing to say and then I'm going to go and find my birthday cake in the fridge and eat it until it's either gone or someone comes and eats it with me.

"You can do what you want, Rigger. Grow the beard back and your hair long again, keep working nights and weekends so that we never see you again. You can do it 'cause you're scared or pissed off or just different.

"And Rock, you can keep on being a mad asshole who hides in Rigger's job and his beard just as much as Rig does.

"That doesn't change how I feel.

"I love you, Rock. And Rigger," Dick took his cheeks and tilted his face so he was looking into blue eyes. "I love you, too, Rigger. You're my family and I want you happy." Dick kissed him hard and then left. Dick stopped at the door and turned back to them. "And I dare you two assholes to deal with that truth."

And then he was gone.

Rig just sat there and looked at the floor, idly wondering how much of the blond was grey and how old he'd be before anyone noticed the difference. Finally he sighed. "Go eat cake with the kid, Rock. I'll be out in a minute."

"You'd better be, because that stupid, fucking kid just poured his goddamned heart out and if you don't join us, he's gonna think you don't give a fucking shit." Rock's hands settled on his shoulders and squeezed. "Kid ain't the only one who loves you, Rabbit."

And then he was alone.

Rig locked the door behind them, cleaned up the hair and the sink and the floor, puked as quietly as he could, turned off the lights, and took a hot shower. Then he brushed his teeth, took some aspirin, and went to find some jeans and a T-shirt and go eat birthday cake.

***

Dick was sitting in the kitchen, staring at the cake in front of him. As far as Rock could see, the kid hadn't so much as dipped a finger in to taste the fucking icing. Big blue eyes turned up to him when he walked in, looking miserable. "He wants me to leave, doesn't he? I screwed up."

Ah shit. Rock sighed and turned a chair around, straddling it. "He doesn't want you to leave, kid."

"Then what does he want?"

"How the fucking hell am I supposed to know?"

The kid shrugged and went back to staring at the cake.

Rig walked in, looked at the table and moved to the dishwasher, pulling out three plates, three forks and a big assed knife. He put them all on the table and then went to the fridge. "Milk or beer?"

"I know I'm supposed to be all about the beer, now that I'm legal and all, but I'm gonna go with the milk."

Rock snorted. "What the fuck -- make it three, Rig."

Rig nodded and poured three glasses out, brought two over and looked at Dick. "Get on with it, kid, you're not getting any younger and that cake's not getting any fresher."

Then he went back to put the milk away and grab his own glass. Dick cut the cake in thirds and dished it out.

"Jesus, kid, you've got to be kidding." Rock went to grab the knife but Dick held it back.

"It's my birthday, Rock. Just eat the fucking cake."

Rig looked over at Dick for a long minute and then shook his head and sighed, pushing the cake away. "I can't do this. Dick was right. I'm tearing us all apart and I hoped that... I wanted you two to be happy enough together that I wouldn't. All I could think in that ambulance was that I was losing you and it happened anyway. I'm sorry."

"No!" Dick shook his head and took Rigger's hand. "You only lose us if you keep pushing us away."

Rock didn't know what to say, he just knew he was more scared now than he had been when Julie had first called that night so many months ago now. He took Rigger's other hand and squeezed. "I'm a stubborn son of a bitch, Rig. I'm not going anywhere."

"I don't know if I can stay, Blue." Grey eyes landed on him, filled with tears. "I'm lost and can't seem to figure my way home." Rig's hand was trembling, holding him tight.

Rock thought it probably would have hurt less if Rigger had picked up the knife and stabbed him with it.

He slid from his chair and pulled Rig's so he could kneel between his lover's legs. His hands found their way into Rigger's shorn hair. "I will do anything, Rabbit. Anything. But I can't let you go. P-please don't ask me to let you go." His voice broke and he laid his head down against Rigger's belly, arms wrapping around the too-thin waist.

He felt like a fucking melodramatic asshole, but it was the truth and he was pretty fucking desperate. Words never had been his fucking friends; he always did speak better with his hands. And so he did. He stroked his way up Rigger's back and then down over his shoulders, ignoring the little voice in his head that kept shouting "too skinny, too skinny, too skinny". He slid his fingers against the sweet stomach that was now gaunt and he raised his head, lips searching for their match.

A soft sob sounded and Rig slid down into his lap, mouth covering his, tongue pushing deep. One hand wrapped around his neck holding tight, holding on. He held tight to the slim form in his arms, kissing Rigger as if his life depended on it.

One of Dick's arms wrapped around him, the kid's heat pressed up tight against him and Rigger.

Rigger cupped his head, pulling out of the kiss long enough to whisper, "I left Texas for you, Blue. Y'all are my home, you and him."

Dick made a soft noise and nuzzled into them and he could tell by the shimmer in the kid's eyes that Dick was verging on tears himself. Just look at them, a bunch of fucking Oprah victims. He wanted to kiss them for the rest of his fucking life. Their mouths all came together, lips and tongues holding, touching, licking, sucking, kissing.

Rig never let his neck go, just wrapped those long legs around him and Dick and let them shoulder his weight. He'd carry it forever if he had to, had faith that if he stumbled, the kid would be there. They were family; they could do anything as long as they were together.

Rig pulled back first, long enough to reach for a plate of cake. He forked out a bite and held it out to Dick. "Happy birthday, lover."

Dick looked like he was gonna start crying for real now.

"It's your birthday, Dick. Just eat the fucking cake."

Half-laughing, half-crying, Dick did.

Chapter Seventeen

The cake tasted better than any he'd ever had.

It tasted even better from Rigger's mouth. Dick was on his knees, holding everything that was truly important to him in his arms. After the up and down night, this was sheer heaven.

Rigger shared another piece of cake with him and then with Rock and then they had yet another altogether. The sweet and his lovers combined in his mouth.

"All right," said Rock with a small groan. "I'm getting too old for this shit -- can we please move this to the bed? Or at least a room with fucking carpet?"

"I wouldn't be opposed to the bed." Rig started pulling away from them with a soft groan, chocolate crumbs dotting his T-shirt.

Rock got up and then put a hand beneath each of their arms and hauled them up as well.

Dick couldn't help himself; he wrapped his arms around both of them again and pulled them in for another shared kiss. He'd thought at one point he was going to be asked to leave; he was never going to take this for granted again. Never ever.

They managed to get the dogs brought in, the cake put away and the house locked up. It took forever because somebody was either wanting a kiss or needing to kiss or holding or being held. At last they were in the bedroom. Dick's hands met Rock's on the bottom of Rigger's T-shirt and he chuckled. "I'll take the T-shirt, you can do the jeans?"

"You got a deal, kid."

Rigger chuckled and raised his arms, stretching up toward the ceiling in a long, skinny line. "I'm all yours."

"Oh, I like the sound of that." Dick pulled off the T-shirt, going immediately for the sweet little nipples that grew hard under his tongue. Rig groaned, pulling Dick's shirt out of his waistband, wiggling slightly as Rock worked off the dark jeans.

The hands against his skin felt so good and he started to moan, letting the sound slide around the flesh in his mouth.

The clothes came away in easy stages, the three of them exploring skin as it was exposed. Rock's hands mapped his back as he explored the nape of Rig's neck, Rig whispered promises over the skin of Rock's belly, while he tasted Rock's mouth. Then they were in bed and he was on top of Rigger, fingers sliding into tight heat while Rock's fingers pushed into his own ass.

Rigger leaned up and kissed him, grey eyes focused. Then those warm, swollen lips found his ear. "I stayed home tonight to be with you, Pretty."

A shudder went through him, half-broken whimper escaping him. He closed his lips over Rigger's, kissing his lover with heat and passion. Rig was right there, lips open and needy, long, thin arms sliding under muscled ones to hold him tight between them. As he slid slowly into Rigger's body, as Rock slid just as slowly into his own, Dick couldn't think of anywhere he'd rather be.

***

He was warm and happy and asleep and somebody was licking his toes. Not a 'gee, I'm horny' kind of licking, either. More a 'gee, Grim ate all the kibbles and I ate one of your favorite socks and now I need to go out back and poop balls of yarn' sort.

"Dick, go let the dogs out."

"Fuck off - 's my birthday."

"No. Yesterday was your fucking birthday. Go let the fucking dogs out."

"Fuck. Rock?"

"Go to hell," Rock muttered.

Dick sighed and got up, dropping a kiss on his belly as he went, complaining worse than Rock the entire time.

"Be good and I'll give you your birthday present when you get back." Rig was already snuggling into Rock's heat, draping over him with a sleepy purr.

Dick snorted. "If I can wake you."

Then Dick was gone, the click of claws and barking following him down the hall.

"Grouch." Rig's cheek found the hollow of Blue's shoulder

and he sighed as he settled, falling almost immediately back into his dreams. He was warm and happy and asleep and somebody was licking his belly.

Not a 'gee, I'm horny' kind of licking, either. More a 'gee you made me get up and let the dogs out and promised me my present so I'm going to fucking well wake you up' sort. He reached up for the headboard, searching out the envelope and handing it down without opening his eyes. "Happy birthday."

He got another lick around his navel and a soft kiss right above his pubes and then the bed bounced with Dick's weight. "What is it?"

"Open it, dork." He hoped the idea of a gay-friendly cruise wouldn't be too fruity for his boys. He'd decided two weeks ago that they needed a little vacation, a little rest and after last night, he was more sure of it than ever.

"Holy fuck! Are these real?"

"No, they're forgeries." Rig grinned, chuckling and waiting for Rock's curiosity to kick in. "Yeah, Dick. They're real. Happy 21st."

Rock's chest rumbled beneath his cheek.

"They're for next weekend!" The kid was bouncing a tiny bit now, making the bed shift. "There's three of them -- can I take who I want?"

"What the fuck is he talking about?"

"I bought three tickets for a little three-day cruise. Thought a mini-vacation would be fun."

One of Rock's eyebrows went up, though the big guy's eyes remained firmly shut. "The kid and I have three day passes next weekend."

He blushed and nodded. "Yeah. I know."

"Oh, man," said Dick. "Please tell me you've got the three days off as well."

Rig looked down at Dick, with the swollen eye and still-bandaged forehead that happened for him, because the boy loved him, feeling something close to normal for the first time in months. "It just so happens that I'm taking a few days off around that time."

Dick bounced in place, looking for all the world like a kid let loose in a candy shop. "I've seen advertisements by these guys on TV -- they're the gay friendly ones, aren't they?"

"Yeah. There's a party Friday night and a big dance

Saturday. All the food you want. Pool, scuba diving, the works." Rigger reached out and stroked the kid's hip. "Figured we'd try it out and, if we all liked it, plan a longer trip next summer?"

He made the offer casually, pushing his hips gently back toward Rock. He'd been scared last night -- hell, he'd probably be scared again today and tomorrow -- but he knew where he belonged.

"This is so cool, Rigger. Thanks." Dick looked over at Rock. "You'll come, right? It'll be all three of us?"

"I figure if Rig's gonna get his money's worth out of all the food you want on those tickets, I'd better go along."

"Yeah, I figured Rock could eat my share of the buffet while I'm dancing and sleeping in the sun."

"You could definitely use the color," Rock said, hand sliding around his hip and pulling him close.

Dick was still half-bouncing, half-vibrating, big shit-eating grin firmly in place. "I don't know how to thank you, Rigger." The grin actually got bigger. "Maybe you've got an idea or two?"

"Maybe." He grinned, nestling back into Blue's embrace. "Come back to bed, Dick. Kiss me good morning."

"Just good morning?" Dick asked, crawling up over him.

"For starters." Rock's hand slid between his thighs, wide and hot, as Dick settled on him, pressing him between his lovers.

"Oh, good. 'Cause I'm really, really thankful."

"Really, really?" Fuck, he loved those riverstone eyes.

"Yeah," whispered Dick against his lips. "Really, really."

Then they were kissing, Dick's mouth hot and loving.

He stretched, letting his back rub against Rock's skin, his belly rub against Dick's. His arm draped over Dick's waist, fingers playing against sensitive nerves as their kiss deepened, melting him like ice cream in the August sun.

"Fuck, you are sexy," murmured Dick against his lips.

"That's my fucking line, kid."

Dick chuckled, the sound bubbling against Rigger's lips. "I'm sure it won't kill him to hear it again."

"Oh God, this feels good." He was fucking made for this, made to be touching hot, smooth skin and tasting and sucking and fucking and loving. Made for it.

"Yeah," agreed Rock, starting to move against him, long, rippling rolls that each ended with that thick cock sliding along his crack. Dick murmured and picked up the rhythm automatically, rubbing their bodies together. Rig just closed his eyes and went with it, let his body take what it needed, reducing his need to lips and tongue and cock and hands and ass and his marines. He shifted, letting the head of Rock's prick push against his hole. Rock got the hint and somehow Dick knew just what he needed to do to help and the kid wrapped his arms around his shoulders and pulled him up, just enough to push him onto Rock's cock as the big guy pushed up.

"Fuck, yeah." He arched, head rolling as the sweet stretchy burn shot up his spine. "Yeah."

As Rock started up a long, slow rhythm, the kid's knees straddled him. He watched Dick's face, pleasure crossing it in waves as the kid impaled himself on his cock.

"Oh! Oh, fuck. Dick..." He reached out and wrapped an arm around the kid's waist, stomach clenching. "Tight."

Dick was making those sweet-as-fuck porno noises, eyes closed as he started to move, falling in with Rock's thrusts. His balls were so tight, aching like he'd not come in days. Rock was nuzzling his neck, tongue and lips playing slowly with his skin. The kid's hands were all over the place: stroking across his belly, tugging at his nipples, tickling along his ribs.

He laughed, head falling back against Rock's shoulder. The sound was a little desperate, a little overwhelmed, a lot happy. He reached for Dick's cock, tugging in time with their hips, thumb sliding over the slit.

"Oh, yeah, Rig. Oh, yeah, that's it." The kid was gasping and moaning and moving on him like a dream. "Fucking perfect..."

Not yet. He shifted his shoulders, tilted his head, groaning as Rock's lips covered his in a hot, hard, fucking sexy kiss. Now it was perfect.

The kid made a sound and started moving faster, pushing him back onto Rock. They sped together, sounds of voices and bodies growing louder, sharper, hungrier. He tightened his grip on Dick's cock, pulling with short tugs. Dick reached out blindly, hand finding his shoulder and following it over to his neck and then up to where his and Rock's mouths were fused together. One of Dick's fingers slid into their mouths and the kid called out, muscles tightening impossibly on his prick as Dick came.

It only took a second of Dick's tight-hot muscles fluttering around his cock to send him gasping into Rock's mouth, filling Dick with his come. He triggered Rock, the solid body beneath him rippling, the thick cock deep inside him losing its load. He shuddered, nerves firing randomly as pleasure moved through him, so fucking good.

Dick collapsed against him, breathing like a steam engine, skin soft and hot and sweaty. Rig wrapped around him and held on tight. Rock's arms slid along his, fingers linking with his as the big guy held both him and Dick in a tight embrace.

"Good morning... afternoon... whatever." Rig leaned in to give Dick a kiss. "Happy late birthday."

Dick grinned and kissed him back, groaning as his cock slid out of the kid's body.

"Oh, somebody tell me it's nowhere near five." Rig snuggled happily, eyes closing. "I'm so not interested in going in tonight."

"You're supposed to go in for seven tonight?" Dick clung tightly. "Fuck, I hate sleeping without you, Rigger. No offence, Rock."

"None taken -- you don't cut it as a Rigger substitute either, asshole."

Rigger nodded, biting his bottom lip. "I... I wanted to see what y'all thought about my going to get my PA certificate at Duke come January. I'd be real tight on cash for a while, working half-time and then schooling, but when I was done, I could have a practice of my own."

He'd been thinking on it since the hospital'd said he'd have to work Christmas. He'd missed last year with Momma and didn't intend on being apart from his family -- any of it -- this year.

"Oh, Rigger, cool!" Dick kissed him with his usual enthusiasm, face full of grins.

Rock's arms tightened around them both. "Your own practice... sounds like something you deserve."

"Yeah. It means my own hours, my own patients." He looked up into Rock's eyes. "It means seeing 'em get better and go on, you know?"

His Blue's eyes smiled at him. "You always did care too much. You're going to be full up in no time."

"Yeah?" He took a kiss. "Thank you."

"Not to mention you're going to have the ladies eating out of your hand with all that southern charm." Rock winked at him and one kiss became two.

He felt his cheeks heat and Rock chuckled and then Dick was right there and two became three.

Chapter Eighteen

Dick bounced on the bed the size of a dime and grinned over at Rigger and Rock. "It's a king-size!" Bounding up, he checked out the bathroom. "Shower's kind of small," he called back to the guys. "Good thing we don't mind a tight fit, right?"

"I bet we'll manage." Rigger's voice was muffled, ass up in the air, pulling out clothes.

"Mm..." Dick walked over to him and rubbed his suddenly hard cock against that bubble cowboy butt. "I see you're fixing to start the party right away."

"Oh." Rig looked over his shoulder, grey eyes shining. He'd gotten his hair fixed and he looked good, slick and sexy, high cheekbones obvious, talented mouth visible and just barely open...

Dick moaned, and rubbed harder against Rigger's ass. "Are we actually going to ever make it out of the room?"

"Shit, yeah. There's a dance tomorrow night! And dolphins and swimming and... Oh, fuck, your cock feels good." Rigger spread his legs. "Up to a little bon voyage fuck?"

"Fuck, yeah."

"Is that all you two ever think of?" asked Rock. Of course the complaint would have been more sincere if Rock hadn't snugged his hips up against Dick's butt.

"Fuck off, Rock. You wanna share your feelings, go wave goodbye to the shore, or get a nice friendly blow job?" Rigger was chuckling, hands pulling off the tight black T-shirt, leaving him in nothing but boots and painted on jeans.

"I'm gonna fuck the kid's ass while he fucks yours -- this is his birthday present after all."

"Actually," Dick said slowly, eyes on the picture Rigger made, "I'm kind of thinking I'll take that blow job. Don't take off those jeans or the boots, Rig."

Rigger stood and turned, hand sliding down his flat belly to cup the straining cock outlined in denim. "You want this?"

"You know it, Rig." Dick leaned in and nuzzled the hot prick through Rigger's jeans.

Rig's thighs parted, the denim stretching. One hands slid over his head. "Straighten up, marine. Want to suck you."

Moaning, he straightened. Rock grabbed his arms, pulling him back against the hard body and hard cock, holding him steady. Rig sank to his knees, hands working open his jeans, lips parted. "Oh, fuck."

Rock chuckled behind him as big hands slid beneath his shirt, lifting it up over his head. "That's our Rigger."

"Yes, sir. Y'all's through and through." Rigger grinned, pushing his jeans down and sliding those hungry lips over the head of his cock.

Dick moaned, pushing into Rigger's mouth, hardly noticing as Rock slid his jeans down the rest of the way and helped him step out of them. Rigger's mouth was teasing, light licks and gentle suction combining with barely-there strokes to his balls to drive him mad.

"Just watch him, kid. Look at that face -- he fucking loves this." Rock's voice was low, vibrating against the skin of his neck. "We are two of the luckiest fuckers in this whole damn world."

Rig's hands slid around him, fingers working open Rock's jeans even as those lips worked their magic on his cock. Rig looked happy, grey eyes bright, lips pulling. Then he was trapped between their bodies, Rock hard and hot behind him, Rigger's mouth tight and hot around him. Fuck it was good. So fucking good.

There were noises all around, the little cabin echoing with his noises and Rock's noises and Rig's noises and... Fuck! Rig's fingers had Rock's prick, sliding it over his hole again and again. Rock's fingers wrapped around his ass, pulling it apart, the big guy rocking forward every time Rigger slid that thick cock against his opening.

Pulling off Dick's cock, Rig's head dipped, ducking between Dick's legs for a second. Rock moaned and then when Rig's lips returned to pulling and sucking, the cock pushing against his asshole slick and wet. He moaned and his hands found Rigger's shoulders as he spread his legs and bent slightly forward. Rig's lips pulled him in deep as Rock's prick pushed inside, stretching and filling him. Thick fingers tugged at his nipples while slender ones manipulated his balls. He was nothing but a ball of sensation.

The pressure and pleasure kept growing, rocketing through him, making him fly.

He pushed back and forth between them, riding back onto Rock's cock and then forward into Rigger's hot mouth. Rig's lips took him in deep, nose buried in his curls. The suction increased, Rig pulling and sucking and humming and sucking. He moaned and whimpered and groaned and just fucking loved every second of it.

As he watched, Rock's hands slid around his waist, Rigger's hands moving up to join them. Long fingers twined with thick ones and when he reached up with his own, his fingers fit right in. Fucking perfect.

He shot his load down Rigger's mouth, muscles clenching around Rock's fat prick. Rigger took him all down, Rock fucking him hard, cock pushing in sharp jerks. He just shook and shuddered, calling out nonsense words that said how good it was.

Rig stood up and took a kiss, tongue pushing deep with a harsh moan. Fuck, he could taste himself there and the barest hint of Rock and all that pure Rigger, filling his mouth. Rigger was whimpering, pressing into him, denim-clad cock rubbing against him, hands keeping their mouths fused.

His own hands slid around to Rigger's ass, finding Rock's already there, the big guy still pounding into him, pulling Rigger tight against him with each thrust. Rig's thrusts matched Rock's, soft, needy sounds pouring into his lips. He pushed one hand between them, finding one of Rigger's nipples and tugging. The other hand slid around to find Rock's ass, just touching his other lover's hard, working muscles.

"Shit, yeah. Good, fuck." Rigger muttered against his lips, hips jerked against him.

"We're gonna make him cream his jeans, kid."

Oh, fuck, yeah. His own cock was coming back to life, caught as he was between the two of them.

Rig was humping against him, slim body shuddering as they rubbed together. He gave up kissing Rigger's mouth, leaving that for Rock as he bent and fastened his lips around the sweet spot on Rigger's neck, sucking hard. Rig convulsed in his arms, groaning and grunting, shooting a load into those painted-on jeans.

"Mm, got him," murmured Rock, still pushing into him with hard jerks. Dick chuckled against the warm skin in his mouth.

"Now it's time to get you, Rocketman." Dick chuckled again as Rock's thrusts stuttered when Rig took the big guy's mouth in a deep, long kiss.

As his hard prick slid against the front of Rigger's jeans, he thought being between the two of them was just about the best place in the world to be.

***

Rock lay on a deck chair, every muscle in his body relaxed. He cracked open an eye and all he could see was blue, blue sky above him. The sun was hot, the smell of ocean salt carried on a cool breeze.

He was stuffed full of good food and good drink and Rigger had just given him a massage under the guise of spreading on suntan lotion. Not that they'd needed a ruse, the cruise was gay-friendly and it was an interesting feeling, not having to worry about what people might think if you kissed the guy next to you or held his hand.

Rigger was sitting in the chair next to him, watching and shouting out comments to Dick as the kid swam and played. He hadn't heard that light-hearted note in Rig's voice in a long time. Sounded good. Rig was already starting to bronze up, the grey tinge to that skin warming to the familiar gold. Laughing grey eyes swung over to him, fucking sexy and happy and relaxed. "Having a good time?"

He nodded. "Food, sun and sex -- what's not to like?"

"Good point." Rig stretched out, a few white curls peeking out of the top of his swim trunks. "Very good point."

Rock reached out and slid his hand along Rigger's side. "What about you, Rig?"

Rig's eyes popped open and he started, making Rock grin. Rig worked so hard at never touching either of them where they could be seen, was so aware of keeping space between them, that the old boy was constantly surprised at any public caress. "Yeah. I've got no complaints."

"Feels good, doesn't it," he said softly. Retirement was starting to look better and better. Just a couple more years and they could do this kind of thing a little more often.

"Yeah." Rig blushed, cheeks shining. "Yeah, it does."

He grinned and would have leaned in for a kiss but a quiet voice interrupted him. "I'm sorry, but I was wondering if you were using this chair -- these are the only two next to each other..."

Turning, he found a good-looking Latino kid holding hands with an older thin man in dark glasses. On closer inspection, the kid probably was closer to his age than Rigger's. It was Dick's chair, but the kid hadn't used it since he'd dropped his towel on it when they'd first come out.

"Go ahead," he said, grabbing Dick's stuff and putting it between him and Rigger.

They settled down into the chairs, the Latino waiting for the tall guy to settle before he took the far seat. The thin guy, hair clipped closer than his, looked over in his direction. "Thanks for the chair, man."

"Yeah, no problem. Dick can share with Rigger if he ever decides to get out of the pool."

Rigger leaned over Rock, arm brushing over his crotch so nonchalantly as he held out his hand. "I'm Rig. This is Rock. The young buck that we've lost to water volleyball is Dick."

The Latino leaned casually past the tall guy, shaking Rigger's hand. "Pablo and this is Marc."

Marc grinned and nodded. "Nice to meet you."

"Same here." Rig leaned back and stole a sip of Rock's beer, before flipping onto his stomach, giving Rock a view of that tight ass. "Are y'all enjoying the boat? I'm thinking I could get used to sunning and eating and watching dolphins and being a bum."

The Latino guy, Pablo, giggled and nodded. "It's pretty nice."

Rock smiled politely in their direction before he let his gaze get distracted by that sweet ass again. He wondered how long they'd have to stay before they could go back to their cabin without seeming rude. Rig let his legs spread slightly, back stretched out and gleaming under the sun. Rock could fucking smell him now, coconut oil and sex and sunshine, the combination familiar and good. So fucking good.

Fuck, he was going to be giving their new acquaintances a fucking show in a second. He turned quickly over to his own front, turning his attention away from Rigger, who was fucking doing it on purpose, he was sure.

"You need me to put sunscreen on you, Rock?" Rig's voice was low, teasing, full of laughter.

"If you want." He buried his face in his hands, but Pablo was asking Marc the same thing.

"I do." Rig's weight settled on his ass, cock pressing against his crack. Hot oil poured over his back before Rig's hands started spreading it. "I'd hate for you to get sunburned."

He buried the strangled noise he made in his hands. Shit, Rigger was trying to kill him. Being able to hold hands and touch in public was one thing, practically humping him was quite another. To Rig's credit, he didn't push it farther, rubbing the oil into his back and arms before that hard cock moved away and those hands smoothed the lotion into the backs of his thighs. Not that he wasn't just about drilling a hole in the cushion on the deck chair, his prick was so hard. He was going to have to wait until Dick got back and hope the kid was feeling mischievous enough to dunk cold water on him.

"You going to do me next, Rock?" Rig moved off him, settling back on the lounge chair. "I mean, do my back." He shot Rig an incredulous look. The fucker was doing it on purpose. Rig blushed again, eyes flashing out over the ocean for a second before returning to him with a wink. "I'm just playing around with you, Rock. You want another beer or water or something? I'm thirsty as hell."

"A Coke would be great and I'm gonna hold you to that thought later on," he added quietly, letting Rigger see how much he'd been affected by the touches.

Next to them, Pablo was just finishing up and Marc's cheeks were pink. Rock couldn't help but chuckle. It was probably a miracle there was anyone on deck at all.

Rig stood and shrugged on a tank top -- one of his, it looked like -- and grinned over at the couple beside him. "Y'all want anything to drink while I'm up?"

"Oh, that'd be great, thanks. I'll take a Dr. Pepper -- Marc?" As he watched, Pablo slid his hand along Marc's arm, the touch unselfconscious, easy.

"Water, thanks." It was weird; the guy seemed to be talking to Rig's left armpit. Rig nodded and headed off, greeted on the way by a group they'd had supper with the night before.

He watched that fine ass go for awhile before turning back to

Pablo and Marc. "So what are you guys back in real life?"

"I'm a sculptor and Pablo's a writer." Marc grinned, reaching out for Pablo. "In other words, we fuck around a lot and pretend to be grownups."

Rock chuckled. "So this is what -- just a change of venue?"

"Our honeymoon, actually." Marc's grin widened. "The first leg of it, anyway. But yeah, I love the water and wanted to smell the ocean and Pablo's humoring me."

"Your honeymoon? Congratulations." He glanced over at Rigger who was chatting up the guy at the bar, laughing and smiling. He had to hold back his laugh as he thought of the expression on his good old boy's face if he ever suggested a "wedding".

Pablo was blushing, but there was a grin on his face and he squeezed his partner's hand.

"Thanks." The guy sounded satisfied, happy. "What do you do, Rock?"

He opened his mouth to answer when Rig's face caught his eye. A group of playful, joking guys had crowded around the bar, jostling and loud. Rig was pale, stiff, grabbing the four bottles and hightailing it out and onto the deck. He stiffened, was halfway up when he realized that Rig was just fine. A little freaked out maybe, but coping. On his own. He took a breath and settled back down.

"Sorry, what was that?" he asked, still watching Rig.

"Oh, just wondering what you did." Marc had turned to look at his partner, the look on the long face vaguely confused.

Rig was making his way toward them, relaxing as he got closer. He felt himself relaxing as well.

"I'm in the Corps. A lifer," he admitted as he watched Pablo lean over and whisper something to Marc.

"Hard job." Marc relaxed again, face turning back toward him. "Is your friend in the service too?"

"Not a chance." Rig handed Pablo a bottle and handed the water out toward Marc. "I'm a nurse."

Rock's eyebrows rose as Marc totally ignored the water. The penny dropped when Pablo took it and put it in Marc's hand.

"Thanks, babe." Marc opened the bottle and took a drink. "Thank you, Rig, that hits the spot. A nurse, huh? There's no stress at your house, is there?"

Rig laughed, sitting back down and handing Rock his Coke.

"Well, given that Dick is a marine, too? Nope. None."

Rock sat back up properly, erection gone thanks to Rigger's little adventure. Rig seemed fine now though, so he let it go after a last, lingering look to make sure everything was how it should be. It was. Rig looked like a million dollars and Rock felt that erection fight to come back.

Rig smiled at him, nodding toward his drink. "Drink up, Rock. You're flushed."

That had Pablo giggling and Marc chuckling and Rock felt his face get even more flushed. Dick was suddenly plopping himself down on the bottom of Rock's chair, all wet and dripping and happy smiles. He'd never been so happy to see the kid.

Rigger handed Dick a bottle of water and a towel. "Hey, kid. Did y'all win the game?"

"You know it. Kicked some ass." Dick shook out his hair like a great big dog, getting them all wet, before grabbing the water and gulping it down.

Rig lifted one eyebrow, lips pursing as he fought a grin. "And this perfectly mannered mutt is Dick. Dick, be a good boy and shake hands with Marc and Pablo."

Marc laughed, holding his hand out, grinning over at Pablo. "See? I told you we should have brought Piet."

Dick shook their hands. "Who's Piet? You guys a threesome, too?"

Rock swore the fucking air pressure changed from everybody's jaw dropping -- well, everybody's but Marc's. He just laughed and shook his head. "Only in the oddest sense of the word, I guess. Piet's my guide dog."

"You guys are a threesome?" Pablo asked.

Dick nodded. "So you're blind," he asked Marc. "How come you didn't bring the dog -- Piet?"

"He doesn't like to fly and we're city hopping. Besides, I've got my husband here, I'll manage."

"Husband? You guys are married? Cool." Dick turned a sly look on him and then Rig. "You and Rig ever talked about getting married?" Dick asked.

Rig gave a snort. "No, Dick, and somehow I don't foresee it happening in the near future."

The kid just gave them both a shit-eating grin and drank the rest of his water.

"Okay, I'm going to go take a shower and a nap before

supper." Rig grinned and winked. "The dance is tonight and I figure I've got to rest up. There's lots of men on this boat."

Dick gave him a look and hit his leg with the back of his hand. He glared at the kid but cleared his throat. "Save a spot on your card for me."

The look on Rig's face was worth it. Rigger looked like he'd just been beaned by a baseball, utterly stunned. Those wide eyes looked at him for a few seconds and then Rig shook his head like he was trying to clear it, taking a shaky breath. "Tease."

He nodded. "I guess maybe I am at that. All right, Texas -- you save that spot for Dick, 'cause the rest are mine."

With that he winked at the kid and said goodbye to Marc and Pablo and sauntered off toward the workout room.

***

By the time the dance actually started, he'd convinced himself Rock was joking. Or humoring Dick. Or losing his mind. They'd been together eight and a half years and hadn't so much as danced in the front room. There was no fucking way Blue was going to dance with him in front of God and everybody. Still, he'd worn his best shirt -- the soft grey one that made his eyes stand out. And his good jeans and his ostrich boots. Shaved real close, too.

Just in case.

He wandered toward the crowded ballroom, following the music and the sound of applause. He hadn't danced in months. The mixture of nerves and anticipation had kept him away from the dining room at supper, but he gathered up his nerve and now... now he just had to find a willing partner. He moved into the room, sliding along the wall until he found a good spot to watch from.

He could see Pablo and Marc dancing together, along with one of the couples they'd sat with the night before. The dance floor wasn't that busy yet, probably only about half full. Dick and Rock were over by the food table, Dick in a new pair of jeans and a soft green sweater; shit, the kid looked good.

Then he saw Rock. Rock was wearing... he'd never seen Rock in the clothes he was wearing before. His Blue had on a pair of black dress pants and a light blue dress shirt, a couple of buttons at the top undone. He wore dress shoes and, even from this distance, Rigger could tell the man had shaved.

Fuck.

He got goose bumps -- so long, so many nights of fucking and fighting and laughing and loving and he'd still follow that beautiful son of a bitch anywhere.

Rig made his way over to his boys, giving them both a warm smile, his stomach full of butterflies. "Hey. Fuck, you both look good enough to eat."

"That's why we're standing by the buffet." Rock grinned at him.

The kid laughed and bounced. "You wanna show me how to two-step before they change the music, Rig?"

"I'd love to." He held out his hand and led Dick to the edge of the dance floor. "You having fun, kid?"

Dick grinned at him, squeezing his hand and then giving him a quick hug. "The best time, Rigger. Thank you."

"Good. I'm glad. I've got to make my men happy on their birthday, yeah, Pretty?" He showed the kid the steps a few times and they were off, laughing around the dance floor.

They danced through two songs and the kid somehow managed to have them back at Rock when the music changed to something soft and slow. "He's all yours, Rock."

"Thanks, kid." His Blue stepped forward, arms open. "You gonna dance with me, Rigger?"

He wanted to say yes. He wanted to say please and thank you and that he'd wanted to do this from the very first day. He wanted to say lots and lots of things and his mouth just wouldn't work. So he just looked into those amazing blue-blue eyes and nodded.

Yeah, he was gonna dance.

Rock's eyes never left his as those strong arms went around his waist.

"Oh, wait a minute," said Rock, letting go of him and stepping back, even as those blue eyes continued to gaze into his own.

He arched an eyebrow, half-expecting Rock to have found his excuse not to dance. "Everything okay?"

Rock nodded, hand shoving into the pocket of his pants. "I've got something that's yours and I think it's about time you took it back."

"Mine?" He leered in the general direction of Rock's zipper, playful. "You sure you want me to take it here? I'm not sure these people are that friendly."

Rock chuckled and shook his head. "Not that, asshole. I meant this."

Rock held out his hand, a ring sitting in the middle of the large palm. His ring.

"Oh..." He smiled up, wanting like anything to kiss his Blue. He'd thought Rock had it, but he couldn't remember for sure, and didn't want to ask, and he'd missed it so. His ring.

"You want me to put it on you?"

"I've been missing it something fierce." He reached out his hand, casual enough that Rock could slip it on or he could put it on himself.

Rock slid the ring onto his finger. "Should have said something."

"Yeah, probably." He grinned, wiggling his fingers slightly. "Still looks damned good. Love this ring."

"Good." Rock's arms opened, his Blue stepping forward again. "We gonna dance or just stand here yammering?"

"We're gonna dance, Blue." He slid into those arms like he was made for them. Rock sort of shuffled him back onto the dance area and then pulled him in close.

"Oh. Blue." They moved together to something sweet and soft and all he knew was that he was dancing with his lover. He rested his cheek against Rock's and closed his eyes, lost in the sensations.

He could feel Rock's arms, hot and hard and right around him. He could feel every breath that Rock took, his lover's chest shifting against his. He thought he could feel Rock's heart, beating against him. And he knew he could feel that fucking hard prick, nudging him.

It was everything he had thought it would be and maybe even a tiny bit more. Rigger tilted his head, lips close to his Blue's ear. "I love you, Jim. Thank you."

Rock stood absolutely still and drew back to look into his eyes. His Blue looked so very, very serious and then he smiled, eyes crinkling. "Ditto."

And they were dancing again.

Chapter Nineteen

The dogs were running around chasing each other, their own tails and, only sometimes, the green ball Dick was throwing for them. Rock was pulling a double shift, making up some time, paying back a favor. He didn't know where Rigger was but for now he had the house and the furry beasts to himself.

It was fun. For the first five minutes.

Now he just missed the guys.

"Hey, Pretty. Want a cup of coffee? I've got two." Rig was wrapped in a sweater, leaning against the doorframe.

Dick nodded, even as he mentally shook his head. Rig had started calling him pretty just around the time of the cruise. He didn't get it. He headed for the door and took the mug from Rig, along with a soft kiss. The dogs barked at him as the screen door closed behind him, trying to convince him to stay outside with them. "I'm not, you know."

"Not what, kid?" Rigger snuggled up to his side and stole another kiss.

He grinned and offered another. "Pretty."

Rigger licked his bottom lip, warm hand sliding under his sweatshirt to stroke his belly. "Are, too."

He made a soft noise. "Horny as fuck -- yes. Pretty -- no."

"Don't argue, kid. When your lover says you're pretty, accept the compliment." Rig kissed the soft spot below his ear.

He laughed softly and pressed closer. "Even if it isn't true?"

The nip was firm and hard. "Come here, I'll show you."

Then Rig started walking him down the hall.

"Show me what?" he asked, laughing as he followed Rig.

"How pretty you are." Rig tugged him into the bedroom, standing them in front of the bureau mirror. Rig's eyes grinned at him from over his shoulder. "Look, Dick. Pretty."

He just shook his head and laughed, wondering what had gotten into Rig. "You're a nut, but I'm keeping you anyway."

"Well, that's good to know." Rig started pulling up his

sweatshirt, hands long against his stomach. "But you're still easy on the eye, Dick. Muscles and smooth skin and riverstones for eyes and oh... your cock."

He felt his cheeks get hot. "I never said I thought I wasn't good-looking. But riverstones for eyes? Pretty? There's a word for that. Exaggeration, but that's not the word, it's hype or something."

"Truth, Pretty." Rig pulled away his sweatshirt and then nuzzled his shoulder. "I love your eyes. I think your eyes are pretty."

Turning, he met Rig's eyes, reading the love and the earnest belief there. Shit, he loved this man. Turning back to the mirror he gasped softly. His love for Rig, his happiness to be in this house with Rig and Rock, it was there in his eyes, making them glow.

"See? I'm not shitting you." Rig's hands moved over his body, tweaking his nipples, counting his ribs, circling his navel.

He moaned and watched as Rigger's hands slid over his skin. It was like watching a porno, only the stuff he could see happening was happening to him -- he could feel it as well as see it. A soft shudder went through him, making all his muscles ripple. He grabbed one of Rigger's hands and pushed it down to his waistband. "What was that about my cock?"

Rig's warm fingers teased along the waistband. "Long and sweet. Love the sounds you make when I run my tongue along the ridge."

He shuddered again and whimpered, watching as Rig's fingers continued to tease. He moved his hands back, sliding them into the back of Rig's pants, grabbing the sweet ass. Rig hummed, snuggling closer, fingertips sliding into his sweats. One finger trailed over the slit of his cock, pulling just slightly. "Love how it feels when you push inside me, fuck me deep."

Oh, fuck... Rigger was gonna have him coming just from his fucking words. And the sight of Rig's hand disappearing into his sweats...

"Love how your mouth feels, the way your balls press against mine when we fuck, the way you're always up for a little midnight action, slow and quiet." Rig's other hand cupped his nuts through the sweats, squeezing just slightly.

"Fuck me..." His eyes wanted to close, his head wanted to fall back against Rig, but he wanted to see, wanted to watch as

Rig's hands slid over him, making his sweats tent strangely.

"Is that a request or an exclamation?" Rig pumped and squeezed and licked and nuzzled, those grey eyes gleaming at him the entire time.

He laughed, but the sound came out as a squeak and a moan. He pushed ineffectually at his sweats. "Wanna see," he complained, hardly recognizing his own voice.

"Good. I want you to watch." Rig pushed his sweats down, moaning softly as his cock bobbed into view. "See, Pretty? Fucking edible."

Then those hands wrapped around his prick and began stroking. He'd never watched himself before, not like this. Suddenly he wanted to fuck Rigger, get fucked by him, and he wanted to watch Rock fuck him as well. Oh, fuck, he could just imagine what all three of them would look like.

Shit, he was close and Rigger wasn't even breathing hard. All he could do was open and close his hands around Rig's ass.

Rig purred against his ear. "That's it, Pretty. That's what I see when you're loving me, when you're loving Rock. So fucking hot, so good. So right. My pretty lover, making me fucking fly."

Those long fingers never stopped moving.

"Shit, Rig, I'm gonna... "

"Fuck, yeah. Let me see, Pretty. Let me see." Rig's voice was sheer fucking sex, fingers tugging and sliding and working him hard. His mouth opened, a cry coming out as he came, spunk hitting his stomach and Rig's hand and the floor. The motions of Rig's hand slowed, eased, spreading his come over his cock and then his belly. "See? Pretty."

He rubbed back against Rig's hard prick. "Fuck me."

"Fuck, yes." Rig's fingers pushed inside him, slick and wet with his own come, sliding deep. It didn't take Rig but a second to shimmy out of his pants and replace fingers with cock. "You like watching us, Pretty? Like watching me fuck you?"

"Fuck, yeah." He spread his legs further and held on tight to Rig's ass with his hands. It was awkward as fuck but he wasn't willing to stop long enough to move forward and grab onto the dresser. "You think... we can put a mirror on the ceiling?"

"If... fuck, you're tight." Rig bent his knees, searching for a good angle. "If you can get the big guy to say yes, I'm... love fucking you, Pretty... He says yes, I'm easy."

"Shit, Rig -- you're always easy -- one of the things I love about you." He groaned as Rig kept searching for the best way in and finally staggered forward and grabbed onto the dresser, bending over it and spreading his legs wide.

"Oh, better!" Rig pushed in deep, hands gripping his hips. "How do you want me, Pretty? Slow and easy? Hard and fast?"

He opened his mouth to answer, but only sounds came out. Probably just as well -- he couldn't decide. He heard Rig's chuckle and then Rig stretched out over him, hips thrusting in steady, deep motions.

"Oh, fuck!" He watched the mirror, watched as his body moved back into Rig and Rig into him. Shit, he wanted to see Rig's cock go into his body, but there was no way they were going to manage that, not without acrobatics.

Rig's eyes were hot, staring at him in the mirror as Rigger fucked him hard. "So good, fucking you. Oh, Pretty, 's so goddamned good."

He made a noise in response and then another, bracing himself, watching as his muscles worked, as his cock bobbed, as Rigger fucked him. The angle of Rig's cock changed, the hot flesh sliding over his gland. "Oh, fuck!"

He pushed back hard, forgetting to breathe, and he watched and felt and fuck it was good. So fucking good.

"Yes." One of Rig's hands grabbed his cock, tugging hard as those thin hips slammed into him, Rig's face stunned and needy and sexy as fuck.

That was it, he was going to come. He held on as long as he could, just watching their bodies move together, watching the raw need on his own face and the echo of it on Rig's. Then he was coming, spunk spraying the mirror as shudders moved through him, climbing up from his toes and shooting out his cock. Rig rode him hard for a few more thrusts before pulling their bodies together with a low cry, heat pulsing deep inside him.

He was panting, out of breath and barely able to stand, but he didn't look away from the mirror, catching Rig's face through the whole thing. They were both sweaty and flushed now, almost glowing from their fucking orgasms.

Fuck they did look good. Both of them. Rig and him.

"See?" Rig grinned, kissing his shoulder blade. "Pretty as fuck."

"Pretty fucking anyway," he murmured, turning his head for

Rig's mouth.

"Quit arguing, asshole." Rig's lips covered his, warm and lazy and sweet.

He laughed as the kiss ended. "I don't know, Rig, so far arguing's done me well."

That earned him a sharp slap on the ass as Rig backed away. "Come on. Shower and then we'll order some Chinese -- I rented "Pitch Black" and "Resident Evil.""

"All right -- fucking to horror, my favorite!"

Rig smiled at him, mischievous and warm and happy. "Never let it be said I don't know my boys."

He laughed and chased Rig into the bathroom.

Maybe being pretty wasn't so bad after all.

Chapter Twenty

Rig had wanted to drive down to Momma's, just like always, but Rock put his foot down in the form of three roundtrip tickets to Dallas and a receipt for a rental car.

"We get there two days before Christmas -- we can pick up gifts once we're there." And with that any of Rig's objections had been squashed. He wasn't going to have his Rabbit stuck in a car for twenty whatever fucking hours, his leg and ribs twinging on him.

The drive from DFW was uneventful and it wasn't long before they were pulling up the familiar lane. He grunted and nodded with satisfaction as he noted Bobby's car wasn't in the driveway. They could do without that asshole's input for as long as possible. "We're here."

Momma came hurrying down the steps, all damp eyes and wide smiles, Deuce behind her looking like a fucking linebacker -- damn, the kid had grown. Rig was still shaking off the effects of his nap, but got out of the car for his hug. "Hey, Momma."

"Baby. Oh, Baby. You're home and I'm not letting you go again for days." Momma just sort of held on, Deuce looking uncomfortable as hell.

"Sorry, Uncle Jimmy. She's been fretting on him."

He clapped Deuce on the shoulder, leaving it up to the kid if he wanted the usual hug or not. "She's his Momma, Deuce -- it's what they do."

"Yeah, and she's the best." He got a wide grin and a hard hug. "Glad y'all're here. Last year just wasn't right and after April we... well, I'm sure glad to see all y'all."

He nodded and then winked. "Go say hello to your Uncle Richard and help him with our bags, I'll rescue Alex long enough to get him inside."

"Yeah. Hey, I got a new forty-aught I want to show you, too. Won it at a shooting competition. Took all-around champion." The kid gave him a proud grin, then hopped over to Dick. "Hey, Uncle Richard! Man, you can tell you've been working out with

Uncle Jimmy!"

"And who have you been working out with? Holy sh--ugar!" Dick cleared his throat and threw Momma an apologetic grin. "Congrats on the shooting championship."

Rock let them be and went around the car to join Momma and Rig. "Give me my hug, Momma, he'll still be here after."

He got a grateful look from Rigger as Momma turned to him and folded him into a tight hug. "Hey, son. I've been missing you, too. Merry Christmas, Jim."

"Merry Christmas, Momma." He gave her a tight hug and then put an arm around her shoulders and the other around Rig's and led them up to the house. "Deuce is looking good."

"Isn't he though? He's going to start on the varsity team next year, I'm thinking." Momma looked up at him with a little frown. "My Alex is looking thin, Jim. Y'all not feeding him?"

"Momma, let him be. I'm fine. Don't start."

"Don't you use that tone of voice on me Jeremy Alexander. I'm not speaking to you. I'm talking to Jim."

"He just needs a little of his Momma's home cooking, Momma. You'll have him put to right in no time." He gave Rig a look -- if Rig didn't want her to fuss he shouldn't have come; it was simple as that.

Rig stuck out his tongue and rolled those eyes, but Momma nodded, silver curls just bobbing. "I've got a turkey and a ham for Christmas dinner, gonna fry up chicken tonight. Oh, I am glad to have you boys home where you belong. Oh!" Momma stopped short. "Are y'all going to be able to make the stairs in the garage apartment? I'll give y'all my room if you need it..."

"Christ, Momma, I've been working for months. You know -- hospitals, emergencies, on my feet all damned day? I'm not broken."

Momma arched an eyebrow and snorted. "And, I tell you what, working that hard hasn't done a damned thing for your good-nature."

He swallowed his smile and nearly choked on his laughter, but he managed to keep a straight face and stay out of it. "Deuce and Dick can take our stuff to the garage, Momma -- we won't put you out of your bed."

Dick came over and stopped them just before they went in. "Deuce is going to show me his rifles once we've put the bags up. We might get in a bit of target practice if that's okay Ma'am -

- I mean Momma."

"Oh, that's fine, Richard. I'm going to get y'all boys to help me with supper, let Alex rest, but you're free 'til then."

Deuce's eyes twinkled, just as full of life as his uncle's. "What about Uncle Jimmy, Ma-maw? He don't have to help?"

Momma chuckled. "Oh, he's gonna help, boy, don't you fret. After all, someone's got to make sure your Uncle Alex sits and rests and eats, don't they?"

"Momma!" Rig's voice rang out over their laughter.

Dick got a quick hug and then took off with Deuce, the two of them still chuckling. He just manhandled Rig and Momma in through the door. "Front room or kitchen, Momma?"

"Kitchen -- it's nice and cozy warm. I'll make coffee and y'all can have some pecan cookies. I just made 'em this morning."

"Oh, cookies."

The kitchen was nice and warm and he helped himself to three cookies and got out three coffee mugs for Momma before sitting down at the table. He was just waiting for the interrogation to start.

"Mmm... There's nothing like a nice warm cup of coffee when the weather's cold." Momma gave Rig a side-ways glance. "How's that leg doing you, baby? It still twinging you?"

"No, Momma, it's fine." It was a sick entertainment, watching the world's most stubborn cowboy and his endless energy momma go at it.

"Really? That's why y'all went so far as to fly out? And the lungs, they're okay?"

"Fine, Momma."

"You stop that nasty smoking, yet?"

"Momma..."

"Jim? You still letting him smoke?"

"I'm a grown man, Momma."

"That all depends on whether or not I've found all his hiding spots, Momma."

"Oh, good Lord and butter." Momma rolled her eyes. "Check behind the toilet tank and in the very, very back of the linen closet. Those were his favorites when he was a teenager. His daddy tended to hide his in the tool shed behind the lawnmower."

Rig's cheeks were bright red, eyes focused on the table. "Momma!"

He just chuckled and snagged himself another cookie. "It's the jeep and his locker at work I can't search."

"You're not helping here, Rock." Rig gave his momma a look. "I'm okay. Honest. I'm starting school next month, I'm going half-time at the hospital. I'm just fine."

"You don't look fine, Alexander. You look sick. You're skin and bones and all grey. You look like you're fixin' to keel over."

"I'm just tired, Momma. Working nights has always been hard for me, you know that." Rig reached across the table. "I'm okay. Ask Rock. He'll tell you. I'm just fine."

"I'm staying out of this one, Rig." He was no fool; Momma was a force to be reckoned with.

"I'm not looking to be a bitch, baby. I'm not." She took Rig's hand, squeezed it. "I love you. I worry about you. Jim's worried. Richard's worried. You've got to let yourself heal up, you've got to sleep and eat like a normal man."

"I do, Momma. I eat. I sleep. I work. Hell, don't you want to know about the college I'm starting?"

"You going to go to your own graduation and invite me this time?"

Rig nodded. "Yes, Momma. I promise. We'll have a party and everything."

"We should have you down and let you plan it," Rock suggested. Hell, it was Christmas; he could afford to throw her a bone. He tucked his legs well to the right, hopefully out of range of Rig's feet.

Charlene's eyes lit up and she nodded. "Oh, I'd love that. Spend a week or so just vacationing and cooking and visiting."

Rig's kick hit the chair leg, vibrated his chair. He gave Rig a grin. "That'd be great, Momma -- 'cause I can't plan a party for shit."

"Oh, Alexander's a fair hand at it, but I'm in the mood for a good party and I have two years to work at it." She gave Rigger a happy smile and Rock could *see* Rigger give in. That man loved his momma more than just about anything.

"You shouldn't have to plan your own party, Rig." He nudged Rig's leg with his own foot and gave his Rabbit a little smile.

Rig scooted closer, free hand petting his thigh under the table. "That's the truth. You know you're always welcome, Momma. When's Sissy coming?"

"They'll all be in late tomorrow night, early Christmas eve morning. Means y'all will have to go shopping tomorrow, I reckon."

"Or we could go Christmas Eve morning and duck out on all the kids." He gave Rig a wink and waited for the heat to be turned on him.

"Jim South! Those baby girls have been nothing but wanting to see their uncles since we told them y'all were coming. Y'all haven't even seen Maddie since she was a baby -- she's two now. Walking and talking and everything."

Rig was drinking his coffee, hiding that shit-eating grin.

"Yes, ma'am." He gave Rig another wink. Rig chuckled into his coffee, flushed and happy.

"Oh, you two brats!" Momma laughed and took a cookie. "Have one, Alexander. Tell me if they're good and tell me all about who's watching those pups of y'all's."

Rig took a cookie without complaint, leaning against his shoulder and chattering away with Momma. He sat eating cookies and drinking coffee. It was warm and good and smelled like Christmas. Almost like normal.

***

It was weird, sitting and snuggling with Rock on the pew along one side of the table, watching Momma and Dick and Deuce cooking. Weird, but kind of nice. Dozy. Peaceful, with one of Rock's arms around him and no one saying anything if he floated off every now and again.

Momma kept trying to spoil them, too. Coffee'd been replaced by thick hot chocolate. Sugared pecans and peanut butter fudge slid in next to the cookies. And now, fried chicken and mashed potatoes and gravy.

"I'm going to have to work out five times as much as usual to make up for this," mumbled Rock. Didn't stop his Blue from taking another handful of pecans though.

"You can work out with me." He nuzzled, hand on Rock's belly. "Momma, you sure you don't want help?"

"No, you rest with Jim. These boys are doing just fine. Richard, crack some eggs into a bowl for me and stir them up." Momma looked right in her element. Dick flashed him a grin and did as he was told.

"Living with Momma's done Deuce a lot of good, hasn't it?" He kept his voice low, soft, shaking his head at the pecan Rock held to his mouth.

"Yep. He's growing up into a fine young man. Looks happy, too."

"Momma has that affect on kids." Rig settled closer. "Momma was saying he wanted a bird dog to hunt with. You think we ought to?"

"Coming from your Momma it was a hint that we should -- she know of anyone around here with a litter?"

"Yeah, the Pilands down in Greenville. Pups aren't quite ready, but we could get a picture and Momma can take him to pick one out at new years."

Rock nodded. "Cross one off your shopping list. Your Momma have any idea what the girls want?"

"Yup-- the two older ones want CD-players and one wants the Powerpuff Girls movie and the other wants a dart board. The twins want baby dolls that crawl. The baby wants a lawnmower that blows bubbles."

He had Elvis' greatest hits on CD for Rock, along with the Indiana Jones movies and a couple three nice sweaters. Dick was getting a big assed gift certificate to the game store. Rig never could remember what the kid had or didn't have.

"We'll hit the malls tomorrow." Rock straightened up and gave Momma a grin. "Everything's really smelling good, Momma. Like a slice of heaven."

Dick mouthed "suck up" at Rock.

"I got to get my baby boy fattened up. Are you paying attention, Richard? Jim? I expect y'all to feed him."

He rolled his eyes. Rig knew she was his momma and knew she worried, but damn, he wasn't that skinny.

"We try," Dick told her earnestly. "But we can't cook like you do and short of holding him down and shoving the food into him..."

Rock nodded. "'Course I could do that. If it was orders 'n all."

He elbowed his Blue about the same time Momma lifted her head. "Well, now. I'm a civilian, so I outrank you, yes?"

"I believe you do, ma'am." Rock blocked his next elbowing attempt.

"Momma!"

"Hush, now. Jim, I want this boy fed and rested and well cared for, and I expect you to see to it. That is an order, marine, and I will personally come kick your butt if you don't do it."

Rig groaned, leaning his head on the table.

"Yes, ma'am." Rock snapped her a smart salute, but his voice was dead serious.

Dick was standing there watching them, looking like a deer caught in the headlights. As soon as the kid could, he turned back to the dishes he was rinsing up.

Rig looked at Rock, then at Momma. "Y'all are out to get me."

"No, son. We're here to love you. Now hush and relax and be grateful I didn't order Richard, too." Dick froze and then kept washing, as Rock chuckled.

He glared over at Rock, giving the big jackass his firmest look. "You're enjoying this."

"Are you kidding? It's great not being the one in trouble for a change." Rock gave him a wink and a grin.

"Wow, Ma-maw... You're really good at that." Deuce looked admiring and stunned all at once, Momma just preening.

He was so screwed.

***

Dick woke up Christmas Eve morning, wrapped around Rig who was wrapped around Rock, one of the big guy's hands on his hip, holding him snuggled close to Rig.

They'd run all their errands the day before and even managed to wrap everything before going to bed. Which was just as well, given Sissy and her gaggle of girls were scheduled to arrive today. Seeing as they had missed out on them last year, Dick had a feeling the girls were not going to give them a moment to themselves. Which also meant that any loving was going to have to happen now. He was so up for that.

He leaned his head in, mouth sliding over the skin of Rig's neck, finding that one really sweet spot.

"Mmm..." Rig stretched, rubbing slow and steady between them. "Mornin'."

"Mmmm." He hummed back, his cock sliding along Rig's ass. Rock grunted, snuffled and kept snoring. Rig shivered, head falling forward, lips trailing along Rock's shoulders, legs spreading and letting him close.

"Oh... gonna let me fuck you?" he asked, cock jerking.

Rock grunted again. "Nothing too energetic."

He rolled his eyes.

"Mmm... yeah. Deep and hard." Rig pushed back against him, mouth sliding down Rock's torso.

"Yeah. I can do that." He reached up under the pillows, finding the lube Rock had put there the day before. He shifted, helping Rig to find his knees, angling them on the bed so Rig could suck Rock off while he fucked Rig.

"Mmm... " Rig was licking and lapping at Rock's belly, curls bobbing as soft moans filled the air. "Smell good, Rocketman."

Rock snuffled, petting Rig on the head.

"So do you," Dick murmured, diving into Rig's ass, opening Rig with his tongue.

"Oh!" Rig jerked, head coming up, thighs parting wide. "Oh, damn! Hot!"

Rock rumbled unhappily and Dick grinned against Rig's skin. "Better get back to it," he teased before sliding his tongue into Rig again.

"Get back to... Oh... Blue, need your cock..." Rig dipped his head, taking Rock down to the root. Rock's whole body rippled and he moaned, low and long.

"Mmm, he likes it," murmured Dick.

Rig gave a soft, sharp noise, body pushing back toward him, making him laugh. Dick wasn't sure if that was an "of course he likes it" noise or a "shit, Dick, don't stop" noise. Either worked though and he kept plowing into Rig with his tongue, wetting and preparing that sweet hole. Rig was hot and moaning beneath him, rocking and shifting, body fucking begging for it. If his own cock wasn't so hard, he might have just kept doing it, but he wanted, so he slicked himself up and pushed up against Rig. Rig's hips shifted, hungry hole just taking him in deep, sucking his cock right in. He moaned and whimpered, starting to thrust gently.

"Oh..." Rig pushed back against him, wanting more. He moved faster, giving Rig more. That got him a groan and Rig started whimpering, riding back against his cock. Moaning and groaning, he reached around for Rig's prick. Rig arched, cock wet-tipped, sliding against his palm. Those curls bobbed faster, wet, hungry sounds floated up.

It was a beautiful thing, the three of them working together for pleasure and he squeezed Rig hard, not wanting to tumble over the edge on his own. Rock grunted as Rig swallowed, that tight fucking hole milking his cock. Rigger came hard, wet heat pulsing over his fingers, long back rosy and flushed. He cried out, his own orgasm like getting hit by lightning and he poured his spunk into Rig.

He slumped over Rig's back, Rock's hand sliding over his head along with Rig's. Rig hummed, head moving slow as he cleaned Rock's prick. He pulled out carefully, whimpering slightly as he lost that snug fit, and lay down curled around Rig, head on Rock's thigh.

"Feels good, Dick. Damned good. Merry Christmas Eve." Rig gave him a long, Rock-flavored kiss.

Oh, that tasted good, Rig and Rock all wrapped up together. He cuddled closer, arm around Rig.

"Mmm... Wanna go again?" The skinny body scooted closer, warm and cuddly.

He chuckled and tweaked one of Rig's nipples. "Count me in."

"You already were," grumped Rock. "It's my turn."

"Oh... yeah." Dick got a grin and a snuggle. "My hungry marines."

With that Rock's stomach growled loudly, sending him and Rig into peals of laughter. God, it felt good -- to snuggle and relax and laugh, all curled up together in a big pile. It was a great Christmas gift.

"Merry Christmas Eve," he murmured.

Chapter Twenty One

Rock headed into the main house ahead of Rig and Dick -- giving his Rabbit a chance to get his footing before being mobbed by the girls. He was hit by the smell of coffee and sausage and biscuits. "Merry Christmas Eve," he called out.

"Uncle Jimmy!"

Four little girls barreled toward him, all grins. Rachel, the one redhead in a pile of blondes, reached him first, shorter and wider than her sisters, but even tempered and her pretty face was always happy. "Oh, Merry Christmas!"

Lisa and the twins were next, peppering his hands and face with kisses, while a tiny wee toddler peeked at him from behind Momma's jeans.

He gave hugs all around and stood with the twins hanging off him. "And who's this little princess. This can't be Maddie -- she's just a baby!"

Those white eyebrows lowered fiercely and he got a look that was so familiar -- stubborn and headstrong and temperamental -- as one tiny foot stomped. "Am NOT a baby!"

"Oh ho, you are Maddie then. Well, come and say Merry Christmas to your Uncle Jimmy -- I was your favorite when you were a baby, you know."

"You were not!" countered Dick, coming in the front door with Rig.

"Sure I was -- I'm all the kids' favorite."

Lisa launched herself into Dick's arms with a squeal, making the kid laugh hard while Rig moseyed on over to Maddie and held his arms out. "C'mere, young'un."

Maddie tilted her head and went, arms out. Rock knew Julie had pictures of Rig up in the house, knew Rig'd talked to those kids more than was reasonable. ""Lex!"

"Yes, ma'am." Maddie was lifted and hugged, Momma given a warm kiss. "Mornin' Momma. Sissy still sleeping? Come here,

Miss Maddie, and say hi to your Uncle Jimmy. He gives the best pony rides on Earth."

Rock held out his hand for the wee thing to shake. "Maddie isn't a baby," he told Rig solemnly.

"No, sir. She's a big girl. Got her own bed and everything." Rig nodded, eyes twinkling for him.

"And panties." Maddie leaned down and kissed his palm, chubby little cheeks nuzzling his hand.

Rock held back his chuckles. "Have you now? Wow, you are a big girl."

Dick came over with the rest of the girls, who swarmed around Rig and Rock turned his attention to Momma. "Merry Christmas Eve, Momma."

"Merry Christmas Eve, son." The kid got a kiss on the cheek and a happy smile. "So good to have y'all home. There's sausage and gravy and biscuits. Y'all want eggs?"

"I do, Ma-maw. Please." Deuce came stumbling in, hair all stuck on end, blinking slow. "'s there milk?"

Rock grinned. "I bet you dollars to doughnuts he eats me under the table this year."

"He's growing like a weed. Goodness, Momma, are you feeding him growth hormones?" Rig went to sit, holding Maddie in his lap and getting kisses from Presley and Tammy.

"Nope. Just good honest food and good honest work, right boy?"

"Yes, ma'am. Want me to bring you the eggs?"

"I'll help," Dick piped up. The kid suddenly looked concerned. "There's no milking involved for getting eggs, is there?"

The room filled with laughter, all warm and happy and easy. When the noise died down, Deuce looked over at Rig. "Does he make eggs as good as Ma-maw, Uncle Alex?"

Rig gave Dick a grin. "He does passable well, but let me or Momma make Uncle Jimmy's. He's particular."

"I am not particular, I just like things a certain way."

"Now there's a Jim-ism if there ever was one. Hey, y'all." Sissy came in, grinning and happy, giving him a long, hard hug and a kiss on the cheek. "Mmm... good to see you, Mr. South. Richard."

"Merry Christmas Eve, Sissy. Now if we've all said hello -- there's coffee and food, right?" Big families were great and it was good to see everyone, but he was hungry.

"Yes, son. Robert, bring me the eggs. Jim, fix you and Alex a plate. Sissy, the kids have had oats already, see if they want biscuits."

"Yes, ma'am." He gave Momma a wink before she could object to the ma'am-ing. It wasn't out of place either; Rock had thought more than once that Charlene would have made an excellent and scary as hell drill sergeant.

"I just want coffee, Mom..." Rig got two glares -- one from Momma and one from Sissy -- hot and sharp and pointed and damn, those women were good at that.

"Biscuits and sausage and I'll make you both some eggs, Jim."

"Oh, check it out, Rig -- there's sausage gravy for the biscuits -- your Momma sure does spoil me." He dished both himself and Rig generous helpings. "You want to get our coffee?"

"I got it, Jim. I'm pouring out anyway." Sissy poured five cups of coffee and brought two over to him, leaning close. "Momma said he was hurt bad, but I didn't think... And this is better than it was?"

He snorted. "One hundred and ten percent better, Sissy."

"Jesus..." She gave him a disbelieving look. "I'd have come, you know that, right? All y'all had to do was ask and I'd have come out."

"Your kids needed you and you know how he feels about being fussed over. He wouldn't have thanked you or me for calling you in. And you didn't need to see him like that." His jaw got tight as he remembered seeing Rig in the hospital the first time. He would still dearly love to have had some one-on-one time with the perpetrators.

"Y'all just hush now, before Maddie loses his attention and he figures you're talking about him." Momma's look was stern. "This is talk for after the kids are sleeping. Not now. Now's for making things right." She lifted a spatula full of eggs and started filling plates.

"Yes, Momma." He handed over his and Rig's plates, letting her put their eggs on them and then headed out to the big table. "All loaded up, Alex. Bring your admirer and come eat."

"You gonna help your Uncle Alex eat his breakfast, sweet baby?" Rig got an enthusiastic nod, the toddler wriggling down and tugging Rig over to Julie.

"Momma! Is 'Lex!"

Julie nodded and gave Rig a tight hug. "Yeah, Maddie-girl. It's your Uncle Alex. You go take him to Uncle Jimmy and y'all eat."

He ignored Rig's glare over the amount of food on his plate, sat and dug in. Rig might not want to eat, but he sure as hell wasn't going to pass up Momma's cooking. Maddie and the twins hopped up and helped Rig out, stealing tastes and bites and bits. Lisa was sitting on the kitchen counter, talking Dick's ear off and Rachel was sitting as close to him as she could, nibbling on a biscuit, watching him.

He worked his way down to one biscuit before giving her a smile. "Something on your mind, little lady?"

She nodded, pursed her lips a little. "Why didn't y'all come to Christmas last time? It wasn't near as good without y'all and Momma cried. Are you gonna be here in the morning?"

He grunted and thought carefully. He didn't figure "because your Uncle Bobby is a lowlife scum" was an answer folks would appreciate him giving a ten year old girl, even if it was the truth. "Did you ask your Momma or Ma-maw why we didn't come?"

Rachel nodded. "Momma said y'all were too busy working, but I don't believe her. Y'all were never too busy to come before and Uncle Alex says y'all love us better than anything. He says so all the time."

"Well, he's right -- we do. And I wish we had come last year." He looked over at Rig and Julie for help. He didn't like having to dance around this. The truth was that Bobby was an asshole with beliefs that were just plain wrong and Rachel had a gay cousin and a gay uncle and she needed to decide for herself how she was going to handle that.

"We do love y'all better than anything, but sometimes, even when we really want to be here, we can't. The important part is that we're here this Christmas and we'll all be a family." Rig's voice was sure, strong.

He nodded and looked back at Rachel, figuring she was going to accept that this time. But she wasn't always going to and he figured it was a good thing there was one of them willing to call a spade a spade. Rachel nodded, not happy, but willing to accept things. "But y'all will be here in the morning? 'Cause... Cause I heard Momma tell Daddy you almost went to heaven to be with Jesus and if you had, we wouldn't have had a one more Christmas morning."

"Oh, baby." Sissy and Rig both made the same sound, said the same thing, but it was his arms she burrowed into.

"Oh, no. That's enough of that malarkey. Y'all stop worrying about last year and start thinking about cookies for Santa!" Momma's voice brooked no argument, husky and firm.

He gave her a squeeze and didn't try to make her sit up and finish her biscuit. "We'll be here," he told her gruffly, glaring at just everyone. And it was a good thing Bobby hadn't showed yet -- it was him and his ilk that had gotten Rig beaten in the first place.

Rachel nodded. "'kay. You going to help make cookies?" He got another hug and a tremulous smile. "'member when you and me made the biggest star cookies and Uncle Alex kept stealing bites?"

Rock nodded and gave her a wink. "He was just trying to make ours smaller so his were biggest. Bet we do the biggest again this year."

Tammy and Presley shook their heads in unison. "Nuh-uh! Robert says he'll make them with us!"

Lisa's laugh was happy. "Nope. Uncle Richard and me will be the biggest!"

Rigger nudged Maddie. "C'mon, wee one. Tell them we'll do the biggest one."

"Big one!" The little laugh had them all rolling with laughter, tension eased.

He gave Rachel another wink. "Don't you worry -- I'm not accustomed to losing."

He got a full grin and then a hard hug. "Oh, I love you, Uncle Jimmy, so much. Can I go outside and see the baby goats, Ma-maw?"

"I reckon, wait to take Deuce with you."

He petted Rachel's head and picked up his plate. "There enough for seconds, Momma?"

"Always. You and Deuce can share the last bit." She grabbed his plate and split the last bits between him and the teenager. "Richard, hon? Can you and Sissy go fetch the Christmas decorations from the attic? I reckon y'all can decorate this afternoon."

"Yes, Momma. Take your time, Julie, I'll just get started

since I'm done eating." Dick drank the last of his coffee and headed upstairs. Rock put away everything on his plate and stole half a sausage going to waste on Rig's.

"What all do you need me to do, Momma?" Maddie was cuddled close, eyes drooping a little.

"Why don't you take the twins and Maddie into the front room and watch over them? Maybe get them to rest? Then when Lisa and Rachel are done with dishes and chores, we'll make cookies." Damn, Momma was good at that.

"You've got lifting stuff for me to do, I'm sure, Momma." He didn't mind hanging out with Rig and the girls, but Momma usually had a couple of dozen little chores for Rig and he'd rather take those this time out. "Or does Deuce have that job now?"

"He does a lot of it, but some need doing by someone careful." Momma's cheeks grew pink and she watched Rig wander into the front room with the girls. "I have a list of things I was hoping to get help on, yeah. My baby boy spoils me, doesn't he?"

"Works both ways, doesn't it?" He gave her a quick hug. "Come on, give me your list before Rig gets wind of it -- the kid and I'll take anything involving heavy stuff, let Rig do the rest."

It didn't take Charlene long to dig out the long list -- with things from 'fix the leaky faucet in the master bath' to 'rehang the back door' to 'check the transmission in the truck' on it.

"Hank can help, too. He's sleeping off driving all night, but he'll help." Sissy nodded, looking over Momma's shoulder. "We'll get it all done between us, I'm sure."

He gave them a nod. "I'll go get started -- send the kid out to help me with the back door once he's got all the decorations down."

With that he headed out, taking a look at Rig first, playing with the girls in the front room, looking pretty good. The food and company were obviously doing him well.

***

He was a bum.

A lazy, layabout, slacker, snuggling with the babies, snoozing while his marines worked bum.

Rig would feel ashamed about it too, if Momma didn't find something for him and the girls to do every time he opened his mouth.

"Son, untangle these lights?"

"Baby, help the twins write their Santa letters?"

"Alexander, can you help all the girls wrap their presents?"

"I can't find my sugar cookie recipe -- look through these boxes for me?"

It was ridiculous and silly and really, honestly? Kind of relaxing and good. Neither Rock nor Dick looked upset any of the times they passed him on their way to do this or that. In fact they looked happy to be doing it, occasionally snagging one of the girls to help them. Maddie stayed close by, periodically wandering off to get this baby doll or that color book. She was a sweet little thing, looked just like her momma.

Speaking of her momma...

Rig grinned up from the recipe cards as Julie turned the corner, baby cup in her hand. "You want a drink, Maddie-Girl?"

He chuckled as the crayons were discarded, chubby hands reaching. "Want!"

"She's something else, Sissy. Real sure of herself."

"Takes after Momma, I'd say." Julie moved to pour herself a cup of coffee. "You need a refill?"

"I'm okay, thanks. Momma keeps foisting hot cocoa and juice and shit on me. My back teeth are floating." He shook his head at one of the recipe cards. "Mayonnaise cake? Ew."

Julie chuckled and sat down next to him, idly going through one of the recipe boxes. "She's just trying to fatten you up -- I can't ever remember seeing you this skinny, Bubba."

"Don't you go on about it, too, now. I've been through a rough patch and I've never been huge and God knows I was getting a belly on me. I'm down to my fighting weight, is all, and y'all aren't used to it." And God knew he'd been trying. It just seemed sort of... hard, worrying on eating when there was other stuff to worry on and the smoking always had killed his appetite.

"A belly on you?" Julie laughed. "You fool those men of yours with that talk?"

"Yeah, sometimes. Rock more than the kid." He winked, scooted closer. "So, how's things up in Arkansas? You enjoying the ranching life?"

She nudged his shoulder. "Things are good. And you're changing the subject."

"I..." He grinned, blushed dark. "Yeah. Yeah, I am."

She gave him a hug. "I'm just worried about my Bubba."

"I'm managing. I... Oh, hell, Sissy, it was hard. The hardest fucking thing ever. You don't know how many times I almost just packed up, came home to hide. I didn't though. I managed." He took her hand, squeezed it. "I managed."

"You just look so different, Bubba. So gaunt and... haunted. You have no idea how badly I want to make you come home to stay, let Momma fatten you up and take care of you."

"I can't. They need me. You know that. They need me at home, going, living. It's what I do." He grinned, patted her hand. "You know that you can't go back home."

"You're not fooling anyone, Bubba. You need to take better care of yourself."

"I'm fine, and don't you go getting Rock and Dick all het up, either. They don't need any shit to worry about." He met her eyes, not sure whether to be firm, adult man or sweet little brother.

She snorted at him. "They have eyes, they don't need me to get them all het up."

"Don't make me beat you, Sissy. I'm right as rain and that's that. You just enjoy your Christmas with me, would you?" He grinned and settled Maddie between them with her colors. "At least until Bobby shows, anyway."

They shared a look, both rolling their eyes.

"I'm not convinced that he is going to show. Or that he's going to be civil if he does." Sissy frowned. "Is Rock gonna sit by if he starts?"

"I don't know." He shrugged. "Dick will be fine and Rock ought to, assuming Bobby watches his mouth. Rock... Rock's itching for a fight and I'm not up to one on my own." Rig gave Julie a half-smile. "Can you believe it? Me? Thinking on letting Rock fight my battles for me?" He hadn't asked anyone to stand up for him in thirty years. Thirty fucking years. But if Bobby started in and it got ugly, he'd look to Rock.

She took his hand and squeezed. "There's no shame in knowing your limitations, Bubba." She grinned suddenly. "Maybe you are growing up, after all."

"Bitch." He popped her hip gently, rolling his eyes.

"You kiss your Momma with that mouth?" she asked, laughing.

"Mm-hmm. Big sexy marines and teasing old sisters, too."

He leaned over and smooched her, laughing hard.

She got serious all of a sudden, eyes warm and sympathetic and his own laughter faded -- he knew what was coming. "What happened, Bubba?"

He shook his head, acid bubbling up in his belly. "Nothing you want to hear about, Sissy. I was stupid and I got caught by it, simple enough."

"Momma said you got beaten, bad enough you almost d. i. e. d. I want to know what happened, Alex."

"I did. I was at a club with some girls, dancing. Some as...jerks overheard us joking and jumped me in the bathroom, beat me good. Then they left and the bartender found me, called an ambulance." He spun his cup around on the table, feeling just about grey.

"God, Bubba..." Her hand slid over his, stilling it. "It must have been awful."

"Yeah. Think it was worse on Jim, though. Sometimes I wonder if everything will settle back where it was. Mostly though? I just keep on keeping on. Reckon that's what Daddy'd tell me." He looked down at the table, swallowing hard. "He was there that night, you know. Talked to me. I heard him. Thought... thought he'd come for me."

"Oh, Bubba..." She squeezed his hand tight.

"Yeah. I didn't tell Momma, but it felt kinda good, knowing Daddy was waiting." He held on, watching Maddie scribble.

"He's watching over you."

"Yeah." He nodded, smiled a little. "Daddy was good at that. Even when I didn't want him to be."

Julie chuckled. "Just like Santa."

The laugh was surprised right out of him. "Now there's a creepy thought. I reckon I have a few habits he doesn't want to know about."

His sister raised an eyebrow at him. "He knows you suck..."

"Down too many beers? Yes." He gave Sissy a look. Nosy old bitch. "You want details? Go nag Rock."

"You think I won't?"

"Go for it. He won't tell you a goddamned thing."

"The kid might."

"Dick? Bah. He'll just blink at you and blush, then run." God, this was fun.

She tilted her head and then gave him a wicked grin. "I could always get Deuce to ask."

"Oh, you are an evil woman." Rig chuckled. "'Course, y'all have five girls... That's years of questions..."

She laughed and nodded. "And I'll give them each the phone and their Uncle Alex the Doctor's number."

"Oh, I do love you, Sissy." He squeezed her hand, holding tight. "You're good for my soul."

"Any time, Bubba -- you know where to find me." She gave him a hug and a kiss on the cheek. "You're my favorite brother after all. Even if that isn't much of a contest."

"Yeah." He chuckled as Maddie pushed up, demanding her own kisses and hugs. "I'm her favorite uncle, too."

"Give her time; she'll fall in love with Rock like they all do." Sissy looked over to the hall where the girls were crowding around a pair of red-cheeked marines. "Although Dick does seem to be giving Rock a run for his money."

He grinned and nodded. "They're good men, Sissy. Damned fine men, and they're good to me."

"So long as you're happy and healthy, Bubba."

"I am, as much as I can be." He squeezed Julie's hand. "They're my family, just as much as Hank and the girls are yours."

"I know, Bubba."

Dick came quietly into the kitchen, going for some coffee and giving them a wide berth, the kid obviously thinking he was giving them some privacy.

"Y'all ready for some help trimming the tree, Dick?" He tilted his head, offered Dick a grin, admiring the way Dick looked -- flushed and happy, warm and easy. "Or are we making cookies first?"

"You better ask your Momma that -- she's in charge."

Rock came in, chuckling. "The kid learns the important stuff, I'll give him that."

"He's a bright one, all right." He smiled at his Blue, nodded. "Momma done giving you all my chores?"

"You think those were your chores? You should see the list she's holding back for you." Rock gave him a warm smile and slid a cold hand down his shirt.

"Oooh! You're chilled through! Maddie! Uncle Jimmy needs hugs and kisses 'fore he freezes!"

Maddie gasped and jumped up into Rock's arms. Rock

chuckled and threw her up into the air, catching her again on the way back down. "Oh! Oh, Momma! Flyin'!" Rig shook his head, laughing softly. Lost another one. "'Gain! Do 'gain!"

Rock did and then held her around the waist and ran through the house, holding her head first as he made airplane noises.

Dick came and sat down beside him. "You know you'd never guess to see him back home, how good he is with the kids."

"He's a good man, kids can tell stuff like that, straight up." Momma's voice was fond, warm. "Kids can smell bullshit fast and our Jim? There's just none there."

Dick nodded, though he also looked faintly shocked at Momma's language. "Yeah, he doesn't have a lot of time for bull."

"Or a lot of patience for it, either." Rig stole a sip of Dick's coffee.

"I can pour you another," Dick teased.

"I bet he'll get you another handful of pecans too, if you asked him nice," said Sissy.

"I'm okay. Just wanted a sip." He stole another drink. "Maybe two."

Dick chuckled and pushed the cup on him and went and got himself another and the tin full of sugared pecans.

Momma patted Dick's cheek as he walked by. "Such a good boy."

Dick blushed and puffed up a bit, even took out a pecan and held it out to his lips. He grinned and took it, studiously avoiding Sissy's eyes. "Thanks. Come sit with me, Dick. You've been busy all day."

Dick sat, feeding him another pecan and taking a handful for himself. "It's all those little girls. Julie, I don't know how you keep up with them. I mean, they're just little girls, but I bet they could outlast a platoon of marines any day."

"Tell me about it." Sissy shook her head. "Rachel's a little mom and Maddie thinks Lisa hung the moon or held the ladder for the one that did. Without my big girls? I'd be crazy."

"Did someone say pie?" asked Rock, coming in with a twin girl in each arm.

Rig laughed, shaking his head. "Not even close."

"In the fridge, Jim." Momma's voice ran right over his.

Rock just beamed at her. "Can I get anyone else a piece? Rig?"

"God, no..."
"I made him a cherry pie. Get him a piece."
"Momma..."
Dick nudged him. "It's easier not to fight a force of nature, Rig."
Rock put a slice of pie and a fork down in front of him. "Whipped cream?"
"Ice cream?"
Momma's grin was worth it, ear to ear. "Of course, son. There's some in the fridge."
"I got it," Rock murmured, voice smug. A scoop of ice cream landed on top of his pie, a quick kiss on top of his head. Rock settled across the table with a very large piece of chocolate pie and a coffee. He really didn't need it, but... Oh... nobody made cherry pie like his momma.

***

Dick was exhausted.
Thank goodness the girls were finally all in bed, because he couldn't possibly have dressed another doll or done another round of ring around the rosie and then he would have lost important uncle points. He wandered into the kitchen and grabbed another piece of fried chicken.
Hank and Sissy were finishing up the dishes, Rig and Rock and Momma looking at photo albums at the table. Sissy gave him a grin and a wink. "Beer's in the fridge. You look worn through."
He went for the beer when he noticed there was cherry pie left, so he took a piece of that and a glass of milk and sat down with Rig, Rock and Momma. "Baby pictures?"
Rig pinked and nodded. "Momma insists on pulling these stupid things out every year."
"How come I missed them the first year I came?" He leaned over, eager to see Rig as a baby.
"Because Alexander distracted me. Look at that pretty baby boy." Momma pointed to a tall, broad man who looked like Rig holding a laughing, clapping little boy with white-blond curls.
"Look at you! How cute." He nudged Rig and grinned.
Rig stuck his tongue out and rolled his eyes. "I was a just a baby."
"Yes, and a sweet one. Oh, and I have some great ones of

Jim from his first Christmas here." Momma flipped, grinning wide. "Here, this is my favorite -- Jeremy and Jim napping, side-by-side."

Sure enough there were two laid back recliners, two buzz-cut heads, two sound asleep men. He laughed at that one. "Two peas in a pod."

Rock growled. "Let's go back to the baby pictures."

Momma kept flipping back and forth --pictures of Rig curled up around a stuffed bear, octopussing just like now, pictures of a teenaged Rig doing barrel racing, pictures of a wee boy in too big boots and his daddy's hat holding up a string of fish, Sissy standing behind. He oohed and ahed over all of them, laughing and nudging Rig. "Damn, you were a cute kid. Should have known by how cute you are now."

Rig turned bright red, neck to hairline and Sissy just hooted. "Look at that! Somebody thinks Bubba's cute! Come on, Rock. How 'bout you? You think that old boy's cute?"

"I wouldn't kick him out of bed for eating crackers."

"Like Rig would be the one eating crackers in bed," Dick snorted. Oh, fuck, had he just said that? His cheeks heated. "I mean..."

Everybody just cracked up, Rig's head landing on his shoulder, Sissy ending in Rock's lap. "Oh, oh, damn, Pretty. You... You are a funny man." Rig squeezed his fingers, held tight. The blush didn't go away, but he didn't feel so bad, holding hands with Rig.

"So, come on... do y'all share one bed or do you make the cover hog here sleep in the guest room?" Sissy's eyes were wicked, dancing.

"Julia!"

"Julie!"

"Sissy!"

Momma, Hank and Rig looked like they'd just swallowed live goldfish.

Sissy, of course, looked utterly unrepentant. "Well? Inquiring minds want to know."

He didn't know what to say, but Rock was chuckling. "You do have a pair, Julie."

Hank rolled his eyes. "Tell me about it. Woman, you and your mouth are going to get you in trouble one day."

Julie giggled, leaning up to kiss Rock's cheek. "Jim loves

me."

Rock just grinned. "I do -- but your brother saw me first."

"Lucky boy." Julie grinned wide. "Course I was already taken when you showed up or I might have turned you to the straight and narrow."

Dick laughed at that. Rock popped him one, but he was unrepentant. There was nothing straight about Rock.

Rig was laughing and Charlene's hand came across the table, stroked Rigger's forehead. "There's my Alexander. I thought... I was afraid we'd lost you."

"He's right here, Momma," Rock answered her gruffly.

Dick didn't say anything, but he smiled. Rig looked happy, more normal than anything since the cruise. Rig nodded, holding her crepe-paper hand for a long minute. "I am. And it's Christmas Eve. Where are the cards? It's time for poker!"

He groaned. "There goes my money."

"Oh, I bet Momma will front you a nickel or two, Richard." Sissy hopped up, heading for the sideboard where the cards were. "She likes you."

"I just might need those nickels -- you guys play vicious poker."

"Pool is the kid's game," Rock noted.

"Jeremy was a pool player." Momma nodded. "Me? I like cards. So much easier. But Jeremy? The man could shoot pool."

"Rig speaks highly of his dad."

"'Course he does. Daddy was a good man." Sissy gave Rig a long look, a smile. "He watched out for us, yeah, Alex?"

Rigger nodded. "Yeah. Yeah, Sissy. He does."

"Your own guardian angel?" Dick asked quietly, nudging his leg.

Rig pinked a little, but nodded. "Yeah, maybe."

Dick gave him a little smile and slid their legs together again. "Cool."

Rock grunted. "Are we playing or what?"

Rig pulled out his wallet and tugged out a ten dollar bill. "I'm in. Gimme chips, Momma."

Dick grinned and pulled out a twenty. "This way I'll still be in the game in an hour."

"Ah, Richard, I'll let you share in my pot." Sissy settled in Hank's lap, long hair trailing down her back. "Can I have some money, honey?"

"Oh, I should have tried that -- then it wouldn't have mattered if I lost." He grinned over at Rig and then at Rock.

"Won't matter anyway, Pretty. All the cash stays to help pay some of Momma's grocery bill." Rig leaned over, kissed his cheek and slid a crisp hundred dollar bill under the rest without a word.

"See nobody's explained that to me before." He gave Rig a really quick peck on the cheek back and avoided looking up into any teasing eyes.

Momma sat next to Rock, Hank keeping Julie in his lap as Rock shuffled and dealt. One of Rig's hands was resting in his lap, not groping, not playing, just there. Like it was supposed to be there. It made him feel good. Like he belonged, like they all belonged together like this. It was pretty nice to belong to a family. To really belong because they wanted him there, not because he happened to be born into it.

It didn't take long for the laughing to start, Julie flitting around the table as she played, sitting on Rock's lap, on his. He was actually doing pretty well tonight -- winning almost as much as he was losing. "I think I'm starting to get the hang of this."

"Nah, kid, I'm just dealing you good hands." Rock gave him a wink.

Rig started fading early, leaning against him, folding one hand out of three, hand warm and heavy on his thigh. Dick noticed no one was hassling him either, just nudging Rig along.

Around two, he folded and yawned. "I don't know about anybody else, but I'm beat. Momma, do you mind if I head off and get some sleep before the girls are up looking to see what Santa brought them?"

He figured maybe Rig'd come with him and Rock could help Hank and Sissy with the presents and stockings.

"I don't mind, Richard. In fact, I'm thinking I'll insist. Take Alexander with you."

He looked down at Rig, sound asleep, head on his shoulder. "Oh man... " He should have decided to go sooner. He nudged Rig. "Hey, let's go to bed."

"Hmm? Game over?" Those grey eyes blinked up, sleepy and dazed. "Bedtime, yeah?"

"Yep, come on, you can make sure I remember the way." He stood up and took Rig's hand, hauling him up. "Night everyone."

"I'll be along in a bit," Rock said.

Momma stood and gave him and Rig a kiss and then they toddled out, Rig warm and snuggly against his side.

***

Rock helped Sissy and Hank get the stockings stuffed, the presents under the tree and the cookies all amply sampled. They headed for bed once it was done and he went to the kitchen to help Momma with whatever it was she thought needed doing at three fucking a.m.. He found Charlene sitting at the kitchen table looking at the photo albums again, big tears rolling down her cheeks.

Well, fuck. He wasn't any good at this kind of thing. He cleared his throat and went and put a hand on her shoulder, patting awkwardly.

"Oh, shit. You caught me being maudlin." She wiped her cheeks and rolled her eyes. "Bring a silly old woman a glass of water and come amuse me for a few? How's things at home with y'all? Better?"

He did as he was told, grabbing himself a beer before sprawling across the table from her. "We're getting by."

"Thank you, son." She shut the album and took a long drink. "He still nightmarin' pretty bad? You ever get him to go talk to somebody? You know, somebody professional?"

Rock snorted. "We are talking about the same Alexander Roberts, right?"

"Yeah. The one stubborn as his daddy. That one." He got a sad grin. "I just worry."

"We all do, Momma. He's doing a whole lot better'n he was. He'll be fine."

"How 'bout you, son? You gonna be fine? Things going good for you?" Momma gave him a smile, reached out for his hand and held on. She was looking her age these days, eyes dark.

"Just fine, Momma." He patted her hand with his free one. "It's been a bad year though and I'm happy to see it over. Lots of bad things happening to lots of people."

"Yeah? I can't say it's been particular good this direction. Could have been worse, though."

He nodded. "Take that carload of marines out on the highway. Wrapped themselves right around a tree. No survivors. Like I said, a bad year all around."

"A whole carload? Boys you knew?" Momma tilted her head, eyes suddenly sharp.

"Nope, can't say I ever did meet them." He gave her a small nod though -- she knew what he meant.

"Well, they say what comes around goes around. I reckon they're right." She teared up again, patted his hand. "You're good people son. My boy chose well."

He grunted and picked up the cards, dealing out some blackjack. "Come on, I'll keep you company waiting up for Santa."

She nodded and stole a sip of his beer. "Yeah and tomorrow? Julia and Alexander can cook breakfast. Merry Christmas, Jim."

"Merry Christmas, Momma."

Chapter Twenty Two

Christmas morning had been perfect -- Rock and Dick had been snuggled up against him when he woke, the air was crisp, the fire blazing when they'd all gotten dressed and headed in. He and Sissy'd thrown a farmer's breakfast in the oven -- the sausage and eggs and cheese cooking up nice and rich, biscuits rolled and covered and waiting -- while the little ones squealed over their stockings. Then he poured three cups of coffee, let Sissy do the same and they went in to settle and watch the mayhem.

He got a good seat between Dick and Rock, pulling a blanket over them. "Mmm... Merry Christmas."

"Merry Christmas," murmured Dick, hand sliding along his thigh beneath the blanket. Rock grunted his greeting, burying his face in his coffee. He leaned against Rock, watching the wee ones squeak and squeal over this and that, laughing as each present was brought over to them for approval. It was nice and fun and just about right.

Momma had got them all sweaters -- blue and green and grey. Heavy and warm and soft. They all had them on and it just added the warmth and goodness of the morning. Which of course he needed as soon as Bobby's knock came to the front door. "Hey Momma, Julie, Hank. I brought the boys."

The greasy bastard and his moonfaced wife came in, Jake and Louie trailing along behind, all smiles. "Ma-maw! Robert! Merry Christmas!"

He felt Rock tighten up next to him, though his Blue didn't say a word. Dick wished them all a Merry Christmas though. He got a quick hug from Louie and a handshake from Jake, as did Rock and Dick, the boys obviously eager to get back to their oldest brother, exclaiming over the photo of the puppy and the deer stand Momma'd gotten him. Rock even relaxed a bit as Bobby seemed intent on ignoring them.

It didn't take long before Maddie weaseled up into his lap,

lifting her face for a kiss, then her new baby doll for another. "'Lex! Sugars!"

"I don't know that I'd let one of mine that close to him, Julie. He looks like he's got AIDS." Bobby met his eyes, sneered. "Course, you didn't, did you? Not unless you were lyin' to your momma and are just into rough stuff with big groups..."

The entire fucking room went dead quiet. Rock got very very still beside him and then his Blue stood up and walked right up to Bobby. "I think you and I had better step on outside."

"Jim, you sit. Bobby, you apologize to your brother right now." Momma's voice was sharp as a whip, full of fury and tears.

"Sissy, why don't you take the kids into the kitchen and feed 'em. Breakfast's ready." He kissed Maddie's cheek and set her down. "Momma, you, too."

Rock looked like his namesake, immovable and solid, the anger fairly pouring off him. Dick was tense and still next to him, waiting and watching. Bobby stood, looking up at Rock, face still. "I won't apologize, Momma. Alexander's nothing better than a fucking whore. You get what you deserve and if he'd been living a decent life? He'd have been at home where he belonged."

Rig winced, every bone in his body aching.

"Outside," Rock growled. "Where the children won't have to see this."

"You're just going to sit there, Charlene? And let this... this huge thing speak to your son that way?" The stupid bitch stood, staring at Momma.

"Momma. Momma, please. Hank?" Sissy looked three-quarters panicked and Rig finally stood, headed toward the door.

"Come on, Bobby. You've been itching to kick my ass for fifteen years. You might just have a chance now. Let's get it over with so the young'uns can play with their toys."

Dick got up and his men shouldered Bobby outside after him. He felt sort of... quiet inside. Not mad, not panicked, hell, not even sad yet. Just quiet. Dead fucking quiet.

They walked out to the pasture out where Momma wouldn't have to see -- him and his marines and Hank and Bobby and... "Deuce, you'd best go on in. Your ma-maw will be needing you."

"No, sir. I reckon I'm old enough to stay, see things through."

Rock touched him on the shoulder. "He's right. He's got a stake in this, too, Rig."

Dick and Rock stood shoulder to shoulder with him, facing off against Bobby. "So what do you have to say? You want to kick my ass? Beat the shit out of me? I'm here. Say your fucking piece."

Bobby flushed red, walked right up to him. "You were a lousy slut when you were a kid, and now you just flaunt it in front of decent men. You're nothing but a lousy piece of shit asshole and your kind deserves what it gets. If you were a real, God-fearing man? Nothing would have happened -- you'd have been home with your wife and kids, not catting around looking for another cock or five to suck."

Rock hammered Bobby one in the face, just hauled off and slugged him.

Rig blinked, tilted his head, waiting to get pissed off at Rock. Nope. Wasn't happening. "You see, you lousy bastard? The man that just hit you and who is going to beat your ass? That man is mine. My lover. My family. And the one next to me? He's mine, too. And if I was out without them? It was because of worthless motherfuckers like you who spend too fucking much time worrying about who I choose to love."

Bobby snarled, blood pouring from his nose. "Daddy would be disgusted by what you've done, you fucking fag."

Rock hit Bobby again, in the ribs this time. "I met Rig's Daddy. He was a good man. You aren't."

Bobby swung, punch connecting right on Rock's jaw, big head rocking with the blow, ham-handed fist answering it, the sounds of flesh on flesh making Rig sick and furious.

Rig stepped forward, grabbing his brother by the arm. "Fucking let it go, you stupid bastard. Let it go and go home."

"This *is* my home and you're not welcome." Bobby turned to him, one punch taking him hard in the breadbasket, one connecting solid on his jaw, sending him stumbling backwards a step or two.

It was Dick that steadied him, but Hank that stepped up and blocked the kick that was coming. "No, I don't think so. You want to fight? Fight someone fit. After all, there were five took Alex and they weren't bare-handed. You just got Jim and his hands. It's a fair fight, I'm thinkin'."

"Come on, you bastard," growled Rock. "Come here and

fight like a man."

"You're not a man. You're a fucking piece of shit queer." Bobby rushed Rock, screaming. Rock laid Bobby out with a single blow, big body crashing to the cold ground, T-shirt showing the dark hair scattered around a beer belly.

Hank nodded. "Well, then, that takes care of that. Deuce, you go tell your momma your daddy's waiting for her to drive him home and that your Aunt Julie will bring Jake and Louie around tomorrow morning. Richard, you grab one arm, I'll take the other. Jim, you got Alex?"

"'m fine."

"Sure you are. Jim? You got him?"

Rock's body settled against his back, hands on his shoulders. "We're fine. Get that piece of shit out of my sight."

Hank nodded. "Y'all go on up to the room. Momma will send Richard with ice and shit. Come on, Rich, let's haul some trash."

Rig reached out for Deuce's arm as he passed by. "I'm sorry, son. I wouldn't have had you see that."

"I know." Deuce was pale, but his voice was steady. "I know where my family is, Uncle Alex. I got good family. I gotta go get Momma."

He nodded, leaned into Rock, the quiet starting to shatter. Dick gave him a quick, hard hug and then helped Hank with Bobby.

Rock's arm went around his shoulders and he was led toward the garage. "Come on, Rig. Inside."

"I'm sorry, Jim." He wasn't sure exactly which part he was sorry for, just that he was. "Did he hurt you?"

"Yeah. I'm hurt he didn't fucking stand up longer. I could have gone another dozen rounds with him."

He nodded as they went into the old garage, looking up at the stairs he and Daddy had put in. "He fucking hates me. I mean, really hates me. Fucking bastard."

Oh, man. The dead quiet was just dissolving, leaving shuddering fury behind.

"He's an asshole, Rig. If it wasn't your being gay, it would be something else -- it's the fact that you exist." As soon as the door closed behind them, Rock started undressing him, pulling the sweater off. He blinked, stunned, watching Rock's fingers move.

"Gotta make sure you're okay," Rock murmured, working

open the buttons on his shirt. Rig nodded, all out of words and shaking. He was okay. He was. He had to be.

Rock just growled softly and kept undressing him, big hands warm and sure. When he was naked, those hands moved over him gently, lingering over his stomach and his jaw. He closed his eyes and leaned into the touches, hands reaching to search out Rock's face, Rock's skin. Rock growled again and then his Blue's mouth closed over his, the kiss hard and needy. He whimpered, sobbing low and pushing hard into Rock's arms. There wasn't anywhere on earth that he could find the comfort he could find there.

He was wrapped in Rock's arms, held close to that solid body.

"Blue..." Rig met those blue on blue eyes, holding that gaze, wanting to say ten thousand things and not having but one fucking word. "Blue."

"Yeah." He was walked backward to the bed and pushed down, Rock following him, blanketing him with that strength. Yes. Yes. Blue. He whimpered, lips parting, fastening onto Rock's, tasting heat and love and need all wrapped together.

The door opened and closed and the bed dipped, Dick sliding up next to him. He had to force one hand to let go of Rock's head. The only reason he could was because it was his Pretty, his Dick, their lover, needing them as much as they needed him. Dick pressed into their kiss, hands sliding over his skin and pulling at Rock's clothes.

He needed. Each touch eased him a little more, each stroke of fingers against his belly, his jaw, each kiss, each sound. They eased him and he let them, wrapped himself in his men and held on tight. Dick got them all naked and then long, slick fingers were sliding between his legs. Soft moans and Rock's grumbles the only sounds in the room.

He spread, eyes focused on his men, holding onto them, onto their strength. Dick opened him for Rock, fingers barely out when that fat prick pushed in, taking him.

"Yes." He whispered the word against Rock's lips, giving his men everything he was, everything he had. Rock started to thrust into him with long, smooth strokes that went deep. Meanwhile, Dick's mouth moved down his chest to his belly to his cock, his Pretty's mouth wrapping around his need.

Theirs. Theirs and it didn't matter who hated it, who didn't approve. He was theirs and they were his family and he needed them. Loved them.

Dick hummed around his prick, Rock just kept moving, those blue eyes holding his, pouring everything Rock was into him. It filled him until nothing else would fit and he came, crying out, eyes fastened onto his Blue, hand on Dick's head. Dick swallowed him down as Rock kept moving, stretching the pleasure out, making it go on and on. Finally Rock moaned, coming deep inside him.

He settled, cuddling, letting the shudders move through him in slow waves. Dick curled up on one side of him, Rock on the other.

"I brought ice," Dick said softly, hand stroking his belly, which was bruising up nicely, and Rock jaw, which was promising to bruise as well.

"Thank you. Momma okay?"

"She had her 'dealing with it' face on. Was organizing everyone like crazy. I told her you were okay, but I don't know if she was convinced." Dick's fingers stroked his belly. "She said to take your time though, come down when you're ready. Jodie took that piece of shit home. And I'm sorry, Rig, I know he's your brother, but he is a piece of shit."

"Yeah. He is. I... I can't believe he did this on Christmas morning."

Rock grunted. "I don't know -- now it's over and done with. You can enjoy the rest of the visit."

"Yeah." He stroked Rock's jaw. "You going to defend my honor any more today, Blue?"

"If I need to."

He met those blue eyes and nodded. "I can live with that."

Rock just smiled and rubbed a cheek against his hand.

"We should go back," Dick murmured. "The girls are going to start fussing if we don't."

"Yeah. Let's get that jaw iced, Rock. You're gonna swell otherwise."

"You gonna play doctor with me?" Rock asked, a hint of twinkle in his eyes.

"Until the end of fucking time, marine. I gotta rig up what's mine." He grinned, taking a quick kiss.

Dick chuckled, nuzzling his neck. "You okay, Rig? I mean really?"

"We just checked him over didn't we?"

Dick rolled his eyes. "I know he's fine physically, Rock."

"Gonna make it, I think, yeah." He held Dick for a second. "Sorry you had to see that."

"Yeah. I'm sorry you did, too." Dick hugged him hard.

"Come on, let's go eat Christmas dinner and play with the boys' new video games and make Momma happy." Enough of this emotional shit. Rock was going to get hives.

"Yes. Food. Knocking out assholes always makes me hungry and I was fucking hungry to start." Rock was the first up, grumbling as he got dressed. Dick just grinned at him and gave him another soft kiss before getting out of bed and getting dressed, too.

He sat up carefully, belly aching some, and started pulling on his jeans and his new sweater. Coffee. He really needed some coffee.

"You okay?" Dick asked soft enough that only he could hear, the kid's eyes far too sharp.

"Yeah. Little sore. Happens." He squeezed Dick's hand and stood. "Let's go down and be social, marines."

"Yes, sir." Rock gave him a wink and a smile and slapped his ass. Dick chuckled and slung an arm around his shoulders. Together they went back down to the main house.

***

Dick took a deep breath, following Rig and Rock in. He'd gone in, grabbed the ice and hightailed it out earlier, but the tension was high -- he figured it wasn't going to be any easier now.

It was Sissy that met them at the door. "Y'all all good?"

Rig nodded, "Yeah."

She hauled off and decked Rig right in the jaw. "You get your ass in the kitchen and apologize to Momma for wrecking her Christmas, you bastard. Leaving me in here to deal with shit while y'all got to go be all macho and shit outside. I am going to... Goddamnit, you scared me."

Rig sighed, "I'm gonna need more ice."

Rock growled at Sissy. "Touch him again and I'll forget you're a girl."

Dick bit his lip.

"Oh, don't fucking growl at me you big jackass. I'll kick your ass so hard you'll shit through your shoulder blades. I'm PMSing, angry and you left me with Momma!" Sissy might possibly have the biggest balls of anyone Dick had ever met.

Of course, Rock never backed down, even when it might be the smart thing to do. "You leave him alone and I won't have to growl at you. He didn't fucking start this -- you want to hit someone go fucking knock out your other brother."

"If you hadn't done it for me, I would. You big jerk." Then Sissy threw herself into Rock's arms, sobbing.

Rig shook his head, sighed, and headed toward the kitchen. "Hank, come fetch your wife. She's leaking all over one of my marines. They're not fucking wash-and-wear."

He followed Rig, feeling Rock glaring at his back the whole way.

"He'll be fine. Sissy's cried on him for years. I need a beer."

"It's too early for beer, son. You haven't had breakfast." Momma was red-eyed, tight-lipped, shaking just a little.

"Yes, ma'am. You want some coffee?" Rig's voice was careful, easy, his actions almost painfully gentle as he walked around the kitchen.

Dick grabbed a plate and filled it with breakfast and grabbed himself a glass of milk. Sitting down next to Maddie, he gave her a smile. "What'cha drawing?" he asked quietly.

Maddie smiled up and pointed to red scribble next to a green one. "Baby an' Lex. Bite?" Her mouth opened wide.

He chuckled, smile growing. "Sure, Baby." He gave her a forkful. "Is it good?"

"Uh-huh." She chewed, watching Rig, who was sitting and speaking low and quiet and serious to his momma. "Lex eat?"

"I bet he would if you asked him, too. Tell you what. You give him this plate and I'll make you and me another one?"

He got a nod and she scooted down onto the floor, little hands held up. He handed her the plate and watched her carefully toddle over. "Lex! Eat!"

Rig and Momma stopped talking, both blinked down at the little girl. "Why, look at you! Did you make me breakfast?"

Maddie nodded. "Me and... and..."

Rig grinned. "Uncle Richard."

"Uh-huh."

He gave Rig an unrepentant grin and went to fix himself

another plate.

Rig took a few bites, then went back to talking, holding Momma's hand, face so serious. "...never will apologize for it. I love them, Momma, They're my family. Bobby's not your fault, Momma. He's fucked up, mean."

Dick nodded without hardly even realizing it. Even his own asshole of a brother wasn't as bad as Bobby.

"He's still my son." Momma's voice was quiet, broken.

"Yeah and so am I. And if you want me to go, I will, but I'm not apologizing for being proud of who I am."

"No. No, of course not." Momma sniffled and picked up her head. "And there'll be no talk of leaving. You and Jim and Richard are welcome here. Bobby was out of place. I just wish... I wish it didn't have to be this way."

"You can't choose the family you're born into," Dick said softly. "But you can choose who you make your family." Rig had told him that.

"That's right." Rig gave him a grin. "See, Momma? He's a good man."

He blushed and ducked his head. "I've got good role models."

He got a nod and a teary grin from Momma. "Yeah. Alexander is a good boy."

"Yes, ma'am. Momma. He is." He gave her a smile. "You raised a good boy."

"Yes." Momma sighed. "I think I'm going to go take a nap for an hour or two before I have to start on Christmas dinner. Can y'all help Julia with the kids?"

"Of course, Momma. You rest. I love you." Rig helped her up and hugged her.

On impulse Dick stood as well and gave her a hug. Momma hugged him tight. "You don't let anybody make you feel unwelcome, Richard. Bobby's got problems, is all."

"Thank you, Momma -- you've made me feel welcome here right from the start."

"You're a good boy." Momma patted his shoulder and then headed off, leaving Rig to sit down with a sigh.

"You okay?" he asked softly, taking his own seat again and letting Maddie feed him a bite of food.

"Been a long day, yeah? And I don't know about you, but I vote nobody else hits me for at least a month."

"No, I vote a year. Maybe even two or three."

Rock came in then, going for the coffee.

"Sissy okay?" Rig didn't sound even a little pissed off, more amused than anything.

Rock snorted. "I didn't hit her back, if that's what you mean."

"That didn't even cross my mind, actually. She's just tired. Did Ha..." Rig trailed off as a set of twins and a little boy wandered in.

"Uncle Jimmy? Me and Presley and Tammy are hungry. Is there more breakfast?"

"There'd better be or your Uncle Jimmy is going to be very unhappy." Rock tousled the kids' hair and pulled out four plates, starting to fill them.

Maddie frowned over and pointed to Dick's plate. "Eat?"

Rig chuckled and nodded. "That's right, Maddie. We're going to eat."

Rock got the kids sorted out and piled his own plate high. "I don't suppose your Momma would approve if I had a fu- beer?"

"Momma's taking a nap. I don't see how she'd know." Rig scooted over for the twins and Louie, who were fighting over who got to sit next to who. "Y'all stop it and sit. There's enough Uncle Richard for all y'all."

He grinned. "I think it's you they want to sit beside, Rig."

Rock got out three beers and set one down in front of him, another in front of Rig and the third at his own place.

Maddie frowned, eyebrows lowering, making a little growl that would make Rock proud. "Mine Lex!"

He bit his lip and watched Rock give Maddie a considering look. "My Alex, but I tell you what I'm willing to do for you -- he can be your Lex while we're visiting."

Rig went pink, eyes fastened on the table, and Maddie tilted her head, then nodded. "Yes."

"Good, deal." Rock held out his hand, waiting for one of Maddie's little ones to wrap around his fingers and they shook on it. Then he dug in, eating like a man starving.

Louie chuckled and started nibbling, the twins sharing a plate. Maddie shared Rig's breakfast and they all sort of relaxed. It wasn't long before Lisa and Rachel wandered in and Dick kept thinking that nobody but nobody at the barracks would believe this -- six kids, two marines and a nurse, eating Christmas breakfast after a nice morning fistfight. He hardly believed it himself, and as they ate, everything just seemed more and more normal. Which was kind of nice, to be able to put it behind them like that.

He started teasing the girls, nabbing bits and bites off their plates. Presley and Tammy were giggling at him, Maddie protecting Rig's plate with a stubborn persistence, at least when she wasn't busily playing "Itsy Bitsy Spider" with her Uncles...

Man, what he wouldn't give for a video camera.

He offered to do the dishes once they were all done, figuring he could avoid Sissy until she was done crying.

"Yeah. I'm going to get the ham into the smoker out back. Rock, will you go get the fire box filled and started for me? The turkey's been in the oven since early." Rig stood, patting little blond heads. "Y'all take your dishes to the sink, now."

"Are there potatoes or something they can peel, Rig?" He could remember being little and always wanting to help and never being allowed to.

"The older ones can, yeah, and the wee'uns can put the vegetable tray together." Rig looked at Louie, "Boy, run in and fetch your brothers. We got supper to make."

Dick watched, wondering how Louie was going to react to the order coming from Rig after the way Bobby had dissed Rig in front of all the kids.

"If they won't come, can I say you're gonna send Uncle Jimmy in?" Louie was grinning, bouncing on the balls of his feet.

"You can," Rock told Louie. "And you tell them I eat marines for breakfast so they'd best not make it come to that."

Dick bit his bottom lip to keep from laughing.

"Cool!" Louie hit the front room running. "Robert! Y'all going come help cook or Uncle Jimmy's gonna eat you!"

Rig started wheezing, hand covering his mouth as he fought the laugh. Rock just grinned, patting Rig on the back. Rock got a look, Rig's eyes dancing. "Merry Christmas, old man."

Rock gave Rig a quick hug and kiss. "Merry Christmas, Rigger."

Dick smiled and started doing dishes.

Chapter Twenty Three

It was quiet this morning -- Sissy and Hank had left with the girls early-early and Deuce was still sleeping. Right now it was just him and Momma and coffee. "You want me to take down the tree before I go?"

Momma shook her head. "No, baby, I'll get Robert to do it."

"Oh, okay." He finished his coffee. He hated this part. It sucked, saying goodbye.

"Y'all have to be at the airport when?"

"Noon. Our plane's at one." He reached out and patted her hand. "You'll have to pray for me, Momma. I'm going back to school."

"You'll be fine, you're good at schoolin', when you focus. Always have been."

He blushed. "I try, Momma."

"That takes care of that wonky gate, Momma," said Rock, coming in with Dick. "And the car's packed up. You got coffee on?"

"There's a fresh pot, Jim. Y'all want me to make you a meal before you go or are you stopping in Dallas?" Damn, Momma was looking old. Broke his heart.

"I thought I'd make a couple of turkey sandwiches, Momma." Dick was already rooting around the fridge, pulling out leftovers. Rock poured out two new cups of coffee and topped up his and Momma's.

Momma chuckled and grinned at him. "They're almost self-sufficient, your men. You're going to work yourself out of a job."

He blushed, didn't meet Rock's eyes. "I don't think that's an issue, Momma."

Rock didn't say a word and Dick almost managed to swallow his laugh.

"I think we'll keep him around," Rock assured her as he sat at the table.

"I would hope so. He's a good boy and someone needs to keep you two outta trouble." Momma gave him a wink.

"That's a pretty tall order," said Dick with a grin.

"Good thing I'm not a short man," he teased, smiling back.

Dick laughed and Rock just shook his head. "You see what I have to put up with, Momma?"

"Oh, Jim. I had him when he was a teenager and so sensitive you didn't know if he was gonna yell or laugh or sulk." She ruffled his hair. "We're just lucky he's good-natured, our Alexander."

He rolled his eyes. "Oh, stop it. I don't sulk." Rock snorted. Rig kicked his Blue under the table. "Hush, you."

"Hey! I didn't say a word."

Dick was biting his lip.

"I could hear you thinking."

"That would be a first, wouldn't it?" Dick asked, ducking Rock's hand.

Momma started chuckling, clapping a little. "Oh, you boys are something else."

"The Dean and Martin show," Rock suggested.

"Who?" asked Dick, ducking another swat. Rig and Momma where laughing hard now, the sad, painful tension gone from the room, replaced with warm happiness.

"I'm gonna have one last piece of cherry pie, anyone else want one?" Dick got up, heading for the fridge again.

"There's one piece of chocolate left for Rock. Maybe..." Rig considered. "Maybe half a slice of the cherry for me..."

Rock and Dick both gave him a surprised look.

"What? I haven't had breakfast yet. There not enough?"

"It's just these days you don't usually volunteer to put food in your mouth," Dick noted quietly.

He felt his cheeks start burning and pushed his chair back. Well, he wasn't starving now was he? No. "I'm going to make some more coffee. Y'all need more?"

Rock rolled his eyes. "Sit down, Rig, we all have enough coffee."

Dick was standing at the counter, looking stricken, eyes full of apology. He got up and started pottering anyway, nudging Dick with one hip as he passed. "You'd best fix y'all your plates, we're fixing to have to think about going, yeah?"

"I made the turkey into sandwiches to bring with. We'll just eat the pie now." Dick put a hand on his. "You're having a piece too, remember? Us all sitting together, having one last bite and chat before going."

"Half a piece, I remember." Their fingers twined together for a second and he gave Dick a grin and a squeeze. Dick leaned against him for a second and then got the pie served up and herded him back toward the table, putting what had to be a piece and a half of cherry pie in front of him. Of course Rock's piece of chocolate pie was at least twice as much, so technically this was half.

He blinked and opened his mouth, but Momma gave him a look. "Just eat, Baby. It's good."

Right. Just eat.

Rock started talking to himself, more mouthing words than saying anything. Looking up and noticing him looking, Rock shrugged. "Sorry, was just practicing."

"Practicing?" He tilted his head. "Practicing what?"

"Just eat, Baby. It's good."

"You bastard." He kicked Rock under the table, all of them laughing good and hard.

They ate their pie and then Rock was checking his watch. "It's getting to be that time."

Momma sighed. "Y'all going to move down this way when you're done soldierin', Jim? I miss y'all something fierce..."

"You know we would if we could, Momma. But enough folks believe like Bobby do. I'm getting tired of hiding who means what to me just to save people's feelings." Rock took her hand and squeezed it. Rig swallowed down the lump in his throat and nodded. Yeah. Yeah, Blue. One day they wouldn't have to, either.

Momma nodded. "It's a damn shame, people being evil."

"If people weren't evil, there wouldn't be marines." Rock petted her hand and then stood up. "It was really nice seeing you again, Momma."

"You know you're always welcome, son. I'll plan a visit in the summer, maybe bring Robert with me. He's talking to the marine recruiter at school, you know." Momma stood up and hugged Rock tight and then turned to Dick. "And you, you take care 'round these mean old boys, don't let them hassle you."

Dick gave her a warm grin. "I won't." He hugged her tight. "Take care of yourself, Momma."

"I do." Then those sad eyes turned to him. "I don't suppose you'll leave life and love behind and come home?"

"I don't suppose I will." He shook his head and grinned.

"I raised you right."

Rock chuckled and then sobered. "We gotta go, Rig."

"I know. I know." He gave Momma a hug. "Love you."

"I love you. You take care of my baby boy. He's important to me."

"They do take care of me."

Rock nodded, hand on his shoulder, squeezing. "You know it."

Dick nodded, too.

He moved from Momma's arms to stand between his men, hand on Rock's waist. "I'll call you when we get home."

Dick's and Rock's arms came around his waist and his shoulders.

Bringing him home.

Chapter Twenty Four

The kid was humping his ass to get everything perfect. Chili and cornbread for supper. Hot cider mulling -- Dick had been very sure about the use of the word, had spent a good three minutes explaining why it was called mulling -- on the stove. Peach cobbler was ready to go into the oven as soon as they started supper so it was ready and hot when they were done eating.

Dick even had Rig's fucking slippers warming by the oven. "You know how he gets cold."

Rock grunted. "It's not the first cold day we've had. It's not even the first cold day we've had this year."

"No, but it is the first day he's come home from classes." Dick continued setting the table. "I just wanted to make it special for him."

"I bet a blow job and a thorough fucking would have been enough to make it special."

"That's your arena, Rock -- and I think it's an excellent idea. After my supper."

He chuckled and shook his head. The kid was nearly as bad as Rig himself when it came to marking special days.

The dogs went nuts as the Jeep pulled into the driveway and Rig stomped onto the front porch. "Good lord, you two monsters act like I've been gone a month of Sundays!"

"That's probably my fault," Dick called out. "I've got them thinking it's a something special day."

Rig chuckled low. "Something smells damned good. That's one hell of a drive, I tell you. Man, Clinical Med's going to be a bear, but not as bad as pathophysiology. Pharmacology, though? I'll ace that. I know about drugs, I tell you what."

Rock stayed put while Dick fussed over Rig, making him sit at the table and bringing the warm slippers over along with a sweater. "Chili and cornbread. You want a beer? Happy first day of classes."

He rolled his eyes and leaned in, giving Rig a kiss, looking to curl his cowboy's toes. Rig moaned low, opening right up to him like he knew his Rabbit would. Slut.

Dick tsked and bopped his arm. "After supper, remember?"

He licked Rig's lips and sat back in his chair, feeling smug. Rig blinked, the look dazed and happy. "Mmm... You're next, Pretty. Welcome me home again." The drawl was pure honeyed sex.

The kid grinned and sat in Rig's lap, hands framing their cowboy's face. "Welcome home, Rig," Dick murmured, sliding their lips together. The kiss was fucking hot and he was pretty fucking hard by the time they were done.

Rig was flushed and smiling, nipples hard under the starched grey shirt. "Mmm... welcome home."

"Yeah." Dick rubbed their noses together. "You ready to eat? 'Cause if you aren't, stuff'll keep..."

Rock chuckled and he was pretty damned sure he was looking more and more smug.

"Let it keep, Pretty. I'm hungry for my marines." Rig pulled Dick in close again, hands wrapping around to tease Dick's lower back. A shudder moved through the kid, Dick pushing in close to Rig.

He grumbled, left out in the cold. One of those long hands immediately reached out for him, the one with his ring on it. Rumbling, he got out of his chair and took Rig's hand, thumb sliding along the warm palm. He pushed close to them, hands on their shoulders, massaging rather suggestively.

"Mmm..." Rig's moan sounded good. Hungry. "Bed? Sofa? Somewhere soft?"

"Uh-huh. Bed." He grabbed their hands and tugged.

Rig chuckled as he tried to untangle himself from the kid. "Neanderthal!"

He snorted. "I'm just trying to help my favorite slut out."

Dick climbed off Rig and helped him get Rig up. Rig sashayed past them, giving them a view of that ass in tight jeans as they headed down the hall. He and Dick took one look at each other and then gave chase, nearly getting tangled up in the doorway, which gave Rig just enough time to get to the bed before he was tackled. Still, Rig made a satisfying oomph as they landed on him, ass pushing right back toward them.

"This ass is mine," he growled.

"No fucking way," countered Dick, "I was here first."

"I'm bigger."

"Yeah, okay, but think of how much more special it would be if you sucked him while I fucked him?"

"It's not his fucking birthday." Dick hit him hard on the arm.

Rig started snorting, turned beneath them. "Come here, you jackasses. More skin, less bitching. Touch me."

Dick chuckled and started stripping Rig down while he worked on his own clothes. The kid was fucking quick with buttons and zippers though and had himself and Rig undressed as quickly as he had his own self naked. Rig curled toward them both, lips brushing over the closest bit of skin he could reach. He rumbled happily, enjoying the eagerness of his slut. Maybe he would give Rig that blow job after all.

Rig shifted until their lips pressed together, tongue sliding in to fuck his mouth, sure and slow, those grey eyes watching him. The man could make him feel like a fucking god, just like that. He broke the kiss and pushed Rig down onto the bed, kissing his way slowly down to Rig's prick.

"Oh, cool!" Dick got in bed with them and started shifting Rig onto his side. "This way we can both do him."

Rig was shivering, eyes hot as they watched him, hands drawing soft circles on his head. "Oh, fuck. Want y'all."

"You've got us," murmured Dick, hands sliding on Rig's skin. The kid grasped Rig's cock and fed it to him.

With a soft growl, he wrapped his lips around Rig's prick. Rig's lips parted, long body shuddering hard. "Oh... Blue..."

He growled around Rig's prick, sucking harder, swiping his tongue around the tip. He could see in the tightening of Rig's stomach when the kid started slicking that tight little hole. The cock in his mouth twitched, salt drops sliding from the slit. He found Rig's balls, rolling them in his hands. Rig spread, moaning low, velvet-soft skin sliding over his fingers, his palm.

"Oh, fuck, Rig... you're so tight." Dick's voice was low, wanton.

It made his own prick jerk and he sucked harder. The low keening that filled the air was fucking sweet, Rig's hips pushing that hard cock on his tongue. "Oh. Fuck. Rock. Please. Turn around? Let me suck you? Want us all together..."

He growled. Yeah, he could fucking do that. He pulled off

Rig's prick and shifted, pushing his own hard cock toward Rig's mouth. And, fuck, but his Rabbit was hot and hungry for it, that hot mouth dropping over him like a fucking Hoover and giving him just what he liked. He groaned and managed to get Rig's prick back into his mouth, sucking as hard as he could. Dick was humping Rig, pushing that hot cock deep into his mouth again and again.

Rig's arms were wrapped around his hips, nose nudging his balls as low moans vibrated along his cock. It made him suck harder, even as his hips found Dick's rhythm, pushing into Rig's mouth while Rig's cock pushed into his. It was hot and fucking perfect -- moans and slurps and slapping skin and scent of sex and sweat and men, all together and fucking and good.

He reached for Dick, petting the kid's thigh, his other hand finding Rig's balls again and rolling them. Rig cried out around his cock, spunk spraying on his tongue.

He groaned, swallowing it down like a pro. Rig's climax was taste and sound and feel on his tongue and it sent him over the edge. His cry and Dick's came together, filling Rig.

Rig purred around him, cuddling close, hands stroking his skin. He let go of Rig's cock, let it slide out of his mouth as he panted.

"Happy first day of classes," murmured Dick.

"Hell, yes." Rig brought Dick's hand to those hot lips, kissing it. "Y'all are good to me."

"Goes both ways," he muttered, shifting so he was right side up again.

Dick guided them into a three-way kiss. Yeah, it went both ways. Or three ways. Whatever -- it was fucking good.

Chapter Twenty Five

The nice thing about having a pool table downstairs was that he could go down and listen to Alan Jackson and sing along and play on all those long nights he couldn't sleep because his schedule was screwed.

He thought about taking a pill to wind down, especially now that school was hot and heavy, but he figured that was a road he'd best not wander down. Besides, Pretty was kicking his ass at pool damned regular these days. He needed the practice. He sank the 7-ball and two-stepped his way around to try to get the 2 in the corner pocket.

"The kid finds out you're practicing in the middle of the night and your ass is grass." He looked up to find Rock lounging in the doorway, arms crossed, naked as the day he was born. "Hell, your ass is already grass with me. Middle of the fucking night, Rabbit. You should be in bed."

He scratched the shot, giving Rock a sheepish grin. "Not that the practice is helping. Couldn't sleep, Blue. My time clock's all out of whack."

"Then come back to bed and let me fuck you into oblivion."

"I was trying to let you sleep, Blue." He grinned, setting the cue aside. "You think you can help me sleep?"

"I think we can have fun trying," said Rock, straightening. "Come on, bed."

"No, Blue. I'm Rig." He moved straight into Rock's arms, knowing right where he belonged. "How's it hanging, Marine?"

"Better now that I've rounded up the missing man." Rock winked at him and kissed him on the nose before moving them toward the bedroom. He went eagerly; even if it didn't put him to sleep, fucking was better than pool any day.

***

Rock woke up with a start, shooting up into a sitting

position.

Something was wrong. Rigger wasn't in bed.

A glance at the clock proved it was late -- almost two in the morning. He sighed and got up, heading for the kitchen. Sure enough, there was a light on in there. And there was Rig, books spread out across the table, face planted in front of him, drooling on his notes.

This school thing was going to be the death of all of them, but especially Rig, who was supposed to be working part time, but who still hadn't learned to say no when the hospital was in a bind. Shaking his head, Rock went over to Rig and slid his hands over the stretched back, kneading automatically against the tight muscles.

Rig gave a soft little purr, pushing back into his hands immediately, still sound asleep. Grimmy and Lucy both lifted their heads, Grim's tail hitting the floor a couple of times before they settled back down together, Grim's muzzle resting on Lucy's belly.

"You think this good ole boy is going to make me carry him into the bedroom?" he asked the dogs. Their ears perked up, but they had nothing to say on the subject. Rock chuckled. "If I do, I'm going to claim a reward."

Grimmy shifted and Lucy gave a low whine, almost as if she was asking Grim to stay put.

Rig patted the table gently. "Sh, sh. 'sokay, pups. Don' wake my boys."

Rock snorted. That settled it. He shifted around and grabbed Rig up, one arm under his knees, the other at his shoulders. He grunted as he stood, pleased that Rig was putting on a little of the weight he'd lost.

Arms circled his neck, Rig's mouth trailing over his skin. "Mm... my Blue. So good."

"Hey, sleepyhead." He carried Rig into the bedroom and dropped him lightly onto the bed next to Dick, climbing up after him. He lay down on Rig, letting his lover take all his weight. Arms and legs wrapped around him, Rig searching for his mouth with hungry lips.

He closed their mouths together, pulling Rig's tongue into him and sucking. His hips started to rock, body eager. Rig met him head on, interested and hungry and wanting. That was one thing about his favorite slut -- Rig could always be counted on to be eager and ready.

He let go of Rig's tongue and slowly moved down along the lean body, giving extra kisses to the pale scars on Rig's chest. It had been close. Too close. With a grunt he pushed those thoughts from his head and went straight for Rig's cock, sucking it in and pulling hard. He needed the taste of Rigger's want and need and life inside him.

"Oh..." Rig's hands slid over his head, hips pushing into his mouth with an immediate and automatic hunger. "Blue. Oh, God. So hot."

He murmured his agreement around Rig's cock, letting the sound really rumble over the hot flesh. Rig jerked, pushing into his lips with a soft sob. So hungry, so needy -- fucking was never a spectator sport with his Rig. Hot and hard, like burning silk in his mouth and fuck, yeah, there was that flavor he'd been looking for, that taste that said his Rigger was alive and fucking his mouth with all that he was.

"Oh, fuck. So good, Blue. Love your mouth." Rig was pushing deep, whispering to him, stroking him, cock leaking one drop of pre-come after another onto his waiting tongue. He rocked his own hips against the bed, cock sliding over the cool sheets. "Want you. Fuck, want you in my mouth, Blue. Come here."

He moaned. Oh, fuck, yes. Shifting, he managed to get his hips up near Rig's head without giving up his prize. Rig groaned, that sweet, amazing fucking mouth surrounding his cock, hands gripping his ass. He sucked hard, finding a rhythm before Rig's mouth made him forget how.

Rig's moans vibrated along his cock, happy and wanting. Rock could fucking feel it when they clicked, when their rhythms joined and they were moving together, lips and tongues and hands and cocks.

It was fucking fantastic, a circle of pleasure. Every time he moaned it made Rig moan which made him moan and on and on and he wasn't sure where he started or Rig ended and so he just kept sucking, just kept thrusting with his hips. Rig's hands cupped his balls, tongue fucking the slit of his cock every time the blond head pulled back.

Oh, fuck. Oh fuck, oh fuck, oh fuck. He made some sort of inarticulate screaming noise around Rigger's cock, totally losing his fucking rhythm, just sucking for all he was worth now, humping to beat the band.

He came at the first touch of Rig's salty spunk on his tongue. Fuck he loved this. Loved the way Rig moved beneath him and over him and around him. Loved the taste and the feel and the sound of him. Loved shooting into that talented-as-fuck mouth.

Rig swallowed him down, mouth slowly going lax. Those lips just sucked at the crown of his cock, pulling out each shudder, each aftershock. He returned the favor, sucking long and slow on that sweet head. Just fucking loved this.

They settled side by side, Rig's head heavy on his thigh. The suction became soft licks, warm and sloppy. Dick snuffled beside them, shifting, arm wrapping over Rig's belly, his shoulders. Yeah. Just about fucking perfect.

He let Rig's prick slip from his mouth, eyes closing, things set back to right. Now Rig could sleep.

Now he could sleep.

Chapter Twenty Six

He stumbled into the house just before dawn, tired down to his bones. His schoolbooks were waiting for him at the table, his hour-long drive to the university looking less and less appealing. Rig started the coffee, the dishwasher, pulled the chili meat out of the fridge and threw it in the crockpot. Christ, he was tired.

He hadn't been sleeping, hadn't been able to do much but study and work and drive and work and study. A year -- it had been a year since... Since shit got complicated. A whole frigging year.

His thigh twinged and he winced. Damn.

"Rig? Is that you?" Dick wandered up the hall and into the kitchen, naked as a jaybird and yawning.

"Nope. Random axe murderer. Hey, Pretty. I'm just doing the between work and school thing." He pulled down three cups -- one travel, two not. "You sleep good?"

Dick shrugged. "You weren't there." His Pretty peered at the clock on the stove. "Shit, Rig, it's not even 6 a.m. and you haven't been to bed yet."

"Yeah. Sucks to be me. I got an eight o'clock class." Rig shucked off his work shoes and scrub top, tossing the shirt in the washer. "You want some toast?"

"No, I want you to get some sleep. Sit." Dick pulled out a chair and pushed him into it, hands rubbing at his shoulders.

"Oh..." He leaned forward, rested his head in his hands. "Oh, shit..."

Dick leaned over him and kissed the top of his head before going back to the massage. "You've got to slow down, Rig -- something's gonna give and I don't want it to be you."

"I'm okay. I am. Just... just tired." He needed to stop doing extra shifts every time they called. He needed to have a bath and a nap and a peanut butter and blackberry jelly sandwich. With milk. Cold milk.

"You got the number of someone in your class?" Dick asked. "You could get the notes off them and just go to bed now instead of making that drive."

Oh, there was a tempting idea. "It's only 'til noon and I don't think I have to work tonight. God, tell me tonight's my night off..."

"I don't know, Rig. We never see you anymore -- from what I can see you don't actually ever get a night off. It's Friday. The seventh. Ring any bells?"

"Uh... No. Not really. April. It's April, right? Maybe I need to take a weekend off..."

"Shit, Rig -- you don't even know what month it is." Dick sighed and pulled out a chair, sitting next to him. His hair was pushed back off his face. "You know if Rock figures out how hard you're burning that candle at both ends he's going to kick your ass."

"That's why you're not going to tell him." He met Dick's eyes. "God, when did things get so fucking hard?"

Dick just shook his head, riverstone eyes full of love and concern. "You've got to ease up on something, Rig. Hell, just stop saying yes every time they call you for extra shifts at work. They know they've got a sucker in you and I'll bet they try you first every single fucking time. You stop pulling so many doubles and then going to school and back to work for another double and I'll bet things'll seem a lot less complicated."

"I try to, but I hate leaving them short-handed and God knows I'm pushing to make my end of the bills these days, much less save anything for after..." Christ, he must have contracted diarrhea of the mouth in his old age, sitting and whining.

"So you don't save anything -- come on, Rig -- you don't think we'd rather have to pay a few more bills than see you work yourself into an early grave. Fuck that -- I miss you. Rock misses you, even if the asshole won't ever actually say it."

He nodded, sighing again before going to pour coffee. "I miss y'all. I miss sleeping. I miss fucking. I miss mowing my lawn and my dogs and my life and..." He shook his head. "It's not forever. It's not. I just gotta hang on."

"Tell you what -- you stop saying yes to the extra shifts and I won't tell Rock how little sleep you're getting." Dick had his look-at-me-I'm-just-as-stubborn-as-Rock look on.

He looked over, eyes wide. "You sorry son of a bitch. You

wouldn't."

Dick wouldn't. Rock would be so fucking pissed. Dick flinched but his face set in stubborn lines. "It would be better than watching you kill yourself. Have you looked in the mirror lately?"

"What? Of course. I shave." He reached up, pinking a little at the stubble he encountered. "Well, most of the time. And what does that have to do with anything anyway?"

Dick sighed. "You just look like shit, Rig. Like death warmed over. Almost worse than... before."

Oh. Oh, that hurt. He pulled himself up, hand going to the scars on his chest. "Yeah. Well, you can't break something, glue it together and expect it to go back to right, can you? I'll stop taking so many hours, you keep your mouth shut and we'll all be fine."

"Rig..." Dick's hand slid toward him on the table, palm up. "I'm just worried about you."

"I know." He took Dick's hand, more because it would hurt Dick if he didn't than because he wanted to. "Don't you know I'd go back in a heartbeat? I'm so fucking tired of being broken and fucked up and dreaming about that night over and over. I don't want to be like this. I don't want to..." He took a deep breath, closing his eyes. "I have class."

"Don't go," murmured Dick, squeezing his hand. "I'll ditch work. We can just... I don't know. Hold each other?"

"Rock'll kick your ass..." His head started dipping again, so tired.

"I'll risk it." Dick got up and started massaging again. "You need to sleep, Rig. You need me to hold you to do that? Then it can be arranged."

"I..." What the fuck was he supposed to say. He didn't need? He didn't need the rest and the touch and the comfort? Lying to his men wasn't his fucking job. "Take me to bed."

"Cool. I'll even give Rock his wake-up call." Dick gave him a hand up, arm going around his waist as they went down the hall.

"He'll know something's up..." He stumbled over his scrubs, body tipping forward. "Shit." Great, asshole. Way to not worry Dick.

"Shit, Rig." Dick's arms came around him, steadying him. "You let me worry about Rock -- you just get horizontal and sleep."

"You'll stay for a bit?" He sat down hard on the bed, eyes burning in his head, sobbing softly as Rock's big hand wrapped around his waist, tugged him in close.

Dick pushed him down and slid in beside him, hand taking his, holding on tight. "Long as you need."

He held on, eyes closed, only barely registering the soft, quiet kiss. "No dreams."

"Just sleep."

Rig nodded, or tried to. Nodding and dreaming at the same time was hard, hard work.

***

Dick got Rock up in the usual manner and made up some excuse for not going into base with him, called in one of the few favors he had and went back to bed, wrapping around Rig. He hadn't been sleeping all that well himself, missing this, missing Rig, and it wasn't long before he was fast asleep.

Soft, panicked little cries woke him, Rig twisting for a moment before sitting straight up, eyes wide open, fighting to breathe. He sat up as well, wrapping his arms around Rig. "Hey. Hey. What's the matter?"

"I... Oh. Oh, nothing. Nothing. Sorry. Dream. Fuck. Oh. I'm fine. Damn." Rig blinked, easing them back onto the mattress. "Damn. Sorry."

He stroked a hand along Rig's side, nuzzling into Rig's neck. "'s okay. Just a dream, yeah?"

Rig nodded, petting him awkwardly for a minute as the skinny body relaxed. "What day is it?"

"Friday. You skipped class, remember?"

"Oh. Right. Yeah. Chili meat in the crock pot and I'm not answering the phone 'til Sunday." Rig curled into him, rubbing. "Thanks for staying home. You didn't have to."

"Yes, I did. Or you would have gone to school and fainted or something." He gave Rig a soft kiss to take the sting out of the words.

"I have never fainted in my entire life, marine." Rig rolled those blood-shot eyes, giving him a wink. "I didn't mean to worry you this morning, honest."

"I've been worried more than just this morning, you know.

You look so tired all the time."

"I am. I'm tired all the damned time. I've been tired for a year." Rig sounded a little pissed, a little sick, a little sad.

"I wanna help. What can I do?"

Rig sighed, shook his head. "I don't know that you can. I don't know how to fix the shit that's been broken and healed weird, you know? I reckon there'll always be a limp."

"Something healed wrong? I thought you were okay. Why didn't you say something?" He started searching Rig, hands moving over the scars that were still there.

"I'm fine, Pretty. I meant up here." Rig tapped his head, then his chest. "I meant in here."

"Oh." He held Rig close. "Did we do something wrong? Me and Rock?"

"No. God, no. Y'all are fine. Y'all are just fine. It's just hard, to be one way and then another. I don't think anyone could have the... the shit that happened to me happen and not be a little off-center. Not be crackly on the inside." Rig was talking to his chest, voice muffled.

He wrapped his arms tight around Rig, holding on. "You never... what happened?" he asked, voice hushed, scared Rig wouldn't answer. Terrified he would.

"You don't want to know, Dick." Rig shivered, pushing closer, almost clinging.

"You're right, I don't. I want it over, behind us. I want everything back to normal." He wrapped his leg over Rig's, eyes closing tight. "But maybe you need to tell someone. I don't think you can tell Rock. I just... if you want -- need."

"No, I can't tell him. It... It was bad and he's still so angry." Rig shook his head. "It took fucking forever. I mean, there's bits I can't remember, but there's parts that I dream about every fucking night, over and over and over."

"That's why you can't sleep." He didn't know what to say, what to do. So he just held on.

"Yeah. And it's the weird shit that eats at me. The way they laughed, the sound that fucking pipe made when it hit me, the smell of piss all the fuck over me. I couldn't move, when they left. I just sat there, dripping piss and blood and I could hear the bubbling where the knife got me." Rig sighed, so cool and still in his arms. "I kept waiting to die."

"But you didn't."

"No. All five of those motherfuckers beating and stabbing me and I still didn't die. They meant to, you know that? They wanted me to die. They said... They kept laughing and telling me they were going to cut my balls off, gut me."

He closed his eyes tight, held Rig tighter. "Why didn't they?"

Rig's laugh was bitter as ashes. "They were scared of the blood after the first cuts. Scared the fag would give them AIDS."

He bit his lip to keep from crying.

"And what if they had? Can you see Rock, dealing with that? I'd have been better off dead." Rig shook his head, voice full of tears.

"Can you see Rock dealing with that?" he asked, his own voice thick.

"He has you; he'd have managed. Y'all would have had to hire a housekeeper to keep from living in filth, but you'd have managed."

Dick shook his head and squeezed Rig as tight as he could. "I don't even want to think about it."

"Yeah, me either, but it sure keeps coming around, don't it?"

"Except you're not dead. You're not, but you're still not all here, are you?"

"I told you, I don't think I'll ever be right again, not altogether." Rig gave a long sigh, pulled away a little. "But I'm managing."

"No. You aren't managing at all, Rig. You're barely surviving." His voice was thick and damn it he wasn't going to cry -- Rig needed him to be strong. But not so strong he couldn't hear. Not distant like Rock. He cleared his throat. "You know you can tell me anything, right? I'm not going to bail if you get all... emotional and stuff -- you know that. I want to help."

"I know." Rig looked up at him, gave him a sad, sweet little smile and cupped his jaw. "Our sensitive one, always worrying about our hearts. Don't you know, Pretty? Me and Rock? We don't get emotional and stuff if we can help it."

He nuzzled into Rig's touch, pulling it in, needing it, craving it. "I think it's time you can't help it."

"I just want to take it all back -- all of it." Rig shook his head, grey eyes wet and blood-shot. "I should have been smarter. I should have paid attention. I should have stayed home. I should have fought harder. Something."

"You can't change what happened, Rig. And I know it

sounds corny, but if you don't move on and live then they might as well have killed you, 'cause they win. Even though they're not here to see it -- they win."

"Don't you go there with me, too, man. I am moving on. I'm functioning, I'm working, I'm going to school. I haven't fucking fallen apart." Oh, there was a flash of pure pissed off Rig.

"No? That's why you could hardly stand this morning, right? 'Cause you've got it so together..." He hated Rig being mad at him -- hated it. But it was more Rig than he'd seen since Christmas. Almost since their cruise.

"No. That was because I've worked almost sixty hours this week, on top of school." Rig pulled out of his arms. "There's been plenty of nights I've babied y'all through shower and bed after a bad bit in the field, you know, and I don't give you shit about it. Y'all never used to give me shit about it either, not until after that night. Now y'all circle around me like vultures, waiting on me to break. Well, I'm not fixin' to. Just because I couldn't hold my own against a slew of you doesn't mean I can't carry my weight here."

"That's because it never used to be all the fucking time, Rig! When was the last time you didn't work a sixty hours plus week? When was the last time we just sat around doing what the fuck ever and enjoying ourselves? I can't remember the last fucking time we all watched TV together or spent the afternoon fucking."

"Jesus, Dick. I'm broke. My savings are gone, my Jeep needs a new transmission, I still owe money on the hospital stay, not to mention my books are running me a fortune. You don't think I wouldn't like to just go to class and then come home and study and spend my free time on my men? Two of the full-time girls are out on maternity leave, they're short-handed and they need me."

He glared at Rig. "So you're just going to work yourself to death then, is that it? You don't think Rock and me wouldn't be willing to rework the budget so you could pay stuff off faster? Or give you a fucking transmission for Christmas or your birthday? But you're so fucking stubborn sometimes."

"I'm not going to be a burden to... " Rig gave him a frown, eyebrows lowered. "I am not stubborn!"

That almost made him smile. Almost. "I only know one person in the entire world more stubborn than you, Rig."

"Rock's more endlessly set in his ways than stubborn."

"That leaves you as the most stubborn person in the whole world." He sighed and reached out for Rig again, pulling him close. "Let me help. I know you need to work and study, but let me help with the other stuff."

"I... How? Tell me how and I'll do it."

"I don't know! I keep... I keep trying and you just keep getting..." Ghost-like, further away, more gaunt... "Thinner."

"I know. I know, Pretty. It won't stop." The whisper was soft, broken. "None of it stops."

Suddenly he was scared. Like right while they were still all in the middle of it scared. "It has to stop, Rig. Please. It has to stop."

Long fingers pet his spine, held him tight. "Oh, now. Hush. It'll be okay. You know me, I'm tired and whiny. Don't you fret, now. It'll all come out in the wash."

"I don't know, Rig. We've been washing for a year now... and it's still not coming out." He was probably twisting the saying all to hell, but he figured Rig would know what he meant.

"Yeah, but I'm still here and I'm still trying and I'm still y'all's."

"I know... it just feels like you're slipping away standing right there sometimes. I'm worried about you." He looked into Rig's eyes.

"I know. I'm worried about me, too." Those grey eyes filled with sudden tears. "Why do you think I work so fucking hard?"

He pulled Rig back close, hand stroking along Rig's back. "Something's gotta give, Rig. I'm just scared it's gonna be you."

"It won't be. I got too much to live for. Y'all need someone to take care of you." Rig's cheek landed on his shoulder, tears falling silently.

He nodded. "We do. And you're the only one who gets Rock's eggs right."

He kept stroking Rig's back, just holding his lover. Rig slowly relaxed, tears replaced with soft, snuffling snores, breath slow and steady as Rig snuggled in and slept. He lay there for a long time, ignoring the tears that made tracks on his own face.

***

Rock pulled into the driveway, surprised to see Rig's jeep already there. It wasn't even five p.m. yet, his Rabbit was never home before five. Even on a fucking Friday. In fact it was usually later in the evening on Fridays that Rig broke it to him and Dick that he'd picked up a couple of double shifts for the weekend.

Stupid fucking proud cowboy.

Like he didn't have the cash to keep them all going for awhile if Rig actually refused a few shifts. He hadn't even gotten his fucking blow job that morning. All right, he'd gotten one, but not from Rig. And the kid was good, but Rig was right there next to them in the bed...

He grunted at the pups and, when the living room proved to be empty, followed his nose to the kitchen. Dick was standing over a pot, stirring. "That smells like chili."

Dick gave him a grin. "Nothing wrong with your nose. How was your day?"

He grunted. "Fine. Grapevine had you at home though."

Dick shrugged. "I pulled in a favor."

"You don't look sick."

Dick shook his head. "I'm not."

He grunted again. Rig's jeep in the driveway, Dick not sick, but calling in favors to get out of going in and Dick making chili. He wasn't fucking stupid. "Where is he?"

"In the bedroom. Sleeping!" added Dick as he headed down the hall. He ignored the kid. And sure enough, there was Rig, passed out under about ten comforters. What the fuck? He sat down on the bed about the same time Dick showed up in the doorway. "He's sleeping, Rock. *Sleeping*."

"He sick?"

"Well, no... just tired."

"So what else is new?"

"Rock..."

Rig groaned and shifted, body curling around his ass, sure as fuck, snuggling and hot to the touch.

"He's never home this early."

Dick rolled his eyes. "So be happy that he is today."

"You're home all day, he's home early. Sleeping in the middle of the day instead of sitting at the kitchen table with a fucking pile of books open. You're making the goddamned chili. I just want to know what the fuck is going on."

"No...nothing. Just tired. 'm getting up." Rig sat up, wincing at the light. "Lemme grab a quick shower and I'll make the cornbread."

"I can do the cornbread," Dick put in.

"Good. Then you and I can shower together." He gave Rig a smile, cock starting to fill at the sight of his Rabbit naked.

Rig blinked and gave him a slow, little smile, then looked over at Dick. "Recipe's on the fridge. You don't have to, Dick. Just... I need to get wet and awake first, yeah?"

Dick gave them both a smile. "Oh, I think you need to get more than just wet and awake." The kid winked and sauntered off, wriggling his ass.

He snorted. "He means you need a piece of the Rocketman."

Rig arched an eyebrow and smiled. "You think?"

He nodded, hand sliding over Rig's chest and belly. Rig hummed and pushed closer, wrapping around him, sitting in his lap. That skinny ass settled on his thighs, heat rubbing against him.

"Been awhile since we've started the weekend like this." It was more a noting of the fact than a complaint, though if Rig wanted to take it as a complaint, that worked, too.

"Yeah. Been busy. 's hell having bills." Rig reached up and wrapped long arms around his neck, holding on. He grunted, mouth taking Rig's, more interested in the doing than the talking about why they hadn't been doing. Rig opened up to him, right and easy as anything, tongue sliding against his own.

He growled into Rig's mouth -- there was nothing like fucking with his favorite cowboy. Closest thing to fucking perfect he knew. Hot and cuddly, Rig was plastered against him, cock slowly filling against his belly. Oh, yeah, that was what he was fucking talking about.

He wrapped his hands around Rig's ass and tugged his Rabbit closer, kiss growing hard.

"Mmm..." Rig arched, rubbing and purring, long hands holding his head close. He pushed Rig back onto the bed, stripping off his BDUs before pressing down against the long skinny body. "Hey, Blue." Rig licked at his lips, moaning. "Feels good."

"Yep. 's gonna feel even better soon." He took one of Rig's titties in his fingers and started tugging.

"Oh..." Rig groaned, sliding and twisting beneath him, lips open, soft little cries sounding. That was what he wanted to hear. He bent and took the other little nipple between his lips, sucking hard.

"Blue!" The sound was low, overwhelmed, fucking delicious, and Rig's hips snapped up against him, spunk spraying everywhere. He purred, rolling his fingers in Rig's spunk, hand drifting lower as his knees spread the long legs. His Rabbit opened right up to him, easy and good, just like always. He teased that tight little hole, middle finger sliding over the hot, wrinkled skin as his mouth tickled at Rig's neck.

"Mmm...Blue..." Rig followed his finger with those slim hips, trying to tempt him in.

"You wanting something, Rabbit?" he asked, fingertip dipping in for just a second before going back to feeling up the skin around the hot little hole.

Those grey eyes met his, sure, serious. "I need you."

He nodded. Yeah, he knew that. He slid his finger in, groaning at the way Rig's ass pulled him in.

Rig nodded, riding slow and easy. "More."

"Yeah, there's a whole lot more where that came from." He pushed a second finger in with the first, knowing just how to curl them, just where to press. He felt every bit of the ripple that shook Rig's body, heard the long, shaky breath. He did it again and then again, reaching under the pillows with his free hand for the lube to slick up his prick. Rig's face was buried in his throat, moans coming fairly steady, body rubbing, tight hole riding his fingers.

He got himself slicked up, but didn't pull his fingers out right away, just stayed right where they were, Rig riding his fingers like there was nothing else in the world.

"Oh... Oh, Blue... " Rig's face tilted, lips by his ear. "Tell me we can just do this for fucking ever."

"I'm in." Yeah, for fucking ever sounded like it just might be long enough.

"Now we just have to sign Dick up and we're good to go." Warm, breathless laughter tickled his ear. "Fuck, you make me happy."

He grunted. "'S what I fucking **do**, Rig." He pulled his fingers away and lined up, grinning down at Rig. "And I can guarantee you the kid'll sign up. For this? He'll sign his soul away."

He sank in to perfect heat.

"Oh, shit. Yes." Rig gave him a smile, body flushed and

warm, hands moving over his chest. He grunted and started thrusting, fucking Rig with nice long strokes, finding just the right speed where he could fucking go forever. Rig just went with it, body moving with his, hands encouraging him to move, fingers tweaking his nipples, petting his belly.

He growled and groaned, the pleasure settling in his balls and the small of his back, jolting each time he thrust. Then Rig leaned up, took his mouth with a single-minded intensity that made him ache, those grey eyes staring into him. Fucking perfect.

He found Rig's cock with his hand, fisting it. A whimper pushed into his mouth, Rig moving faster, eyes rolling, grey shining now. He increased his pace, fucking Rig harder, faster, more. "Anytime, Rabbit."

"Yeah. Oh, sweet fuck, yes." Rig's body tightened almost painfully as spunk spilled over his fingers. With a roar, he jerked hard, filling Rig with come. His Rabbit held him close, face against his shoulder, hands petting.

He let Rig take a lot of his weight, keeping some of it off with his knees and one hand. "Good," he muttered into Rig's neck.

"Yeah. Yeah, Blue." Rig settled, still and snuggly and quiet.

"You gonna get some more sleep?" he asked. Not that he was complaining if Rig was, he wasn't stupid -- he could see Rig was pushing himself too hard.

"Prob'ly need to get up." Rig octopussed some more, clingy bastard, breath slowing. "In a minute."

He snorted. "You need to sleep, just say so."

"Need you. Talk to the kid, yeah? Tell him I'm okay?" Rig curled up under him, snuffling and half-asleep again.

Rock snorted again. "I'll tell him. Don't make me a fucking liar."

Rig nodded. "Gonna be fine. Just tired in my bones."

"You could try sleep. I hear that's really good for that tired thing."

"You find me the spare time, marine, and I'm so there." Rig nipped his shoulder. "I'm not giving up fucking, though."

"Better not. It's all about priorities." He nudged Rig. "If you'd let me take care of your fucking jeep for you, and pick up the goddamned grocery bill, because fuck knows you don't eat, you'd be able to sleep, instead of working all those fucking double shifts."

Rig tilted his head, looked up. "I don't want to be a burden for you. Never have. You didn't ask me to come here and now... Shit, now things are weird. We're not weird, just things are."

"Things are only fucking weird because you're too fucking stubborn and proud to let me and the kid carry you. It's not a fucking sin to let people do for you. Fuck, most of the guys on the squad's wives don't fucking work and they aren't anywhere near as good a cook as you." He gave Rig a shake. "I'm not letting your pride kill you, cowboy. A dead corpse ain't gonna blow me every morning."

"Rock, that was gross. I mean, just disgusting." Rigger was chuckling, pretty eyes bright and almost dancing. "And like I told Dick this morning, I am not stubborn."

"Yeah, and I like vegetables."

"You... I didn't know it would be so hard -- take so much out of me. It sucks, getting older, getting tired." Rig shrugged, blushed a little. "I thought I could manage, no sweat, but the job and the classes and the drive? It's kicking my ass."

"Then fucking back off something, or I'll kick your ass for you." He glared down at Rig.

"Are you throwing your weight around, marine? Don't make me kick your butt." Rig met his glare head-on, but those grey eyes weren't pissed, not really.

"I'm just saying don't be more stubborn than I am -- it's not attractive." He gave Rig a wink.

Rig rolled his eyes, shook his head. "If you'd pick up the groceries, help me a little on the bills, I could cut back to thirty hours a week. That'd get me my weekends back..."

"Done." He gave Rig a quick, hard kiss to seal the bargain. "'Course when I'm old and grizzly, I'll expect you to return the favor."

"Anytime." Rig stroked his face, hands warm and sure. "Wanna come take a shower with me? Someone made us chili and cornbread and, since I haven't answered the phone, I got a night off."

"Now that's an offer I can't refuse." He grinned down at Rig. Fucking shit -- they hadn't had a good old-fashioned Friday night in far too long. He got up and put a hand out for Rig. "Yo, Dick. Get your ass in the bathroom. We've got a nurse to play with."

Chapter Twenty Seven

Garth was playing and he was standing. Waiting. Looking at himself in a huge, plain piece of mirrored glass. He was wearing his dove grey hat, his dark blue shirt with mother of pearl buttons that Sissy got him.

He wanted to move, to get the hell out of Dodge. Hell, he needed to move. They were coming. He could hear them -- the stomp of boots on the hardwood, the sound of jeers and snorts.

'Move, Alex. Come on. Move. Now. You gotta.' He could hear himself jabbering, hear it somewhere deep inside him, young and scared and breathless. 'You *gotta*!'

But he couldn't.

He couldn't.

He just watched as slow trails of dark started spreading -- his ear, his nose, staining his shirt. They didn't stop, just got bigger and bigger. The door to the bathroom started opening and suddenly he could move, except he was falling and he couldn't breathe anymore and he couldn't make his fucking legs work and they were fucking coming.

He called out for Rock, for Dick, for anybody, but in his heart he knew it didn't matter. He was alone and no one was coming. Still, he tried, screaming for all he was worth, praying to God that this time things would be different.

And this time it was different.

"Rig!" Dick called out to him. "Rig, wake up!"

His eyes popped open and he bolted from the bed, heading straight into the bathroom to splash some water on his face, wake his ass up. His heart was pounding, going ninety miles an hour, just slamming in his fucking ribcage. Shit. Fuck.

Dick's hands slid over his back, found his shoulders, and began to rub as the warmth of his Pretty's body moved against his back. "You okay?"

"Yeah. Just a dream. Damn. What time is it?" He let his head fall forward, trying to get the tremors to ease.

"I don't know. Two, maybe three in the morning." Dick kept touching him, soothing him. "You want to talk about it?"

He shook his head. "'s nothing. Just a dream. Sorry I woke you. Go on back to bed, yeah? I need a shower."

Dick shook his head and wrapped warm arms around him, pulling him back into his Pretty's warmth. "Seems to me you've been dreaming a lot and most of it not good."

"Yeah. Been working hard. Been studying hard." Been trying so fucking hard to heal.

"You had a nightmare about work or about school? Or both?" Dick's voice was soft, but there was a hard edge to it that he usually didn't hear from his Pretty.

"Huh?" He shook his head. "Neither. It was just a dream. Not about working."

Dick turned him, looked him right in the eye. "Come curl up on the couch with me. And talk to me. I mean really talk to me."

He dropped his eyes, feeling a little shaky, a lot sick. "You don't want to go to bed?"

"Rig... I just want you to be easy in your skin again and you're not." Dick was whispering, holding him tight. "I used to make your nightmares go away, remember?"

He nodded, pushing close and if his eyes were teary, nobody'd see anyway. "You did. I do. I'm trying, Pretty."

"Come with me, Rig. We'll sit and I'll hold you." Dick turned, heading them into the front room, arm around his waist, keeping him close to his Pretty's long, warm body.

Rig followed Dick -- how was it that he was always looking to curl into one or another of his men these days?

They sat in the dark room, wrapped together in a quilt, his cheek on Dick's shoulder. Dick's hands slid over his skin, offering love and comfort and warmth.

"Mmm... I'm sorry I woke you up. I know you need your rest..." He moaned and snuggled, Dick's touch was so good.

"You need yours, too. More than me." Dick dropped a kiss on his head and his Pretty's voice was thick when he continued. "Talk to me, Rig. Keeping it bottled in obviously isn't helping."

"I don't know what to say. I keep dreaming about that night, different parts, different bits. I know what's coming, know I need to run and I don't." He shook his head. "It's pointless."

"No it's not. You don't run because you're keeping it all inside. You've never told anyone what all happened, have you?

You've got to tell someone, Rig. And I'm right here."

"I don't want to." Rig brought his fingers up to Dick's lips, frowning, shaking his head. This was his hurt, his shame. His. And he'd be damned if he spread it around, like a sick disease. "You don't need to know."

Dick kissed his fingers and squeezed him tight and he felt as much as heard the sob that shook his Pretty.

"Oh. Oh, Pretty. No. Love. No, don't. Please. Please, don't..." He pushed close, heart just breaking. "Please. I'm trying so hard to make sure they don't hurt y'all. Please."

"But we're losing you, Rig. Just as surely as if they'd killed you." Dick sniffed hard, tears falling into his curls. "You remember how you said you were healed up wrong? I think it's because you're trying to do it all by yourself. I think you have to talk to someone. *Have* to, Rig. And it doesn't have to be me, but then you need to go see someone, like a shrink or something." Another quiet sob shook Dick's chest. "Please, Rig. Please."

"I'm not taking this outside the family, Dick. I can't. I can't sit and tell some stranger about... about that night." He petted and held and stroked and rocked and didn't know what to do.

"Then you're going to have to tell me." Dick rubbed at his eyes and sniffed hard again and held him tight. "I love you, Rig. Now tell me."

"I... Pretty... It was ugly. I was about to take a piss and they came in all at once, slammed me into the mirror and..." He turned over, facing out into the front room, unable to face his lover. "And I went down sorta like a bull at the butchers."

Dick's arms were like bands around his chest, holding him tightly against solid heat. "I think you need to tell it all to me, Rig. I'm sorry, but... so far sparing me has left you hurting and I can't take it anymore."

"And telling you is going to do what? Let you know how weak I am? Let you know that after all these years of fighting Rock and proving myself that all it took to fuck my world was five marines and a length of pipe? God damn it, Dick, they hit me and stabbed me and you want to know about it?

"It hurt. I would have died rather than take another blow from that pipe -- when my femur broke? I fucking begged them to stop. Is that what you want to hear? I cried and I begged and all I could fucking think when they stabbed me was that they were going to win and I didn't care, so long as it all stopped." He was growling, as furious and hurt and shamed as ever, voice ringing raw and broken through the room.

Dick was crying again, arms so tight around him. "You think that makes you weak, Rig? To go down under five men armed with a pipe? Nobody wins on their own against five, Rig. Not even Rock."

"I'm not talking about winning. I'm talking about breaking. I'm talking about begging and sobbing and bleeding out over a public toilet smelling of other men's piss. I didn't lose. I broke."

"And what the fuck were you supposed to do? Lie there and take it like a fucking man?" Dick snarled at him. "Would that make a difference now, Rig? You didn't break then -- you're breaking now. Bit by bit, every day that you hold onto the hurt and the shame and your stupid fucking pride."

He sat up, pushing out of Dick's arms as he stood, ice fucking cold except for the fury burning in him like a bonfire. "I didn't ask you to worry about me and my stupid fucking pride. Sometimes that pride's all a man has, sometimes that's all I have to hang my hat on. You want to be pissed at me? Be pissed. I'm fucking tired of working my ass off and never being enough. I'm working too much. I'm moping too much. I'm too skinny. I'm never home. I'm prideful and stubborn and this and that and goddamnit!"

He picked some stupid fucking knick-knack up from the end table and threw it, letting it shatter against the wall. "Y'all aren't happy with me? I'll fucking move to Raleigh and you two can take care of yourselves and quit worrying about what I'm fucking up!"

"Since when has pride been all you had?" Dick's voice was quiet, almost no more than a whisper, his face pale.

"Don't you dare."

"Don't I dare what? Expect you to love me more than your pride? Well, I fucking do."

He turned and stared at Dick, shaking with fury. "I love the two of you more than life itself. I am here for y'all. I feed and clean and work and plan and stay for you and him. Don't you dare suggest I live like I don't love you. I love you and Rock better than anyone ever fucking will."

"I know that, Rig, I do. But something's wrong. Something bad's got hold of you and won't let go and it's got to be from that night." Dick wasn't looking at him now, was looking down at the hands twisting up together in Dick's lap.

There was a noise from the hall and Rock stumbled in, glaring and growling, butt naked and blinking in the moonlight coming in through the window. "What the fuck is going on?"

"Nothing. Why the fuck would anything be going on?" He threw his hands up. Fuck, he was tired. "They should have killed me and then y'all could have gone on with your fucking lives and I wouldn't be a fucking thorn in your sides."

He pushed past Rock and headed down the hall.

Rock's hand reached out and snagged him, pulling him back against all those muscles. "Fucking shit, the two of you wake me up in the middle of the fucking night with shouting and goddamned smashing things and you tell me nothing's going on and you wish you were fucking dead?" Rock growled. "Dick? You want to tell me what the fuck is going on?"

"I'm an arrogant jerk who thought he could help, that's what's going on. I'm sorry, Rig. I shouldn't have said anything."

"I can't do this. I'm tired of being a fucking disappointment. I'm tired of fighting so hard and it not being enough. I can't do it anymore. I lost my fucking life, Dick. My job, my friends, my health -- all taken by five motherfuckers who tried to fucking kill me because I love y'all. That's all I did. I had the fucking audacity to follow my old man across the country and love him and then find you, too!" He was screaming, tears pouring down his cheeks, so mad he couldn't see. "My fucking brother hates me because of it. My daddy was ashamed of it. Y'all don't have a single friggin' family member left between you and I'm done! I want it to fucking stop!"

Rig pulled away from Rock and shook his head. "I need a shower."

Now. Right fucking now.

"Who's a fucking disappointment?" Rock asked, a confused frown pulling down his face.

"No one." Dick came over and touched his arm for a moment. "You aren't. You never have been. Ever."

"Go back to bed." He sank to the floor, feeling like a fucking moron basket case. "Just go to bed."

"Jesus fucking Christ." Rock grabbed his arm, pulling him up. Dick's arm was taking in Rock's other hand. "We're all going back to fucking bed."

He closed his eyes, head fucking throbbing. "I need a

shower."

A cigarette. A valium.

"Bed. We're going to fucking bed and we're staying there if I have to fucking sit on the two of you." Rig blinked over at Rock, just sort of stumbling alongside them down the hall. "Would you look at the fucking time? Three goddamned twenty a.m.. What the fuck is wrong with you people?" Rock kept growling, all but tossing them into the bed.

Dick gave him a sad look. "I'm sorry."

He shook his head, scooting over to one side. "Me, too."

God, him, too. So fucking sorry.

Rock got in on the other side of him and Dick tentatively put an arm around him, hugging him tightly. He turned, pushed into Dick's arms, slow, silent tears sliding down his cheeks. Dick held him, one hand stroking along his back. One of Rock's hands slid over his hip, just holding.

He cried until there wasn't anything left to cry, then he just lay there, empty and silent, listening to his men sleep. When he could, he got up and packed a bag, leaving a note that said he was staying in Raleigh for a week or two, just to get his shit together.

He wasn't going to let this destroy him. He wasn't.

He couldn't.

***

Rig dialed Dick's cell phone, knowing his Pretty should be home, needing to talk. Ten days he'd been gone. Working. Thinking. Talking to Momma and Sissy. Maybe even doing a shitload of praying. He sat in his Jeep, listening to the rings. Come on. Pick up. Talk to me. Come on.

The phone finally picked up, Dick's voice coming on the line. "Rig? That really you?"

"Yeah, Pretty. You busy? I was thinking we could get together and talk, just us?" He was grinning, he couldn't help it, Dick sounded good.

"Of course! Are you okay, Rig? I've been worried. And Rock's been like a bear with a sore paw and... are you coming home?"

"Yeah. Yeah, I am. I... I just want to talk to you first. Somewhere not the house. Somewhere easy where it can be about talking, you know? Not about all the other stuff." He wasn't sure if he was making sense, but it was so hard to keep all the hurt and anger away in the safety of the house. Out in public, he had to think.

"Okay. Tell me where." Dick sounded cautious, worried.

"Hmm...Well, there's that little coffee shop near the house? The one with the cushy booths and good hot chocolate?" He was already sitting in the parking lot, after all. "I'm coming home, Pretty. Honest. I just want to talk first. Trust me."

"I can be there in five minutes."

"Thank you."

"I love you," whispered across the line before the phone went dead.

Rig went in and got them a table in the back, ordered two hot chocolates and waited. He listened to the idle chatter, to the sounds of people laughing and greeting each other, just sort of floated. It wasn't very long before Dick came in, looking around and smiling and heading toward him. He gave Dick a warm smile, almost vibrating in his seat. "Hey stranger! You're a sight for sore eyes!"

God, he'd missed that grin.

Dick nodded and one hand made an abortive reach for him. "Hey, Rig. Miss you."

Dick sat, gazing at him. He sat too, hand reaching out under the table to stroke Dick's knee. "How're y'all doing? I've missed you something fierce."

"Yeah. Miss you. Rock's... well, Rock." Dick looked down at his hot chocolate.

"Yeah." He looked at the table, then waited until Dick met his eyes. "I've been thinking a lot, Dick. A whole lot. Been thinking that maybe you were right and maybe I was too and maybe we ought to come to terms with that." Rig took a deep breath and trudged on. "I know you think I'm a prideful bastard, and you're right. I am. I want to be strong and want to be everything my daddy wanted his son to be. And I've thought and thought and I don't think that's wrong. I don't think I can change it if it is, and you need to know that."

"I'm sorry I said you were too proud, Rig. I never meant to hurt you. I'm just... I worry."

"I know. And that's the part where you were right. I'm... It hurts me that I lost so much. It hurts me that they took me down and I wasn't expecting it. I hate knowing that I'll wear their scars forever." He refused to drop his eyes. "They broke something inside my soul I believed nobody could break and I'm having a bitch of a time dealing with that."

"What can I do to help?" Dick asked. "I can't, can I?"

"That's just it. You do. You listen. I can tell you things I can't tell Rock. Things like how scared I was they were going to fuck up my mouth. Things like how they wanted to know who I was fucking and I lied and gave them names of people from when I was a kid." Dick blinked and his Pretty's hand met his under the table, squeezing tight. "It's not the big stuff that's eating me. The physical stuff? Christ, I work the ER. I know all about trauma and pain. It's the little stuff -- the way I feel old or how I lost my favorite hat or how they ruined Garth Brooks for me." Rig shrugged, words just pouring out of him.

"I'm trying to deal. I'm trying to deal with the fact that I hurt Rock by letting them go. That I'm never going to move as easy as I did. All sorts. But sometimes? Lots of times? I'm just trying to muscle through the day with too much to do and not enough time."

"I want to help, Rig. So you don't have to deal alone. You can tell me anything. And there isn't anything I wouldn't do to help take the load off you. The only one pushing you to do too much every day is you."

"But don't you see? Before all this happened? I was doing all this and playing and laughing and not exhausted in my bones. I don't want them to have everything, to have taken everything." He took a big drink of hot chocolate, forced himself to relax, to chill the fuck out. "I guess what I'm saying is it's easier to know it's what you ought to do than to do it."

Dick shook his head. "Bullshit, Rig. Before this happened you were working. And less hours most of the time, then you are now. But that's it. Now you're working, and you always pick up at least an extra shift every week, plus you're going to school full time. So is it any wonder you're tired at the end of the day?"

"Now, I'm only working half-time, three-quarters sometimes, tops..."

"I don't think so, Rig. Add up the hours you worked last week. And then add up the hours you actually attended class and the hours you spend studying." Those eyes were looking at him earnestly. "I'm not saying you should quit or anything, okay? I don't want you to think I'm telling you what to do. And I'm not trying to say you're neglecting anything else, 'cause that's so not what I mean. But you think you're doing the same as you used to only not cutting it and I think if you add it all up you'll find you're doing way more than you used to so no wonder it's taking a toll on you."

He thought on it. After two or three twelve-hour shifts, and fourteen hours of class, and seven hours driving time and... oh, the whole thing made his head spin. He met Dick's eyes head on. "I'm too fucking busy and tired to figure out how to make it right. Hell, I went and spent ten days in a roach-trap just to be able to slow down enough to know what I needed to tell you, to know what I think."

Rig shook his head. "Christ, Pretty. I'm what? Heading toward thirty-one and looking to you for advice? You're supposed to be partying and having fun and shit."

"You can worry about me later. I'll help you make a schedule if you want -- we'll pencil the worrying in, okay?" Dick gave him a smile. "I think you've been keeping yourself too busy on purpose, so you don't have to think about it. Which worked for awhile, but..." Dick shrugged. "It's not working anymore, is it?"

"I had a long time in that bed thinking on what happened, Dick. You can't blame a man for wanting it behind him."

"I know and I don't." Dick sighed. "But you never talked about it -- not until now and not talking about it? That's not putting it behind you, that's ignoring it." Dick laughed. "Now Rock's really good at that and somehow it works for him. But most of us aren't like Rock."

He chuckled, nodding and feeling a warm ache in his belly that meant it was time to get home. "God, no. There's only enough room in my world for one of him."

"Can you... do you think you can try to come talk to me when things are getting to you? And I'll try and be patient and not bully you into it? Would that work?"

He'd been waiting on this, been thinking on it hard and Rig nodded, just like he'd decided he would. "Yeah. But I have a favor. I... I need to do this kind of talking where it's not all about hurting and where I can think. It's so easy to just yell and slam shit and let it be about my temper at home in private and I don't like that."

Dick bit his lip, considering what he'd asked. Then his Pretty smiled. "You know... we could do something like this once a week. Just take a bit of time out and have a bite to eat somewhere, talk, not necessarily about what happened or how you're feeling, but just... touch base?" Here the smile became a grin. "It could be like a standing date."

"A date, huh?" He felt a big old grin growing. "I'd like that. Something easy and ours. I'd like that a lot. I've been missing you. More than you know."

"Oh, I know all about missing, Rig." Dick stroked his fingers beneath the table.

"You 'bout done?" He nodded to Dick's cup. "I'm thinking it's time I get home where I belong."

Dick grabbed his cup and drank down the rest of his hot chocolate. "Yeah, I'm done. And more than ready to have you home. We can wake Rock together."

"Yeah. Sounds good." He nudged Dick's knee with his own. "We good, Pretty?"

Dick nodded. "As soon as I can get you home, and kiss you blind, yeah."

"Cool. I'll meet you there." He finished his hot chocolate and followed his lover out, heading home.

Chapter Twenty Eight

There were days when the only reason he was able to get up at all was because of Rig's magnificent mouth. More than once, that morning blow job had saved his butt by waking him up and getting him hauled out of bed on time.

Sometimes on the weekends though -- when he knew there wasn't anywhere he had to be, not even his morning blow job woke him up enough to get out of bed and he'd throw his arm over his eyes and go back to sleep, hand still stroking through Rig's hair in a thank you. Especially when they'd been up most of the night fucking. Like they had last night.

"Come on, Rock -- 's almost noon."

He grunted and turned his face into the pillow, ignoring Dick. He didn't care what time it was -- he was sleeping.

He heard Rig's chuckle, felt the cool, long fingers on his back, on his ass. "Mm... let him sleep, kid. He was working late last night." Oh. His Rabbit was home, not working and not studying. Fucking A.

A hot, soft tongue touched the top of his spine, then a smooth freshly shaved cheek brushed his ass. He rumbled, not quite growling, as he pushed up into the sweet touches. He still didn't give a fuck what time it was, but maybe he wasn't quite so sleepy.

"Hey, I'll do all the work now, but it'd be nice if he was conscious for it," complained Dick.

"Hush, now. 's not very often I get to admire this fine ass while he's dozing." Rig's tongue slid along the top of his crease, fingers easing his cheeks apart to stroke over his hole.

"Hedonist," accused Dick, but the kid's voice was fond.

"Slut," he corrected the kid, voice slurred, still more asleep than awake, though his cock was tipping the balance the other way, responding to Rig's touches.

"Yours." Rig's fingers and lips were hot, easing him while

they pushed him from relaxation to hunger. Those fingers started pressing inside, slick and smooth.

The dogs started barking and Dick sighed. "I'll see what's got them riled up."

He moaned, toes curling as his cock jerked.

Rig's purr was hot, needy, fucking pure sex against his spine. Those fingers found his gland, played it like a fucking harp as open-mouthed kisses wandered up his body. Fucking shit, he was awake now. He grabbed onto the sheets and tried to find enough leverage to push back into Rig's touch.

"Shh... you were sleeping, remember?" Rig's voice, rough and hungry, brushed his jaw, fingers sliding again and again, leaving every few breaths to return slick, to push deep.

He snorted, but turned the sound into a fake snore. The least he could do for Rig was pretend to be asleep. His body pushed back again, meeting the thrust of Rig's fingers -- there were some things a man couldn't pretend.

Rig chuckled, licking at his neck. "You're so hungry this morning, Blue, hot and tight."

"Always hungry for you, Rig."

He felt Rig's shudder, hard cock sliding against his thigh. Those fingers kept moving, kept playing. "Ditto. Want you."

He growled. "Then you'd better fucking take me before I flip you and nail your ass to this mattress."

"Neanderthal." Rig bit his shoulder hard.

He growled louder, body tensing, getting ready to take matters into his own hands.

"I don't think so, Blue." Rig's hand pushed between his shoulders. "You were sleeping and I was enjoying your amazing fucking body and you can just lay right there and relax and let me enjoy, you hear?"

"Tease," he accused, sliding his cock against the sheets under the guise of moving up into Rig's fingers.

"Pushy bastard." As he moved up, Rig's fingers were replaced with the width of that hot cock.

"Asshole." The word ended on a groan, Rig's cock stretching him. He buried his face in the pillow.

"Yeah, but you're my asshole." Rig pressed close, making it feel like they were fucking touching everywhere. Rig's cock burned and it was fucking sweet, the slide of their skin together even sweeter and he was fucking moaning. Those hands were sliding over his belly, down to cup his balls. He could feel Rig rocking behind him, motions slow and fluid against him, inside him.

The burn gave way to sweet pleasure, Rig nailing his gland now and sending him slowly into orbit. Rig pumped him, hand and cock moving in unison. Then that sweet mouth fastened on his shoulder and started sucking, picking up the rhythm. He rumbled, fisting his hands in the sheets, not wanting to come too fast, wanting to last for his Rabbit.

"So fucking hot, Blue." Rig's whisper was desperate, breathy, but the steady thrusts continued, Rig trying to drive him out of his fucking mind.

He half-raised his ass and spread his legs wider, making a noise that sounded awfully close to a whimper as Rig slid deeper. "Fuck. Harder."

"Yeah." Rig started moving, nailing his gland over and over, teeth scraping over his shoulder as their low, hungry cries sounded. He pushed back and forth, rocking between cock and hand, feeling the pleasure begin to settle at the base of his spine, building and building.

"Oh, Blue. Yeah. Fucking sweet." Rig started jerking, slamming into him, working his ass with a passion.

Roaring, he threw back his head and came hard. Rig's hand was still pulling out aftershocks then his Rabbit stiffened, crying out as heat pulsed inside him. He collapsed onto the bed, Rig heavy and loose on top of him.

A soft moan brought his attention to the doorway where Dick leaned, spunk-covered hand slowing its movements. He gave the kid a cocky grin and got a warm smile in return.

"See, Pretty. He's not hard to wake up." Rig moaned as he pulled out, staying close and warm. "Just gotta know the right things to say."

Dick chuckled and stumbled to the bed. "Or not say, as the case may be."

He grunted, making room for the kid. "Fucking's better'n talking any day."

"Rocketman, fucking's better than anything." Rig cleaned them both up, mouth sliding over his shoulders again. "Let's do it again."

He chuckled and pulled Rig up, taking that sweet mouth in a long kiss. He hooked a hand around the back of Dick's head and made it a three-way.

There were days when the only reason he was able to get up was Rig's mouth. Other days it took two mouths.

Chapter Twenty Nine

Rock didn't have nightmares. He didn't dream about killing and being killed and losing loved ones. Not him. Not Rock, the Marine Gunnery Sergeant. Sometimes he woke up in the middle of the night though and he needed. Not often, but more than once in a blue moon.

Tonight was one of those nights and he reached out and there was Rig, all sleep-warm and pliant and he spooned up behind him, fingers already traveling down to open him up as his lips closed over the back of that sweet neck.

Rig gave a soft moan, head dipping forward, hips shifting into his hands. "Mm... Blue..."

"Want you," he whispered, sliding a finger into tight heat.

"Yours." Rig shifted, body pressing back against his finger, hot and tight. Willing. Ready.

He didn't linger long, Rig was ready for him, wanted him, and he needed. He pushed one of Rig's legs forward and held open the sweet ass with his hands, pushing himself inside. Rig's hole pulled him in, body hungry for him, clutching at his cock. The soft, breathy moan seemed to almost fill the room.

Fuck, yes. This was what he needed, to lose himself inside the grasping heat of Rig's body. He started to move, sliding in and out with long, easy thrusts. He wrapped his arms around Rig, earning another hungry noise, Rig's fingers twined with his and held them close together. He took a deep breath, pulling the scent of Rig and sex into himself and just kept moving. So easy, so good, so right; the hot grasp of Rig's body was where he belonged.

Rig rocked with him, hips moving against him, fluid as fuck. "Good, Blue. Hot."

He had no idea how long they moved together; time didn't matter. This was better than sleep, better than anything and he just kept moving. Rig brought their joined hands up to that mouth, lips nuzzling over his inner wrist, kissing and nibbling.

He groaned, easy and right becoming hot and urgent just like that, Rig's tongue working its magic on him.

"Mm... Blue..." The whisper was needy, insistent. "More."

He growled and rolled, pushing Rig onto his stomach, sliding the long legs apart with his knees. His cock went deeper and he started pounding into Rig, loving that fucking tight heat.

Rig pushed up, cheek rubbing against his. "Yeah! Fucking love this. Love your cock."

"Yeah." He kept pushing, shoving into Rig, giving his lover everything he had.

Rig arched, groaning and jerking beneath him. "Close."

He nodded, licking at the back of Rig's neck and then leaning forward to lick at Rig's lips. "Anytime, Rabbit."

Rig's fingers tightened around his, ass clenching as Rig convulsed, his name cried out into the bedroom. That sweet ass milked his own orgasm from him and he groaned out Rig's name, shooting deep inside that sweet heat. Fucking perfect.

Rig relaxed beneath him, holding his cock, his fingers.

"Mm... Rig." His head dropped to Rig's neck, his body dropping slowly, carefully down onto Rig.

"Yeah, Blue. 's good." Rig's cheek was resting on his hand, soft snuffles already starting.

He didn't even pull out of Rig, just stayed snug and held tight inside his lover, letting Rig hold him inside and out. Rig's chest rose and fell slowly, giving his own breathing a rhythm. Yeah, he didn't have nightmares, he had Rig.

Chapter Thirty

Dick ordered himself a Coke and Rig a coffee and told the waitress he'd wait to order.

He was enjoying his "dates" with Rig. Hell, half the time they didn't do more than eat and talk about fun stuff, but if Rig needed to talk... they were there and there was no pressure. The odd time he'd even had stuff to get off his own chest. They usually met Saturdays for lunch, after Rock's blow job and early enough that the big guy was still sleeping in. Rig pretty much worked evening and night shifts these days, so they almost always had the time off together.

He smiled as he saw the skinny form outlined in the doorway of the diner for a moment, cowboy hat making it unmistakably Rig.

Dick had gotten Rig the hat for his birthday and it was gratifyingly worn at every possible moment -- the dove grey making Rig's eyes shine and stand out. Rig was looking good, draped in a western shirt and a pair of ironed blue jeans. The man took their dates very seriously, cologne and all. He even shaved, except for the little moustache that they all knew was just worn to see how long it would be before Rock noticed.

"Hey, you. How's it going?" Rig slid into the booth, giving him a smile. "You order me coffee?"

"Yeah, I did. Told the waitress we'd order food when you got here." He slouched just a little, legs spreading out so their knees touched. "You're looking good."

"Yeah?" Rig preened a little. "Feeling pretty good. Three weeks 'til finals and then Christmas break. Woo."

"Mmm, yeah -- I know what I want under my tree this year." He grinned and winked, sitting up a little as the waitress came with their drinks. They ordered -- he got a big burger with fries and Rig got the Caesar salad with chicken. "So how're you doing?" he asked once the waitress was gone again.

"Not bad. Sort of wishing we weren't making the trip home

for Christmas, just because I could use some money from working the overtime. Then I feel guilty for wishing. Classes are going good, though. I'm thinking real serious about applying for a fellowship for when my clinicals start." Rig settled back with his coffee, looking relaxed, sort of peaceful.

He smiled. It felt really good, seeing Rig looking so at ease. "Would that mean you wouldn't have to work while you were doing your clinicals?"

"You know it." Rig nodded. "I was giving it a good hard think and see? These clinicals? Well, they're what it's all about -- learning my trade better and if I want to learn all I can and be good at what I do? Well, I figure I need to focus on it and not worry about County General. Hell, to be honest? I'm so fucking tired of the politics there it isn't funny."

"Yeah, you've been looking a little green around the edges whenever you come home from there. I thought there was maybe some hard cases coming through."

"Some, but that's pretty normal. It's the constant bullshit -- somebody not doing their job, somebody else bitching about the schedule. It's getting old and I'm less and less apt to deal with it." Rig stirred a little more sugar into his coffee. "How about you? You happy?"

He nodded. "I am. You're good, Rock's good. I'm not the grunt of the week for picking on -- haven't been for awhile actually. Yeah."

"Well, Corporal, you're not exactly a cherry anymore, are you?" Rig winked. "Hell, Rock says you're damned good at the communications shit. He's impressed."

"Yeah?" His cheeks heated just a little. Fuck, he was still an eager little soldier when it came to Rock's approval sometimes. But then look at Rock and who could blame him? "I do my best."

"Well, Rock says you're the one he'd want at his back in combat, kid. There's no higher praise from the career man." Their food came and Rig unrolled his silverware, peppering his salad liberally. "Oh, what did the vet say about Lucy's paw? Did she step on something or did something bite her?"

"Something bit her -- a spider or a hornet or something. We should spray the yard, but it's going to mean keeping the pups inside for a few days if we do, so they don't eat anything with the poison on it. And you know how Rock's gonna feel about that." He added ketchup and mustard to his burger and salted up his fries.

"So set it up while we have them kenneled over Christmas. That ought to kill two birds with one stone and keep Rock happy." Rig stole a French fry with a wink. "One day, I'm gonna find that man a dog to fall in love with. Mark my words."

He chuckled and turned his plate so the fries were closer to Rig. "I bet you will yet. And you know it's going to be the mangiest, ugliest mutt ever."

Oh, his burger was good, though he imagined it had a lot to do with the company.

"Either that or some girly yippy beast, though I can't hardly see that." Rig stole another fry or two as they ate.

They ate their meal, making small talk between bites. Rig really did look good, smiling and happy and like he finally really was putting the attack behind him. "I suppose you've got study group this afternoon and work tonight?"

Rig shook his head, wiped his mouth with a napkin. "I'm working three to eleven today. The study group wanted to meet this morning at 10:30 and I told them I had plans."

Oh, fuck, that made him feel good. Special. "Thanks," he said softly, hand sliding over Rig's knee under the table.

He got a slow, sexy grin, those thighs parting for him, just a little. "It's for me as much as you."

He just beamed at Rig, wanting more than just the simple touch of fingers on denim in the worst way. Of course he was coming to appreciate their dates and putting up with the wanting for a bit until they could get home. The sex once they got to it was usually pretty fucking good. Not that it wasn't always, but having to wait... well, it gave it an edge. "You want to share a dessert with me?"

"Cherry pie with ice cream?" Those grey eyes were hot, happy. Hungry.

"Yeah, that sounds perfect. Maybe later we can just have some cream."

Oh, fuck that was a great blush. "I'm thinking a pre-work appetizers and then a full-course meal late tonight..."

That drawl could make him go zero to sixty just like that. He bit his lip to bite back his groan and he squeezed Rig's knee. "Oh, yeah... I bet even Rock'll volunteer to cook for that."

"I'm sort of counting on full participation, yes sir." Rig winked, shifting in his seat, adjusting himself.

He laughed, but the sound was husky and pretty fucking wanton, even to his own ears. He had to clear his throat to order the cherry pie a la mode.

***

There were days when being a nurse was harder than others.

There were days when it was useless, pointless, unrewarding, hard, underpaid, evil fucking work. Days where death and pain and tears and stench filled up every part of him and made him sick to his stomach and sad. Then, there were days like today when it was right and there was pain and stench and filth and, at the end, lives were saved and he felt like it was worth it.

He pulled up into the driveway and grinned as he saw the back porch lights were on. He'd called, left a message for whoever was home first to please fire up the portable hot tub and stick some beers in the cooler for him, he was in need of a little celebration and a lot of relaxation.

Rig didn't even bother to go in through the front, just went through the back gate and unlocked the door of the privacy fence surrounding the deck. "Hey. I'm home."

Rock and Dick were in the middle of the Jacuzzi in the middle of a clinch. Their lips parted and they turned together, similar grins on their faces. "Hey, Rig."

He smiled and started stripping straight away, wanting nothing more than to slide into the hot water with a cold beer and soak for the next thirty years. He stepped into the water, butt hitting the seat, and groaned, eyes closing in pleasure. Okay, maybe forty years.

Four hands slid over his skin, two mouths sealing with his. Oh, they felt good, tasted sweeter than Tupelo honey and just fed a hunger that he didn't even notice anymore it was so constant. Rig moaned, lips parting, tongue sliding against theirs. They each slid a hand beneath him, cupping his ass and Dick's fingers tugged at first one and then the other nipple, while Rock's hand circled his cock, squeezing him tight.

Oh, fuck. Never let it be said his marines weren't focused or dedicated to their particular brand of relaxation. He didn't fight them, didn't say a word, just held on and fucking went with it. Fingers met on his asshole, one of Dick's and one of Rock's pushing into him. Laughter filled his mouth.

Rig grinned and bore down, riding both fingers with ease and the beginnings of real hunger, happy and relaxed. "Y'all doubling up on me?"

"You sounded like you needed to relax," said Dick.

"And you interrupted the showdown for who got you first," added Rock.

"Oh, darn. Guess you'll have to share." He gasped as someone's finger quirked, jerking, splashing the water. "I'm all yours."

"We can always hope," said Dick, mouth moving to wrap around his collarbone.

He cried out, the sound low and needy and Rock smothered it with a hard, hungry kiss that tilted his head and made him dizzy. They worked his asshole and his cock and his titties and his mouth and his skin, leaving him a ball of pleasure.

"God... fuck." He whimpered and twisted, crying out into Dick's neck, Rock's mouth moving faster, riding harder. He'd stopped trying to catch his breath, to focus, to touch back -- to do anything but feel -- ages ago.

They were relentless, working together to make him lose his mind. They were doing a damn fine job of it. He lifted his head, body tensing, searching for his orgasm. His hips worked furiously, balls feeling as tight as a drum.

Rock pushed another finger inside him, Dick's mouth moving to suck hard on one his nipples, fingers still working the other one. He shot hard, hard enough that it would have hurt if it wasn't sheer fucking pleasure. Better than drugs, better than anything -- Oh, yeah, this was his own personal fucking nirvana.

Dick hummed around his nipple and Rock chuckled into his mouth. "Feeling better, Rig? More relaxed?"

"Oh, sweet fuck, yeah. Yeah." His head was lolling, floating on bubbles and endorphins and pleasure too sweet to be real.

"I think he liked it," Dick murmured.

"Yep," agreed Rock. His Blue was nudging his legs open, settling between them. "I figure you're about ready for me, Rig."

"Always, Rocketman. Always." He was more than willing to ride that thick cock; as relaxed as he was, Rock should fit right in. Dick took one of his legs and pulled it up over the kid's thighs and he could feel Rock's heat against his hole. In no time at all Rock was pushing in, slow and steady.

"Mm..." He hummed and stretched, toes curling as he was filled, spread wide. "So good to be home, here, now."

Dick was sitting next to him, close and nuzzling against his neck, fingers playing over the soft skin of his inner thigh. "Yeah, s'great having you."

"It sure is." He shivered, moaned softly, nudged Dick with his chin. "Kiss me."

"Anything you want," Dick told him with a smile. Those eyes were twinkling at him happily as Dick's lips closed over his, tongue sliding along his own. He hummed low and easy, shuddering as Dick's kiss deepened, Dick's earthy, rich flavor filling his mouth as surely as his Blue filled his body. As Rock began to move, in and out in an easy rhythm, Dick slid a hand around his cock, the other tugging on his nipple.

"Oh... oh. Pretty." He wasn't quite ready to get it up again, not ready to move from floating to aching and wanting, but Dick and Rock were just taking him, fucking him, sending him to the fucking moon. Dick's teeth scraped over his skin and Rock increased the power of his movements, coming into him harder, faster, stronger. The water was all around them, warm and bubbling, buoying. He started pushing against Rock, hips tilting so that Rock hit right... "There! Oh, right there, Blue. Yeah, fuck. Right there."

"Anything you want, Rig." With that, Rock picked up the pace again. Man was part fucking machine, hitting him hard and fast over and over. Dick's suction increased, the hand on his cock moved faster.

His eyes were wide open and, fucking God, how could they do this? Get him so close, so fast? He leaned back and caught Blue's gaze, breath catching, watching those eyes. They were focused on him, blue and dark and happy. He felt his body begin to tighten, shake and then Dick's tongue pushed into his mouth again, forcing his orgasm from him with a cry. Rock thrust a few more times, graceless pushes into his body that spoke of need and want and then his Blue came with a low growl.

Rig reached up, stroked Blue, Pretty, sighing softly. "Y'all are gonna kill me one day. I'm a lucky man."

Rock chuckled and Dick laughed, the kid rubbing a hard, hard prick against his thigh. He reached down to pet the hot flesh. "Somebody's still wanting."

He leaned his hand over, licking at Dick's lips. He may never get it up again, but that was no reason to leave his Pretty high and dry. Dick moaned, the sound vibrating in his mouth. He rubbed slow and easy as he floated, Rock almost light against him, still held inside. Rock's lips licked at the skin of his neck and shoulders, sucking softly. On the other side of his neck, Dick's breath came faster and faster.

"So good. Hot." Rig rubbed his thumb along the ridge at the tip of Dick's cock, teasing, sending sparks through his lover.

Moaning, Dick reached for his lips, mouth closing over his with hunger. He opened, tongue sliding lazily, shifting and tightening around Rock's prick. A rumbling growl made the skin along his neck vibrate and Dick jerked against him. Rig's cock twitched and his hand and body tightened again, a soft moan sliding into Dick's mouth. Oh... Oh, fuck...

Dick pushed soft sounds into his mouth, lips wrapping around his tongue and sucking. He reached around with his free hand, tugging Dick closer. His legs were wrapped around Rock's waist, keeping them tight together. Dick was starting to move against him, pushing that long cock into the tunnel of his hand, driving the rhythm quickly.

"So good. Pretty. Make me so hungry..." He whispered nonsense, tugging hard on Dick's cock, hips moving slow and unconscious against Rock.

Rock was still rumbling, starting to meet his soft movements, and then his Blue's tongue pushed into their kiss. He closed his eyes, fingers losing their rhythm, the three-way stealing his focus, his breath. Rock was sliding into him and Dick sliding along his thigh, both men working together, moving slowly.

So good. So fucking good. He didn't know where to put his hands, what to touch, who to hold. That didn't seem to bother his marines though, they just kept kissing, just kept moving, blowing his fucking mind.

"Oh... Oh, I..." He gasped, hard again, hot water keeping him relaxed, dizzy.

Dick's hand found his prick, sliding over it, thumb catching his slit again and again. Oh, right! He reached down, fingers tugging Dick's cock, murmuring a desperate 'sorry' into Dick's lips. Rock's chuckle filled the air along with Dick's soft moan, neither of them missing a beat.

He pulled Dick's tongue into his mouth, sucking in time with his hand. Dick's hand. Rock's prick. Oh, fuck, yeah.

Now this was the fucking circle of life.

Dick came first, the kid shouting into his mouth and shooting against him, the water soon carrying the hot spunk away.

"Pretty..." He was going to die. No question. Right here in the hot tub. "Blue..."

"That's us, Rig and I'm not shooting again until you have," Rock murmured. Dick was nuzzling lazily at his neck.

"Not..." He shook his head. "Already come twice, Rock. Getting old."

Rock changed angles, hitting his prostate again. "Not as old as I am, Rig."

"But... oh... Oh, fuck..." No fair. Rock had only... and he'd... oh, fuck, right there. Rock kept nailing him right where it counted, Dick kept pulling on his fucking prick. He looked up, blinking hard, gasping, words lost. Those blue eyes bored into his own, saying everything that Rock never vocalized.

He arched, coming with a broken cry, completely fucking lost. Rock and Dick wrapped around him, his marines holding him close as they all floated in the water. He just let them hold him, keep him afloat and together and there. So good, his marines, his lovers, his men.

A little celebration, a lot of relaxation. It didn't get much better than this.

Chapter Thirty One

He turned the page, jotting down notes as he went. Nerves. Bones had been challenging. Muscles a little harder, but nerves? Fuck. He was too old to learn this shit.

Rig sighed, absently rubbing Grimmy's back with his foot, forcing himself to focus. He was on his fourth pot of coffee today, sequestered in the kitchen while the boys took their day off. Right. Nerves. Focus, Rig. NERVES.

Rock came in and poured himself a cup of coffee, setting it down on the table next to him. Then his Blue went into the cupboard and found a stash of Momma's pecan cookies and put them on a plate, setting that on the table, too. Finally, Rock came and sat and ate a cookie. He reached out with his foot, rubbing it up Rock's calf, loving on his Blue, slow and easy. Rock looked at him and he'd be goddamned if the man wasn't pouting. "Does this mean you'll take a break and come fuck?"

Rig arched an eyebrow, then shut his book with a nod. He reached over, stroked his Blue's bottom lip. "Yeah. Want you."

Rock nipped at his finger. "Yeah? Really?"

He got a grin. "Good. The kid's been moping."

"I can't have that. It'll give him premature wrinkles." Rig grinned and stood, pulling Rock to his feet. He was going to say something smartassed and clever, but he got caught by those lips and took a nice, long kiss instead, licking the pecan and brown sugar and coffee flavors from his Blue.

Rock growled, hands sliding around his waist and pulling him in close to that hard body. Oh, yeah. That's what he needed. He reached up, wrapped his arms around Rock's neck and held on tight. Their bellies rubbed together, tongues sliding against each other, slow and deep. Almost without him noticing, Rock moved them, pushing him up against a wall and rubbing their cocks together through their clothes.

"Mm... Blue. Good." He hummed, holding on tight, pleasure filling him, slowly becoming edged with sheer need. His Blue kept on rocking against him, hips moving slowly, just like the tongue that was fucking his mouth. He hooked one leg around Rock's hip. Fuck, he loved the strength and heat and... oh, fuck, the package was Grade A perfect.

He got a growl for his troubles, a low, perfect rumble that set his lips tingling. One of Rock's hands slid around and gripped his ass, pulling him tighter against that perfect heat. He slid one hand down, shoving their sweats low enough that their cocks slid together.

"Oh... Fuck, yeah..." He pushed up into the kiss again, keening softly, trusting Blue to keep him steady. Rock just growled again and deepened the kiss, pushing into his mouth like he owned it, body hard and tight against his own. Rig rose up on his toes, hips moving faster, taking as much as Rock would offer him. The wall was solid against his back, wall of muscles in front of him heated steel. One of Rock's hands slid between them, wrapping around both their pricks and stroking.

Oh, yeah. Just what he fucking needed. Right fucking there.

He cried out into Blue's lips, back arching as he shot hard enough that his calves hurt. Rock's hand slowed, still pumping them together, making him shudder and shake with sweet aftershocks. Reaching back around to his ass, Rock slid one come-slick finger into his hole.

"Oh... fuck, yes." Rig pushed into the touch, riding his Blue slow and easy, warm and happy and right where he fucking belonged.

Rock growled for him, another finger pushing into his body. "Want you."

"'m yours." He took another long, hard kiss, pulling Rock's tongue into his mouth and sucking in time with the fingers spreading his ass. "Take me."

Rock slid his other leg up around Rock's waist and spread his ass wide with large, warm hands. Rock's fat prick was hot as the tip teased his hole.

He smiled at his Blue, eyes fastened together. "Fucking live for this, Blue."

Rock nodded, pushing that hot cock inside him in one long easy stroke. He moaned, forehead against Rock's, stealing hot little kisses and watching those blue-blue eyes as that cock spread him wide. "So fucking good, Rig."

Rock started to fuck him, slow and easy, making his skin

hum.

"Al...always is. Always has been." He nipped Rock's bottom lip, then sucked on it, tongue sliding. Rock rumbled, moving faster, taking what they both needed. Rig angled his hips, shoulders pressing hard against the wall, letting Rock in deep, hard... "Oh, fuck. Sweet."

Growling, Rock pushed harder, deeper, taking everything he offered, demanding more, demanding everything he had and returning it with each thrust of that sweet cock. He held on tight, panting and keening, feeling the flush that covered him. Then his Blue got one hand between them, wrapping around his cock and pumping in time with the hard thrusts into his ass. He just let that hot fucking hand tug his ass right on over, shooting over Rock's fingers, ass squeezing that fat cock tight.

"Fuck. Yeah." Rock grunted, shoving in hard and coming in his ass. He rested his cheek on Rock's shoulder, trying to catch his breath, tongue sliding slow and easy over the hot skin. Rock murmured and then chuckled. "You still got some time, Rig? The kid's gonna be upset he missed your break time."

"I'm thinking too much work and coffee and not enough Rock and Dick makes Rig a grouchy boy, Blue. Y'all busy until, say, tomorrow morning?"

"Yep. Busy fucking you." Rock grinned and took a kiss. "Can you spare the time? Really?"

"Yeah. Need my men." Needed to spend a little less time studying how the nerves worked and put in some practical study on where the good ones were.

"Well, all right."

Rock pulled out, but didn't put him down. Instead, his Blue called for Dick and carried him off to the bedroom like he was the prize of some barbarian raiding party.

He chuckled, held on tight and went with it. Being the kidnapped desert prince was way sexier than overworked college student any fucking day.

***

Rock was home alone. Not that unusual an occurrence these days, though usually by midnight, Dick was home. Tonight Dick was out with his buddies for a little Saturday night pool and Rig had gone straight from a seven a.m. to seven p.m. shift at the hospital to a study group meeting. Rig was taking his studies fucking seriously and doing really well and Rock knew Rig was going to be a fine doctor, but in the meantime their time together had shrunk back down to a few hours in the evenings, if they were lucky, and Rig had to study for most of those.

He made another round through the channels, wanting to wait up for some quality time with Rig, but there was nothing on. He'd just turned off the TV when he heard a vehicle pull in to the drive.

It didn't take any time for Rig's key to sound in the lock, that good old boy already shushing the dogs as he muscled in. "Hush, now. Don't y'all dare wake Blue up. How're my babies doing? Y'all want out? Thank the Lord above I got tomorrow off. I think I'm gonna start pissing chemical combinations, Christ knows I'm fucking dreaming about bones..."

Rig looked tired, tight, but that grayness was gone. The limp almost unnoticeable. The intensity and laughter and energy back.

"I've got a bone right here for you to dream about." He grinned at Rig's startled look. "Course might be more fun if you're not dreaming while you check it out."

"You're up!" Rig grinned, the look happy and horny as backpack and bags got thrown on the coffee table. Then Rock found himself with an armful of tired, hard redneck. "Christ but you're a sight for sore eyes, Blue. How's it hanging, marine?"

He took a handful of ass in each hand and tugged Rig tight against him, letting his hips rub up a bit. "You tell me."

"Mm... hard and ready as always, Blue." Rig leaned forward, licking at his lips. "Oh... somebody had apple pie for dessert."

He chuckled and unsuccessfully tried to capture Rig's tongue with his lips. "I didn't think I'd get caught."

Rigger chuckled, teasing him with nipping tastes and quick, almost-there licks. It felt good -- playful, happy. He countered by threading his fingers through Rig's belt loops and tugging, haphazardly bringing their hips together, randomly rubbing their pricks together. Laughter mixed with moans and gasps slid over and into his mouth, Rigger's hands holding his head.

He let Rig lead the kiss, happy to follow. Rig finally settled in, melting against him with a purr, tongue sliding deep. It was what he'd been waiting for and he slid his hands between them, undoing first Rig's and then his own buttons and fly.

"Mm... yeah." Rigger nodded, groaning low. "Yeah, Blue."

When their cocks touched, Rig whimpered into his lips, hungry. "You like that, Rig? You like that enough or you want to ride me?"

"Oh, fuck. Live for your fucking cock." Rig leaned up rubbing that sweet prick against his belly, that ass nuzzling back against his hands.

He pushed at Rig's jeans, Rig helping him get them off before settling back down onto his lap. "Oh, fuck..."

"Yeah, Blue. Please." Rig was vibrating, rocking in his hands. Wanting him.

He slid his hand down around Rig's ass, finding that sweet hole and pushing two of his fingers in. Shit, Rig was hot there. Hot and grasping and clutching at his skin. So fucking good he couldn't wait to get his prick in there. Rig groaned, nodding, nibbling against his lips as his fingers were ridden like the class A slut that his Rabbit was. Those grey eyes were shining at him, fucking hungry and needy and right and his.

He pushed another finger in, loving the way Rig's eyes half-rolled back into his head for a moment before finding his again.

"So fucking good, Blue." Rig's hands slid over his shoulder, down to his pecs, tracing his abs, all the while riding his fingers. "Love touching you."

He rumbled happily, feeling the sweet touches in his balls, his cock, his toes. Sliding his free hand up along Rig's spine, he brought that mouth back in for a kiss. Sweet and spicy all at once, sort of like Rig's apple pie, but sharper and hungry and fucking **Rig**, that tongue pressed deep, fucking his mouth in rhythm with his fingers driving into Rig's body.

He could do this forever. He wanted to do this forever. Just kiss and rub and fuck with this man. They settled into it, Rig's eyes watching, tongue sliding, fingers touching. He held on tight, kept the pressure and friction on their cocks, kept fucking his man, fingers pushing deeper and deeper.

He wasn't sure how long they would have kept it up, but they were interrupted by the door, Dick coming in, locking up behind him and then coming to a full stop. "Whoa, isn't that something to come home to?"

Rig lifted his head, grinned. "Hey Pretty. Missed you. Wanna play?"

Rock chuckled -- Dick was already half-undressed, T-shirt gone and jeans open. The kid got rid of the rest of his clothes and came to straddle Rock's lap as well, snuggling up behind Rig. Smiling at the kid, Rock leaned forward and they kissed over Rig's shoulder for a moment.

Then Rock settled back -- it would be Rig's turn now and there wasn't much prettier to look at than these two men kissing. Rig smiled, turning his head for his kiss. Those long, thin arms stretched up, wrapping around Dick's neck, giving Rock a beautiful view of Rig's body pulled taut against Dick's muscles. He slid the fingers of his free hand over Rig's sides and his belly, teasing the tip of the sweet, hard cock, before sliding his hand back to touch Dick.

Rig hummed softly, leaning against Dick, soaking up the warmth and the exuberance of their young pup. The whole time that sweet body never stopped moving on his fingers. Fuck, but Rig was a slut. Just the way he liked it. Dick's hands slid around Rig's waist, wrapping around their cocks.

"Oh, shit. Dick. Oh, yeah." Rig jerked, that full bottom lip caught in white teeth.

"Gonna let me in, Rock?" He nodded and grunted, letting his fingers slide from Rig's body.

Rig whimpered and pouted -- fucking *pouted*, the little slut -- at him. "What, you want me and the kid, Rig? Greedy, greedy."

Dick laughed, shifting and pressing, and then moaned, sliding into Rig, if the look on Rig's face was anything to go by.

"Oh..." Rig's hands landed on his shoulders, head falling back on Dick's shoulder. Rig's body started to move, stomach muscles clenching and rolling for him. The kid was still stroking their cocks, finding a nice, solid rhythm, leaving him both hands for touching and stroking and sliding over taut muscles and smooth, warm skin. Rig's moans were less intense than Dick's, quieter, but each one was breathed onto his lips, Rig leaned forward to kiss, to lick, to watch him with those passion-drugged, fucking eyes.

The kid would come first, he usually did, but tonight Dick was also setting the rhythm, keeping it long and slow and sweet, making them all sweat. Draping over him, moving with Dick, moving against him, Rig sort of melted. The blond head settled on his shoulder, lips moving on his neck.

So fucking good.

Dick leaned in to kiss him, coming back every now and then for another as he slowly, almost imperceptibly, moved them faster and then faster. He could see it in the kid's face when Dick was getting close, could smell it in the strong odor of sweat, could feel it in the way Rig's body started to jerk against his own, the hand around his cock losing its smoothness.

Rig pushed back, head lifting as that bubble butt ground back against Dick. "Yes, Pretty. Right there. Right fucking there."

"Yeah," Dick agreed, nodding and moving faster, harder. Rock found himself nodding, ready to blow right along with them. His lips were taken in a long, hard kiss, Rig close and needy, body jerking, tightening. Oh, fuck, he knew so well how that felt, sweet ass working his cock.

Dick's sweet noises got loud and then louder still, the kid slamming into Rig, now, shoving against him with every thrust. The kid came with a cry, hand tightening hard on his prick.

Rig grunted into his lips, eyes flying open wide, heat splashing against his cock, his belly. Rock flew into those grey eyes as he came, the pleasure blocking everything but grey from his mind. Rig melted against him again, breathing slowing down, completely relaxed.

Dick grinned at him over Rig's shoulder and leaned forward for a quick kiss before moving back carefully and standing up. "You got him?"

Rock nodded. "I do."

"Cool, I'll go turn down the bed and then wash off the smoke and beer."

Rig didn't move, already snoring softly. God, the man was tired. But tomorrow was a day off. There were fresh sheets on the bed and a half-dozen cans of chili courtesy of Momma. He figured they'd keep Rig fed and in bed, sleeping definitely optional.

He shifted and slid his hands around Rig's thighs. It was enough of an effort to stand to make him grunt, but all in all, this was one burden he wouldn't ever put down.

Chapter Thirty Two

Rock smiled as Rig and Dick explored the beach house, their voices ringing out from room to room, full of happiness and enthusiasm. Fuck, but that sounded good. Made it worth the extra expense of staying in a house instead of at the hotel; they still had all the amenities available to them, but with the added privacy of four walls that bordered on nothing but air. The boys could be as loud as they wanted.

He was planning on giving them plenty of reason to be very loud indeed. They came back out into the living room, matching shit-eating grins on their faces. Very, very loud.

"Oh, Rock! You did *good*, Blue. It's fucking perfect!" Rig bounced into his arms, grinning from ear to ear.

He tried not to look too smug as he bent and took a kiss, wanting a taste of that happiness for himself. "Happy fucking anniversary, Rig."

"Yeah. Happy anniversary, Rock." That got him a long, hard needy kiss, Rig's excitement leaking into every motion.

Another set of arms came around them, Dick dropping kisses on their cheeks. "I'm gonna go check out the beach and stuff."

He growled just a little and put his arm around Dick, keeping the kid in place.

"I don't think you're going anywhere quite yet, Pretty." Rig's voice was smug, body wriggling between them. "I think somebody wants something."

"I just want to make sure you guys don't decide you shouldn't have brought me along."

Rock grunted and smacked the kid's ass. "We didn't want you along, we wouldn't have brought you."

"I know, I know -- it's just *your* tenth anniversary."

"Yeah, it is." Rig nodded, turning his head and resting his cheek on Rock's shoulder. "But we wouldn't make Rock celebrate a birthday alone, just because it's not ours, would we?"

"Well, no, but you guys aren't alone...ah hell, I'm just trying to be subtle and let you guys have some special together time, is all."

Rock snorted. "And you're not paying attention."

"We want you here, Dick. Here, now. Family, remember?" Rig turned and gave the kid a long, hungry kiss that made Rock grin. He could hear the good old boy's mind working. Kissing was better than talking any damned day. Dick's arms tightened, a soft, muffled moan coming from the kid as Rig's mouth opened his up wide. Rock rumbled happily and rubbed his cock against Rig's ass.

Rig was focused, holding Dick close, fucking the kid's mouth with that talented tongue and assuring Dick that he was where he was fucking supposed to be. He stroked them both, one long body for each hand. Yeah. They were all right where they were supposed to fucking be.

When Rig finally came up for breath, Dick's eyes were glazed and the kid was gasping, making those little 'come back here, I wasn't finished' sounds.

He grunted, happy to have that settled, and pulled them both toward the couch. It was time to give the facilities a proper workout. Rig settled in his lap, straddling one leg, tugging Dick up alongside. Then the two best mouths in the settled worlds bent to kiss him. There was nothing quite like a three-way and he happily just sat back and let their tongues invade his mouth. Fuck, it was going to be a hell of a Valentine's Day this year.

Rig's hands were wandering -- over Dick's ass, stroking his cock, cupping his balls. Tweaking their nipples. The kid's hands were as well, and he wasn't one to let everyone else do the work, but fuck if they weren't short-circuiting his brain. Rig's mouth disappeared, body sliding down, those long fucking fingers opening his jeans like an expert.

He groaned happily, letting Rig know how much he liked it. One hand slid over Dick's back, the other grabbed Rig's head, holding, guiding as Rig swallowed him down. He could remember the first night they were together, ten years ago now and he'd been worried Rig wasn't getting anything out of sucking him off. It made him chuckle fondly. The fucker probably enjoyed sucking more than he himself liked to get sucked. And he sure as hell liked being sucked.

Rig worked his cock like a master, sucking and licking, humming happily. Warm hands pushed his jeans down and away, fingers sliding over his nuts. Dick grinned at him and then dove back into their kiss, the two of them using their mouths to drive him high. Rig's hand slid behind his balls, teasing his hole, pushing as that hot tongue fucked his slit.

Oh, yeah, that was good. He shifted, hips moving as much as they could between the two sensations. Dick just kept on kissing him, tongue fucking his mouth. Then Dick's hand slid down to join Rig's, two fingers teasing him. He shouted out into Dick's mouth, hips bucking, shoving his prick deep into Rig's mouth and then he pushed back, riding both fingers, taking them in, both of his lovers together. Shit, they were sex on legs, both of them.

Someone's finger quirked, stroked his gland again and again, while those tongues pushed him higher and faster. He could feel his own heartbeat pounding, he imagined he could feel theirs in his ass and in his mouth and around his cock and he roared into Dick's mouth, shaking as he came hard.

He relaxed into the sofa, Rig's mouth still hot and sucking on him, Dick still kissing him.

The next ten days promised to be fucking awesome.

***

Dick still couldn't quite believe they'd brought him along. Sure they'd celebrated the last years all together, but a lot had happened in the past year and this was a big anniversary for Rock and Rig. Ten years. That was a long time. At the same time, he could feel the rightness of it. He belonged here with them. He was a part of what they were now. More so than he had been even the year before.

So he knew it was silly to feel like a third wheel, and for the most part he didn't. Still... they deserved at least a couple of hours alone to fuck together. Just the two of them.

He'd set himself up on the deck of their private beach house, slathered on the suntan lotion and put on Rig's cowboy hat, pulling it low over his face. Even if he wasn't asleep, he'd look it and they could have as much time as they wanted.

Rig's giggle sounded about a quarter second before the good old boy was straddling his waist. "Hey, you! You sleeping?"

"Well, if I was, I'm not anymore." He tried to sound annoyed, but the truth was that he wasn't and how could anyone complain about having a real live cowboy of their very own pressed up close and personal?

"Rock's napping on the bed and I'm bored. Amuse me." Rig's voice was full of mischief, utter fucking sex.

He chuckled and slid the cowboy hat back on his head. "Don't tell me we managed to tucker Rock out on the first day?"

"He's gathering his energy." Rig chuckled and winked. "Plus, I sucked him off in the shower. Made him dozy."

"Well, I guess then it'd only be fair if I sucked you off on the deck."

"Oh, you are a brilliant thing, Pretty." He could feel Rig's cock throb against his belly, full and eager. "Then whatever will we do for you to make it fair..."

"I'm sure you'll come up with something, Rig."

"I'm good that way." Rig leaned forward, sucked on his bottom lip.

He made a soft noise. "Yeah, you are."

He looped his arms behind Rig, fingers sliding over warm skin. There were definitely advantages to the warmer climate. Lack of clothing was one of them.

Rig hummed, rocking against him. "Mm... your hands feel good."

"Good." He tugged gently, encouraging Rig to rise up onto his knees. "Wanna taste."

"Oh, yeah." Rig's voice lowered, a shudder passing through the thin frame as his lover straightened, cock swollen and pushing at the swim shorts. He pushed the bathing suit down Rig's hips, eager to get to Rig's prick.

"Fucking sweet," he murmured before licking at the tip.

Those grey eyes were watching him, fingers sliding over his forehead. "Fuck, but you're a sexy man, Pretty. You make me ache."

He smiled up at Rig, taking another swipe at the tip of Rig's cock. "As long as it's a good ache."

"It's a fucking fabulous ache. More, Dick. I need more." Rig's hips pressed closer, brushing the heated head of the heavy cock against his lips.

"Anything you want, Rig. Anything at all." He watched Rig's eyes as he opened his mouth wide and took in Rig's cock. Rig's lips parted, tongue sliding out to trace those swollen lips, a soft cry sounding. He closed his lips around Rig's prick, pulling hard, sliding up and down along the hard flesh, wanting more of those noises.

"Oh, fuck! Yeah, Pretty. So fucking good. So hot..." Rig was whimpering, hips rocking slow and easy. He slid his hands around to Rig's ass, squeezing that awesome butt, fingers dancing along the hot crack.

"Mmm... Pretty..." Rig shuddered, ass pushing back into his hands before that cock was pushed back into his mouth. He hummed happily, knowing the vibrations from the sound would lodge themselves right in Rig's balls.

"Shit! Oh, yeah, Dick." Rig started to move faster, endearments pouring down over him. He sucked harder, head sliding up and down along the sweet heat. Rig jerked, coming for him with another of those long low cries. He drank it all down, still sucking, pulling shuddering aftershocks out of Rig, just the way the man had taught him how. He loved being able to do this, giving it back. Sucking cock made him pretty hot, too.

Rig pulled away, sliding down his body to give him a long, sloppy kiss. "Fuck, Pretty. You melted me."

He grinned, hands sliding over skin. "That was the idea."

"Yeah? You like having you some melted cowboy?" Rig was chuckling, snuggling, fingers playing on his belly.

"Fuck, yes." He chuckled some himself, mouth finding Rig and pulling the flavor of that happiness into himself.

Rig settled at his side, nuzzling at his jaw, fingers sliding lower. "You wanna go into town later? Buy cheap silver and piñatas?"

"Piñatas? Wouldn't it be easier to just buy some candy?"

"The piñatas aren't for breaking, Pretty. They're for decorating the house."

"No candy?" He tried very hard not to pout. "Rock's not going to appreciate that."

Rig's chuckles were tickling him now, Rig loose and relaxed and so happy in his arms. "I'll buy candy, Dick. I promise."

"Well, that's all right then," he said with a grin.

"I don't know, kid. You've gotta keep an eye on him or he's gonna come back with low-fat, no sugar, wax would taste better shit that has the word healthy stamped all over it." Rock's voice was amused and relaxed, the big guy lounging in the doorway wearing nothing more than the tiniest pair of shorts Dick had seen. Ever. And considering some of Rig's cut-offs, that was saying something.

Rig chuckled and turned. "I'm telling you, Rock, fruit is nature's can... Sweet Jesus in Heaven!"

"Is there a problem?" Rock asked, looking for all the world as if he didn't have a clue. Dick chuckled as Rig's spent cock took a definite interest.

"A problem?" Rig's eyes were sharp, hungry, focused.

"You're the one swearing up a blue streak."

Dick laughed harder.

"Hmm?" Rig was rubbing against him now, cock filling. "Lookin' good enough to eat, old man."

His laughter faded, and he grabbed Rig's hips, guiding him over just a bit to the right. Oh, yeah, right there. "Rig's right, those things are unfuckingbelievably hot."

Rock preened a little for them. Chest puffing up, Rock turned slowly. Shit, the man had a body to die for.

"Okay, Pretty. Which side do you want -- cock or ass?"

"Hell, there's no loser there -- you pick, it's your anniversary after all."

"Mmm... I take that sweet cock, you get the tight ass. We'll make him fly."

"He's in the room," drawled Rock.

"No you're not. This isn't a room, it's a deck, and you're barely on it."

Rock rolled his eyes and Dick grinned at Rig. "You get off me right quick and we can tackle him by the time he reaches the bedroom."

"You got it." Fuck, that redneck could move when he wanted to.

Apprised of their plan as they were making it, Rock kindly let them catch him in the bedroom where they all went down in a heap beside the bed. Rock glared. "I'm getting too old for this shit."

"Then you shouldn't be wearing the world's tiniest shorts, Rocketman." Rig was already sliding down and licking Rock's naked belly. "Not old, Rock. Sexy as fuck, maybe. Not old."

Rock made that deep, rumbling sound that meant he was happy. "I'd still rather be doing this on the bed."

Rig made a non-committal noise, hands sliding up and spreading Rock's thighs. Dick took a few seconds to assess the situation and then stood, grabbing Rock beneath his pits. "Come on then, Marine -- let's get onto the bed -- there isn't enough room for a good fucking on the floor."

Rig scrambled up along with Rock, mouth not leaving Rock's skin. Rock let him manhandle him and he caught the wink the big guy aimed at Rig. He settled Rock on his side, cuddling up close behind him, hands stroking over skin and the teeny shorts that left very little, but just enough to be sexy as hell, to the imagination.

The sound of the button and zipper sliding down immediately preceded the loosening of those shorts, Rock's groan telling him that Rig's lips had found their target. He was falling behind. Dick reached back onto the side-table and grabbed the lube. Rig worked the back of Rock's shorts down, exposing that strong, chiseled ass.

"Sweet," he murmured, nipping at Rock's neck. Rock groaned, hips pressing back. He could hear Rig's purr, feel the long fingers running up Rock's spine. He met those fingers with his own, sliding over Rig's skin and Rock's skin, and then letting his own drop down to Rock's crack.

One of Rock's legs bent, resting against Rig, opening to him, for him. He made a noise and pressed his fingers against Rock's opening, teasing. Rock was moving between them, slow and steady, the slurp and suck of Rig's mouth driving the thrusts of those hips. He let one of his fingers slip into Rock's body as the big guy moved back against him. One of Rig's hands slid between Rock's legs to stroke his cock, moving in the same rhythm as Rock's hips.

They were all moving together, three shifting and pushing and pulling and sucking and fucking and stroking with the same rhythm. Together. The motions of Rock's hips grew jerky, rough, and Rig's voice sounded, breathy and hoarse. "Now kid. He's fixing to come soon. Take him."

Rock grunted an agreement and Dick shifted, removing his finger and pushing against Rock's hole. Rock's own motions pushed the big guy back onto his cock, swallowing him up. Rig's hands were there, holding Rock open, fingertips stroking at his balls, his cock as it moved. He reached around, finding Rig's face with his hand, stroking the hollowed cheeks. Oh, yeah. This was the best fucking closed circuit ever.

They started moving faster, Rock directing the speed, the strength of his thrusts. He was making noises, unable to stop, not wanting to stop. It felt so good; Rock was so tight and Rig's hands were touching him and he could feel Rock's muscles moving against him. He felt Rig's come splash against his calves an instant before Rock roared, ass tightening around his cock. That sweet ass milked his own orgasm from him, and he cried out as he shot.

Rig's arm was draped around him, holding them both, when his head cleared. He kissed the back of Rock's neck and then leaned over, finding Rig's mouth. Rig pushed up into the kiss, sharing the salt of Rock with him. He groaned, cock jerking within the grasp of Rock's body.

Rig's chuckle tickled his lips. "Tastes pretty fucking good, doesn't he?"

"You said it."

He licked at Rig's lips again and gave Rock another kiss before settling down behind Rock, snug along the big guy's back. Rig curled up in Rock's arms, cheek pillowed on his arm, eyes already closed. Rock's soft snore told its own tale and Dick grinned, feeling satiation stealing his own energy.

Maybe he felt they should have some time alone together; that didn't mean he wasn't ecstatic they'd chosen to have him along.

Chapter Thirty Three

Rigger two-stepped around the dance floor, grinning up at the cowboy leading. The boy was fine -- not Rock or Dick, but then again, who was? Moved like a fucking dream, too. God, he loved dancing. They danced to the end of the song, moving and laughing over sea air being good for rednecks, then a slow, sweet waltz started up and Rig nodded and grinned, taking a step back. "Thank you, son. You were built to dance, but my buckle-polishing dances are all taken."

Right on cue, he felt the tap on his shoulder. The kid looked disappointed, but he backed off, leaving Rig to turn into Rock's arms.

"You look like you're having a good time."

"Yeah." He couldn't stop grinning, couldn't remember ever having felt so good and not fucking. "You know me, Blue. I'd dance forever, if I didn't have to stop for fucking and coffee."

Rock chuckled, moving him around the room with military precision: one two three, one two three, one two three, one two three. He just melted into Rock's arms, following easy as breathing, his body giving their dance a bit of a drawl. "You ever regret me delivering you that pizza, Blue?"

"No, I can't say as I ever have." Rock danced them a few more turns. "What about you, Rabbit? The last ten years been worth leaving Texas?"

"You know it. I know where I belong, always have." He grinned up into those eyes, letting his hips rub against his Blue's. "Besides, you can take the cowboy out of Texas, but you can't make him a Yankee."

Rock laughed, the sound low and sexy. "Nobody would ever mistake you for a Yankee, Rig."

"You don't think so, Rocketman? You think this old redneck'd still make it as a Texan?" God, Blue smelled good, warm and sun-kissed and musky. Made him want a kiss. Made him want things that would get his skinny ass tossed in a

Mexican jail.

"Aside from the pair of Yankees he's got attached to his ass, I sure do." Rock was almost growling, the look in those blue eyes intense. "And if you don't stop that your dancing's going to be cut short."

He shivered, pressing close with a low moan, cock coming to full-fledged attention. "Stop what, Blue?"

"Teasing me, Texas."

He met Blue's eyes, full-on. "I'm not teasing, Blue."

"Then you'd better be fixing to leave."

As if he'd just gotten some signal he'd been waiting for, Dick slid an arm around both their shoulders. "Tab's paid up, you guys ready to go?"

He grinned at Dick, bumping their hips together. "I'm ready. Rock?"

"I was ready three bars ago when you performed that little hip maneuver of yours."

He smiled, leaning into Dick's arm, feeling sexy and loose and easy and right where he needed to be. "Were you watching my ass, Rocketman?"

"When doesn't he?" asked Dick, earning himself a half-hearted swat.

"That's what the tight jeans are for, Dick. I keep telling you, I have to work twice as hard to keep my Marines' attention." He slid out from beneath Dick's arm, moving ahead for a little wiggle and then scooted off to avoid the inevitable pinches. Laughter followed him.

"I don't know where he thinks he's going," said Dick. "I've got the keys to the car."

"Just enjoy the show, kid."

He grinned and sashayed all the way to the rental, garnering a few whistles and catcalls from a few of the guys heading into the club.

"Look all you want, boys. He's going home with me," called out Rock.

Rig stopped short, cheeks blazing. Oh, fuck... Rock was maybe going to retire soon and possibly Dick was going to finish his tour and then this in-public lovers thing was going to be full-time and he was going to burn up with fucking lust.

"And me," complained Dick.

Rock chuckled. "No, no, that's not how it works, kid. You're both coming home with me."

"Don't argue, kid. What matters is we're all headed to bed and there'll be hot kisses and hard cocks involved." He slid into the backseat, giving Blue the roomier passenger side and letting the kid drive and leaving both men where he could kiss and touch.

Dick grinned back at him and started up the car. "This has been the greatest vacation ever."

Rock chuckled. "You're easy."

Dick snorted. "And you're not?"

He could hear Rock's grin from the backseat. "Not as easy as you and Rig."

"Is that a challenge?"

"If you want it to be."

"Boys, if you want to have a pissing contest, go down to the beach and wrestle sharks. **I** am easy. No question. And horny. And I need my men." Rig punctuated his words with a caress to Dick's nape, a long lick to Rock's ear. Two hands reached up to caress his face.

"Save that thought, I've got to get us back to the beach house without going off the road."

"You don't have to save mine," said Rock, turning to take his lips. Rig hummed, leaning over for the kiss, lips parted and ready. Rock kissed him hard and deep, arm coming up to hold him in place. Like he was going anywhere. He threw himself full-force into the kiss, letting Rock taste how good this was, how happy he was, how fucking hot he was.

Dick whistled. "Fuck, you two are hot."

He reached down and stroked Dick's leg, hand sliding toward his Pretty's cock while he focused on the amazing fucking kiss Blue was giving him. Blue tasted like beer and hot sauce and sheer, unadulterated hunger. Dick's hand came down over his, twining their fingers together and keeping his hand on one solid thigh. Rig rumbled into Rock's mouth, complaining, wanting his Pretty, that long, hard cock.

"Five minutes," said Dick, squeezing his hand.

Rock chuckled, pulling out of the kiss to lick at his lips. "Slut."

"Mm... yes." He nodded, chasing that hot tongue. "Y'all's." Dick and Rock's laughter filled the car. He grinned, "You wouldn't want me any other way."

Dick's hand squeezed his again. "Absolutely."

Rock tilted his head. "I don't know..."

Rig arched an eyebrow. "Oh?"

Rig was going to bite the teasing old bastard right on the tit, if he made a crack.

Rock chuckled. "I'll take you any which way I can get you -- you know that."

"Yeah." Rig took another kiss, this one lighter, more playful. Those blue eyes were watching him, warm and happy. God, he loved two of the most beautiful men... He groaned, tracing Blue's lips with the tip of his nose, squeezing Dick's thigh. "Pretty, please... Aren't we there yet?"

"Slut," whispered Rock, kissing his nose.

"It's just around this corner, Rig." There was laughter in Dick's voice. And a whole lot of need.

"Yours." He smiled into his Blue's eyes, hot and ready and feeling so fucking good.

"Yes." Rock smiled at him, hand stroking along his cheek.

The car turned a corner and slowed right down and then finally stopped and that hand holding his down against Dick's thigh slid up his arm in a long caress. "We're here."

"Good." He was breathing hard, aching. "Need my men."

Dick leaned back to him and kissed him with the kid's usual enthusiasm. "That works out well."

"Yep, it does." Rock was out of the car already, both their doors opened for them. "It'll work even better inside."

"Yeah." He got out of the car, pressing against Rock, shoulder to hip. "Bed."

Dick was ahead of them, key in the lock, pushing open the door. "Last one to the bed has to bring the lube."

"Isn't the lube on the headboard?" He licked Rock's jaw, rubbing slowly.

"Yep." Rock grabbed his ass and shifted him slightly, directing his rubbing.

"Cool." The hollow below Blue's ear was salty, soft. His. Rock rumbled for him.

"Guys! That meant get your butts in here and share the joy."

"He should really be more clear about what he wants, especially when it comes to fucking." He fastened his lips over his spot, bringing the blood up to the surface. Rock jerked against him, hands pressing him close. Oh, yeah. That's what he wanted to feel. He pulled harder, marking his Blue, sucking on that sensitive spot.

"Making sure the world knows I'm yours?" Rock asked, voice a growl that Rig could feel against his belly.

"Yes. Mine." He bit down again, sucking and nibbling. "My Blue."

One of Rock's legs pushed between his. He rocked against that hardness, groaning against Rock's throat. Rock's hands on his ass kept him moving and warm lips pressed against his ear, touching and tickling and making him tingle. "Love you."

He gasped, eyes flying open. His lips parted and all that came out was a harsh whisper. "Oh, my Blue."

Then he turned his head and answered Rock in the best possible way, with a hard, hungry kiss, hands holding those strong shoulders tight. Rock kissed him back, giving him everything. He was shaking, entire universe fading to a sharp point, body flying. Rock rumbled into his mouth, a satisfied noise, the big hands continuing to hold him. He came with a cry, shaking like a teenager, trusting in Rock to hold him up, keep him close.

Oh, fuck. Oh...

The world spun as Rock picked him up and carried him in, their mouths never parting. He held on, legs wrapping around Rock's waist. Oh, going to get their Pretty. Going to get the rest of their family. Going to make them whole.

They were soon inside and then in the bedroom.

"I was wondering if you guys were going to show up or if I was going to have to play alone." Dick's voice was warm and wanton and Rig did a double take as he glanced on the bed where Dick was spread out, naked, hands wandering restlessly over the long body.

"Fucking sexy... and all of it ours..." He groaned, nipping Rock's lips. "Want to eat him up."

Rock grinned and dumped him on the bed. "Go for it."

Never let it be said he didn't follow direction. Rig crouched over and swallowed Dick's cock down to the root, sucking hard. Dick screamed, hips humping up hard. Rock's hands slid over him, working at removing his clothes. He groaned, hands wrapping around Dick's hips as soon as Rock freed them, the earth and need flavor of Dick teasing his tongue. Dick's legs spread further apart, the kid's hands finding his head and pressing him closer. He hummed, taking his Pretty all the way in, swallowing around the tip.

Dick shouted his name out, shooting down his throat. Rig drank him down, pulling each pulse from his Pretty's cock, drawing those sweet porno noises out, making them ring through the room. Dick was making soft, coming down noises, hands stroking through his hair. The noises were suddenly muted, Rock's mouth covering Dick's.

He just snuggled into Dick's legs, continuing to suck and lick, cheek resting on that sweet, warm skin. One of Rock's hands joined Dick's in his hair, stroking, caressing. Oh, that was nice. Rig let his eyes close, just focused on the touches and smells and tastes. God, he was happy, just as simple as that. In bed with his men -- that was all he needed.

"This is good," murmured Dick. "Fucking good. Thank you."

He purred softly around the soft flesh in his mouth, hand petting the hollow of Dick's hip.

"It's how it's supposed to be," said Rock, voice low.

One of Rock's legs was warm against his back, Dick smooth against his belly, two hands in his hair, full of peace. Oh, yeah, Blue, no fucking regrets.

Chapter Thirty Four

Six days and this was the first one they ventured out into town aside from the dancing. They'd meant to come earlier, but somehow kept getting distracted before they got to the car. They'd almost made it yesterday, but Rig had been wearing a sinfully short pair of cut-offs and Dick had tackled him on the deck. Rock himself had only been a half-step behind and it wasn't long before bed was the only place Rig was interested in going to.

They'd stopped and picked up some candy and now Rig was just bouncing and the kid grinning infectiously. Rock chuckled, just happy and pleased the trip was such a success -- they all deserved a little happiness after the last couple of years. It wasn't long before Rig had his arms filled with gifts for Momma and Sissy and all the girls and every fucking friend they had. Dick was holding some wool blankets for the back of Rig's jeep and a string of ceramic onions and peppers.

He was grumbling every time he was given a new package to hold, but he could see that Rig was taking him about as seriously as he meant it. It was the kid who suggested dumping everything in the rental so they could have lunch and then they'd be fit to load up again.

"Ooooooh! Guacamole! Margaritas!" Rig bounced even higher as they headed to the car. "Maybe flan for dessert..."

"I don't think you're enjoying yourself enough," he told Rig, giving the kid a wink. Dick laughed and opened the trunk, dumping in his parcels and then taking Rock's from him.

Rig shot him a flirtatious glance. "Does that mean it's time to fuck again, Rocketman?"

"It's always time to fuck."

"Maybe we ought to wait 'til we get home though," suggested Dick, voice still full of laughter.

"Spoilsport." Rig winked at Dick and shook that fine ass at him and then was off again, be-bopping down the street, garnering stares and grins.

Rock shook his head fondly as Dick fell into step with him, the two of them trailing Rig.

"He's happy," Dick said softly.

Rock nodded. "You?"

"Yeah, Rock. Me, too."

"Good."

Rig just moved on, bartering here and there, his Spanish rusty, but functional. Happiness looked good on Rig, erased the tension and worry of the last two years, took five years off that tanned face.

They'd almost made it to the taqueria when Rig stopped short and grinned over at Dick. "Oooh! Look Pretty! You could get a tattoo! A little Latina shaking her hooters when you flex."

Dick laughed. "Or a heart with 'Momma' across it."

Rock chuckled and stood back, watching the two of them.

"There's always a skull with 'Death From Above'" Rig's eyes were dancing. "Or a rose with 'Lucy' underneath."

Dick shook his head, suddenly serious. "If I were to get one, it would have to mean something."

Rig winked at the kid. "As opposed to mine, which means, don't get shit-faced in the Philippines?"

Reaching out, Dick touched Rig briefly on the shoulder. "You get me shit-faced you can probably talk me into anything you want, but sober…" Dick shook his head.

Rig nodded, eyes warm enough to make Dick shiver. "Guess we don't have to worry about our Dick coming home pierced and tattooed, Rock."

"Not unless you find him something like a truck full of boulders to tattoo onto his ass."

"As attractive and symbolic as that sounds, I think I'd vote to keep that sweet ass as it is. I'm a bit fond."

Dick's facc picked up some color. "Just a bit fond?" he teased.

Rig's eyebrow arched. "Fond enough not to mar it with a drawing of a rock-hauler."

Dick grinned and nodded. The kid turned back to the window of the tattoo parlor, face growing serious again. "Almost seems like the occasion needs something though, doesn't it?" Dick shrugged. "I don't know, it's just, all joking aside... "

Rock rolled his eyes. If the kid suggested they get wedding

bands, he was going to plop them both back in the car and drive them home and then fuck their brains out until they couldn't remember their own names.

Rig tilted his head. "What's rattling around in your brains, Pretty? What're you plotting?"

Dick shrugged. "It's just that we're all here for your tenth anniversary and we've come through a pretty rough time and we're all here and solid and..." Another shrug. "I'm not suggesting we get married or nothing, just... "

"I'm not adverse to the two of you getting 'property of Rock' tattooed on you."

Rig rolled those eyes and popped him one on the shoulder. "As soon as you get "Rigger's" inked on your dick, asshole. Or we could just put a big assed ring through the head of that big piece of meat, lead you around with a leash."

He could feel his balls try to climb up into his stomach just at the thought. "I don't think so, asshole." He shook his head and tried to resist the urge to cover his balls. "No needles anywhere near my prick."

"Don't worry, Blue. I wouldn't let anyone fuck with perfection and you know it." Rig reached over and flicked Dick's nipple casually. "Besides, I might chip a tooth."

The kid gave a half gasp/half laugh.

He just chuckled and shook his head. "I'm not wearing any fucking earring either."

"You could get your bellybutton pierced like the teenybopper girls do..." Rig moved behind Dick with a grin, avoiding the swat.

He settled on glaring and growling just a little.

"He'd look silly," said Dick, shaking his head. "You know... he'd look nice with a nipple ring through."

"How did we get from you getting a tattoo to my getting my nipple pierced?"

Rig was staring at him, eyes hot. "Fuck, that would be sexy as hell. A little gold ring keeping that nipple hard all the time."

The same look appeared in Dick's eyes. "Oh, fuck, yeah."

He held up his hands and shook his head, backing up a couple of steps.

"No, wait, Rock -- it won't be just you, we'll all get one. A private symbol just for the three of us." Dick's eyes got even hotter. "Can't you imagine one of Rig's sensitive little titties constantly stimulated by the ring? He'd be a fucking ball of pleasure."

He froze where he was; he had to admit, that didn't sound half-bad.

"All of us?" Rig squeaked. "Oh, fuck, Pretty. I couldn't... It would drive me fucking crazy. You know how I am."

"It would be fucking sexy, Rig." Dick turned to look at Rig and Rock could see the kid make the effort not to melt into the good old boy.

Rock planted his feet firmly and crossed his arms. "All of us or none of us, Rig. That's the way it works."

Rig gave him the calculating, bargaining face. "You can't touch it, then. No fucking playing and teasing in public. The ring's off limits unless we're fucking. I'll be shooting in my jeans otherwise and that's just wrong."

"I have never played in public," he growled, thinking about it.

Dick just waited quietly between them, looking from him to Rig and back again.

"But you will." Rig's look lightened, cheeks flushing. "Fifteen months, Blue. Just fifteen months left."

He nodded. Yeah, Rig had a point; they left Bragg and the marines behind and his Rabbit was going to find himself hunted. The kid, too.

"All right -- off limits in public but in private the ring's as available as the rest of you." He was aiming to test Rig's shooting in his jeans theory and though he wouldn't admit it, he thought maybe he'd even go for the ring through his prick in exchange.

"It's a deal. You go first."

He nodded. "Then you, then the kid."

Dick bounced. "It has to be the same ring for all of us."

"As long as you don't expect us to recite anything, kid, you can pick any ring you want."

Rig pouted at him, "But I wanted to hear you singing Mary had a Little Lamb while the needle went in."

He snorted as Dick chuckled, the kid looking pretty fucking happy. "Don't push your luck."

Rig was laughing as he opened the door to the shop. "Y'all still owe me lunch after this."

"We'll get you room service," he promised. He had a hunch

the first pair of jeans Rig was going to cream were the ones he was wearing now.

Rings in their fucking nipples.

That was fucked up.

Still it seemed oddly right and in the end, there wasn't anything he wouldn't do to make his two boys happy.

***

The tattoo parlor was small and empty. There was a single counter with a glass top, inside of which were rings of all shapes and sizes, various studs and barbells. There was no other furniture. The walls were covered with artwork, everything from simple black peace symbols to elaborate and colorful dragons.

Dick couldn't really believe they'd actually come in, that they were going to leave with matching nipple rings, but he guessed if Rock went ahead and did it, it would be real -- there was no way he and Rig were going to refuse if Rock got it done. He could feel his heartbeat in his nipples, which had gone hard the minute the nipple rings had been mentioned. Actually, they'd gone hard when Rig had teased Rock about getting a ring for his cock -- that was just fucking explosive.

The dark red curtain at the back of the shop was pushed aside, an older man, maybe even older than Rock, stepped out. "Can I help you?" he asked in lightly accented English.

Rig smiled. "We're looking for nipple rings. What do you charge for... which ones do you like, Dick?"

Dick headed for counter, checking out the rings.

"Keep it simple, kid," warned Rock and he nodded. A plain gold band was what he wanted, no matter how silly or cheesy Rock thought it was.

"These," he said, spotting a small plastic bag with a number of plain gold rings in it.

"Forty a piece."

Rig nodded. "I like them. Let me see -- are they solid? 10 or 14 carat? I don't want any bad reactions..."

Dick grinned at Rock. That was their Rig, always looking out for them.

They bickered and bargained, words flying furiously in Spanish and English until Rig finally nodded and handed over his MasterCard. "Okay, $125 for all three, with the better quality metal rings and brand new needles each time. Let's do this thing."

The guy, who introduced himself as Berto, led them through the curtain where there were two dentist type chairs and a table along with a bookshelf filled with tools and bottles of ink. Rock sat down on one of the chairs, pulling his T-shirt up to his pits. Fuck, but the man had a beautiful body. Rig spared a glance at Rock and then watched Berto closely, nodding as hands were washed and gloves snapped on, alcohol brought out for the clamp and ring. The guy turned to Rock, spray bottle in hand. "Right or left?"

Rock turned to them and raised an eyebrow. Dick looked at Rig and then nodded at Rock's chest. "Left -- over his heart."

Rig nodded and smiled. "Yeah. That works."

Berto marked the holes, got Rig's nod of approval and then sprayed a short burst of liquid on Rock's nipple, making it hard and making those muscles jerk. It didn't seem to take any time before he had clamped Rock's little nipple and slid a needle through. The ring slid in without a hitch and then he swiped off the tiny drops of blood. "Okay. Next."

Rock hadn't made a sound, hadn't even winced. Dick took a deep breath, biting his bottom lip as Rock got off the chair and grinned at them both, flexing his muscles and making the ring dance before pulling his shirt back on. "You're up, Rig."

Rig gave Rock a quick look, an 'I don't know about this' look, but Rock didn't look away and then Rig slid into the chair, pulling up his T-shirt.

"You been fighting, I see. Them knife fights are bad things. Left or right?"

Dick felt himself stiffen, watched as Rock did, too, big hands curling into fists. He held his breath, waiting for Rig's reaction. Rig nodded, cheeks heating, long fingers fluttering over the scars. "They aren't to be recommended, sir, that's for fucking sure. Left, just like Rock's."

Dick relaxed and he could feel the stress leaving the big guy as Rock's fists uncurled. Rig didn't say another word as Berto sprayed, rubbed, and clamped that sensitive little titty.

Dick watched Rig closely, knowing how sensitive his nipples were. Out of the corner of his eye he could see Rock paying even closer attention and suddenly the whole thing seemed hugely sexual. He took another look at Rock. He could see the big guy's nipples through his T-shirt, both of them hard, one with the ring through it. His cock got fucking hard.

Rig's nipple was stretched out and Rig's hips shifted, thighs parting slightly, then closing again, A dark flush moved up that tanned belly as the needle went in, Rig's eyes flashing open, wide and desperate as the ring was tugged in.

Oh, fuck. Dick had to bite back his gasp, but he couldn't stop himself from going forward, from reaching for Rig's hand. Rock's was already there, warm and solid. Rig held on as the blood was wiped away, giving a hissing little moan as he pulled his shirt back down and stood on shaky legs.

Berto looked up, completely oblivious. "Next."

Dick gave Rig's hand a little squeeze and then sat down himself. Fuck he was nervous and horny and damned embarrassed, 'cause his little tits were already hard, just like his cock.

Rig was standing close to Rock, blinking slow, spots of color high on his cheekbones. "Pull up your shirt, Dick. Let's finish this and go home."

That voice was pure, distilled sex.

He managed not to shudder, somehow, and did as he was told. The air seemed cold against his skin, the silence in the small shop almost overwhelming. The spray on his nipple was cold, shocking, almost as shocking as the pressure of the clamps and the firm tug of his nipple. "Left for you too, right?" The needle was right there, silver and shining.

"Right. I mean yes -- the left." He took a deep breath, muscles clenching.

The needle slid in easy, the pain bright and sharp, but damned far from unbearable and then, as he exhaled, the ring was put in with a tug. Fuck, he could feel that all the way to his cock; he could only imagine what it was going to be like for Rig. This was going to be fun.

He was cleaned off and that was it, Berto turning to clean up his little table as Dick pulled his shirt down, humming at the slight burn in his chest.

Rig's eyes were dark, hooded. "Home. Thank you, Berto. Good job."

Then their Texan pulled them out into the sunshine. He stumbled along after Rig and Rock. As far as he was concerned, they couldn't get home fast enough.

From the silent dash they were making to the car, it looked like he wasn't the only one.

***

He was vibrating, aching, never so glad that his men were in the front seat and he was out of reach. Beach house. Inside. Bathroom to clean up and jack off before they got hold of him. If he got himself off twice more, he'd keep a smidgen of dignity. Maybe.

Nipple rings.

Fuck.

He'd never thought Rock would agree.

Dick stopped the car and he was out in a flash, groaning at the sensation of fabric against his sensitive, sore, burning, hot, hard, sparking, oh-fuck-it's-nice nipple. They tackled him in the hall, Rock shoving him up against the wall, mouth hard on his, fucking hard as diamonds cock rubbing against him. Dick was behind Rock, doing a lot of rubbing of his own.

Dignity was fucking overrated.

He opened with a sharp needy cry, hands reaching up to hold Rock close, keep their lips together. Fuck, yeah. More. The big hands pushed between him and the wall, grabbing his ass and pulling him hard against Rock's body.

Dick was making urgent noises, hands on his shoulders, touching just to touch and then the kid cried out. He bit down on Rock's bottom lip, coming hard, body on fucking fire. Rock growled for him, shoving hard against him a few times before his Blue was coming, too.

"Fuck, yeah. Bed. More, Blue. Pretty. Now." He was still hard, still wanting. Dick moaned and made an affirmative sounding noise. Rock just chuckled, but it was his Blue who hustled them into the bedroom and the hands that were working his clothes belonged to Rock.

He got Rock's shorts down and off, when Rock pulled his t-shirt up over his nipples. He keened softly as the air brushed across the hot, swollen flesh.

"You in pain?" Rock asked, voice low, rough.

"Warned you. Told you it would make me fucking insane, Blue." His hips were jerking, breath coming in panting gasps. Dick pushed him back on the bed, mouth swallowing him down.

"Fuck, yes!" His hands found Dick's head, hips moving to take that hot mouth.

Rock's hand was rough on his jaw, turning him to look up into a hard blue gaze. "Good fuck-me-now-I'm-coming-pain or pain pain?" His Blue looked ready to rip the ring out then and there if he had to.

"Fuck, I'm never going stop coming, kiss me, Blue pain." His lips were parted, entire body tight.

"I can live with that." Rock's mouth covered his, the kiss hard. One hand came to rest on his belly, solid and hot. He cried out, pressing up into his lovers, body convulsing. Dick sucked him dry and then just kept on sucking, making his cock throb along with his nipple. Rock lay down next to him, solid and warm, lips nuzzling against his ear. "Good thing we've got another five days here," his Blue murmured.

"Mm...yeah?" His head was swimming, shivers rocking him.

"Yep. If you're fixing to be a walking orgasm, I want to be off work so I can enjoy it."

Dick's laughter vibrated around his cock.

"There's no fixin' to be about it and the rules are no touching, remember?" Sweet God in Heaven, they were going to drain him dry.

"The rules are no touching *in public*." Rock grinned at him and the kid pulled off his cock, sliding slowly up his body, stopping to blow on his ringed nipple.

"Rock's right -- the deal was no touching in public."

He'd have argued, but fuck! -- his entire world short-circuited.

"Besides," added Rock, sounding smug. "I don't believe anyone's actually touched it yet."

"No... no touching it." He was going to fucking catch his goddamned breath, he was.

"It only counts as touching if it's done with fingers, right, Rock?" asked Dick, blowing more air over his nipple.

"Pretty..." He twisted, moaning as he felt the skin of his nipple slide over the metal piercing it.

"You look like the littlest thing is going to set you off again," murmured Dick, licking a line up his breastbone.

"It will," rumbled Rock, fingers painting a wide circle around his nipple. He was whimpering now, lips parted, cock full and hard and not listening to his insistence that he was too fucking old for this multiple orgasm shit. Dick used the point of his tongue to trace around Rig's nipple.

He jerked, a sob leaving him. "Oh, fuck. Fuck."

"That's the idea," whispered Rock into his ear.

Dick managed to get his tongue under one edge of the ring, flipping it up.

"Fuck!" Electricity shot through him, settling in his cock, come shooting over his belly, hot and wet.

"Mm... nice." Dick settled along his free side, warm and hard and pressed close. His marines grinned at each other over his chest.

"What's that? Three?"

Dick shook his head. "Four if you count the one in the tattoo shop."

"Fuck we're good." Dick laughed at that, the sweet sounds joining Rock's chuckles.

"Who said I came at the store?" he argued, or thought he did. He was really fucking dozy and really fucking relaxed and really, really fucking... He cuddled next to Rock, humming softly.

Dick and Rock pressed close on either side and a light blanket covered him.

"Happy fucking anniversary," murmured Rock, a soft kiss punctuating the words.

"Yeah, Blue. Yeah." He was asleep before he could quite remember what he was agreeing to.

***

Rock lay out on the deck chair, wearing the shortest shorts he had with him and nothing else. The sun was shining down, good and hot, the smell of coconut oil and Rig and Dick all around.

It made him hard, those smells. Well, the little bit of metal through his nipple that was growing heated under the sun's rays wasn't hurting the state of his cock's hardness either.

It ached. Constantly. According to Rig that would settle out just a bit, which was good, because right now even the material of his shirts against it made him hard as nails. He had no idea how Rig with his super sensitive titties could stand it. He chuckled and glanced to his right where his Rig was sleeping;

man's cock was still hard, pressing against the fly of his cut-offs.

They'd done nothing but make love, sleep and eat for the last three days. It was fucking awesome.

Rig's nipple seemed to throb beneath his gaze and Rock figured the man would come in his sleep if he so much as tugged it. He wanted to know. Hell, maybe he even needed to know. He got up and knelt quietly next to Rig's chair, winking at Dick as the kid turned to look at him.

Taking the ring between his lips he tugged.

Rig moaned, hands coming up to hold his head, hips snapping a few times before the sharp smell of spunk filled the air. He murmured happily, dragging the flat of his tongue across the top of Rig's nipple, hand sliding down the flat stomach to push into Rig's shorts. He pulled it back up, bringing his head up and grinning at Rig as he licked the come from his fingers. "Taste good, Rig."

Dick's moan filled the air.

"Y'all are... Blue... that's fucking cheating." Those grey eyes were dazed, stunned, almost fucking drunk.

"All's fair in love and war," he murmured. "And I do believe I know how to wage either."

Dick got up and came over to them, settling on his knees on the other side of Rig. The kid's own nipple ring glinted and Rock reached out for it -- the kid's reaction had fallen somewhere in between his and Rig's. Rig's lips surrounded his nipple as he touched the kid's ring, pulling and tugging.

"Oh, fuck..." He tugged hard on Dick's nipple ring, the kid gasping, back bowing. Dick started making those sweet porno noises, hips rocking as he kept tugging at the nipple ring, following the rhythm Rig'd set.

Rig purred, tongue sliding over the tip of his nipple, again and again, lip nudging the ring. He was about to lose it and if this had been a war he'd be dead, but it wasn't war and that made him a winner.

He closed his eyes and pushed his hand into his own shorts, Rig's tongue sending him flying. Rig's teeth just barely scraped against his skin, making him fucking soar. He shouted out, coming into his hand, fingers tugging hard on Dick's ring. The kid was right behind him, the air filling with the scent of their spunk.

Rig's hands wrapped around his waist, cheek falling to

nuzzle against his belly with a moan. Dick was panting, watching them with glazed eyes and he chuckled. "We are all so screwed."

"I warned you both." Rig's voice was husky, still hungry.

"I wasn't complaining," he pointed out.

"Me either." Dick's hands were reaching for Rig's shorts, opening them up and wrapping around Rig's prick. "Not complaining at all."

Rig whimpered against his belly, lips parted and moving over his skin. He slid his own hands over Rig's skin, loving the feel of his lover, the smooth heat that responded and pushed into his touch. His little finger caught on Rig's ring, tugging hard. Rig made this desperate sound, hands grasping him as that long body convulsed.

Yeah, one hundred percent screwed and he wasn't complaining one little bit.

Chapter Forty Five

Rig stumbled in from the library about 2:15, right about the time he needed to be getting his scrubs on for his shift at the hospital. He worked until eleven tonight, then he could study 'til one, sleep until six, get up and study again until his final at noon.

He needed a fucking shower and a snack and another nap and a brain transplant. He was too fucking old for this shit, no question.

"Hey stranger." Dick was in the front room, playing video games. His Pretty put the controller down though, coming over to give him a hug and a kiss.

"Hey, Pretty. How's it going?" He gave Dick a hug, resting for a second. "Come chat with me while I get dressed for work?"

"What the fuck?" Rock's growl came from behind him, one big hand coming to rest on his shoulder. "Work? We haven't fucking seen you in weeks."

Rig nodded. "It's finals week -- I can't pull any of my normal shifts but Wednesday, so I swapped with Carol for today and Monday night. It's a shit schedule, but I couldn't do better."

Dick gave him a squeeze.

Rock didn't seem so sympathetic. "When's your final? Because you don't look like you can remember your own name right now, let alone whether or not Mrs. Sick-as-a-Dog had her meds or how many bones are in the hand."

"I have one tomorrow at noon, one Wednesday afternoon and two Thursday." He sighed and shook his head.

Rock crossed his arms. "Find someone to take your work shifts this week."

He arched an eyebrow. "I tried to get a better schedule, Rock. It's a shit time of year to get off."

"Did you even try?"

"Excuse me?" He blinked, shook his head. "What the hell do you mean?"

"I mean did you ask for time off or just to work around your exams? Because you should have asked for time off, but I know you. You'd rather work yourself into the fucking ground than take help."

Dick winced, hand rubbing his back.

Rig bit his bottom lip, hard enough to draw blood, biting back the sarcasm that wanted out. He didn't need this, not today. "I'm going to get changed."

Rock shook his head but got out of his way. "It's your life."

Oh, fuck, he was pissed. Finals. Fucking finals and he was at the top of his class and damn it, neither one of them had gone to college, much less grad school and he was trying so hard to juggle shit and nothing was right enough for anybody anymore.

Fuck it. He'd grab a pair of jeans and a few shirts and just go stay with one of the girls until his tests were over and he could have a nice long break.

Rock followed him into the bedroom, looming in the doorway. "I'm worried about you."

"I'm not working more than twenty-five hours a week, Blue. Thirty tops. I've got to get through these tests. I... I'm not trying to worry you. I'm just trying to survive." His head was throbbing, skin itching with nerves. He'd been doing okay until finals had hit.

"You're not surviving," Rock told him, moving forward, hands dropping onto his shoulders, rubbing, massaging. "You're all wound up."

"Oh..." God, those hands felt so fucking good and it had been days -- DAYS -- since he'd felt them.

Rock kept working his shoulders, blue eyes gazing into his own. "You remember how to fuck, Rig?"

"Uh-huh." He had to go. Really. Had to. Go. Work. Oh... He took a step forward, lips brushing Rock's jaw.

"I think we should make sure you do." Rock bent, nuzzling his face, lips just brushing his as the big hands slowly worked their way down his back.

"I... Oh, fuck... I'm s'posed to... Oh, Blue..." He dropped his scrubs, hands wrapping around Rock's neck, spine fucking melting.

Rock was hard and warm against him, all muscles and heat. "Just say the word and I'll stop, Rabbit." The words were spoken against his lips.

Oh, that was so cheating...

His lips parted, tongue sliding out to taste. One kiss. One kiss and then he'd go. Rock purred into his mouth, tongue sliding in. His ass was cupped, his body sliding against Rock's. Rig whimpered, a mixture of painfully hard and completely melted and all fucking want.

"Hey, Rig, I made you a ... oh. Sandwich." Then Dick was behind him, warm and almost as solid as Rock, his Pretty pushing into the kiss with a soft whimper.

Oh, God. Oh, good. One. Just one more minute. Oh, he wanted them...

He rubbed between them, cock hard as nails, heart pounding. Dick and Rock's hands met on his prick, the two of them rubbing and squeezing him. He could feel Dick's cock like a brand along his ass and Rock's, just as hard and hot, against his hip.

"Gonna... Oh, sweet fuck. 's good. Your hands. Fuck, love your hands..." He went up on his toes, balls going tight and hard. They kept working him, Rock's hand moving down to cup his balls, Dick's staying at his cock, thumb stroking over the tip through his jeans. He groaned into their mouths, shooting hard, creaming his jeans like a desperate virgin. "Oh..."

Rock growled softly, breaking the kiss. "There you go - that's the edge gone. You need our hands now. On you, around you, inside you."

Rig blinked, mouth following Rock's instinctively, shaking with the aftershocks. "Mmm... Need you. Need my men..."

"Call him in sick, Dick," Rock ordered and the heat behind him slid away.

He should have argued, but... Oh, fuck. Who wouldn't want them? Need them? Rock's thick fingers made quick work of his shirt, undoing the buttons and pushing the material from his shoulders. Immediately, Rock started to nuzzle his neck, tongue teasing the sweet spot.

"Blue..." He lifted his chin, arching his neck and offering himself over to sweet pleasure. "Good..."

Rock rumbled and then Dick was there, too, his Pretty working off his jeans before starting on Rock's clothes.

"He wants our hands," Rock muttered against his collarbone.

"Oh, I want to go first."

"First?" His hands trailed over Rock's head, petting, stroking. "Oh, so hot..."

Rock nodded. "Yeah, kid -- you can get him warmed up for

me."

Rock pushed him down onto the bed, spreading him out like he was a feast. Rig stretched, back popping, hips shifting on the bedspread. He didn't know exactly how he got derailed from his plan, or his snit, or his studies, but he'd be dammed if he didn't love the way it felt, his marines touching him.

"Do you want to get cleaned up first?" Dick asked him, fingers playing on his skin, not really settling anywhere -- dancing.

"Hmmm?" He chuckled as Dick's fingers found a sensitive spot. "Tickles!"

Dick laughed, fingers lingering. "I can go get the tubing ready if you want, let Rock bring you in after a few minutes. It's more intimate that way, isn't it? I thought so."

Tubing... Hands... Oh.

Oh.

He blinked up into his Blue's eyes, body beginning to thrum, brain just fucking shorting out. "Oh." He licked his lips. "Yeah."

Dick licked his lips too and then kissed him. "I'll be ready in two minutes."

Then his Pretty was gone and Rock was kissing him. "Tonight's just for us, no school, no job, no exams. Just three men."

"Yeah." He met Rock's eyes, holding onto the promises there with all he was. "Just you and me and him. I need that."

"I know." Rock kissed him again, long and hard and as full of promises as those blue eyes. "Come on, the kid'll be ready for us."

"'kay." He stood up, cuddling close to Rock as they moved into the bathroom where Pretty was waiting on them, the room already warm and comfortable. Dick kissed him when he came in and then he was guided to his hands and knees, his marines' hands on him, touching him all over and keeping him warm.

His face was buried in Rock's chest, eyes closed, just relaxed and trusting and feeling the soft, hot touches.

"I'm going to start now, Rig," murmured Dick, fingers sliding down his spine.

"'kay." He took a deep breath, let it out and cuddled close, thighs parting. One of Dick's fingers slid into him, pushing in, thin compared to what was coming, holding the promise of that. He rode the finger, humming softly, hips shifting and sliding, showing his men how much he needed.

"Fuck, you're so tight, Rig. How long has been since we did this? How long since we fucked properly?"

"Too long. Too fucking long..." He moaned, toes curling. Dick slowly worked a second finger in as well, twisting and sliding them deep. "Oh!" He shook, thighs parting farther. "Damn. Again."

"Yeah, and again and again." Dick's fingers followed his words, sliding in over and over again, nudging his gland. Rock's hands were still moving over him, warm and solid and sure. Electricity was riding his spine, hot and bright and so fucking fine. "I'm putting the tubing in now," murmured Dick.

He nodded, still drowning in the pleasure filling him, cheek sliding along Rock's skin. Dick's fingers slid away, leaving only the tube, the plastic not cold, but not hot like skin, not his lovers. The water started filling him, hot and heavy, the sensation strange, making him shift and moan. His Pretty's hand slid across his belly, stroking and massaging while Rock murmured wordlessly to him. The pressure got harder and he started panting, toes curling. "Dick..."

"I feel it." The water flow stopped and Dick's hands were on his ass. "I'm taking the tube out now, Rig."

"Yeah." He nodded, sweating, shivering against Rock's heat, cramps threatening as the water filled him.

Dick's hand returned to his belly, the other one moving on his spine. "You want a shower after, Rig? Or just off to bed?"

"Want a quick shower. Want to be clean, yeah?"

"Quick?" asked Rock. "So you want to take it on your own?"

Dick chuckled, hands working magic against his abdomen.

He whined softly, rolling his eyes. "You know I don't."

"Sh, sh," murmured Dick. "You know we'll go in with you. You ready to move yet?"

"Yeah. Yeah." He rolled his eyes, "Feel like a water balloon."

"Okay, Rock'll help you -- I'll get the shower going." Dick put a kiss in the small of his back before getting up and going to the shower.

He hated this part -- the momentary loss of control, the emptiness, the cold sweat shaking. Still, Rock was there, helping him to the toilet, find his feet, stumble into the tub and it didn't take any time before he was held between them, water sluicing the sweat away.

Both marines sudsed up their hands, making them slide slickly over his skin, smooth and warm. Rig moaned, fucking melting and happy and warm and wet and there. There. God, he'd missed them. The water was hot, falling down on him, on them, washing away the soap as it was applied.

Dick found his neck, licking the water away, while Rock went for one of his nipples, sucking it in. He made soft little noises, hungry and wanton and wordless. It was like a dream, all the heat and mist and sucking mouths driving him crazy.

"This is what's been missing," Dick murmured against his skin. "Me and Rock... we're good together, but it's still not the same -- the showers have definitely been undermanned."

"Miss you both. So tired of being alone, Pretty." His hands were wrapped around his Blue, holding on, stroking.

"You're almost done now," Dick murmured. "And then you'll be Doc Roberts."

Rock grunted, nodded, those blue eyes turning up to him. "Proud of you, Rabbit."

Oh. He groaned and pulled Rock up for a kiss just aching, his heart was so full. Rock's big hands tilted his head as his Blue deepened the kiss. He could feel his men's cocks, hot and hard against his hips and ass, Rock and Dick rubbing. He shifted and slid, letting his body touch them both, love them both.

"You want a little taste?" Rock asked him.

"Always." He slid down, shifting Dick around until he could have them both, sweet heavy pricks red and hot for him. Fuck. Yes. His. They both moaned, Dick's a little higher pitched and followed by Pretty's sweet noises. Two hands landed on his head, one Rock's, one Dick's, both familiar and loved. Rig opened wide and took them in, humming over the hard, sweet cocks. His tongue licked and lapped, pulling their salt into his mouth. He could hear the wet sound of their kisses above him, could feel their hips tensing, holding back from taking his mouth hard.

Head bobbing, Rig made love to those cocks -- one fat and wide and thick, the other thin, but so fucking long. He knew them intimately, the taste and shape of them in his mouth, the feel of them inside him. He knew Dick liked the barest brush of teeth along the ridge of that flared crown. He knew Rock loved the shock and burn of his tongue, pushing into the tight little slit. They both liked pushing deep, filling his throat.

They started moving together, hands going hard on his head, holding him in place as they thrust, not as hard as usual, aware he was taking them both. He relaxed and let them have everything he had to give. Dick came first, his Pretty's cry echoing. Rock's roar slid over it as his Blue's thick cock jerked, sending more spunk shooting down his throat. He took it all, hands stroking two thighs, two hips, encouraging each little jolt of sensation.

They pulled out together, each hooking a hand beneath his arms and pulling him up. Rig licked his lips, smiled at them both, warm and flushed. "Taste good."

Rock chuckled and took a taste, Dick turning the kiss into a three way. "Mm, we do."

His chuckles were joined by his marines'. "Bed. Water's getting cold."

Rock grunted and Dick nodded. The water was turned off and he was led out, dried and flanked by his marines as they made their way to the bedroom.

"You ready for us?" Rock asked, lying him out on the bed again.

"Always." Hell, he was in a better mood than he'd been in for weeks, lazy and relaxed, his men still on his tongue.

Rock and Dick started to touch him, to lick and nuzzle him, making his skin vibrate. He returned the favor as best he could, petting and stroking, loving on them, nibbling on whatever bit of body neared his mouth. A finger slid into him, slick and wide -- Rock's finger fucking him.

"Mmm..." He spread, riding that finger slow and easy, wanting it. "Hot."

"And tight," murmured Rock. "Like a virgin."

Dick chuckled, the sound turning into a moan as one of his Pretty's fingers joined Rock's inside him.

"Mmmm..." He stretched, arms going above his head as his hips rocked and shifted. "Feel you both. Love your touch."

"Gonna fill you so deep," Rock murmured. "Dick first and then me. Going to put us both right there with you for days."

He moaned and shivered, ass clenching hard around their fingers as his cock throbbed. Oh. Oh, both of them.

"Oh, I think he likes it." Dick smiled down at him.

Rock grinned. "Yeah? You think?"

"Mmm... we'll have to see if it stays good..." His tease would have been better had it not been so husky, almost purred.

Rock chuckled. "You let us know if it doesn't."

The fingers inside him pulled away and then returned, doubled. Two of Dick's and two of Rock's, sliding in together just like that.

"Oh..." His mouth fell open, toes curling up tight. "Oh, sweet fuck."

"Still good," murmured Rock. Dick just moaned, fingers sliding with Rock's.

He ran his hands down his body, stroking his skin, fingers slipping over his own nipples, the metal of the ring hot from his skin. "Good..."

Dick whimpered and bent, nose sliding across his nipple and then his Pretty's tongue danced over it. His ass clenched again at the burst of heat and pleasure and electricity. They stayed like that a long time, four fingers from two lovers inside him, Dick's tongue teasing his skin, Rock's free hand moving over his legs.

Rig was floating -- spread wide and supported, stretched and touched and loved and held. The fingers inside him disappeared again and Rock shifted, sitting behind him and pulling him up against that hard, hot body. "Kid's going to take you now."

He draped his legs over Rock's, letting his Blue cradle him, spread him wide. Rock rumbled, chest vibrating against his back. Those big hands cupped his ass and tilted him slightly.

Dick whimpered. "Oh...oh, fuck."

God, he felt sexy, hot. Fucking wanted. "Touch me, Pretty. I want you."

"Oh, yeah. I want you, too." Dick gave him a smile and a hard kiss and then slicked up his hand and settled in close between Rig's legs. The tip of one finger teased him open, the others slowly following. Rig worked to relax, eyelids drooped as he breathed deep and slow, feeling everything. Dick was making those sweet noises, filling the air with the sounds of love and lust and need. Dick's free hand stroked his belly, fingers inside him, pushing, insisting gently that they would all go in.

"Oh..." He leaned hard into the curve of Rock's body, muscles clenching restlessly, body spreading so wide, so fucking wide. Dick bent and sucked the tip of his cock into that pretty, hot mouth.

"Relax," murmured Rock. "We've got you."

"Yeah." He stretched again, cock throbbing a little, body

opening wide and then wider still. "Y'all's."

Dick hummed around the tip of his cock and then just like that, Dick's hand pushed right in, stretching him unbelievably wide. A low, rough sound was pressed out of him, Dick's hand filling him so that nothing else fit. Dick licked at the tip of his prick before pulling off and looking down at his ass. "Oh, fuck... my hand... it's inside you. Tight. So fucking hot and tight."

"Yeah. So full. So much..." So good. Oh, fuck. So much.

"Look at that," Rock murmured into his ear, hands squeezing his ass cheeks. "Look at Dick's arm, disappearing right into your ass."

Rock's words made him whimper, made his ass clench, made him shiver. His eyes were fastened downward, looking at his Pretty's arm, his balls resting against it. "Oh..."

"Yeah, oh." Rock nuzzled his neck, breath warm on his skin.

Dick's face was full of bliss, eyes half-glazed. "Oh, Rig..." Dick's hand slowly closed and opened inside him. His stomach jumped, electricity shooting through him. "More?" Dick asked, voice breathless.

"Uh-huh. Please. Oh, fuck. Please." Dick moaned, hand closing into a fist again, then beginning to move, fucking him. His mind shorted out, went all pleasure, all need. "Pretty. Oh. I feel you."

"I sure hope so," Rock murmured into his ear.

"Me too," Dick told him. "I feel you, too. So tight. Fuck, it's amazing..."

He nodded, tongue wetting his lips, just spread and open and gasping and so fucking hot. Dick kept moving the hand inside him. Then his Pretty bent and took his cock back into that sweet, hot mouth. Tremors shook him, hips moving a little, shifting and aching and needing. "Oh. Oh, fuck. I... Oh..."

"Just let go," Rock whispered as Dick sucked harder.

He arched a little, his Pretty's knuckles rubbing him deep inside, and he groaned, cock spurting into Dick's mouth, body shuddering.

"Fuck, that's beautiful," murmured Rock.

Dick kept sucking, pulling tremors out of him as the hand inside him opened and started to pull out. He whimpered, lips open, body stretching again, muscles holding Dick's hand tight. Dick let his prick go and peppered his belly with soft open-mouthed kisses. "Gotta let me go, Rig. Let Rock have his turn."

He gave an almost chuckle, body finally relaxing and letting Dick's hand slip free, leaving him empty. Dick crawled up his body, kissing him softly, deeply, rubbing a hard prick against him. He tried to rub back, but he was still a little passion-drunk, still leaning into his Blue. Dick didn't appear to need too much help though, his Pretty crying out and coming all over him. He kissed Dick, feeding on the soft cries, the heat. Dick collapsed against him, nuzzling. "Oh, fuck, that was intense."

He nodded, holding and petting his Pretty, humming soft and low. Rock waited patiently until Dick stirred and then his marines switched places, Dick's body cradling him, holding him while Rock settled between his legs.

"You want more?" Rock asked, holding out a large hand to him. "You want this?"

He blinked at his Blue, taking that hand and bringing it to his mouth, licking and sucking those thick fingers. "Always want you, Blue."

Rock purred for him, the sound deep and good. "That's what I like to hear."

He let his mouth trail to the web of veins on Rock's inner wrist, sucking and licking. Needed this man with all he fucking was.

Dick moaned softly, hands stroking his belly. "Too fucking sexy."

Rock's hand cupped his face, fingers stroking softly. He whispered soft, silent secrets onto Rock's palm, breathing out his love, his need. Rock's thumb slid across his lips and then his Blue was kissing him, tongue sliding in deep. Oh, yeah. He opened wide, leaned back against his Pretty, drowning. Blue. My Blue. Fuck.

Dick's mouth was on his neck, working along his jaw when Rock ended the kiss, settling between his legs, finger teasing his sensitive hole. He jerked a little, biting his bottom lip. "Oh. Oh, fuck. 's hot."

"Mm... yeah, hot and swollen, stretched for me." Rock's finger pushed in, slick and hot and oh, fuck.

"Oh. Oh, fuck. Oh..." He shifted, toes fucking curling, eyes wide, breath coming quick. "Oh, Blue..."

Dick's fingers slid down to his nipples, touching them gently as Rock slid two more fingers inside him. It was so big, his body shuddering, heat and pure sensation threatening to overload his nerves.

"So fucking tight," murmured Rock. "You gonna let me in, Rabbit? Let me put my whole hand inside you?"

"Anything." He fought to catch his breath, focused on Rock. "All of me."

Rock's fingers disappeared and then returned, that big hand pushing into him. His world just dissolved, the stretch burning and deep, his Blue so wide. Those blue eyes caught his, held his gaze as Rock's hand moved into him, inexorable, filling him.

Everything stopped, stilled. He couldn't think, couldn't move, just let Rock in and in and in. Rock stopped moving when his hand was all the way in, he could feel the thick fingers deep inside him, his muscles squeezing tight around the heavy wrist.

His breath was coming quick and light, entire body shaking, hands opening and closing over and over. Rock was moaning, Dick breathing heavily in his ear. It was overwhelming and hot and the three of them all wrapped together in Rock's hand.

"Please..." He reached out, shaking hard. "Oh, Blue... Please."

Rock grabbed his hand, the one inside him starting to move, wrapping into a fist and fucking him. He held on tight, the contact of that hand and Dick solid behind him the only things keeping him from shattering. Dick's hand found his cock, slid around and began to pull as Rock's hand slid over his gland. The sounds that poured from him were deep, broken, so full of need and want and love that they hurt his throat as they fought their way free.

"That's it," Dick whispered. "Just let go, we've got you."

"We always have," murmured Rock, hand still moving.

"Always..." He sobbed, arching as his balls tightened, world going grey.

When it came back again, he was shattered and put back together again, cradled between them, held, loved. He cuddled in, something deep inside him throbbing, beating in time with his heart.

"Sleep," muttered Rock, big hand on his hip.

He nodded, whispering soft nonsense words as he sank into dreams, telling his men everything in his heart.

Chapter fifty

Late Sunday mornings were for lazing.

Rock was sitting at the kitchen table, coffee in one hand, sports section in the other. He'd done his duty, made pancakes for breakfast -- and mighty fine pancakes they'd been, too. Rig and Dick had done the dishes and then headed out back to do one industrious thing or another. Not him. He was reading his paper and drinking his coffee. It was what Sunday mornings were for.

He could hear them -- Rig laughing as the lawnmower started, Dick dragging the washtub over the deck for the dogs. He shook his head and turned the page. The most work he was willing to do on a Sunday was fucking.

By the time he'd finished the baseball stats, Rig had finished the yard and was helping Dick with the dogs. They were both damned near naked, both wearing little shorts and soaked, shining in the sunshine and laughing. It was almost enough to make a man go out and join them. Of course what he wanted to do with them wasn't possible outside, so he'd just wait until they were done. He knew it wouldn't be long before Rig made a beeline for the shower.

He heard it in Rig's voice as the soap and grass started to make his Rabbit itch. First Grimmy was irritating him, then the laughter slowed. Finally he heard the magic words. "All right then, I've had all I can take. I'm fixing to jump in the shower, Dick. You comin'?"

Rock snorted and folded his paper, tossing it on the table. Like the kid would be anywhere else. Dick knew the best part about a shower was never the soap and water. Sure enough, the kid was making happy joining noises.

Rock got up and ambled out into the bathroom, shedding clothes as he went. He started the water and stepped in, ready to be jumped.

Rig's hands grabbed his ass a half-second before a kiss brushed his neck. "How was the paper, Blue? You have to wait on us long?"

"Long enough. Sunday's are for relaxing, Rig." He didn't let his Rabbit answer, turning and taking that fucking fantastic mouth with his own. Rig just melted, rubbing against his body, tongue pushing and fucking his lips. Immediate and hungry, there was never any doubt that his class-A slut wanted him, needed him. Then Dick's hands found his hips, sandwiching Rigger between them, Rig's moan low and desperate.

Correction, needed them both.

He reached for the kid's head and brought Dick into the kiss. There was nothing better than a three-way. Rig shifted, wrapped an arm around them both with a soft hum. Two tongues slid over his, pushing and licking and tasting. He put his own arms around each of them, bringing them into a triangle. With just a little work, their cocks slid together, all hard and hot, slick in the water.

Rig's grey eyes were dancing as the kiss broke, hips bumping them all together. "Can't decide whether to watch or bend down and suck you both off. Pretty fucking cocks, marines."

Rock growled. "Much as I want to be all noble and say we'll all get off together -- you start offering blow jobs, Rig and that's all I can think about."

Rig chuckled, the sound warm and happy. "That's because I'm fucking good at what I do, Rocketman."

Then his long, tall Texan sank to his knees, tongue licking at his prick, then the kid's. Oh, yeah, that was worth waiting for. He grabbed the kid's head and pulled him in for another kiss as Rig went to work on their cocks. His cock was sucked once, then that mouth disappeared, but before he got a chance to complain, Rig had them pressed together, mouth wrapped around them both, tongue flicking wildly.

Dick was pressing all sorts of noises into his mouth and he had a groan or two of his own to add to it. Fuck, but their slut was a pro. He had to look down, had to watch the fucking master at work.

Rig's eyes were closed, hair plastered against his head, lips red against their cocks. He could see Rig's prick, too -- hard as fuck, dark, curled up against that flat belly. Happy, the son-of-a-bitch looked happy and horny and like he knew just where he wanted to be.

Rock figured he was one lucky asshole. He stroked Rig's hollowed cheek, other hand solid on Dick's neck. Yeah, fucking lucky.

He groaned, letting Rig know how fucking good it was. Rig hummed, head starting to bob, taking them both halfway with a strong suction. One thin hand landed on his hip, the other on

Dick's, holding on. Dick provided their soundtrack, with his moans and groans and needy little noises.

Rig's mouth was fucking good around his cock, Dick's cock hot and slick and solid against his. They started pushing, Dick pulling back as he nudged in, rocking together in slow thrusts, taking that tight mouth together. It was a thing of fucking beauty, made even better by how much they were all enjoying it. As he watched, Rig looked up, met his eyes, and... Oh, fuck, yes.

He squeezed Dick's shoulder and the two of them moved faster, still gentle, still careful, but faster and Rig just took it, took them and those grey eyes begged for more. With a shout, the kid came, spunk hot around his prick before swallowed away by Rig and it was enough to send him over as well, his own load pushing down Rig's throat.

"Mmm..." Rig's hum was loud, cheek rubbing against his belly, hand petting Dick's thigh.

"Slut," he whispered, knowing Rig would hear the words he didn't say.

"Ours," added Dick, kid's voice just as soft.

Rig nodded, dropping a kiss beneath his navel, stroking Dick's inner thigh. "Yours."

He wrapped his hand beneath Rig's arm. "Get up here and share the taste."

Dick took Rig's other arm, steadying him as they took his mouth. Him and Dick, strong and almost bitter and Rig's sweet mouth beneath that. Fucking good.

Long and thin, hot and hungry, Rig moved between them, rocking hard and steady. He reached down, meeting Dick's hand and their fingers twined together as they wrapped around Rig.

"Oh... fuck, yeah!" Rig's head fell back, hips moving up into their grip. He licked at Rig's lips, lapped water off his cheeks, his neck, tongue tangling now and then with Dick's. All the while they worked their slut's cock as ably as he'd worked theirs. Rig moaned, pushed, hummed long and low as he arched beneath the shower spray. "Oh, shit! So good."

"You know it," he growled against Rig's skin.

"Yeah. Yeah." A soft cry sounded, then Rig jerked, coming over their hands. Yeah, fucking good.

They stood under the spray of the water, together and warm and sated.

Fucking perfect for a lazy Sunday morning.

Chapter Thirty Six

Rigger was in fucking heaven.

Cold beer, beautiful, clear cool night, radio playing soft, hot bubbling water -- fucking heaven. He should've put in the hot tub years ago. He lifted himself up out of the water enough that his nipples tightened from the cold and then sank back down. There was a tiny hickey, right next to his left nipple, black as a politician's heart. He touched it with his finger, moaning softly. Dick had given it to him.

Speak of the devil and there he was, squinting in the darkness. "Rig? You out here?" The kid walked out to the deck, nearly tripping over the hot tub. "Shit -- I still say the stupid thing's a health hazard."

"Yeah, I'm soaking. What's up?" He leaned back, letting his body float up, let Dick see what was up.

"Rock's um... gonna be... late." Dick's eyes finally dragged themselves back up to meet Rigger's eyes. And oh, the kid was hungry. "How's the water?"

"Lonely." He reached down, stroked his cock as his fingers traced the tiny mark. "Really lonely."

Dick groaned and then made a soft noise. The kid could get undressed pretty fucking quick, given the right motivation. Fuck, but the kid was looking good, sleek and hard little muscles all framing that long, long cock and heavy balls. He pumped his cock again, groaning as he waited.

"Shit, it's cold out here." The kid hightailed it into the water, landing practically on top of him. "It's pretty hot in here though."

Rigger nodded, pressing up into Dick with a groan and lifting his head for a kiss. Oh, yeah, it was getting plenty warm in here. Dick's mouth met his; the kid was hungry, fucking starving. The long body rubbed against him. "What is it about water that makes everything seem so easy and smooth?"

"It's wet?" He grinned, nipping at Dick's bottom lip. His hands slid down the slick back to cup Dick's ass and then back up. "Fuck, love touching you."

"That's handy, 'cause I fucking love it when you touch me." Dick's eyes closed and he pressed close, cock hard and even hotter than the water, pressing against his own.

Oh, playing one-on-one with Dick was something else. He spread his legs, ass resting on the little ledge, and began rocking his hips, working their cocks together.

"Oh, fuck!" The kid's eyes were still closed, his mouth open, face slack with bliss. Dick's hands held tight to the edge on either side of his head, providing leverage for the kid to keep himself pressed down. The sweet fucking noises had started, all for him. He rose up, licking and sucking at Dick's jaw line. He hooked one leg around Dick, using his weight to keep them together. The combination of hot water and hot cock was making his fucking head spin. Dick was writhing against him, eyes opening, the blue dark, glazed. "Fucking amazing," muttered the kid.

"No, Pretty." He bit Dick's earlobe. "You're fucking Rigger."

Dick gasped and laughed and moaned all together. Rigger kept nuzzling, fingers moving over the smooth, sensitive skin at the small of Dick's back.

"You're gonna make me come." The words were softly spoken, Dick's eyes back to half closed as he slid against Rigger.

"Good." He shuddered, moaning into Dick's ear, hips moving faster. "Come on me, Dick. Want to watch you."

"Oh, fuck, oh, fuck, oh, fuck." Dick made a few more soft, desperate noises and then shuddered, head arching back with the force of his pleasure.

Fucking beautiful. Rig licked a long line up Dick's throat, his hips still moving, pushing hard and fast. "Make me fucking hard. Make me ache."

Dick's mouth found his, opening wide for him and then the kid pulled back, still dark eyes on him. "Wanna fuck me?"

"Does a bear shit in the woods?" Toes curling, Rigger groaned, tugging Dick back down for a hard, deep kiss. "Ride my cock."

Dick shuddered against him and groaned and then was shifting, pushing himself upright. Dick got his cock sliding along the kid's crack, rocking just enough to tease them both. "Like this?"

Rigger pressed up, thrusting steadily. Fuck, he was hard enough to cut glass. "Tease. More. Inside."

Dick laughed, the sound soft and thick and aroused. "Make me."

He reached for Dick's hips, trying to hold the kid still so he could push inside. Dick had better leverage now though, the kid's knees on the bottom of the hot tub, hands on the edge. Dick just grinned down at him and kept sliding back and forth. "Shit, you feel good."

"Yeah. Fucking good." His hips were answering Dick's motions, his focus wavering as the kid's ass cheeks squeezed his shaft.

Dick laughed again, grinning down happily at him. "I thought you were gonna fuck me, Rig."

"Was. Am. Fuck, kid, 'm gonna shoot if you don't stop." Rigger leaned up, nuzzling Dick's wet skin as his hips worked.

Dick stopped and chuckled breathlessly at his sound of protest. "You said stop."

"You are an evil motherfucker." He nipped hard at Dick's skin, chuckling. "I'm boiled down to a wet noodle, hard enough a cat couldn't scratch me, and you want to play mind games?"

Dick grinned. "I was just going for getting you riled up enough you'd fuck me through the deck."

"Oh, that I can do." He slid out from beneath Dick, groaning at the loss of friction. He turned the bubbles back on and then draped himself over Dick, their fingers wrapping together on the edge of the hot tub. His cock pushed against the kid's hole, pressing and retreating again and again. When the kid pushed back, the head of Rig's cock popped inside. Fucking A. "Deck's too fucking cold, Pretty. This'll have to do."

"Uh-huh." Dick pushed back some more, moaning softly. "It'll do great if you actually get down to the fucking part."

"Smartass." Oh, but Dick was getting mouthy in his old age. Rig leaned up and pushed into Dick's heat, not waiting for the kid's shivers to stop before beginning to fuck him hard and deep, water sloshing all around them. He could feel the kid shifting beneath him, trying to get a foothold or kneehold or something to get some leverage to push back. He grabbed Dick's ass, pulling him onto his cock over and over, the bubbles tickling his ass, his balls. He whimpered. Fuck, he should have bought this thing years ago.

Dick was moaning and groaning and making those sweet fucking noises, pushing back against him as best the kid could.

"Fuck yeah - more, Rigger, harder."

"Yeah." He bent his head, resting his forehead against Dick's nape and slammed into the hot tightness, groaning as he moved. "Fuck."

Dick wasn't talking anymore, just making noises and writhing, body tight and grasping. Oh, fuck. Sweet, Dick was tight and sweet and fucking shit he was going to come in that tight ass. He bit down on Dick's shoulder as he shot his load, grunting loud, hips jerking.

"Oh, fuck!" Dick let go of the edge with one hand, balancing precariously as he worked himself. Seconds later his muscles were squeezing Rig's cock tight.

"Dick... shit..." He moaned, aftershocks shooting up and down his spine.

"Fuck that was good." Dick rested his head on the edge of the hot tub, breathing hard. "Damn those bubbles are nice -- I know I say it every time, but you should have gotten this thing years ago, Rig."

"No shit." He chuckled, pulling out of Dick's body and settling on the seat again, pulling the kid into his arms for a kiss. "Couldn't have said it better myself."

Dick wrapped one arm around his head and pulled him down for a kiss. Lazy and sloppy and happy Dick kisses were quite the lovely thing.

Sheer fucking heaven.

Chapter Thirty Seven

They'd been gone for weeks -- it wasn't the first time they'd been called out, but it was the first since... His hand went to his chest, tracing scars. And it was the first time since their anniversary and so close to the possibility of them both being free and part of him worried that fate was just mean enough to promise him something and then snatch it back.

It was the first time since he hadn't been on post, too. Wasn't even allowed on post. Hell, they'd call Momma if something happened to Rock. With Dick? He'd never even know. But there were rumors -- girls at the hospital with husbands coming home soon and Rig just cleaned and worked at his clinicals and prayed.

And waited.

He was out in the backyard, topless and sweaty, mowing the grass, thinking about giving the pups a bath and maybe running down to the Home Depot for some roofing tiles, when Grim and Lucy started barking at something. "Hush now. Y'all just let those squirrels be now, y'hear?"

They didn't hush though and both of them were going half out of their minds now. He groaned and killed the mower, wiping the grass and sweat off as he went to see which stray dog or cat had wandered over. "I swear, y'all are enough to drive a man to drinking."

"Gee, I thought we'd get a better welcome home than that."

"Didn't you get the memo, kid? The romance is gone."

Their voices were weary, their BDUs muddy and torn, their faces drawn, tired, but they were home, Rock and Dick, standing on the back deck, looking like they were holding each other upright.

"Oh." He forced himself to stay where he was, feet planted firmly on the ground. "Well, aren't y'all sights for sore eyes? 's been a while. House has been real empty."

Home. Thank you, Lord. Home and together in one piece.

"Well, it's not anymore." Rock growled. "Get your ass over

here, Roberts and welcome us home proper."

"Yeah." It didn't take any time at all before he was pushing into two sets of strong arms, the privacy fence protecting them from outside eyes, and taking his kisses.

Oh, they tasted good. Weary as hell and God knows when the last time they brushed their teeth was, but good just the same. They each kissed him and then all three of them kissed together, long, wet, sloppy kisses that went on and on until Rock grunted and backed off a bit. "Inside. Bed. Couch. Floor. Hell, I'm not picky I just need to sit."

"Bathtub. Y'all need a bath and a nice scrub and then I'll put you in bed." Rig was already pulling off layers, dropping them into a pile to be cleaned. "When do you have to go back?"

"Tomorrow," growled Rock, clearly unhappy.

"We've been promised at least another week before we're out again though," added Dick. "Just regular hours tomorrow."

Rig nodded, not trusting his voice. He wouldn't bitch, hadn't ever, not starting now. He got them both naked -- he didn't think even he could save those boots -- and headed down the hallway toward the bathroom. Bath. Food. Beer. Bed. The basics of life.

"You're coming in, too." The way his Blue said it, it wasn't a question. He nodded, toeing off his sneakers and popping the fly on his cutoffs.

Food and beer could wait.

It wasn't long before they were all settled, Rock lying against the back of the tub, him sandwiched in the middle between his Blue and his Pretty, all floating. He stroked Dick's belly, Rock's thigh, just touching them both, needing to assure himself they were okay. "Missed you."

"Oh, yeah," Dick agreed, head leaning on his shoulder, riverstone eyes looking back at him. "Missed you so much. And hot water and being clean and the dogs... but especially you."

He leaned down and brushed a kiss over Dick's temple. "I was right here waiting."

"I know." Dick's eyes were soft, the hand that stroked over his cheek even softer. And the truly fucked up part was that Dick did know -- maybe even more than Rock, maybe even more than him. He closed his eyes, nuzzled down into that touch, hand exploring Dick's skin.

Dick made sweet noises for him, noises that had been missing from their home for far too long. Behind him Rock rumbled, the noise sounding soft and happy and half-asleep. He reached back, twined his fingers with Rock's, holding on as they floated.

They stayed like that until the water cooled and then Dick pulled the plug out and added more hot, settling back down against him once the tub was full again.

Rig leaned his head up, kissing Rock's jaw, the broad, strong chin. "You doing okay, Blue?"

"Yeah." Rock's mouth met his in a soft kiss. "I'm getting too old for this shit."

"Just a year left. Just a year, Blue."

Rock nodded. "Yeah. I guess I can put in the time. I just miss my morning wake up calls."

"Missed the taste of you. 's not a good morning without my men fucking my mouth."

Rock's cock was growing hard against his ass, twitching and jerking and hot. Dick pressed against him, sliding that sweet, long cock against his belly. "You make a man forget he's tired, Rig."

"That's my job, marine. Keep you two up and awake and ready." He pulled Dick in for a kiss, deep and hot and long.

Rock chuckled again behind him, lips closing around his skin on his neck. "You're pretty fucking good at your job."

"Yep. Years of devoted practice." He gasped, arching into Dick with a groan. "Blue..."

They were both chuckling, bodies moving against him.

"There's none more devoted than you," said Rock, hands sliding him back along that thick prick.

"You know how it is, when you love what you do." He groaned, thighs parting as best they could.

They rocked together for a moment, the water splashing against the sides of the tub. Rock put a stop to it. "Getting too old for this, too. No acrobatics -- let's just go to bed and fuck."

"Sounds like a plan, Blue." He stole another kiss from Dick before the kid managed to lever out of the tub and helped his skinny ass up and out. Rock followed, hands grabbing a towel and drying him off, bending to wrap hot lips around his shoulder. Dick was busy, too, seeming intent on drying him solely by tongue. He was simply touching, hands running over bellies and thighs, fingers curling around two hard cocks just waiting for his lips. Shuddering, he groaned. "Bed... Oh, fuck. Want y'all so bad."

"Yeah," murmured Dick, tongue hot against his skin.

"Yeah," agreed Rock, teeth scraping.

He cupped Dick's face, tilting his Pretty so he could taste that mouth, take a kiss while Rock shattered him. Dick's mouth opened to his, hungry now where earlier there had only been need dulled by weariness. Rock's fingers were on his ass, sliding, pulling his ass cheeks apart. Those thick thumbs pushed at his hole, shoving right in as his Blue's teeth scraped right down along his spine.

Rig cried out into Dick's mouth, body convulsing, shuddering as he gripped the base of his cock. "Never gonna make it to bed."

Dick pushed his hand away, long fingers wrapping around his prick and stroking, hard and fast. "I think we can help you get it up again, Rig."

"Just enjoy it, Rig, we'll be making demands soon enough." Rock licked back up along his spine, soothing the scraped skin, thumbs still working his asshole hard.

He spread his thighs, working between those two sensations harder and faster, rising up on his toes as the sensation peaked. "Oh! Oh, fuck! Yeah! Oh!"

Dick's other hand slid down to cup his balls, Rock pushing his thumbs deep at the same time. He screamed as he came, head falling back on his shoulders.

"Missed that smell," growled Rock, hands cupping his ass.

Dick brought his come-covered hand up, held it about shoulder height and as he watched, his Blue and his Pretty dove for Dick's hand, licking it clean. He moaned, lips fastening on Rock's throat, sucking hard for a few seconds. Then he groaned and started tugging them both. "Bed. Now. Move it, marines."

"Yes, sir." They said it together, snapping upright and giving him a salute. Dick grabbed his hands, laughing and pulling him into their bedroom, Rock pushing from behind, as if he had been the one holding them up in the bathroom. Not that it mattered. Because as soon as he fucking could, he was going to get one of those hard cocks between his lips and another filling his ass.

It seemed they had the same idea because Rock cupped his chin and took a hard kiss and then asked, "How do you want it, Rig? Aside from hard and fast, I mean."

"Now, Blue. Right fucking now."

"Hands and knees, cowboy." Rock all but pushed him down, Dick grabbing the lube and climbing up behind him. Rock nodded and knelt in front of him, rubbing that thick cock across his lips. "Want you."

"Yes, Blue." He groaned as he opened up, sucked that fat, sweet cock in, hands tangling in the bed sheets. Oh, yeah. Fucking sweet. Dick's fingers were warm and long, spreading him. There was no finesse, no gentle lead-in, his men were hungry. Maybe almost as hungry as he was.

Maybe. He closed his eyes, started sucking in time with the firm finger-fucking Dick was giving him. He was fucking made for this, for these men to fuck. The first hint of Rock's flavor teased his tongue and he pulled harder, needing more.

Maybe not.

Rock's hands were hot on his head, guiding him, holding him, not still, but just where Rock needed him as his Blue started to move, slowly fucking his mouth. Dick was making those sweet porno noises, driving him fucking crazy with fingers that weren't enough. He would have to give up his prize to ask for more, so he resorted to non-verbal begging -- hips rocking, ass clenching tight, tongue fucking the sweet slit of Rock's cock.

Rock groaned, the sound like a caress against his ears, that fat prick moving faster, sliding deeper. Dick must have got the message, or just needed the same thing he did, not that it mattered. All that mattered was that long cock, pressing into him, in and in, sliding across his gland and settling deep. No one stretched him as wide as his Blue, but no one touched him as deep as his Pretty.

Rig lost himself, purring and humming, sucking and fucking and working two hard pricks for all he was worth. Dick's hand slid down along his belly, wrapping around his cock and pulling in time with the deep thrusts. He moaned, pulling hard as his balls tightened, shudders rocking him hard.

Rock groaned and Dick whimpered and they moved faster, harder, taking him, making him theirs again. Rig's nose was buried in Rock's pubes, head spinning as he shot, ass milking Dick's long cock. His men came together, both shooting deep inside him, hands hard and hot and tight on his body.

Fucking made for this.

For them.

They collapsed down around him, pulling him between

them, holding him safe and warm and wanted. He thought briefly about food, beer, setting the alarm for them, taking care of his marines -- then he curled close, stayed happy between them while they all slept.

Chapter Thirty Eight

The sound of water on skin woke him, pulled him out of Dick's arms and the warm covers and onto cold tile. He slid into the shower, grabbing the soap and snuggling up against the beautiful fucking body of his Blue. "Hey, you're home late. Early. Whatthefuckever."

Rock growled, not even answering him, just turning and wrapping those solid arms around him, holding him close. He covered Rock's lips with his own, hands soaping up shoulders and upper arms, melting into Rock and just touching. Rock's lips spread his, tongue invading and taking his mouth, sweeping everywhere.

He moaned, opening wide, his tongue sliding against Blue's, meeting that need, answering it. Rock devoured him, hands sliding to his ass and tugging him close against that hard, buff body. One leg draped around Rock's hip, trusting that strength without question, cocks sliding together, hot even in the water. Rock growled again, the noise lower now, primal.

A keening sigh was his answer, hands gripping hard against rock-hard shoulders. Rock moved them, brought their hips together again and again, sliding that fat prick against his cock. Rig blinked up, smiling into the bluest eyes on earth, telling his Blue how good it was, they were. Telling his Blue everything.

The growl softened, became less hungry but more needy, Rock's eyes holding him as surely as those arms. His hand wrapped around their cocks, holding them together, stroking them off. Rock's hands got tighter on his ass, the kiss growing harder.

He just opened wide, held tight, stroked hard. He gave Rock everything, moaning, hungry. One of those thick fingers slid along his crease, pressed against his hole. He shuddered, jerking against Rock's strength. "Blue!"

"That's it, Rig, let me feel you come."

He gave a soft cry, jerking hard, shooting against his Blue, arching. Rock growled, coming hard against him.

Rig held Rock, hands smoothing over that fine skin until all the shudders were gone. "Come to bed, Blue. Been missing my old man."

"You've got a young man to keep you warm now." The words were accompanied by a soft kiss.

"Yeah." Rig nodded and looked into those blue-blue eyes. "And he'll never be you and I'll never stop needing my old man."

Rock kissed him, long and deep. The water was shut off, a towel wrapped around him and then he was hoisted over Rock's shoulder. "Bed."

"You Ug, me Rig. We go sleep now." Rig reached down, pinched that hard ass as they moved.

Rock grunted and threatened to drop him before setting him down gently enough next to Dick. "Fuck off, asshole."

"Anytime, any place, Rocketman."

Rock chuckled and sandwiched him between his marines. "Go to sleep, Rig. You'll need that attitude in the morning."

"Mm... I'm counting on it, jackass." He pulled the blanket over them all, humming as Dick curled around him with a happy sound. "Night, Rock."

"Night, Rabbit."

It didn't take more than a couple of minutes before Rock's snores started. He snuggled in, warm and surrounded, right where he belonged -- at home between two men who were right where they belonged.

***

The very best thing about cold, rainy days off was being able to curl up on the sofa with Granny's quilt and a cup of coffee and watch movies -- one after the other. John Wayne and Wyatt Earp, Jackie Chan and Arnold Schwartzenegger and Steven Seagal. Robert Redford -- fuck, but that was a fine-looking man -- and Paul Newman, who almost had eyes as blue as Rock's.

Almost.

He hadn't had such a lazy day in months, but his thigh and wrist didn't like the cold and the damp. The jeep was running fine, the house was clean, chili was simmering and his boys were on base. Even the dogs were lounging, Grimmy's head resting on Lucy's belly while they watched Butch Cassidy have a nice little shoot-em-up. At one point he made popcorn for him and the pups. Once or twice he warmed up his coffee, grabbed another quilt, stirred the chili. Eventually he just dozed off, warm and relaxed and right as you please, dreaming of him and his boys, riding the plains, looking for banditos and drinking in saloons.

The motion of the horse changed and he felt more like the horse was carrying him than he was riding and wasn't that just the silliest thing, but dreams were like that. Next thing he knew the horse had put him down and was kissing him, big horsy lips all over his face.

He chuckled, hands reaching up to push the horse off, when his fingers slid over strong shoulders and a thick neck that was familiar even in his dreams. "Mmm... Blue."

"Hey sleeping beauty." He got a long, sweet kiss from Rock, Dick's body sliding alongside his and pressing close, the kid's lips warm against his neck. "You were right, kid, all he needed was a kiss."

Dick chuckled. "That still doesn't make you a prince, Rock."

He purred, stretching out as far as he could along those two amazing bodies, still dozing a bit. "A prince? Nah, Pretty. Was dreaming about y'all being cowboys. Y'all's asses looked **fine** in chaps."

Rock chuckled, warm fingers sliding under his shirt and working it slowly up.

"Just chaps?" asked Dick. "Or were we wearing jeans, too? 'Cause that would chafe, wouldn't it?"

"Hmm?" He lifted his arms so that Rock could pull his shirt off, ending up with them wrapped around Dick's neck. "Nah, y'all had jeans. We were riding. Hadn't gotten to the good part yet."

Dick's mouth covered his, tongue sliding into his mouth.

"Oh, the good part," said Rock, rubbing against him. "Would that be where we came in?"

Rig grinned, rubbing back, lips parting eagerly for his Pretty. Oh, yeah, and Rock knew it, too. The good part was *always* where they came in. Rock and Dick worked to get his jeans off, their fingers tangling, but still managing to work together, teasing as much as anything else.

He managed to do some teasing of his own, licking along Rock's collarbones, sucking a tiny mark beneath Dick's ear. They kissed just above him and then split up, Rock going for that spot on his neck and Dick moving down and down until the kid's hot lips wrapped around the tip of his prick.

"Oh! Oh, 's good." He arched, spine sliding on the blankets, hands finding purchase on Rock's shoulders. What the fuck had he done right to deserve them?

Dick worked his jeans the rest of the way off as that sweet mouth worked him slowly. Rock's hands were moving over his chest, stroking his belly and generally not touching his nipples, though he got close a few times. He was melting, capturing one of Rock's hands and bringing it up to his lips, tongue tracing all the little lines before moving to suck on each finger, one at a time. Rock rumbled against his skin, teeth scraping gently as his Blue nipped at him.

He could feel their cocks, both hard and painting him with liquid heat: one against his hip, the other against his calf, both of them moving with damned near the same slow, lazy rhythm. He wasn't in any hurry himself, spending a good long time exploring the veins crisscrossing Rock's inner arm with his tongue, one hand stroking Dick's head, petting and loving his men. Dick was working his cock a little harder now, head bobbing up and down on him. The kid's long fingers moved over his balls, cupping his sacs and playing with the skin beyond.

"Mm... Feels so good, Pretty. Fucking sweet." He spread his legs, opening himself wide for Dick's touch.

Dick hummed around his cock, fingers teasing over his hole. Rock growled, moving to cover his nipple with that hot mouth, fingers finding the ring in his other nipple and tugging.

"Oh! Oh, fuck!" Rig moaned, shifting to rock between those sweet sensations, caught up between his men and their need and his own. Dick and Rock both sucked harder, working to send him flying. His orgasm slid all the way down his spine, sparks feeling like they were shooting all through him, making him groan and buck and twist. They kept him on the edge, made it last with their mouths and their hands playing over his body like experts at a piano. "Please. Making me fucking fly!"

His toes curled, tremors rocking him. The kid hummed and Rock growled, the vibrations against his cock and nipple exactly what he'd needed. He shot with a cry, entire body convulsing as he came.

"Mmm, very nice," murmured Rock, kissing him.

He murmured his agreement. Oh, yeah. Very fucking nice.

More. Good. Yeah.

"Our turn now." Rock shifted, moved, and suddenly that fat prick was at his mouth, teasing across his lips. Dick moved, too, pushing his legs further apart, heat nudging against his entrance.

"Absofuckinglutely." He took both cocks in, sucking in and bearing down eagerly. Oh, yeah. That was good, two hot cocks, two hungry groans, filling him deep.

They didn't say anything else, just moaned and groaned and fucked him. They twisted, moved until they were settled, Rock sitting in front of him, hard prick spreading his lips wide as he knelt, Dick's hands hard on his hips, pushing in him deep. They moved hard and fast, the time for teasing gone; this was urgent and needy, plain and simple.

He worked them both, tight and hungry and wanting nothing more than to fuck them forever, make them come, feel the slide of skin on skin. Dick shot first, sweet sounds turning into a sharp cry and then heat filled him, shot deep. Rig moaned, purring around his Blue's cock, nose burying in those soft, dark pubes as he swallowed.

It wasn't long before he was hearing Rock's roar, that fat prick shoving in deep and hard, coming down his throat. He relaxed onto Rock's thighs, drinking his Blue down and then letting the sweet motions of mouth and tongue continue, searching out each aftershock. Finally they all collapsed into a heap, Rock and Dick spreading him back out, sandwiching him between them.

He pulled the quilt over them, nuzzling whatever skin he could find. "Evening, boys. Glad you're home."

"Back at you," rumbled Rock lazily.

"Ditto." Dick pushed closer, hands touching him and Rock.

He found his spot, head on Rock's shoulder, Dick's leg atop his, Rock's hand on his hip.

"Don't get too comfy, I smell chili." Trust Rock, once one hunger was fed, the other reared its head.

"Mm... cornbread, too. And there's an apple pie in the freezer." He grinned, licking Rock's skin. "I don't suppose y'all stopped for videos and beer?"

Dick chuckled. "A dozen longnecks and US Marshalls with Tommy Lee Jones."

Rock rumbled. "Just for you."

"Oh, y'all rock!" He grinned, giving one kiss and then

another. Oh, yeah -- chili, quilts, good movies, apple pie, fucking and his marines. Fucking A.

Life just didn't get any better.

Chapter Thirty Nine

Dick checked the turkey and tried to decide if the pumpkin pie was going to need another ten minutes or should come out now. Rig didn't have clinicals over Thanksgiving and between the two of them, they'd gotten everything ready, but Rig had fallen asleep about an hour ago, curled up on the couch with his head in Rock's lap. There was no way in hell Dick was waking Rig. He'd let the pie burn first.

The turkey looked great and smelled better and the pie crust was pretty brown, so he figured it had to come out now. He did that, putting it on the counter with the pecan pie and Rock's chocolate pie and the cranberry sauce. Then he set the table and, following the directions carefully, made the layer salad. The armadillo eggs were beyond him and he figured Rig would either wake up in time to make them or they'd do without.

He washed the dishes, swept the floor and took the garbage out to the garage. Once he was convinced there wasn't anything else to do, though Rig would probably find something anyway when he woke up, Dick grabbed three beers and the chips and dip and went into the living room.

Rock grunted his thanks, taking a swig of the beer.

"What's the score?"

"Nothing yet." Rock stretched, Rig's head moving on his thighs. "It's been a long, boring game."

Rig murmured, turning to nuzzle Rock's belly. Rig needed a haircut; the back of that white-blond head was filled with dozens and dozens of curls.

"Pass me a couple of chips, would you? I don't want to disturb him." Rock's mouth opened expectantly and he had to chuckle. Rig was right -- the man was spoiled. Of course whose fault was that? He grabbed a couple of chips, chuckles turning into laughter as Rock growled "Dip" at him.

Rig was slowly waking up, Dick could see it in the little, random movements, the way Rig scooted enough for him to get comfortable.

He dipped a couple of chips, handing them over to Rock and then settled, sitting with them, warm and good. It was what holidays had come to mean, being with these two men, his lovers. His family.

Rig turned a little, grey eyes blinking over at him. "D'you take those pies out, Pretty? I got all warm and comfy and just fell right to sleep. Sorry."

He stroked Rig's back, smiling down at Rig. "I didn't mind. Not one burned and the turkey looks really nice."

Rig grinned, the look playful and wicked. One lightly stubbled cheek slid across Rock's crotch. "Yeah. Yeah, he does."

He started laughing, which made Rock's eyes narrow. "What?" He could see it dawn on Rock and one big hand went to Rig's ribs, fingers digging in.

The squeak was heartening, Rig's laughter warm and breathless, filling the air. It was amazing what six months of clinicals and a fellowship so the man didn't have to work had done -- their cowboy was still tired, but it was a healthy tired, a tired that found Rigger in bed with them, sleeping and fucking and laughing.

He grabbed Rock's beer and put it down on the coffee table along with his own before joining in, helping Rig to get Rock's one ticklish spot -- under the man's arms. Rig managed to straddle Rock's thighs and they got Rock laughing hard, the pups starting to bounce and bark with excitement. They finally all ended up in a heap, he and Rig leaning against Rock, trying to catch their breath as Grimmy and Lucy attempted to lick them to death.

Rig tilted his head and licked Rock's lips, then Dick's. "Happy Thanksgiving. Lucy, quit biting my toes."

Laughing, he pushed Lucy away. "Go on, both of you."

"Like they're going to listen," muttered Rock, shaking his head.

Dick just grinned as the two pups curled up together in the armchair.

Rig chuckled. "Oh, man, they're something else. Grimmy needed a Lucy around to play with." Rig relaxed against Rock's chest, one hand reaching out to stroke across his belly, warm and good.

"Kind of like you and Rock needing a Dick?"

Rock rolled his eyes and he ducked the swat easily, all grins.

Rig turned and landed in his arms, kissing him soundly. "Kind of. I lick your balls more than Lucy licks Grimmy's."

He laughed as Rock popped Rig's ass. "Hey, he licks your balls, too."

Rig nodded, laughter shaking their redneck. "I do. I lick all sorts of bits and usually don't get popped for it."

"I don't want to be imagining those dogs' tongues next time you're licking anything of mine," complained Rock.

Dick made a face. "That's gross, Rock."

"I didn't start it."

Rig was rolling, grey eyes bright and amused as fuck. "Oh, y'all... Y'all are something else!"

"You hear that -- I'm something else." Rock was looking smug.

"That doesn't necessarily mean something good," he pointed out.

"Rig was smiling when he said it."

"He could have been doing that to put you off the scent."

Rock shook his head. "Do I need to take you out back and beat you?"

"Oh, would you?" He was laughing again, scooting over to stay out of the way of a swat of his own from Rock.

"There will be no beatings until after turkey and cranberry sauce." The pronouncement was given almost straight-faced, Rig stretching to take a long, hard taste of Rock's lips.

"Spoilsport," murmured Rock around Rig's lips.

Grinning, he pushed into their kiss, moaning happily as their tastes mingled together. Rig's arm wound around his waist, holding him close. The three-way kisses were the best, Rig's quick tongue and Rock's growls and heat... Yeah. Damn. Everything else kind of faded, the way it did when they started touching each other, and he moaned into the kisses, whimpered and groaned and fed every little sound he made into their mouths. Fuck, it was good.

Rig started working open their shirts, fingers quick and sure, flicking their nipple rings. Oh, yeah -- that was better and he reciprocated, fingers a little clumsier than Rig's on the man's buttons, given he was pretty fucking distracted by the play of those fingers on his nipple ring. Rock shuddered and helped, pulling Rig's shirt open, sending buttons flying.

"Neanderthal." Rig tugged their rings, nipping at Rock's lips, the complaint toothless and fond.

Rock snorted and tugged on Rig's ring, making Rig gasp, eyes wide and wanton. "Slut."

"Uh-huh. Yours. Do it again." Rig licked their lips -- hungry cowboy. Rock chuckled and tugged on Rig's nipple ring again while he bent and licked at the sensitive flesh where it was stretched and at Rock's fingers.

"Oh, sweet fuck!" Rig took a deep breath, a flush covering that stretched belly. Dick's hands slid down to tease at the waistband of Rig's jeans and then Rock's, making them both move and moan.

"He's such a good boy... So good at buttons and zippers..." Rig whimpered, sucking his belly in so the pants could come undone.

"Ah, so that's why you keep me around," he teased, undoing Rock's jeans first, gasping at the heat of Rock's prick as it pushed out of the jeans.

"One reason of thousands..." Rig took a deep breath, groaning. "Oh, fuck. Blue. I can smell you..."

"Hey, kid -- his nose works."

He rolled his eyes at Rock and kissed Rig again, quick and hard before opening Rig's jeans. He took each prick in one of his hands and started pumping. Oh, fuck, they were hot and hard and solid and like fucking silk-covered steel. He moaned, working them harder.

"Missing one." Rig nuzzled into his neck, working his jeans open. Long fingers fished out his prick and started stroking, low moans vibrating his throat. He whimpered, the sound getting louder as Rock's fingers tugged on his and Rig's nipple rings. It made him gasp and moan, hips pushing into Rig's hand.

They all moved together, Rig's free hand twining with his on Rock's prick, soft, sucking kisses trailing along his jaw. He whimpered and moaned and gasped and cried out, not able to stop the noises even if he had wanted to.

Rig groaned and licked his ear. "So hot, Pretty. Fucking love how you feel in my hand."

He whimpered, shooting at the words, at the way they made him feel.

"Oh, fuck. Yeah." Rig's wet fingers trailed over his mouth and then his lips were taken in a hard, hungry kiss. He whimpered into Rig's kiss, a shudder moving down his spine as his hands moved over hot flesh. Rig was jerking, hips thrusting in rough, uneven motions, tongue pushing into his lips again and again.

Rock rumbled and groaned, moving with them. He squeezed his hands harder, thumbs sliding across the tips of their cocks. Rig shot with a sharp cry, hips bucking up into his hand, heat spraying. As if that was all he'd been waiting for, Rock groaned and shot, too, the scent of all three of them sharp in the air.

"Mmm... 's sweet." Rig snuggled in, reaching for a T-shirt to clean them all up.

"Yeah," grunted Rock. "Working up an appetite."

Dick grinned. "Turkey's not ready for at least another hour, maybe more."

"Oooh... that means we can have a shower." Rig leaned to lick Rock's nipple. "Hors d'oeuvres."

Rock looked down at Rig. "There's nothing horry dovers about my nipples."

Rig groaned, eyes rolling. "We may have to make an exception to the no beating rule for you, Rock..."

"Promises, promises."

"Bitch." Rock laughed, grabbing Rig around the neck and giving him a noogie. Dick just backed away, happy his own head was safe for now. Rig nibbled Rock's pecs, wiggling free. "You'll muss my hair, Rocketman!"

The tease was drawled in the thickest, sweetest voice ever.

"Time to give you a high and tight if you're worried about it getting mussed. You know where the shaver is, kid?"

"Oh, keep me out of this!"

"You always say that until there's sex involved."

"Yeah, well, that's different."

Rock laughed at him. "We haven't done his pubes in awhile -- it's about time that pretty little tat got another airing, isn't it?"

Dick grinned. Rock didn't play fair.

"Perv." Rig was pink, nipples hard as little rocks. "You can't shave my pubes. It's Thanksgiving."

Rock snorted. "Show me the rule where it says we can't shave your pubes because it's Thanksgiving."

"It's under the 'Wholesome Holiday' part." Rig was backing up now, cock bobbing.

Rock snorted again. "Show me one thing about our holiday

that's 'wholesome'."

Rock looked relaxed, sounded relaxed, but you could see in his thigh muscles that he was getting ready to jump Rig.

"Turkey. Dressing. Football. Pumpkin pie." Rig maneuvered around the end table, toward the hall.

"If you don't think those can be perverted, you aren't the slut I know you to be." Rock was up now, taking a single, slow step for every one of Rig's. Dick just watched, licking his lips.

Rig was flushed, hard, eyes shining. "Cranberry sauce is wholesome..."

Those long fingers just brushed through those white curls.

Rock's nostrils flared. "Not smeared all over your ass it isn't."

"No food fights either. Hell, we ought to eat at the table..." Rig licked his lips, shivering a little. Ten to one, there was going to be a break for the bathroom. Twenty to one, Rig wasn't going to make it.

"I'm thinking we should make our own table. After we shave it clean." With that Rock pounced.

Rig squeaked and jumped and didn't even make it two steps before Rock had him, held tight. Rock pushed Rig up against the wall, kissing and groping, pulling Rig's jeans down the rest of the way. Rig wrapped around Rock, moaning into that hungry mouth. Rock broke the kiss to look over and give him a grin. "Come on, kid, we've got some shaving to do. And bring the cranberry sauce."

"No cranberry sauce..." Rig's words were crushed by Rock's mouth, nothing but whimpers left.

Chuckling, he watched Rock manhandle Rig down to the bathroom and then went to grab the cranberry sauce before following -- he wanted to see what Rock had planned.

Rock had Rig sitting on the vanity, kissing their redneck hard every time Rig opened his mouth. Oh, yeah, so cheating. And it was working beautifully. Rig was looking less protestant and more participant.

The hot water was filling the sink bowl, the steam tickling his nose. The clippers and razor and soap were right there, just waiting.

He put down the bowl of cranberry sauce and turned off the water. "Do I get to do the honors?"

He fingered the razor.

Rig opened his mouth and Rock kissed it again, hard enough that Rig bowed into it, prick leaking. Fuck, he was as turned on as Rig was. He stripped quickly, to put them on an even playing field and grabbed a cloth, using it to clean Rig's pubes, hand sliding over Rig's hot cock.

Rig's hips pushed up into his hand, thighs parting wide, giving him access to everything. He moaned, bending to lick the hot, salty drops from the tip of Rig's cock.

Rock growled. "That's not shaving, kid."

"I'll get there," he murmured, tongue pressing into Rig's slit.

"Oh..." Rig shifted, moaning low. "So hot. Fuck."

He moaned again, licking down to Rig's balls. Then he grabbed the clippers and turned them on, the buzz vibrating against his hand.

"Pretty... " The scent was all male and salt and need. All Rig.

"Oh, fuck, this is awesome." It was. The scent and the sounds and the feeling of Rig under his hands. He started cutting Rig's pubes with the clippers, shortening them for the razor. The white curls just melted away, the dark stain of the tattoo just softened by the short hairs left behind. He nuzzled, laughing as the hairs tickled.

Rock growled. "Just do it already."

He shook his head. "I'm having fun."

Rigger chuckled. "Just don't trim anything off, yeah?"

He laughed. "I think I know which bits are important."

"You hear that, Rig? Kid called you bitty."

"You are a punny, punny man, Blue." Rig rolled his eyes, offered him a grin.

He grinned back and took another suck off the top of Rig's cock.

"Oh... Fuck, yeah." Rig leaned back, belly rippling. He lathered the soap in his hands and got Rig all soapy. Slick and wet and warm -- Rig shifted and slid, eyes watching him, wanting. It made him feel like the sexiest man in the world, that look. Well, second sexiest because the sexiest man was the one looking at him.

He started to shave Rig, metal scraping on skin. Rig's fine, soft hair was sheared away, tattoo sharp and so dark over the full prick, balls soft and heavy in his hand.

"Mm... oh fuck, Rig... so sexy..." He leaned in, tracing the tattoo with his tongue.

A soft whimper sounded as his tongue touched that so-soft skin. "Oh..."

Rock chuckled. "You always fight it and then you always get off on it so hard."

One of Rock's fingers started following his tongue. He licked it, licked Rig, enjoying the way their tastes slid together.

"You just like the way I look bare. Always have, even before the ink." Rig's voice was husky as fuck.

"You're the one who gave me the excuse," Rock murmured. Dick licked Rock's finger and then sucked it in, working the pad with his teeth and his tongue until Rock moaned for him.

"Oh, fuck, y'all are so fucking hot. So sexy." Rig shifted again. "Shower now? Bed?"

"You don't want the kid to suck you off?" Rock asked, voice low, needy. Rig whimpered, legs shifting, cock throbbing. "I think that's a yes, kid."

He grinned, letting Rock's finger slide out of his mouth. Tracing the tattoo again, he let the tension build, knew they were all waiting for it.

Rig moaned, brushed his cheek, always willing to need them. "Please, Pretty..."

He looked up at Rig, letting his feelings show in his eyes and then he took that sweet prick in, sucking hard.

"Dick!" Rig jerked and sobbed, come splashing on his tongue. He drank it all down, hands sliding on Rig's thighs. Rig's fingers were trembling on his head. "Oh, damn..."

He nuzzled the soft, smooth flesh around Rig's cock, murmuring happily. The soft moans and touches got louder, Rig shifting. He looked up at Rig, tongue teasing the tip of that fine prick. "Happy Thanksgiving."

Rock chuckled. "Happy fucking Thanksgiving."

"Yeah. Yeah." Rig laughed, so happy, so fucking sexy. "Happy fucking Thanksgiving."

"Now I want to know, Rock. What's the cranberry sauce for?"

"Lube."

"No." Rig shook his head. "No way. You are *not* lubing my ass with Thanksgiving dinner."

He laughed, leaning against Rig. "That's just gross."

"Now, I'm surprised, Rig -- you're the one who's always going on about how fruit's good for you."

"James South, I will beat you with a turkey leg. No cranberry lube." Rig was giggling, belly jerking with each laugh.

He was laughing hard himself, but Rock's mouth wasn't even twitching. "How about as body oil?"

"Blue? Cranberry sauce isn't slick..." Rig gave Rock a huge grin and pushed right into those arms for a kiss. Finally laughing, Rock gave it to him, one big hand grabbing a handful of sauce out of the bowl and smearing it over Rig's chest. Rig 'eeeeewed' and stretched up. "Lick it off. 's only fair!"

"Or we could just have a food fight," Rock suggested, grabbing another handful and getting him full in the face. Dick sputtered, hand automatically going into the sauce to retaliate.

"Y'all! You'll stain the tiles!" Rig squeaked and struggled.

He launched his handful, accidentally catching Rig in the face instead of Rock. "Oh, shit!"

Rig sputtered, blinking. "Oh. Y'all are so dead."

Rock was just laughing and laughing. His second handful got the big guy right in the pie hole. Rig stepped back into the tub, fiddling with the water and grabbing the detachable nozzle.

"Oh, no, he's going to start spraying us. Come on, kid -- attack!" Still laughing, he grabbed a double handful of cranberry sauce, landing one fistful on Rock and the second one on Rig.

"I'm going to make you two eat in the backyard." Rig rinsed himself off and then started spraying. He and Rock fought to get the other into the spray, laughing and slipping, soaking wet and cranberry-y. Rig shook his head. "Man, if I had a camera in here..."

"There'd be pictures of your naked prick wearing that tattoo."

That just made him laugh harder and Dick finally wound up sitting on the tiles, holding his stomach and trying to catch his breath.

Rig rinsed himself off, soaping and cleaning his pubes, chuckling low. "Nutty fucking marines."

"Yeah, I guess we've both got a pair of nuts." Dick rolled his eyes at Rock.

"You've both got a pair, all right." Rig stepped out of the tub and pointed. "You two. In. Clean."

"Hey," complained Rock. "You can't talk to us like we're the mutts."

One white eyebrow arched. "The mutts didn't have a food fight in my bathroom."

"They would if they had thumbs."

While Rock was busy arguing, Dick got into the shower and quickly cleaned up.

"Thumbs?" Rig was chuckling, wiping up the floor with old towels, ass swaying in the breeze.

He could see Rock admiring that ass, could see where it was going. "You better clean off first, Rock, or Rig'll never forgive you."

Rig kept working, wiping the tile down, rinsing the towels out, every time he bent, those tight little sacs swayed a little, the pink, wrinkled line of skin leading up to that tight little hole exposed. He grabbed Rock, tugging the big guy into the shower and then stepping out, intent on Rig's ass. Rig bent deep, cleaning a spot on the floor behind the toilet, those fine, long legs stretched for him.

Rock's growl echoed his own moan and he pushed up against Rig's body, not even taking the time to dry himself off. Fuck, he wanted. Needed.

"Mmm..." Rig rocked back, snuggling right into him, wet or not. God, the man was a slut, just fucking begging for it.

He fumbled with the medicine cabinet door, pulling it open and finding a tube of lube. It didn't take long at all to get his fingers slicked up and two pushed into the tight, grasping heat of Rig's body.

"Mine," growled Rock, coming up behind him.

"I was here first."

Rock just growled, one of the thick fingers sliding in alongside his own as Rock rubbed against him.

"Oh... Y'all's." Rig straightened a little, body going all warm and pink, ass riding their fingers. "More."

He pulled his fingers out and pulled Rock's hand away, pushing in with his cock, gasping as he sank deep.

Rig's body sucked him in, rippled around him, so fucking hot. Those hips tilted, ass working his prick, Rig fucking himself on his cock with low, happy moans. "Oh, Pretty..."

Rock growled behind him and two fingers slid into him, fucking him hard.

"Oh, fuck. Brace yourself, Rig." Moaning, he moved between the sensations, forward into Rig and back onto Rock's fingers. The sound Rigger made was pure fucking bliss, legs parting, arms pushed against the wall. He wrapped one hand around Rig's hip, the other around Rig's hard cock, and when Rock's fingers disappeared and that fat prick spread him wide he was ready.

Rock set the pace, fucking him hard, fucking Rig through him and it was amazing, hard and hot and good. His needy sounds mixed with Rock's deep grunts and Rig's softer moans, making the bathroom echo with the sounds of sex and wanting. He zoned on it, everything else fading away but the sounds and scents and feelings of the three of them. Over and over Rock pounded into him and he pounded into Rig who fucked his hand and it was so fucking good that he wanted to scream.

He could feel Rig's orgasm building, feel it hot and shuddering and rippling around his cock. "Oh, fuck, yeah."

Whimpering, he squeezed Rig's prick harder and moaned as his noises made Rock speed the pace, that fat cock fucking him hard. He did scream as he came, heat pushing out of him and deep into Rig. Heat poured over his fingers, just like the touch of his spunk in that hot little ass brought his lover over the edge. Rock thrust hard and roared, filling him up and there was nothing fucking better than that, was there? Holding two pulsing pricks, his own milked by hot, rippling muscles. Fuck. Good.

Their movements slowed and he rested his cheek on Rig's back, Rock's breath coming quick and hot against his own spine.

"Mmm... it's good." Rig sounded happy, almost drunk with it.

"Oh, yeah." He nodded, hands sliding on Rig's skin.

"Fucking perfect," muttered Rock.

Rig nodded, one hand petting his arm. "Perfect."

He groaned as Rock petted his side and pulled out, leaving him empty. He did the same though, coming out of Rig with a little sound. Rig stretched, back popping. The inside of that sweet thigh was shiny and slick with his come and he knew Rig's belly would be streaked with more spunk. "Back in the shower?"

With a laugh he nodded, grinning as Rock started the water running.

Happy Thanksgiving indeed.

***

Dick groaned.

He was fucking stuffed.

He thought maybe he'd eaten twice his fucking body weight. He'd certainly fucked and been fucked more than twice and he was just boneless, every hunger utterly sated. Rig and Rock were finishing up the dishes and he was pulling a Rock, kind of half-dozing on the couch, not even bothering with the TV, and contemplating whether or not a cookie would make him explode.

He could hear Rig laughing, heard a low rumble from Rock in response. The sounds were good, familiar. Basic and happy.

They wandered in, Rock with a cup of coffee and a plate of fudge and cookies, Rig with two mugs. "Coffee?"

He straightened up with a smile. "Yeah. That sounds just about perfect." The fudge looked perfect too and he bet with a bit of coffee in him he'd be able to manage a piece or two.

Rock sat next to him, nice and close and helped himself to three cookies and two pieces of fudge and Dick had to shake his head. The man had an endless pit for a stomach.

Rig curled up in the armchair, one of his Granny's quilts wrapped around him as he sipped his coffee. "You did good on the food, Pretty. It was damned fine."

"I had a lot of help."

"You're welcome." Rock gave him a wink.

Rigger just grinned, looking at Rock with fondness. "It's hell, being the official taste-tester."

Rock nodded. "Gonna have to work out twice as hard the next few weeks to make up for today."

"Gotta keep that body hard," Dick noted.

Rock nodded again. "Apparently that's how my lovers like it."

And that should have been cheesy and silly, but it made his belly warm, his balls ache and he reached over to stroke Rock's abs. "Yeah."

"God, y'all are something else." Rig's voice was pure drawl, eycs dark.

The warm in his belly ratcheted up a notch and his cock started filling. He nodded. "Yeah, you guys are something else."

Rig chuckled, shook his head. "It's our fourth Thanksgiving together, all three of us. Damn, we're getting old, Blue."

"You might be getting old, I'm getting distinguished."

He laughed and then sobered. "Which makes almost five years since I joined up. Got my papers this week."

"Yeah? You thinking on re-upping?" Rig and Rock shared a

look, then his lovers looked at him, curious.

"I don't know." It was the truth, too. He hadn't joined because he'd wanted to, he'd joined because if he didn't Barker Simpson was going to press charges and he was going to go to jail. But, corny as it sounded, the Corps had made him a man and if he hadn't joined up he'd have never met Rock and Rig. "I thought I'd ask you guys what you thought."

"It's your life, Pretty. Your career. Me and Rock -- we have six more months before we can move, so if they ship you somewhere else, it'll take us time to get to you."

He nodded. "You'd follow me though if I re-upped? Come with me?"

Rock growled a little. "Why the fuck wouldn't we?"

He shrugged, looking over at Rig. Rig tilted his head, a confused little look on his face. "Of course we'd come. We're family. You're ours."

"Okay, then it's not just my life -- if Rock's retiring maybe he doesn't want to be stuck still tied to the military and you're just getting your PA certificate, what if there's no jobs going where I wind up?"

"I'm retiring." Rock's voice was dead sure. "But the Corps is a good place and if you want to stay with it, I'll manage 'being tied to the military'."

Rig got up, pushed himself onto Rock's lap, quilt and all. "Same here. I'm willing to manage whatever, so long as I don't lose my men."

Something inside him eased and he nodded. He got that. He got that absolutely and it was why he'd needed to talk to them before making his decision.

"You going to throw me a party when I get out?" he asked, giving them a grin.

Rock chuckled, but those blue eyes were sharp. "You sure, kid?"

He nodded. "I don't want to stay in the Corps. Nothing personal, Rock, but it's not where I want to be in twenty years. It's not where I belong."

Rig was settled, snuggled and octopussed against Rock. "Where do you belong, Pretty? You going to think about going to school? Or just renting your pretty ass out to us as a houseboy?"

He laughed, hand stroking them. "I like the sound of that last one." He put down his cup and turned so he could use both hands to touch them. "I don't know -- you know? I mean, I joined up because it was that or go to jail for grand theft. I never thought about what I wanted to be when I grew up and now, well, I guess I'm grown up and the only thing I know for sure is that I love you guys." He felt his cheeks go hot as he said the words, but he wouldn't take them back, not for anything.

Rig opened his arms up and pulled him in, kissing him soundly. "Well, then. It looks like we're going to have something to celebrate come Christmastime."

He grinned, bouncing a little. "Yeah."

Rock chuckled, arm coming around his shoulders and he was pulled in for a hard kiss from the big guy.

"We could start celebrating now." He waggled his eyebrows suggestively.

"Horny little bastard." Rig chuckled and pulled him closer. "We ought to start thinking on what we're going to do, if we're going to sell the house, rent it out, what."

"Where are we gonna go?"

"Somewhere without a base," growled Rock, "if the kid's not staying in the Corps. This isn't a place to be a fag. Not if you have a choice."

"Somewhere with a beach." Rig grinned and stroked Rock's belly. "Somewhere with a reasonable winter."

Rock gave Rig a look. "Nothing unreasonable about winter here. You should see Chicago or New York in January."

"Uh. No. Nope. No Yankee country. I don't have to go back to Texas, but can you see me? In New York?"

"You're a people person, Rig, you'd be fine."

He nodded in agreement with Rock. "You would be. That said -- somewhere with a beach and without a snowy, blustery winter? I could so go for that."

"Well, we could go to California. There's work for me there. We sell the house here, it'd be more than enough for a down payment there. We wouldn't be the only gay people in the state." Rig shrugged. "Maybe we ought to take a week in the spring. Go and see."

"Oh, that would be cool!" California sounded like fun.

Rock was frowning. "The house is yours, Rig. Wouldn't be fair to ask you to pay the lion's share."

"This house is ours, Rock." Rig grinned over. "It's not like

I'm going to let y'all up and disappear on me. Beside, you carried me when..." Rig shrugged. "When I needed you to."

Rock nodded. "I've got a nice sum saved up, but it's nothing like what you'll get for the house. Best to be in your name, I guess. You'll have the most cash and the best job."

"I haven't got anything to offer," Dick told them. "A couple thousand in the bank, but not like the two of you."

"Well, I've been thinking on it, Rock. Between the three of us, we could manage to swing a solid, good-sized loan. Buy a little fixer-upper on the beach, get you two that gym you're always going on about. There's a good-sized town south of San Fran. Property's expensive, but we could do it, if we lived tight for a few years, did our own repairs, our own building on."

"I could see myself running a gym," Rock said slowly. "A serious gym, not one of those namby-pamby trendy places."

"Living on the beach would be fucking awesome. Sounds like you've been thinking about this a lot, Rig."

Rig looked down at the floor and bit his lip. "I... yeah. Yeah, I have. I can't stay here in this place. I... I'm ready to go and live somewhere where we don't lie to our friends, where we aren't always watched. Where the three of us can start something together. *Our* house. *Our* home."

"That sounds nice," Dick said. "Hell, it sounds like a fucking dream."

Rock's hand slid beneath Rig's chin, tilted Rig's head up so Rig was looking into those blue eyes. "Whatever you need, Rig -- that's what I want."

"I'll make some plans, then. Work some shit out so we can look." Rig winked over at him. "Or hell, Mr. Free-and-Easy can do it in his spare time and save me the trouble."

Dick grinned. "Oh, shit, I'll have spare time. I can do that -- you guys just let me know when you can get time off."

"I can do it whenever -- Rig's the one on a schedule."

"I get a break at Easter -- ten whole days off. I'm taking my licensing test the second day into that. So that week before Easter? That's good." Rig chuckled. "Man, ten whole days off -- no school, no clinicals. Too cool."

"Oh, and how are we going to fill all that time..."

"Blow jobs. Dozens and dozens of blow jobs."

He laughed, prick jerking hard. "Can we get started early?"

Rock chuckled. "I think that's a wonderful idea."

"Mmm... I'm thinking this is a good plan." Rig licked his lips, hands reaching for them both. "Who's first?"

"Tell you what. You do the kid while I fuck him." Oh, he liked the sound of that. He moaned softly.

"You going to fuck me after, Blue? Let me ride your cock?" Oh, God. Rig was pure sex.

"You fucking know it."

'Course Rock wasn't a slouch in that department either.

And he was the luckiest fucker going.

Chapter Forty

"Rock? I've got the roast out. Is he on his way?" Rigger started the gravy, making sure the butter was on the table. There was a strawberry pie in the fridge, champagne for later. They'd gotten the kid some clothes -- some nice jeans, a suit, four good shirts. Good stuff.

His Pretty wasn't a marine anymore. In six months, his Blue wouldn't be anymore either. Wow. Dick was going to be home.

"There's his ride. He's home," Rock called from the living room. Then his Blue was there, stealing a mouthful of roast.

"Hands off, you." He popped Blue's hand, grinning wide. "Man, we both outrank you now."

Unrepentant, Rock stole another bit of roast. "We hiding under the table and shouting surprise or something?"

"Nah. He knows we're home." He chuckled and whapped again. "You're going to make it ugly and lopsided."

"Nah, I'll even it out," Rock told him, grabbing a bit from the other side.

"Hey, your civilian is home," Dick called out. "Where is everyone?"

"Blue, stop it! Pretty! Dinner's ready!" He grinned and almost bounced. "Welcome home, Mr. Main."

Dick came in just as Rock stole more meat, his Pretty all grins. "What did you call me, Rig?"

"Mr. Main." He moved around the table, right into Dick's arms. "**Mister** Main."

He got a long, warm kiss from Dick. "Mister Main. That's me. Look at this, roast -- all the fixings, too?"

"Of course. And strawberry pie, too." Rig winked. "Assuming Rock hasn't eaten it."

"Not unless you buried it in chocolate pie," Rock told him around more roast.

Dick just hugged him tight. "Thanks, Rig. This was really nice."

"Well, I couldn't make your beer bash, figured we should do something."

"Cool. We should eat before Rock's full." Dick gave him a wink and went to Rock, taking a kiss from their old man.

Rig took the opportunity to grab the roast and get it on the table. "Beer or milk, marines?"

"Beer," Dick and Rock answered together. He nodded, grabbing two bottles, pouring himself some tea.

Dick just looked pleased as punch, pilling his plate high and digging in. Every now and then those riverstone eyes would smile over at him. The food was good, but it was weird, knowing that coming Monday, Rock would be heading on post alone.

They were eating dessert when Dick commented on it. "Feels weird. Like it's not real yet."

"It'll be real enough when you can sleep in, kid."

"You decided if you're going to look for work or just take some time off?"

"I'll look for something. Saunders said they were looking for people over at the gym on Water Road. Figure I'll do something like that while I figure out what I want to do." Dick grinned. "Gotta make sure I have my milk money."

Rig chuckled, scooting his chair out of Rock's reach. "Oh, I was thinking we'd all let Rock support us."

"Oh, I could go for that." Dick squeaked as he caught Rock's whap.

"Oh, yeah. Live on Rock's fortune, grow our hair down to our asses, beards..." Oh, teasing Rock was still his third favorite pastime.

Rock growled. "If I'm picking up the tabs, there'll be no beards. Besides, I thought the two of you were supposed to support me in my old age -- I am retiring in six months."

"No beards? Damn it, there goes my winter fashion look." He chuckled and winked at Dick.

"If I'm keeping you -- I'm keeping you naked, winter or no."

He blushed and grinned, Dick's chuckles making him flush darker. "Perv."

Rock snorted. "Slut."

"Man, you're giving up early tonight." Rig leaned in, kissing Rock hard. "Yours."

"Hey, it's the kid's night -- I didn't want to spend it trading insults."

Dick chuckled. "Does that mean someone's going to call me a slutty perv?"

Rig tilted back to look at Dick, hips rubbing against Blue. "Nah. You get to be a horndog."

Dick laughed and Rock's hand slid along his thigh.

Mmm... that was nice. He rubbed again, leaning farther. "You gonna open your gifts?"

"I get gifts? Cool!" Dick grinned wide, rubbing his hands together. "Are the bows on your cocks?"

"Damn, I wish I'd've thought of that!" Rig winked. "In the front room. There's boxes."

"I should clean up the dishes first." Dick got up and started clearing the table.

"Hey! This is your celebration! Go! Sit. Open. Relax." He took the dishes and headed for the sink. "I'll clean up."

Dick chuckled and bumped hips with him as he went by. "No fun to do all that on my own. I'll help."

"What am I?" asked Rock. "Chopped liver?"

"Nope -- so pick up a dish and pretend to help and we can all go relax and watch me open gifts."

Rig hid his chuckle, just steadily loading the dishwasher. Oh, Rock would either kick the kid's ass or help. Rock grumbled, but picked up the beer bottles and took 'em to recycling, Dick grinning wide as soon as Blue's back was turned. Their eyes met, the laughter good and strong and silent between them. God, he loved his men.

Rock came back and the three of them worked quickly and quietly together, clearing the table and doing dishes. Rock had a couple more mouthfuls of the roast as he put it away and he had to shake his head, wondering if it really tasted better like that leftover off a plate.

"You're going to make yourself sick. Have some broccoli instead." He kept Dick between him and Rock.

Rock snorted. "So this is how it's going to be, is it? The civilians ganging up on the poor beleaguered Marine -- making him clear the table and eat vegetables."

Dick started laughing, nearly dropping the serving platter. He started chuckling, not able to hold it in. Oh. Oh, fuck.

Rock looked extremely put out. "What?"

Dick just petted Blue's arm. "Don't worry, Rock, I won't make a habit of it."

"No, the only habits we're holding onto are the good ones -- morning blow jobs, midnight fucking..."

Rock rumbled happily and Dick moaned softly. "Those are fucking good habits."

Rig nodded and hummed. "Sucking Rock's sweet cock. Riding Dick's long cock..."

His marines got the same looks on their faces, looks that said he should put his money where his mouth was. He licked his lips, eyes hot, fingers unbuttoning his shirt. "Bedroom or sofa?"

"My presents are in the front room."

Rock nodded. "Sofa so we don't have to move after."

"Cool." He headed toward the front room, hips swaying, cock filling with every move. He could feel their eyes on his ass, the heat of them as they sped up to walk right behind him, one at each shoulder, at each ass cheek. "Mmm... my men." He leaned back toward them. "Feel good."

"Thank God some things never change," murmured Dick.

"Never. Gonna need you both for fucking ever." He turned, pushed into a kiss.

Three way kisses were the best, the fucking best. Rock's arms held them altogether, his Pretty working on getting them naked. His hands were busy just touching, stroking every exposed bit of skin.

Dick's sweet noises filled the air, their very own fucking porno soundtrack, Rock's rumbling base running beneath the wanton sounds. He found Dick's nipples, stroking and tugging, petted Rock's belly, just brushing that heavy cock. So good. One of Rock's hands found his ass, squeezing and pulling him and Dick in tighter, closer, rubbing.

"Mmm... yeah." He whimpered, mouth wide. God, they tasted good, hot.

Rock waited until they were naked and then he was pushing them the rest of the way to the sofa. "Want."

Yes. Want." He turned, ass in the air, taking Dick's mouth hard, tongue fucking those pretty lips.

Rock's hands slid over his ass, Dick's found his nipples, fingers tugging on his ring. He rocked, ass pushing against Rock's touch, chest toward Dick's. "You got the lube there, kid?"

One of Dick's hands disappeared and the tube slid along his ribs toward Rock.

"Want you to take my mouth, Pretty. Want to taste you." He

met Dick's eyes, sucking that sweet bottom lip. His Pretty's eyes went hot, needy, a soft noise sounding.

Rock chuckled, hands sliding along his crease. "Slut."

"Fuck, yes. Y'all's." He nodded, encouraging Dick to slide back, feed him that cock. Dick did, hands sliding over his face, cupping his cheeks and guiding him down.

"Mmm... so fucking hard for me." He dropped his mouth over that long, pretty cock, sucking hard. Dick cried out, bucking, a shiver going through his Pretty, as if it were the first time all over again. He reached under Dick, fingers teasing the tight little hole, mouth working hard. Dick whimpered, body starting to move between his mouth and his finger.

"This a private party?" Rock asked, one thick finger sliding into him.

He squeezed tight, moaning loud, encouraging. Wanting. Needing. Now. One finger became two, Rock picking up the rhythm of Dick's movements. Rig whimpered, hips rocking, pushing back, begging for more, lips sucking hard. Dick's noises were getting louder, his Pretty writhing for him.

"He looks like he's enjoying himself," Rock noted. The casual tone would have worked better if that hungry husk hadn't been threaded through Blue's words.

He hummed in response, pulling hard, pushing two fingers deep into his Pretty and curling them. Dick cried out, bucking, hands sliding into his hair and holding him in place. His Pretty's movements got rough, eager.

Rock growled and then that fat prick was pushing into him, stretching him wide. Oh, fuck! Yes! Good! He shuddered, body going all hot. Rock's hands slid up along his sides and then back down, wrapping around his hips. His Blue went absolutely still for a moment and then started to pound into him.

He cried out around Dick's cock, head bobbing faster. Please. Oh, fuck. Good.

They all moved together, writhing and pushing and pulling and thrusting and sucking and there was nothing like it. Nothing at all, ever. Rig looked up along Dick's body, meeting those pretty eyes, letting his lover know how good it was, how happy he was.

Dick slid a hand along his cheek, finger sliding over his lips. "Love you," mouthed his Pretty.

He took that finger in too, nodding, loving with all he was.

Dick whimpered, hips bucking as the kid shot down his throat. Oh, so fucking right. He swallowed, pulling every bit out, moaning around Dick's flesh.

Dick kept moving slowly, sliding that sweet prick in and out of his mouth as Rock went to town on his ass, pounding hard and fast. He balanced himself on one hand, reaching back to pump his prick, matching Rock's rhythm. Rock shifted just a bit, finding his gland and starting to nail it.

His head flew up, eyes wide. "Oh! Oh, sweet fuck!"

Dick smiled at him, eyes soft and happy, hands sliding over his face, prick still working his mouth, even as it softened. It didn't take long, not with electricity sliding right up his spine like a fucking freight train. He squeezed tight, came hard, hips pushing into his own hand.

Rock jerked into him a couple more times, roaring out his pleasure. He cuddled down onto Dick's belly, Rock's weight covering his back. "Good."

"Oh, yeah," murmured Dick.

"Fuck yeah." Rock grunted and pulled out and they all rearranged themselves so they could sprawl out on the sofa together, limbs tangled. He just relaxed, fingers stroking Dick's skin, Rock's muscles, boneless and happy.

They lay there for a few minutes before Dick craned his neck. "Did someone say presents?"

He chuckled and pointed to the stack behind the sofa. "Uh-huh. Can you reach 'em?"

He so wasn't moving.

"I got 'em," growled Rock, making them all shift as he leaned back and grabbed them, tossing them onto the coffee table.

Dick bounced happily. "Too cool!"

Chuckling, he scooted over closer to his Blue, giving Dick room to reach and unwrap. Dick tore into the first box, pulling out the dark charcoal suit. "Oh, wow. Guys, this is... wow."

Rig nodded. Oh, yeah. It would look fine with those eyes. "For interviews and stuff, you know?"

Dick beamed at him and then gave him a hard kiss. "Thanks."

Rock cleared his throat. "They're from me, too."

Grinning, Dick leaned past him to kiss Rock. It made the pit of his belly warm, the heat between his men, the love there that he could fucking see. Dick lingered, pressed against him, eyes closing as Rock's hand held his Pretty's head in place. The kiss ended on a soft moan from Dick. "Thanks," he murmured, smiling at Rock.

Rock grunted. "It's not like I actually shopped for 'em."

Laughing, Dick went for the next gift. The shirts were oohed and aahed over, along with the jeans and shoes and all. Best of all, each one got him a kiss.

"Thanks guys, this is great -- all of it. It sure is going to be weird come Monday though, not to be going in with you, Rock."

"You can ride into the hospital with me, if you want. I work a six hour shift that day and I need the jeep's oil changed and there's a big old mall that you can wander about in." He gave Dick a wink. "Maybe do my last-minute shopping for me?"

"Sounds cool, thanks."

Rock snorted. "Errand boy."

"Yeah, but I bet Rig pays in blow jobs." Dick stuck his tongue out at Rock.

"Hell, yes. I'll even take you out to supper after." He took a kiss, then looked back toward Rock. "You want to meet us at that little steakhouse off the highway after you get off work Monday?"

"Yeah, I like their potatoes."

"Cool." He settled down, snuggling between them. "Gotta put the tree up tomorrow, yeah? Get all Christmassed."

It sucked that they couldn't fly home this year, but he needed some rest, some days of peace and quiet and just them, so Rock had played bad guy and told Momma they were too tight, schedule-wise. Sort of made for a nice thought -- just the three of them, Christmassing together.

"Ho, ho, ho." Rock's voice rumbled and his Pretty chuckled, grabbing the remote before Rock could.

"My day -- remember?"

Rock grunted but seemed unconcerned, one big hand stroking slowly up and down along Rig's arm. Rig hummed and let the touch and the warmth and the quiet murmur of the television send him drifting, floating into dreams where both his men were free.

Chapter Forty One

Rig pulled into the driveway and headed up the stairs, stretching and twisting. He was two hours late for supper -- he'd had a blowout on the highway and had to change the tire. Not a big deal, just an irritation and, of course, he was going to have to kiss Dick's neck and ask him to swap cars tomorrow or drive him in and get new tires put on. Not that kissing Dick's neck was a hardship...

He grinned at himself and opened the door. "Did y'all save any supper back for me?"

"Nope, the kid did real good tonight and I ate it all." Rock looked up from the couch with a grin. "He even made dessert."

Dick rolled his eyes and got up to give him a soft kiss. "I'll get your plate warmed up. You get that tire changed out all right?"

"Yeah. Just a pain in the ass is all." He winked over at Rock, smiling a hello before following Dick into the kitchen so he could wash his hands. Kitchen smelled good -- warm and spicy. "I don't suppose I can get you to have tires put on the old bitch tomorrow? I have three more days in the obstetrics ward and can't miss it."

Dick put a plate full of tamale pie into the microwave and set a small bowl of salad onto a tray. "I can do that for you -- I don't go in until noon. I can't make supper though; I'm working 'til eight with a client. My first so I need to make a good impression, make sure the work out runs smoothly. Beer or soda?"

"Congrats. We have any tea?" He grabbed a glass and headed for the fridge. "How about we all meet at the Golden Coral at nine and then catch a late movie? Either that or I can pick up fried chicken on my way in?"

"Either one works for me, you'd better ask Rock." Dick took the tea out for him and grabbed his plate out of the microwave, his Pretty moving easily in the kitchen, working well with him.

"Hey, Blue? You got plans tomorrow night?" He cupped

Dick's ass, just squeezing and appreciating the whole firm-and-fully-packed aspect of it. Dick wiggled back into his hand and gave him another quick kiss before picking up his tray and bringing it into the front room for him.

"Why?" Rock asked, one eyebrow raised.

"Kid's working 'til eight tomorrow and I figured we could meet somewhere, catch a movie, something. If not, I'll grab fried chicken on my way home." He sat down next to Rock and took a nice, long, hey-you-sexy-bastard-how're-you type of kiss.

Rock growled into his mouth, big hand coming up to hold his head in place and make it an I'm-good-but-missing-the-hell-out-of-you kiss. "My answer depends on what movie we're catching."

"Don't even know what's playing." He groaned a little, way more interested in more kissing than eating.

Dick obviously had different priorities. "Let Rig eat."

Rock grumped but sat back. "I'd rather you just brought home chicken and we'll fuck instead of going to a movie."

"I can so handle that." He picked up his fork and took a bite or two before getting to the good business of touching his men, hands sliding up two muscled thighs. "Did you go see Dick's gym yet?"

"I saw it. Nice enough place if you don't have a home gym. Less... perks." Rock gave him a wink and a grin, spreading his legs.

"Isn't the tamale pie any good?" Dick asked.

"It's perfect." He leaned over to beg another kiss from his Pretty. "You're going to make me fat, you keep feeding me so good."

Dick snorted. "You didn't even have half the plate." His Pretty gave him a kiss though, long and slow and not at all conducive to him eating anymore.

Oh, yum. He shifted and leaned until he was in Rock's arms, Dick sprawled out half on top of him while they kissed. Oh, yeah. That was good. Rock rumbled, the sound vibrating against his back and then his Blue's lips slid against the skin on his neck, just above the collar of his scrubs.

Oh, yeah. Good. He started working off Dick's shirt, moaning low as his men got him nice and hot and bothered. Dick's sweet noises answered him, moans and groans and happy little whimpers. Rock's groans and growls slid over his skin, the thick fingers working up his top.

God, he loved fucking. He lifted his head as Dick's shirt came off, mouth searching for Rock's. Loved sucking and kissing and touching and the whole fucking package.

Rock's mouth came down on his, tongue pushing into his mouth. Dick's mouth attached to one of his nipples, bared by Rock's continued efforts to get him out of his scrubs. Rig cried out, hands holding Dick's head close, lips fastening around Rock's tongue and sucking. Yes. Fuck, yes. More.

Dick and Rock's hands met inside his scrub pants, fighting over his prick. He spread, sucking in his belly to give them room. Their hands tangled together and wrapped around his cock, sliding up and down.

"Mmm..." He panted, rocking and pushing and yeah. Yeah. "Good."

"Yeah." Dick slid down his body, pulling his scrubs off at the same time and then his Pretty's mouth was around him, sucking the tip of his cock as Rock stroked the bottom.

"Oh. Oh, fuck yeah. Damn." He shifted, legs spreading, eyes fucking rolling. "Damn."

"He's speechless. Good job, kid." Rock's hand left his prick, slid down to cup his balls, Rock's free hand moving up to pinch his nipples, tug on the ring.

Dick took him all in, just swallowed him whole.

"Fuck!" He arched up, shaking hard, balls drawing up tight as little rocks.

"That's the idea," murmured Rock.

Dick chuckled around his prick. He stuck his tongue out at Rock, toes fucking curling. Rock chuckled and grabbed his tongue between hot lips, sucking hard, just like Dick was doing to his cock.

Oh. What man could resist that? He groaned and gave it up, coming hard enough to lose his breath. Dick swallowed him down and Rock let his tongue go, but kept their mouths together, kissing him softly, deeply. He relaxed into the caress, moaning into the kiss and smiling up into Rock's eyes.

Rock rumbled softly for him, filling his mouth with the low, happy sounds. Dick finally pulled off, nuzzling his belly, tongue occasionally lapping at his cock.

"Come to bed. Come to bed and let me have my dessert." Lucky, that's what he was. A fucking lucky redneck.

"I'm dessert," Rock said, grinning.

"We both are you greedy asshole." Dick bopped Rock in the arm.

"Mmm... Yeah. I'll do you together. Go get naked on the bed." Boy, his marines could sure move fast when they wanted to. When they had the right motivation.

He headed down the hall after he threw his plate in the kitchen. Mmm. Dessert.

Chapter Forty Two

Rock threw a few things into his duffle and added some stuff for Dick. "Come on, Rabbit, haul ass. We've got to pick the kid up in twenty."

"I'm right behind you." Rig was blinking and moving a little slow, body trying to figure out why it wasn't still sleeping.

"You give him a happy anniversary blow while we're driving down to the beach and then you can go back to sleep." He grinned and gave that sleepy mouth a quick kiss.

"Mmm..." Rig nodded, pushing into his arms. "I can handle that. Do I need my boots?"

"We're going to the beach, Rig -- I seem to remember something about getting yelled at for suggesting sand and your beloved boots in the past." He reached past Rig for his Rabbit's bag. "You need something on your feet though."

He shook the bag. "The gift in here?"

"Oh, right. I got tennies..." Rig bent over in the closet, pretty ass in the air. "Yeah. I think so. Yeah."

He leaned back, taking a good look. "What did we get him?"

"Real pretty watch -- got the date and two 'R's and a 'D' engraved on it."

He grunted. Sounded good, the kid would like that. Rig always knew. "You take much longer and I'm gonna nail your ass to the floor."

Grey eyes looked at him from between those long legs. "Uh... It's gonna be hard to go to the beach with my butt here..."

"Exactly, so let's go before I change my mind and decide we can celebrate at home. In bed."

"Oh! Right." Rig blushed and grinned, slipping on a pair of tennis shoes. "Did you pack lube?"

"Are you kidding? That's all I packed." He grinned and grabbed Rig around the waist, rubbing their cocks together. "Come on, let's go get the kid and get fucking."

Rig laughed and leaned in, gave him a long, wet, fucking

bone-melting kiss. "You do happy really fucking well, Blue."

"I do fucking really happy well, Rabbit." He chuckled and smacked Rig's ass. "Let's go."

They managed to get on the road on time, Rig only running back in twice for this or that. Then they were off, Rig awake and laughing, singing along with the radio and teasing him.

The kid was waiting for him, looking annoyed and then surprised when he saw Rig. "It takes two of you to pick me up?"

Rig nodded and pushed the door open. "You know how Rock gets... all distracted and shit. I'm here to keep him in line."

He reached over and whapped Rig, the kid laughing at them both and settling in the back seat. "You're both in a good mood -- what's up?"

"You, soon." Rig let them get going before the kid got pounced, Rig just tackling him.

Dick gave a soft laugh and then moaned. "Oh, fuck, Rig..."

"No, kid, he's giving you a blow job."

Rig chuckled, the sound of Dick's zipper opening surprisingly loud. "Yep. Tell the kid what he won, Blue. Besides my mouth."

"Won? It's not my birthday..."

Rock chuckled. "We're going to the beach, kid. For three days. Lots of sun, lots of sand, lots of fucking."

Rig's head started bobbing, the low, happy hum making his own cock hard.

Dick was making those fucking porno noises, which also went right to his prick and it made him wonder who's idea it had been to have him drive while everyone else got their rocks off. Oh. Right. That would be him. Damn it.

Rig should have fucking talked him out of it. Dick's noises were fucking sweet and each one made his prick throb.

It didn't take any time before Dick was jerking and coming, throaty cries filling the air. Rig settled down on Dick's legs, breathing hard. "Mmm... fuck, yeah."

He grinned at them in the rear-view mirror. "I had to wake him up to get him out here and promised him a nap once he'd done you."

"Awww, that's sweet Rig. This is 'cause it's been five years, isn't it?" Fucking shit, how the hell had the kid known? It's not like Dick'd had Rig to tell him like he had.

Rig chuckled. "Good call, Pretty. Happy anniversary."

"Yeah, happy anniversary. You guys are lucky I picked up my gifts on the way to work or you'd be left out, kidnapping me like this."

Rig shook his head. "You didn't. I'll be damned."

"What? You thought I'd forget? Like Rock?"

"Hey, I didn't forget! I just didn't think of it."

"He didn't forget, don't let him fool you. He was just iffy on the exact dates." His Rabbit understood him.

The kid laughed and he growled, but Dick's eyes danced, unrepentant, in the rear-view mirror. "So what'd you get us?"

"That would be telling."

"Yes. Tell us what you got us."

The kid just laughed. Fucker.

He watched Rig snuggle up in Dick's arms, wrapping right around the kid. "Mmm... d'you have a good day, Pretty?"

He shook his head. "You're supposed to be pumping him for information, not making nice."

"Oh, right. Sorry." Rig lifted his head, took a long, slow kiss. "So, tell. What did you get Rock?"

Dick laughed, the sound breathless and went back for another kiss. He rolled his eyes and picked up speed. Just a little. Just to get them to the house they'd rented a little quicker.

Rig moaned, hands reaching up to pull the kid closer. Damn. This was going to be the longest drive of his entire fucking life. And it was. He kept glancing back in the rear view, watching as Rig and Dick made out in the back seat like a pair of fucking teenagers.

Dick kept Rig awake, though. Awake and moaning and wanting, never quite pushing his Rabbit over the edge. Had the good old boy whimpering and vibrating. Rig was going to be well-revved by the time they got there. So was he. A good match.

Finally, they pulled up at the rental cottage on the beach, and he didn't even bother with the luggage, just grabbed his men and hauled them up the stairs. The key they'd been given fit just fine and he pushed open the door and then slammed Dick up against the wall.

"Happy fucking anniversary." He took the kid's mouth like he owned it.

Rig's moan almost drowned out the kid's and it wasn't a second before Rig was pushing up his T-shirt, rubbing off against his hip. He got one arm around each of them, never breaking the kiss with Dick, letting the two of them get them all naked.

Rig ended up on his knees, working their jeans down and off, tongue sliding on his thigh, his hip. Oh, yeah, that mouth could make a man forget his own name. He groaned into the kid's mouth, Dick feeding him sweet little sounds in return. Little soft nibbles and licks trailed over his skin, driving him crazy, lips brushing his balls, the curve of his ass. He spread his legs, leaning against Dick.

"Mmm... God, y'all smell so fucking hot." Rig settled behind him, hands spreading him as that hot fucking tongue started working his crease.

"Fuck!"

"What's he doing?" Dick asked, hand sliding behind him, touching where Rig was licking. Dick moaned and grabbed hold of his ass, holding it open for Rig. That freed Rig's hands to circle around, wrap his and Dick's cocks together and start pumping. "Oh, fuck, he's good. He's so fucking good."

He nodded, groaning. The kid was right, Rig was fucking good at this. His hole was licked and kissed and then well and truly fucked, Rig giving it to him hard. Warm hands worked his prick, Rig's face rubbed his ass, Dick was hot against him.

It was hot. The smell of them was fucking primal male sex and he fucking loved it. He pushed back against Rig's face and kissed Dick hard. Rig moaned, thumb rubbing the slit of his prick, then rubbing Dick's, sliding them together. Growling, he pushed back and then forward again. He roared as Dick's fingers caught his nipple ring, the kid tugging on the metal, and came hard.

Rig's forehead was hot on the small of his back. "Fuck, yeah."

Then one of Rig's hands slid away, working Rig's prick while Dick's cock was stroked and tugged.

"Smells like spunk. You two come and it'll be perfect." Dick cried out, pushing into Rig's hand like a madman, coming all over his belly. Rig was shaking, panting against his ass, moving and rocking and moaning low. "Your turn, Rabbit," he growled. "Wanna feel your heat on my legs."

"Oh, fuck. Blue..." It didn't take any more than that and Rig shot for him, keening against his skin.

He fucking purred, letting Dick hold him up, his two men keeping him warm.

Rig's cheek nuzzled his ass. "Nap now? Just 'til supper?"

"Shower first. I'm fucking covered in come."

"Picky, picky." Rig chuckled, nipped his hip.

"Nope. I don't give a shit, but I know a certain redneck who'd want me to clean up before he stole all my heat."

Dick chuckled, eyes dancing and happy.

"Mmm..." Rig grinned against him and stood. "Come on. Water. Kisses. Bed. Nap. Then more fucking and food."

"Yeah. The recipe for a perfect three-day." He put an arm around each of his men and headed in the direction of what he hoped was the shower.

***

Hunger woke him up. Either that or Blue's belly rumbling like it was trying to eat itself to death. Either way. It was dark and they were all wrapped up together and it was time to order pizza.

Rig sat up, leaning over Dick to rummage in the bedside table for a phone book and his watch. 10:30. Cool. Still time for pizza. He found a local chain, ordered a meat lovers and a supreme without green peppers, plus bread sticks and Cokes and a cinnamon dessert thingie. Yum.

By the time he was done, Dick was up, rubbing against his back.

"Mmm... hey, Pretty. Pizza's coming." He stretched, rubbing right back, humming happily.

"Oh, good, Rock's stomach's starting to scare me."

"I heard that," growled Rock.

He chuckled, curling in between them with a happy sigh. "It helps if you think of it as a force of nature, Dick. Sort of like a hurricane or an earthquake."

Rock goosed him for that. His Pretty laughed though, eyes sparkling.

"Mmm... kiss me." He reached up for it, lips parted and hungry, wanting to taste that pleasure. Dick's mouth landed on his, tongue pushing in to taste.

Mmm... Five years he'd tasted this man. Five years and God, Dick had been so fucking green, so young, so nervous and now...

Now Rig trusted him with his soul. Dick's hand slid down his spine, warm and stroking as soft sounds filled his mouth.

"You've got food coming, right?" Rock's voice interrupted them. "Better save it until after. We could do presents while we wait."

"Wait?" He frowned, rubbed his ass back against Rock.

"I don't want to be mid-fuck when your pizza gets here," growled Rock. "And I'm not watching the two of you fuck without being able to participate again."

He winked at Dick, then turned, pushing himself full-up against his Blue, taking a kiss. "No growling, Blue Eyes. I'm not leaving you out of anything."

Rock's arms went around him, pulling him up against the hard body. "Well, good."

"Mmm... yeah. Good." He brought their lips together, snuggling in close. Rock's complaints seemed to be entirely gone, his Blue's mouth opening wide for him. Dick pressed up close behind him, rubbing slowly. He dove into the kiss, determined to drive Rock out of his motherfucking mind.

Rock rumbled and purred for him, but still broke the kiss. "I'm not answering the fucking door with a hard on."

Dick laughed. "I'll get the dammed door, okay?"

"He just wants his present..." Rig grinned wide. "I know him."

"Stuff over sex? Our Rock? Are you sure?"

"Yep. 'Cause he knows he'll get laid after." Rig licked Rock's lips.

"Fucking right."

Dick laughed. "So he wants to have his cake and eat it, too?"

"Fucking right," Rock said again.

"That can't surprise you after five years, Pretty."

"No, but it's still fun to tease the bear."

"Oh, God yes." Rigger nodded, grinning ear to ear. "Love the growling. Love the pouncing even more."

Rock growled and lay back, pouting at them, though Blue'd never admit that's what he was doing. "These better be good presents."

Rig leaned in and licked Rock's jaw. "Go get my bag, Pretty?"

"And yours, kid -- you said you had presents."

Dick got up and got the bags, bringing them over. "Mine

first." He and Rock were each handed a wrapped box.

Rock grinned and tore into his like a little kid. "Oh, wow, awesome." Rock showed him the knife, the blade set in a handle worked into the shape of an eagle's head.

"Oh, look at that!" Rig admired, then unwrapped his own gift, resting against his men.

Rock gave Dick a long kiss. "Thanks, kid -- this is great."

"Cool." Then Dick turned to him, looking eager as he unwrapped a top of the line stethoscope he'd been drooling over for weeks. "I got your name put on it -- see?" Dick pointed out where it had "Doc Rigger" on it. "I know I'm anticipating a bit -- but not really by much."

"Oh!" He took it out, gave it a long look over. "Oh, wow. Oh, I've been lusting after this. Oh, thank you!"

"Yeah, the pages of the catalogue were pretty sticky."

"Bitch." He leaned over for his kiss. "You're too good to your old man."

Dick smiled softly and gave him a long, slow kiss. "Happy Anniversary, Rig, Rock." Dick sat back, that smile remaining. "It means a lot to me, being here with you both. Five years. 'S been wonderful."

"It has been something else, yes sir." He dug out Dick's watch and handed it over. "This is from us."

Dick was almost as bad as Rock, tearing into the gift. "Oh. Oh, Rig, this is... perfect. Thanks, guys."

"Look on the inside, Pretty." He nudged gently.

Dick turned it over, mouth making an o without any noise as he saw the initials. "This is... thank you."

"Yeah." He looked at Rock with a happy smile. "We did good."

Rock nodded and winked. "You did."

"Thanks, Rig. Thanks, Rock. Not for this -- for bringing me home, keeping me."

"Rock brought you home. I just decided to keep you on full-time." He was bouncing a little, happy. "When's the fucking pizza coming? I have two naked men to play with."

As if on cue, there was a knock on the door. Rock chuckled and lay back. "There's money in my wallet."

Rig grinned as Dick threw on some shorts and grabbed Rock's wallet and went to the door. He scooted into Rock's lap, leaning. "I didn't get you anything. Figured we have ours coming in a few years. Fifteen years."

"Didn't we just celebrate ten?"

"Little over two years ago, yeah. Little less than three left 'til the next big one."

Rock chuckled. "Like every day isn't big."

He looked up, nodding. Sometimes? His simple, straightforward, solid man was so fucking right it ached. "You got that shit right, Blue."

Rock grunted and the moment slid away as Dick came back armed with pizza and sodas. His and Rock's belly rumbled in concert and Dick laughed, tossing the boxes on the bed. Rock opened the boxes, grunting and digging into the meat lovers. "Coke? Where's the beer?"

"They don't deliver beer out here, Rock. We'll have to make a run tomorrow, unless you remembered to grab some from home." He snagged a piece of the supreme, nibbling.

"I didn't know it was BYOB," grumped Rock.

"You want me to run out and grab a twelve-pack? There's got to be a store close by."

"No. Come on, Rock, you need a beer more than you need a blow job?" Dick's hand slid on his arm.

"Kid's right, I'll live."

He leaned up and took a quick kiss from both of them and then settled in to eat. He periodically teased one or the other of them, stealing a bite there, offering a bite there. Dick cleared up, tossing them some napkins to clean up.

Rock pulled him back, so he was lying against his Blue. "Don't you two look good enough to eat."

"Mmm... is that an offer, Blue Eyes?" Rig stroked one hand along Rock's belly, lips tracing one strong pec.

"Is that a request?" Rock asked him, purring.

"Am I allowed to make one?" Dick asked, bouncing back onto the bed.

Rock grunted. "Sure."

"A 69? Times three?"

"You want a 207? Kinky..." Rig winked and chuckled.

Dick thumped him. "You know what I mean."

Rock chuckled. "I know I'm not that good at sucking cock, and now I've got both of you wanting it?"

He reached down, circled that fine, thick cock. "You know what I'm wanting..."

Rock purred. "I guess I could suck the kid's cock."

"Such a generous man..." He slid his lips down that sexy six-pack, hunting that heavy prick that was filling for him.

"Anything for my men."

Dick chuckled, shifting him slightly and licking at the tip of his prick.

"Mmm... So fucking sweet." He wasn't sure if he was talking about Rock's prick or Dick's mouth. Either would do.

Dick licked again, head settling on his thigh. His Pretty moaned softly, telling him Rock had started sucking. Rig settled, got comfortable and started dropping hot, sucking kisses to the tip of his Blue's cock, tongue flicking the slit, searching for that flavor. Rock groaned for him, prick jerking. Dick's breath was warm on his own cock, tongue hot. They started moving, rocking together, licks and kisses becoming long, hard sucks and hungry pulls.

It was the perfect circle... triangle. Whatever, it was fucking good.

It felt so good, head and hips moving, fingers rolling heavy balls, feeling Dick's moans deep in the pit of his belly. Rock's prick was a familiar feeling in his mouth, the taste as familiar as coffee and more necessary. He took Rock in deep, taking that fat cock down to the root and pulling hard.

He could feel the muscles in Rock's belly ripple, the balls in his hand draw up. Rock's moan was muffled, translated into one from Dick as his Pretty went all the way down on him. His groan was muffled, low and needy and he sucked with all he had, needing that flavor, needing to come.

Dick's hand wrapped around his hip, one finger teasing along his crease. Rig jerked and shot, hips pumping as pleasure tingled through him. It was as if he'd set off a chain reaction, Dick swallowing him down and shaking and a moment later, Rock's rich taste flooded his mouth.

He took it all, humming and licking and so fucking happy. Loved them. Loved them both.

Chapter Forty Three

Rock pulled into the driveway, grunting when he saw Rig's jeep. Hallefuckingluiah. Maybe he'd get to see his fucking redneck for more than just a few minutes without a fucking book attached now that Rig had done with his NANCE or PANCE or whatever the fuck the damned certification exam was called.

He rolled his shoulder as he went up the stairs, wincing at the pull. He was getting fucking old. Retiring was looking better and better the closer it came. Of course a good long session in bed with a pair of younger men would do him wonders...

He went in the door, petting the damn dogs as they rushed him. He could hear the shower running, hear Rig singing along with some redneck song. Fucking A. Singing meant shit had gone well and that the evening was looking up and up and up. Not to mention the fact that it meant his Rabbit was already naked.

He stripped down, tossing his stuff at the washing machine. By the time he was slipping into the shower with Rig, he was hard. He growled softly, hands reaching out for his Rabbit. "Hey there, stranger."

"Mmm... hey there, Blue." Rig stretched under his touch and pushed right into his arms, all hot and wet and slick and hard as stone. "I was just thinking on you."

He purred. "I can see that." One arm went around Rig to grab that fine ass, the other wrapped around Rig's cock, just holding it in his hand, reacquainting himself with the heat and the weight of it.

Rig spread his thighs a little, tight ass snuggling into his hand. "I'll give you until forever to stop that."

"Oh, you will, will you?" He chuckled, thumb sliding across the slit.

"Uh-huh." Rig bit his bottom lip and then gasped, head falling back a little. Pure fucking sex and his Rabbit just begged for it, wanted him. Growling, he leaned in to lick the water from Rig's neck, tugging on the hot prick again and again. Rig's hands were on his head, holding him close, those hips pushing into his touch over and over again. "Oh. Oh, fuck. Not gonna fucking last."

"Yeah? You gonna come for me, Rabbit? Gonna give it up for me?"

"Oh. Oh, fuck. Kiss me. Please, Blue. Now." Rig pulled his head up, grey eyes wide and wild and hungry as fuck.

He took Rig's mouth, spread those red lips and pushed his tongue in, fucking owning it. Rig shot at the first touch of his tongue, spunk spraying against his fingers, his Rabbit shuddering in his arms before just sinking into their kiss, going all boneless against him.

He gathered Rig in close, the skinny body feeling so good against him. They slid together, Rig still damned hard against his hip. The kiss grew deeper and deeper still, his Rabbit blowing his mind, pouring so much into that kiss that it made him breathless. He pushed Rig up against the tiles, rubbing his cock against that skinny belly. Rig climbed his body, legs around his waist, hands on his shoulders. No hesitation, no worry -- just trust and need and pure want wrapped right around him.

He got hold of the soap, slicking up his fingers and pushing two into Rig's body. Low hums pushed into his mouth, Rig riding his fingers, hole hungry for him, so fucking tight and hot. He didn't want to wait, couldn't and he pulled his fingers out, prick pushing at that sweet hole.

"Yeah..." The word was breathed against his lips, Rig pulling him right in, holding him tight and squeezing.

"Fuck. Rig." He started to fuck Rig, pushing his Rabbit up against the tile over and over again.

"Yeah, Blue. Need this. Need you. So fucking good."

"For fucking ever, Rabbit." For fucking ever. He took Rig's mouth, fucking it just the same as he fucked that sweet, tight ass. Fuck, he could taste it -- the happiness and pleasure just pouring from Rig, the constant stress and tension from the last few years suddenly eased.

"You gonna come on my cock, Rig?" he asked, moving hard and fast. "Gonna pull me over with you?"

"Fuck, yes. Want to feel you shoot, so fucking hot." Rig shifted, jerked a little. "Oh, sweet fuck. Right there. Right fucking there."

Growling, he kept right on pushing into Rig's body, the

sensations sliding along his spine. Rig's orgasm started, that fine body rippling around his prick, pulling hard and milking him, his Rabbit blushing dark as spunk spilled against him. Rig's body worked his cock, pulling the come right out of his balls and he roared out Rig's name.

"Oh. Good. So fucking good." Rig nuzzled his throat, the fucking smile hot on his skin.

"Yeah. Fucking, fucking good." He didn't let Rig go, didn't put his redneck down. Seemed to work just fine for Rig, too, his Rabbit just staying close, holding on tight. "Gonna stay here all fucking night. All fucking weekend."

"I can live with that, Blue. Yes, sir." Rig kissed his jaw, humming happily. It sure felt good knowing Rig didn't have anywhere to be, anything to be doing and he held his Rabbit up against the tiles until the water began to cool.

"Come to bed. We'll order food later after the kid comes home. Come to bed." Rig nuzzled and licked, ass tightening on his prick. He groaned and nodded and regretfully pulled out of Rig. He leaned their foreheads together and gave Rig a kiss before turning off the water. Rig smiled over at him, eyes shining. "I did it. We made it all the way through."

"You did good, Rabbit. I'm proud of you." His voice was gruff as he dried Rig off, patting him down with the towel.

"Thank you." Rig pushed into his arms. "It feels fucking amazing."

"You feel fucking amazing." He grinned down at Rig. The truth was he was proud of Rig. He was also happy the stress was all but over; the last three years had been fucking hard.

They all deserved a celebration, a break.

"Come to bed. I've got hours and hours and hours to worship that beautiful fucking body of yours."

"Fucking A. I'll follow you," he said, wagging his eyebrows and then watching that fine ass move.

Rig pinked right up, but took his sweet fucking time, fucking sashaying to their bedroom, hips fucking swaying. He was hard and growling, balls just aching even though he'd already come. The growl made Rig shiver, made the motions more sultry, more sensual. He did it again, loving the effect he had on his Rabbit.

Rig moaned, heat spreading up the long spine. "Oh... Oh, Blue."

"Fuck, but you're easy, Rig." It wasn't a complaint.

Rig turned and gave him a smile. "I just know what I need and don't have a problem letting y'all know it, too."

He nodded, pushing Rig back onto the bed and climbing on up, pressing Rig down into the bed. "It wasn't a complaint."

"I know." Rig grinned and stretched beneath him. "I know what those sound like, Blue."

He snorted and pressed down hard with his hips. "Are you saying I complain a lot?"

"Nope. I'm saying I work really hard to make sure you don't have to." Rig snuggled up into him.

He purred, bending to kiss Rig softly. Rig opened up to him, the kiss sweet and hot, pulling his breath right out of him. He lost himself in the kiss, enough that when a third hand slid along his back it made him jump.

"It's just me." Dick chuckled and kissed one ass cheek.

"Mmm... hey, Pretty. Happy fucking Friday." Rig grinned, nose brushing his lips.

"Hey Rig. Rock. You two look amazing together." Dick licked a line down his spine, winding up at his ass again, teasing his crease.

Rig grinned. "Oh, someone's being naughty." Fuck, but that sounded perverse in that drawl.

"He is," he growled. "Kid's got a wicked tongue. Learned from the best." He groaned as that tongue slid against his hole.

"Mmmm..." Rig's hands slid down his sides, spreading his cheeks wide. "So fucking sexy."

"Oh, fuck."

Dick echoed the words and licked at his cheeks, Rig's fingers, and then started to push that hot tongue into his hole. Rig was kissing his face, his jaw, his lips. Low words were filling the air, Rig moaning and whispering and fucking promising him the world. He rubbed against Rig, prick sliding against matching heat as shudders rocked him, Dick's tongue fucking him now, making him wet.

"So fucking hot. Oh, fuck, Pretty. You should see his eyes..." Rig took his mouth, tongue pushing deep. The kid moaned and whimpered, sweet sounds vibrating against him, in him as Dick made him fucking shake. Rig moaned, head dipping to wrap lips around his nipple, tugging on the ring.

"Oh, fuck!" He groaned, jerking, moving between the two fucking awesome sensations. The pulls grew firmer, pleasure sparking through him, bright and hot. He slid his cock along Rig's skin, a long, low groan pulled out of him. Shit, he was fucking flying.

Rig scooted down, pulling him and Dick up, slowly working down until that mouth reached his cock, two hot bodies nestled together between his legs.

He growled, head resting in his hands on the bed, hips moving him between the two most fucking perfect mouths he'd ever fucking known. And they loved it -- he could hear them, feel the vibrations of their moans and cries, the heat and pressure of their mouths eating him up. He started to fuck Rig's mouth hard, feeling his balls tighten up, feeling the fucking pleasure barreling down on him like a tank. Hot. Tight. Fucking good. They worked him faster, the rhythm driving him hard. He had no idea how long it went on for -- he got lost in it, lost in the sensations, in them.

When he came, it was almost a surprise, the pleasure suddenly too much for his body to bear and he roared, everything disappearing but the feeling of his spunk shooting out his cock and the lightning going up his spine from his ass. When shit came back into focus, he was on his side, Dick pressed along his spine, Rig licking his prick with a soft tongue.

He groaned softly, hand in Rig's hair. "You wanting, kid?"

He got a soft kiss to the back of his neck. "I'm good."

Rig let his cock slide free, then moved into his arms to snuggle, relaxed and warm, happy little sounds in the air. He grunted, holding onto his Rabbit, Dick's hand sliding around him and grabbing hold of Rig's hip.

"You know what's really great about this," Dick murmured. "None of us have anywhere to be, or anything we have to do before Monday morning."

"Mm-hmm. Going to stay right here all fucking weekend." Rig kissed his jaw. "Right here."

He grunted. Yeah, he could fucking live with that. It felt dammed fucking good.

Not even his shoulder was bothering him anymore.

He wondered if Rig would let them eat in bed.

Chapter Forty Four

Dick waited at the airport, looking for Momma and Robert. Rig's graduation ceremony was in two days and Momma had been planning the party for weeks, calling him and Rock, sending them on errand after errand. He'd never seen anyone organize anything so efficiently -- not even Rig.

Their plane had already landed and he craned his neck, trying to see around the corner, to see if they were coming yet. What he saw stunned him -- Deuce was tall. Like really, really tall. Momma looked sort of like a gnome beside him. A little Texan gnome.

God, he was glad no one could read his mind.

He waved to them, smiling as Momma's face lit up, making him feel really good.

"Richard! Son! Howdy!" Momma bustled right over and kissed him soundly. "Oh, Lord, it's good to see your face! I'm so sorry I couldn't be here for your mustering-out party. Alexander said y'all had a good time."

"Yeah, it was great. 's been good, being out. But you had to save coming down for this -- Rig graduating." He gave Deuce a hug, laughing. "I can't believe how much you've grown! Even Rock's going to have to look up to you!"

"Yup. Was almost too tall to get in, but I leave for Basic the first of August. Ma-maw says she's had a boy in the service for a while now, so she's used to it." The boy's voice was deep and the drawl was heavy and Rig was just going to shit.

"Well, it's a good thing I've got Rock's truck -- you'd never fit in the little tin can I've got. Come on, let's get home and let them get a look at you." He offered Momma his arm and let Robert carry the bags.

"So, how's he doing? He sounds good on the phone, rested, happy. I missed y'all at Christmas, the girls missed you, too..." Man, five whole minutes before the guilt. Momma was **good**.

"We would have come if we could have, Momma -- and you

know having a couple of days at home with nothing to do did Rig good. In fact he's doing really well -- he finished up his exams a bit ago and has just had the clinicals. I think he's really excited about the move. He told you he had a place already, didn't he? They snapped him right up."

"Yes. California! He keeps going on about y'all having a little fixer-upper on the beach proper and his place and his practice." Momma laughed, shook her head. "He's excited, son, mark my words. Nervous, too, I reckon."

He nodded. "We all are. I can't wait to go though -- I've kind of been in a holding pattern since Christmas. Rock finished up last week." He chuckled. Rock wasn't complaining about being retired, not one bit. The big guy was sleeping in and relaxing, taking it easy.

"Is he driving Alexander insane yet?" Momma's eyes twinkled. "Jeremy damned near killed me when he retired -- hanging about and being underfoot."

"No yet, but Rig's been wrapping up his clinicals, so he's not been home that much. Today's his last official day."

They got to the truck and he helped Momma get in, Deuce sitting next to her, and then climbed in behind the wheel. "Of course Rig's been cleaning like crazy every spare moment he's had, which makes Rock nuts. I think he's trying to impress you." He gave Momma a wink.

"I would hope so. I raised him right." She chuckled, patting his shoulder. "Did he wash the curtains?"

Deuce blinked. "Y'all have curtains?"

"Of course we have curtains, we're not Neanderthals." He waited a beat and then added. "Well, two out of three anyway."

Momma just cackled, clapping and laughing hard. "Oh. I tell you what -- Jim'll have your head he hears that."

"Hey, I didn't specify which two. Plausible deniability -- that's what it's all about." He grinned, pleased as punch at making her laugh. They chatted during the rest of the drive, Deuce fairly quiet, letting Momma do the talking.

"Rig should be home by now, Rock, too -- he was running those last minute errands for you, Momma." He grinned as he saw Rig's jeep and his little car in the driveway. "Yep, and I'll bet Rig's really eager to see you both."

The door swung open before he even killed the engine, Rig and Grimmy and Lucy hitting the front yard. "Momma! You're here!"

Rigger was looking good -- tan and healthy, hair a little too long, moustache still avoiding Rock's hand, happy. Still gave him a thrill to see Rig, made his cock take notice, even with Momma sitting in the car with him. Oh, he wasn't sporting big wood or anything, just happy to see Rig. And Rock, who was coming out, too.

He watched Rig and Rock closely, just waiting for their reaction to Deuce. Deuce climbed out of the pickup and Rig stopped short, eyes huge, mouth open. "Good lord and butter. Dick. Are you picking up strangers in the damned airport?"

He laughed, helping Momma out. "Don't you recognize your own nephew? Shame on you."

"Uncle Alex. Jimmy." Deuce grinned and held out his hand. "Y'all shouldn't look so surprised. Ma-maw sent pictures."

"Yeah, but... Damn. Damn, boy. You're all grown." Rig shook Deuce's hand and then tugged him in for a hug. Rock took a hug too, and did it ever look weird, seeing the big guy... not.

Momma was all over Rig, pulling him down into her arms and holding him. Patting and hugging and crying and -- Momming.

Rock had the suitcases and was trying to herd everyone inside. "Dick, get the damned dogs in, before the neighbors complain about the barking."

Grinning, knowing Rock really meant get the people in before it gets any more emotional, Dick did as he'd been told, the others trailing him slowly.

Momma didn't look anywhere near ready to let her boy go, so Rig brought her over to the sofa. "We're going to give you the guest room, Momma. Deuce? Your stuff can go in the workout room and you can sleep out here on the sofa. It'll be long enough."

"Julie and her brood don't get in until tomorrow and they're staying at a hotel," Rock noted. "Anyone want something to drink? Or eat? It's not your cooking, Momma, but Rig and Dick do a pretty good job."

"There's damning with faint praise." Rig rolled his eyes and patted Momma's hand. "There's a roast in the oven for supper. I thought we'd all go out to eat tomorrow. There's plenty of sandwich stuff in the fridge, though, if y'all want."

Deuce headed toward the kitchen almost immediately,

stomach audibly rumbling. That set them all chuckling and Rock shook his head. "What do you put in his feed, Momma? That boy is big."

"His momma comes from big people and Bobby's daddy? Was damned near seven foot tall." Momma grinned at Rock and winked devilishly. "It's no wonder he and I didn't stay together. The logistics just sucked."

"Momma!" Rig shook his head. "Listen to you!"

Dick went beet red, but he was laughing a little. Rock on the other hand was laughing right along with Momma. Dick tried to imagine his mother joking like that, but just couldn't. Well, he couldn't even see her coming to visit him and his gay lovers under any circumstances. Rig was lucky. And so was he, because Momma sure treated him like one of her own.

"So, I'll need to do some shopping, son. And I'll need to see this place y'all rented to hold the party in. And do y'all have something for the girls to do here tomorrow -- those young'uns need to be occupied..." Momma was off and running, questions and errands and stuff just pouring out into Rig's lap. And didn't he and Rig and Rock just scramble to get things done for her? Just as it should be.

***

Good grief. Rock knew they didn't actually take up the Golden Keg's entire dining room, but they did take up an awful lot of room, with who knows how many tables put together. Julie, Hank and the girls were all there, along with Louis and Jacob, a couple of the girls who'd worked with Rigger, Momma and Deuce, him, Rig and Dick. It was going to cost him his retirement bonus just to pay for it. Of course, them eating here meant Rig and his Momma were both relaxing instead of cooking, so he figured it was worth it in the end.

Seating arrangements were a nightmare, with the girls all calling dibs on their favorite uncle and Rock finally just sat down and picked up his menu. They could figure it out on their own -- he was hungry. Maddie was already in Rig's lap, chattering happily and drawing on her placemat, with Rachel snagging the chair beside him, looking near to grown. God, when did she go from pudgy cheeks and pigtail to acne and braces?

Sissy ended up on his other side, leaning against his arm and grinning. "Hey, old man. You really moving to California?"

"Now, how come you get to call me old man, but if I try to call you an old woman, I'll get thumped for it?"

"Because I'm not old, and I'm a sensitive, delicate flower, and if you thump me my husband will break his boot off in your ass." She grinned up at him, grey eyes twinkling.

He chuckled. "I don't know, maybe I'll get the giant here to protect me." He nodded at Deuce who was sitting on the other side of Rachel. "But yeah, we're really moving to California."

"Are you going to live on a beach? Can me and Lisa come in the summertime? Momma says there's lots of cute boys on the beach." Rachel pinked up, but didn't look away, fingers playing with her silverware.

He chuckled. He'd been waiting for this, knew that part of the deal of living in California, on a beach no less, was going to mean visits from relatives. Of course Rig always looked happy when his family was around and, though he'd not admit it to anyone, Rock himself had a soft spot for Sissy's girls. "I daresay your Momma knows what she's talking about when it comes to cute boys. And of course you and Lisa can come -- there's a real nice guest bedroom in the house we bought."

"Yeah?" Sissy ordered a beer and then looked back at him. "Alex said y'all found a place -- a little bigger than what you have now, but needing some work. You like it?"

"It'll do."

"Rock's not overly fond of change," Dick teased from across the table.

He glared at the kid, but Dick grinned unrepentantly. "I'm sure it'll be great once we're in it."

"It's sweet, Sissy. Wrap around porch in the front. Gonna put a deck on the back. One huge bedroom and two others. The kitchen window looks out to the ocean." Rig was almost bouncing -- his Rabbit had fallen in love with the house and its private postage stamp of beach. The house was in need of serious work -- plumbing, floors, roof -- but it didn't matter. Rig wanted it, and now? It was theirs.

The waitress came by then and he ordered himself a nice big steak, baked potato with sour cream and a beer before helping himself to the rolls she'd left on the table. Deuce was right there with him and he grinned at the kid, pleased he wasn't the only one with the hollow leg. In fact, he had a hunch Deuce could eat him under the table now.

Rig and Maddie were sharing a roll, laughing together. With their heads side-by-side, he could tell how grey his Rabbit had gotten over the last few years. Something inside him clenched. He couldn't fucking wait to get out of this town. Rig laughed again and the sound eased him, the anger fading as quickly as it had come.

They made small talk as they waited for their meals to come and then they were busy eating and he was glad he wasn't in a race with Deuce; he had nothing on the kid. Retiring, slowing down, maybe he was getting old.

Right then, Rig looked up, grey eyes happy and warm, smiling right at him and suddenly all he felt was the center of that man's world. Fuck, there was nothing like it. Nothing. And in a few days? They would be on the other side of the fucking country -- all three of them. I n a house in their names. Out of the closet.

Out.

No more fucking hiding or worrying about people beating you to death for who you loved. Didn't seem real.

"He looks so happy." Sissy looked up at him, patted his knee. "You did it. You healed him up. None of us will ever forget that, Jim."

He grunted. "He healed himself up, Julie. All I did was refuse to let him go."

"Yeah, right. Whatever. He still looks happy and I'm blaming you. So, tell me. What did you get him for a graduation present?"

"Oh, shit. I knew I'd forgotten something." He kept his face serious. "What did you get him -- I could give you some money and you could add my name to the card."

"Oh, don't you even go there!" Sissy leaned closer. "Daddy left me his watch and... Well, I can't wear it and thought he'd like it."

"Oh, he'll like that, Julie. He'll like it a lot. Kid and I got him one of those medical bags. All kitted out, well, except for the stethoscope, Dick already gave him that."

He gave her a smile and a wink. "I didn't forget."

"I didn't think you would." She punched his arm and chuckled. "What did he get you for your retirement gift?"

He waggled his eyebrows. "That would be kissing and telling and I don't do that."

"Jim! You old dog!" Julie blushed and shook her head. "You're telling me you retire and that's all you got?"

"I think you're underestimating the power of your brother's... kisses." Oh, it was fun to tease her. Of course he'd forgotten about Rachel on his other side who was about twenty shades of red.

Julie was rolling, laughing hard enough that Hank was shaking his head and Rig was arching his eyebrows. "So, share, Sissy. What's the joke?"

She looked right at Rig. "Nothing. Nothing. Rock was just telling me about his retirement present."

Rig turned a bright, hot red, eyes going wide. Oh, that was worth the price of admission right there and he started to chuckle. Dick kicked him under the table, but he was unrepentant. Rig shook his head, cheeks just blazing. "Y'all... Y'all are something else."

"Yeah, well, you just wait until the kids go to bed. I want details." God, Julie had balls.

"Julia!"

"Sissy!"

"Ju-lie!"

"Mo-ther!"

He just laughed. If he'd been into women, he figured Julie'd be the kind he'd want. Of course, he was pretty fucking happy with the Roberts he had. Luckily dessert was served about then and everyone was off the hook. Including him, as he was pretty sure that one would have come back 'round to him.

He decided to turn to safer waters. "So Deuce, you've signed up?"

"Yes, sir. I go to Basic in August. I'm just under the height limit." Deuce grinned at him. "Talked to all the recruiters, got all the info before I signed the papers."

"Good. You go into this with both eyes open. You sign up for five?" The kid looked proud, happy, excited. Momma'd done a really good job with Deuce.

"I did. I've been working on practicing the basic skills." Deuce grinned. "I want to get President's guard duty, if I can."

"You've got the height for it. You just keep your nose clean and work hard."

"I will, Uncle Jimmy. You know I will." Deuce nodded at him. "I did real good on the DLAB and I was in ROTC all through high school. I did all the things you told me."

"Well, that'll start you as an E-3. Now if you want to be in the President's Guard they're going to want to know you're serious, and if you're doing really well, they may want you to extend early, but you wait until you've put at least three years in. You make sure this is what you want to do for the next twenty years before you give them that, yeah?"

"You sound like Ma-maw. I won't extend before talking to y'all, before thinking on it hard." The kid gave Momma a quick look. "I know I'm still young and that things happen. I know."

Rig nodded. "We trust you, Deuce. We just want the best for you -- heart and soul."

Rock nodded. Rig was right. What's more, Deuce was more like Dick than him and hiding who he was, who he loved, was more likely to grate more on Deuce than it had on him.

"You'll be fine," Dick put in. "If I could make it through, you sure can."

Deuce grinned. "I just want to make everybody proud."

Momma's voice cut across the table. "You've done that, Robert. You've always done that. You're a good boy."

"You can't get a better endorsement than that." He reached around Rachel to clap Deuce on the back. "You're going to make one hell of a marine, Robert."

"Thanks, Uncle Jimmy."

"Well, he's had a sterling example to mold himself after." Rig's voice was proud, eyes shining at him. He had nothing but smiles for his Rabbit. He'd have had more for Rig, but there was too much family around. He settled for letting Rig know with his eyes what he wanted and sitting back to drink his coffee once Rig had blushed again.

Thank God, they weren't all staying at the house.

***

The four of them were sitting around the kitchen table, helping Momma fill cherry tomatoes with cream cheese for the party. Deuce had gone to the hotel with the other kids so he could swim and Hank had made Sissy go too, saving them all from her constant teasing. Little perv.

Rig chuckled and grinned, reaching out to stroke his men with his foot -- first Dick, then Rock.

Dick blushed and fumbled with his tomato, but Rock just grinned at him.

"I think we're going to be ready in plenty of time for the party. You arranged for a place to dance and music, Jim?" Momma was managing twice the appetizers they were, little fingers flying.

"Yes, ma'am. I'd be in trouble if I hadn't, wouldn't I?" Rock grinned, not looking particularly concerned.

"You know it." Momma chuckled and nodded. "You follow orders pretty well, son. Not as well as Richard, but pretty well."

Rock laughed. "Well, ma'am, I followed orders without question for twenty years of my life, I suppose I'm due a little slack."

"Only a little." Rigger chuckled and finished stuffing. "Thanks for all your work, Momma. The party's going to be great."

"Yeah, Momma, it's going to be great thanks to you."

Rock nodded. "I've known plenty a CO who could take lessons from you."

"Well, I've had lots of time to plan. Lots of thinking on it." Momma started gathering the tomatoes, arranging them on trays. "I want to give y'all your gift tonight, while it's just us. It's for all three of y'all."

He stood up and took the tray from Momma, to put it in the fridge. "You didn't have to get us anything, Momma. We have everything we need."

She wiped off her hands and nodded, reaching for her purse. "I know. Here." She handed Rock an envelope. "This is for all y'all."

"You didn't have to do this, Momma. Your being here is enough." Rock opened the envelope and blinked. "Momma, we can't take this."

Rig frowned, headed across the room to look over Rock's shoulder. A check. A check for $10,000.

$10,000.

"Momma?"

She met his eyes. "I sold the back thirty acres. It was time. I can't work it and Deuce is leaving. Your daddy and me paid for Bobby's wedding, for Julia's. It's fair. Use it to fix your house."

Dick went over to Momma and wrapped her in a big hug. "Thank you, Momma. For the money, but mostly for taking me and Rock into your heart like we were one of your own."

Rig was still just blinking, watching Momma hug Dick. Sold the land? Ten thousand dollars?

"The kid's right," Rock's voice was gruff, arm nudging him. His Blue went over to Momma and wrapped her in a hug. "A man couldn't ask for a better mother-in-law."

"You're good men, both of you. I'm proud of you, proud to call you my own." Momma met his eyes. "Almost as proud as I am of the man who loves you."

Rig shook his head. "Momma, you need..."

"I have what I need. So do you. Just take it, baby. It's y'all's."

"Your Momma knows if she ever needs anything she can come to us, Rig. Just say thank you and be glad she's your Momma. You got one of the good ones." It was a long speech for Rock and about as emotional as he knew his Blue could stand.

"I'm always glad she's my momma." He went over and just held on tight, burying his face in her hair. "Never needed anything for that."

Rock patted her shoulder. "We'll go turn in, give you two some time..."

Dick kissed her cheek and slid a hand along his back and then they were gone.

"I did it, Momma. I made it." He wasn't sure exactly what specific 'it' he was talking about for sure. Maybe all of them.

"I know, baby. I'm so proud of you. It's been a hard row to hoe and you did it." Momma sniffled, held him close. "Your daddy would be busting his buttons. He should be here."

"Yeah. Yeah, Momma." He nodded, blinking back tears. "I can't wait for you to see the new house. It's so pretty -- right on the water, nice sized rooms."

"I can't wait. You got a buyer for this place yet?"

"Yeah, we start packing right after y'all leave." He chuckled. "I start work in two months. Want to get the house done first."

"You mad about me selling the land, baby?"

Rig winced. She would ask. Damn it. "I... No, Momma. Not mad. I just... I guess I gotta accept the fact that I'm not going to go back and be what Daddy raised me to be."

"Oh, honey. You're everything your daddy raised you to be. You're strong and smart and clever and a damned good man.

Damn good." Tear-filled eyes met his, flashing and sure and more familiar than anything. "Don't you believe for a second that your daddy wasn't proud. You were his boy. He thought you walked on water."

There just wasn't anything to say on that. Nothing at all. So they didn't. They washed dishes and swept the floor and chatted and let the dogs out and then it was time for bed. "What time do you need me up, Momma?"

"Whenever. Julie and Hank will be here at 10. You'll be up."

Rig nodded. "Yeah. I will."

He took one last hug. "Night, Momma. I love you."

"Love you, baby. See you in the morning."

He made sure she had clean towels and then headed into his bedroom, looking for his men.

Chapter Forty Five

The graduation ceremony had been... well, a graduation ceremony, the highlight being when not only twenty odd family members and friends got up and cheered Rig across the stage, but his classmates did, too. That was his redneck, ever popular. It was because Rig cared about people, it was what was going to make the man a good doctor. And that was why the dance hall was packed. Everyone wanted to give Rig a hug and a kiss and a good luck to you.

Sure, the party was for his retirement as well as Rig's graduation, but it was his redneck who was the center of attention. And that was just fine by him. He had himself a beer, a spot next to the munchies and a rotating harem of little blonde girls all wanting to find Uncle Jimmy the choicest treats. Lisa was ahead because she'd figured out early on he didn't like vegetables. He thought maybe she was what Rig would call a kindred spirit because he couldn't remember ever seeing her put something green in her mouth.

Dick came over, grinning at him. "So this is where you're hiding."

"I'm not hiding; I'm making inroads into the buffet table. With a little help," he noted as Lisa brought him another cocktail wiener.

Sissy came bouncing up, all giggles and flushed cheeks. There had been a huge bout of laughter when she and Rig had seen each other -- both in jeans and dove grey shirts and Stetsons. "Alex says I should get my brothers-in-law to dance with me. Who's first?"

Dick blushed a little and nudged him with an elbow. "She said brothers-in-law."

"I heard what she said." He rolled his eyes, but he was pleased. "You'd better dance with the kid first, I'm likely to maim you."

"You're going to dance with me before it's over though,

right? Alex already did. Momma's got him now." She grabbed Dick's hand and dragged him out.

Lucky Momma.

Not that he had anyone but himself to blame for not dancing with Rig. Maybe after everyone was gone, he'd waltz his cowboy around the front room.

He grinned as he saw Deuce make a beeline for him. "Aunt Julie's looking to get everyone out on the dance floor," Robert warned him.

He chuckled and nodded. "So I noticed. She catch you yet?"

"Uh-huh. Ma-maw, too." Robert leaned forward, looking a little panicked. "And the two ladies? The red-head and the blonde? They keep looking at me."

"You'd better get used to it, kid -- you're a fine looking boy and put you in the uniform." He shook his head. "They're going to be lined up around the block for you."

"And, uh... If that's not what I want lined up for me?"

"Then you give each one a dance and leave it at that. You've heard of don't ask don't tell. They make a good cover."

"That's not like lying to 'em?" Robert sat down next to him, eyes on the dance floor.

"Well, that depends. If you let them think they've got a chance, yeah, I'd say it was. But if you tell them you just want to be friends? How's that lying?"

He nodded to the two gals who were still giving Deuce the eye. "Those ladies adore your Uncle Alex even though they always knew they never stood a chance with him. They still wanted to be friends with him because of who he was; you be yourself and you'll find the same thing."

"Uncle Jimmy... Everybody loves Uncle Alex. He's... I don't know. Ma-maw says he's so busy living that people can't help but want that, too."

"So now you know who to model yourself after." He gave the kid a wink.

Robert rolled his eyes. "Yeah. I sorta figured who I wanted to be like a long time ago."

"That puts you ahead of a lot of us, kid." He clapped Robert on the back. He really liked the kid, who was a lot more like his Ma-maw and Uncle Alex than he gave himself credit for. That was okay though, the marines would help the boy learn how to stand up and be proud.

"Well, well, well... Look at you, South. All grown up and civilian." The rough voice sounded from his shoulder and he looked up into the weathered and leathered face of an old, old friend.

He got up and smiled at the man, going in for a quick, rough, manly hug. "Sarge. Thanks for coming."

"Wouldn't miss it. Knew there'd be good beer." The man settled down in a chair, bones popping and cracking. "There is good beer isn't there?"

"Of course there is. Robert, this is Sergeant Watson. Go get him a beer -- and tell the bartender you want the stuff from the cooler under the table."

"Yes, sir." Robert stood and shook Sarge's hand. "Pleased to meet you, Sergeant Watson. I'll be right back."

"Nice kid. He family?" Sarge grinned over. "You got him to sign up yet?"

"Nephew. And he starts basic in August." He chuckled. "Kid nearly didn't make the height requirement. Can you believe you can get *too* tall?"

"Too hard to fit 'em in the dress blues." Sarge chuckled as Maddie wandered up and crawled into her Uncle Jimmy's lap without asking, cuddling in with a tired little sigh. "Why you're positively domestic, South. This another one of yours?"

He almost blushed, Sarge bringing him back to a time when he was a lot younger, a lot less sure of himself. "Niece. Julie's got five girls. Five."

"And Julie is?" Those pale eyes were twinkling, laughing.

He was about to start squirming. "Sister-in-law."

"Oh? So, which one is yours? Come on, boy. Point him out."

"You see the blond cowboy leading that line dance? Just graduated as a physician's assistant today." He couldn't have held back his proud smile if he'd wanted to and he sure as hell didn't want to.

Sarge looked Rig over, checked him out. "Fine looking man, there... Bit skinny, though. Not a marine. Not like that one."

He almost choked on his beer when Sarge nodded toward Dick. The man still had a fine radar.

"Funny you should mention him..." He grinned and took a swig of his beer.

"Oh, no... You old dog!" Sarge's eyes went wide. "Your cowboy lets you play the field?"

"We used to play it together -- extend the hand that was extended to me, yeah?" He gave Sarge a nod. "But Dick was the last marine I mentored."

Sarge gave him a long look. "You mean you three are committed? How long you been together?"

"Eleven for me an' Rig, five for the three of us." Rock shrugged. "It just... it's how it works for us."

"Damn. Congratulations, South. Not many men find one person to spend a life with, much less two." Sarge nodded and took the beer Robert brought. "Thank you, son. Your cowboy okay? Made it through the bad shit?"

"You tell me," he said, nodding out at Rig. It made him smile, to see that happy look on his Rabbit's face.

Sarge nodded. "He's sure in his element out there."

"He loves life. Would you like to meet him?" It was the least he could do for all Sarge had done for him.

"I would." Sarge nodded and finished his beer. "I need to see what kind of man could hold your interest for so long."

"Deuce, go get your Uncle Alex. Tell him there's someone I want him to meet."

He waited until Robert was out of earshot before leaning close. "Thank you, Sarge. For solving that little problem for me."

"Sometimes a cancer needs cutting out and sometimes a man needs an uninterested party to do the cutting." Sarge's eyes were icy and sure.

He nodded. "You got that right."

"Does your man know?"

"No." The word was short, clipped.

"I see." Sarge said only that much before a laughing, sweating cowboy with shining eyes was deposited in front of him.

"Oh, she's plumb tuckered out." Rig grinned and stroked Maddie's cheek, the girl sound asleep in his arms. "You having fun, Rocketman. Want me to take Maddie upstairs? The twins are already up there sleeping."

He looked down at his lap. Damn, he was turning domestic. He'd forgotten she was there.

"Actually I wanted you to meet someone. Rig, this here is Sergeant Watson. Sarge, Doctor Alexander Roberts."

"Hi there. It's nice to..." Rig tilted his head. "You're Sarge. Rock's Sarge. Well, I'll be! I'm so glad you could come!" Sarge got one of those blinding smiles and a firm handshake. "Very, very good to meet you, sir."

He couldn't help but puff up. His Rig might not be classically handsome or built, but Rig could charm anyone, anytime, anywhere.

Sarge smiled back, eyes twinkling. "I take it you're South's man?"

"Yes, sir. I am." Rig nodded. "I've heard tales about you, sir. It's a pleasure."

"All untrue, I promise." Rock shifted Maddie. The last thing he needed was these two comparing notes.

Salvation came in the form of Dick, the kid coming over with a wide grin, just slightly tipsy and out of breath. "Julie's gonna dance everyone off the floor. It's chasing all those girls around all the time, isn't it?"

Chuckling, he put his arm around Dick's shoulders. "Perfect timing, kid, I wanted to introduce you to an old friend. This is Sergeant Watson. Sarge, Dick Main."

Dick held out his hand. "Hi."

Sarge took Dick's hand, shook it hard. "Hey there, son. You got to watch those women, 'cause damn, they'll run a man ragged."

Dick laughed. "Yes, sir, they sure will. It's nice to meet you."

Rig chuckled. "This is Rock's NCO from way back when. Back when he was as cherry as you used to be."

"Oh, cool! Hi. Nice to meet you."

Rig leaned down and took Maddie. "I'm going to give her to her momma. I'll be right back."

"Thanks, Rig."

"That'll slow her down," Dick opined. "You guys want refills?" Rock handed his empty over to the kid.

Sarge shook his head. "One's enough for now. We old guys have to take it slow. So, South, tell me. Where are you headed now?"

"Would you believe California?" He chuckled. "Can you see this old jarhead in with all those hippies?"

"Oh, good Lord. You going to grow hair down to your ass and start smoking dope?" Sarge gave him a look, one that sent him back twenty years.

"No, sir. Not a chance." He forced himself to relax, chuckling. "Actually, we've bought a nice little place on the beach south of San Francisco. Rig's already got a job with a clinic and the kid and I are going to open a gym."

"A gym?" Sarge nodded. "Sounds like you. Sounds like solid work."

"Yeah. And from what I'm told, you don't have to hide down there, you know. I think I'm about ready to stop worrying someone's gonna find out what I do in my bedroom."

"South, I imagine out there? You're gonna have more troubles with people thinking you got too much in your bedroom."

"Well, that's just too fucking bad for them," he growled.

Sarge chuckled, shook his head. "Oh, boy... You got it bad."

"You've seen them -- you blame me?"

One steel eyebrow rose. "No. No, South, I can't say I can."

"What about you, Sarge? You gonna stay on here the rest of your days?"

"I'm thinking about Florida, honestly." Sarge grinned, the look a little sly. "Jack and me have been thinking on it."

One of his eyebrows went up. "Jack? And you called me an old dog."

The old man actually pinked. "You hush."

Oh, he didn't think so. Not now that he was off the hot seat. "You bring him along?" He made a show of looking around.

"He's at the main bar. He didn't want to intrude on a private party." Oh, man. Sarge was blushing.

"Oh, now, I showed you mine, you better show me yours."

"You saw mine years and years ago, South. It's older and greyer now."

He laughed and nudged Sarge. "So you're saying you're an old man now."

"Yep. But I still got what it took to make you ask for it, and don't you forget it." Sarge winked and waggled his eyebrows.

He laughed. "I'll just bet you do."

"Here's your beer, Rock. And this is Jack, apparently he came with Sarge." The kid gave him a shit-eating grin.

Sarge looked... well, the man looked pleased and stood, giving Jack his chair. "Jack, this here's Jim South. He's one of my old boys."

Jack had a bright smile, dark hair shot through with silver, crinkles around blue eyes. "Nice to meet you, Jim."

"You, too. I didn't know there was a man alive who could

convince the Sarge to settle down, you must be something special." And he must have had too many beers, getting all sentimental.

Sarge laid one hand on Jack's shoulder, eyes sharp. "He's something else."

Rock could hear the "and all mine" in the air.

"You having a good time? We can make sure you're having a good time." Rock winked, some devil riding him to tease Sarge.

Sarge rumbled, hands sliding over Jack's shoulders. "Watch it, marine, before I have you in the front leaning rest position."

"I'm a civilian now, Sarge -- the only one who gives me orders is the mother-in-law. Besides," and he winked again, "mine are better looking."

Sarge snorted and Dick chuckled, Rig's warmth coming to rest near his back. "You going to dance with Momma, Rocketman? She's waiting on you."

He chuckled, leaning back into Rig. "Yeah, I'll go dance with Momma. I'll do my best not to step on her feet." He leaned over and shook Jack's hand and Sarge's. "Thanks for coming."

"I wouldn't have missed it." Sarge pressed something into his hand -- a single grenade pin, bent and blackened. "For surviving."

He clapped the man, pulling him in for a quick, hard hug. "You take care."

"I always do. You keep in touch."

He nodded. "Yes, sir. Now, I'd better be going to find my dance partner before she comes to find me."

He gave one last nod to Sarge and his man, pocketed the pin and went to find Momma.

Chapter Forty Six

"Uncle Alex?"

He blinked over at Robert, breathing in his coffee. "Yeah?"

"How do you tell if another guy is gay?"

"Huh?" He blinked, shook his head. It was too fucking early and he was too fucking hung-over to try and field that question. "You walk in on them fucking another guy?"

"Uncle Alex!"

"Yeah. Sorry. Uh..." He rubbed his forehead. "You're better off asking your Uncle Jimmy, Deuce. The man has dead-on radar. Me? I sort of just wait until they come onto me. I? Am never mistaken as straight."

"Why not?"

"Fuck if I know." He shrugged, stirred his coffee. "Ask Rock. He never once questioned. Just knew, right off."

"Ask me what?" growled Rock, staggering in, wincing. "Do we need all the fucking lights on?"

"Turn the overheads off, Deuce." Rig stood and poured Rock a cup of coffee and handed it over with two Excedrin and a B-12. "Deuce wanted to know how you knew I was queer."

One of Rock's eyebrows went up, his Blue going to sit at the table. "I just knew." Rock shrugged. "It's in the eyes."

"Well, that doesn't help, Uncle Jimmy. Uncle Alex's eyes look just like Aunt Julie's, and she's not gay."

Rig hid his grin and held up a loaf of bread, offering his Blue something to settle his stomach.

"No they aren't just the same -- trust me, she doesn't look at me like he does." Rock nodded at him and his toast. He smiled over at Rock and nodded back, putting a couple of pieces in and grabbing the butter and jelly. Julie looked at Rock like he did and he'd kick her blue-jeaned butt.

When he turned back around, he found Deuce staring at him. "What?"

"Well, I'm trying to figure out what Rock's seeing." Deuce

looked so damned sincere.

Rock made a sound, those blue eyes twinkling at him. Rock cleared his throat twice and drank half his coffee before giving Robert a break. "Look. It's just something you have or you don't. An… instinct. You trust it and it gets sharp. At the party last night -- did you peg Sarge as playing for our team before he introduced his partner?"

"I... Yeah, kinda. I mean, he seemed cool with Uncle Alex and stuff." Deuce shrugged. "I mean, I... Well, there's a guy back home and... Well, you know. But I don't know and I don't know how to know."

"He ever date girls?"

"No. His best friend's a girl, though. She likes him." Christ, Rig was so glad he wasn't a teenager anymore.

Rock rubbed his hand over his face. "It's too fucking early for this shit."

"Let Rock be now, Deuce. He's not a morning person. Go pack your suitcases and shit." It was a dismissal, clear as anything, but they'd be leaving this afternoon. He'd have Rock until the end of time grumping. After the kid fled, Rig brought Rock his toast. "Sorry, Blue."

"Were we ever that fucking young, Rig?"

"Nope. Not a chance." He ran his hand over Rock's head and bent for a kiss, slowly rubbing Rock's temples.

Rock growled softly, eyes closing, leaning into him. "Kid knows how to use his fists, right?"

"You know it." He straddled Rock's lap, massaging gently, just enjoying his Blue. "He'll make it. You did. Dick did."

Beautiful fucking man.

Rock nodded. "Someone'll find him. Teach him the ropes."

"Yeah. He'll be too busy at first too worry about it. Basic's hell on a man." He kissed Rock's forehead, humming at the warmth. Rock's hands came up and slid along his back, warm and solid. "Mmm... you feel good, Rocketman. Good down deep in my bones."

Rock growled softly for him, nuzzling their faces together. He touched and massaged until all the stress lines and frowns were gone, just enjoying his Blue.

There was a groan from the doorway. "You know, I was pretty sure I wasn't that drunk. What was in that special beer of yours, Rock?"

He grinned and took one more kiss before getting up and getting Dick the vitamin/caffeine/aspirin cocktail. "Toast?"

"Um... I'm not sure it'll stay down." Dick sat next to Rock. "Where is everyone? I haven't missed the goodbyes, have I?"

Rig added a big glass of water to the stuff in front of Dick. "Momma's in the bathtub and Deuce has been sent to pack."

One of Dick's eyebrow's went up in a move he'd learned from Rock. "Sent to pack?"

"Uh-huh. He wanted to know how to tell if someone was gay. Rock wasn't in the mood and my gaydar is whacked, you know that."

Dick started laughing and then groaned. "Oh, fuck -- ow! Don't make me laugh."

"Take your pills and drink your water, Pretty." He stood behind Dick, started rubbing the kid's shoulders.

"Yes, Doc." Dick looked back up at him with a half grin and then dutifully took the pills, washing them down with the water. "He needs a Rock of his own."

"He can't have mine. He's retired."

"Ours," Dick corrected softly, smiling up at him again.

Rock snorted. "You've both got it wrong -- you're mine."

He leaned down and kissed Dick. "You're both mine. My men. Mine. Mine. Mine."

"But are you sure about that, Rig?" Rock teased.

"Yep." He chuckled, kissing Dick's nose. "Sure as shit."

Dick reached a hand up around his neck, pulling him down for a real kiss. Oh. Yes. He moaned, lips parting easily. Dick fed his moan back to him, tongue sliding through his mouth.

He scooted around, taking his place on Dick's lap. He could get used to this, straddling both his men's thighs every morning for breakfast kisses. Dick's arms wrapped around him, holding him close as the kiss continued. A soft, happy purr came from Rock.

Oh, hell, yes. He could more than get used to this.

"Uncle Alex, did you see -- oh!"

He sat up, blinking over, knowing his cheeks were hot, but fucking refusing to act like he'd been doing something wrong. This was his goddamned house. "Did... did I see what?"

Robert was blushing hard. "I didn't mean to interrupt, I just... I was looking for my dress shoes."

"Oh, they're up on the washing machine. Lucy likes shoes. A

lot." God, he didn't know what to do.

Rock got up and went to Deuce. "We'll go find your shoes and I'll see if I can wake up your gaydar."

The kid blushed darker. "Yeah. Okay. Right."

Rig chuckled and grinned at Dick. "Gonna take some getting used to, this out of the closet thing."

"Yeah? I think it's going to be nice." Dick grinned, but let him go. "I don't think I want to get caught necking by your Momma, though."

"Chicken." Rig stood, stuck out his tongue and winked. "You want that toast now?"

"You telling me you want to keep kissing here until she comes in?" Dick waggled his tongue back. "Yes, please on the toast."

"Raspberry jam? Peanut butter?" He wiggled his butt as he went to the toaster.

"You?" He could feel those eyes on his ass.

"On toast?" He shimmied again, because he could.

"Any way I can get you," Dick murmured.

"Oh." He grinned, blushing dark, pleased clear on through. They were still flirting with each other when Rock and Robert came back, Momma with them.

"Lead him astray?" Rock was saying. "Now would I do that?"

"Lead who astray?" Rig grabbed Momma a mug. "Mornin', Momma."

"Robert." Rock gave him a grin, his Blue obviously in a better mood.

Rig chuckled. "Rock's all about the straight and narrow, Momma."

Momma snorted. "Don't bullshit me, son. Jim's lots of stuff, but straight's not one of them."

Poor Dick started choking on his toast and Rock pounded Dick on his back. "You're supposed to eat it, not breathe it in, kid."

Then Rock winked at Momma. "I'm not narrow either."

Rig snorted and Momma gave Rock a raised eyebrow and a quirky smile. "Well, well. I knew Alexander was a lucky man..."

That did it and they all dissolved, laughing hard enough that his belly hurt. Dick and Robert both looked a little red around the ears and a little shocked, but they were laughing along.

"Robert won't have time to go astray, Momma. Being a marine's damn hard work, especially the first few months."

Dick nodded in agreement with Rock. "I can remember not caring about anything but sleep for the longest time."

Robert nodded. "I'll manage. I will. I've been training hard."

Rig grinned. "You'll be fine, Deuce. You'll have to write us, let us know how you're doing."

Dick smiled. "It feels weird. Us being done with that, out of it and giving you advice. I've been the kid for so long..."

Momma chuckled. "You're not long in the tooth, yet, Richard. Though you've thrown your lot in with some good 'uns, so you should be fine."

Not just good ones -- the best." Dick smiled at him softly and then looked over at Rock. His Blue rolled his eyes and made a half-snorting noise, but you could tell he was pleased. "Not that I'm biased or anything," Dick added with a wink.

"Of course not." Rig handed Momma her coffee. "You going to have Sissy pick y'all up or you want us to take y'all to the airport this afternoon?"

"Julia will pick us up. Y'all have to get to packing and airports are evil." Momma nodded. "We'll all have lunch together, yeah?"

"Yep, one last hootenanny before y'all go," Rock drawled.

"Bitch." Rig winked over. "Be good or I'll tell Julie you want a cowboy hat for Christmas."

"Just make sure she gets it in your size."

"I wouldn't mind a cowboy hat," Dick noted.

"Just don't go getting any ideas about regrowing that little caterpillar fuzz under the nose so many cowboys seem to like," growled Rock, looking right at him and not Dick.

He arched an eyebrow. "I don't know... there's something sexy about a mustache on a man..."

Momma snorted. "Your daddy hated them. Said they were a sign of laziness."

"Good thing you shave yours then, Momma." He stuck out his tongue and ducked her swat. Dick's jaw was about on the floor, Rock wheezing he was laughing so hard. He leaned down and hugged Momma hard, brushing her cheek with his barely-there morning stubble. "You remember how proud I was to get facial hair?"

She patted his hand, chuckling softly. "I remember a lot of

peach fuzz."

If Rock kept chortling like that he was going to hurt something.

"Peach fuzz! Momma! You're killing my macho reputation here!"

Deuce chuckled. "Uh... Uncle Alex?"

"Shut up, boy."

"Yes, sir."

Dick had to thump Rock on the back.

"I think you're a stud," Dick said softly. "Both of you are."

He stuck his tongue out at Rock. "You hear that? He thinks I'm a stud."

"He's got most of the letters right." Rock winked at him.

Momma chuckled, shook her head. "This is one of those things I don't want to know, right son?"

He nodded. "Right, Momma."

Rock chuckled and Dick went pink again. There was a lightness in today's banter, an openness that was slowly beginning to flavor everything. He met Rock's eyes, smiling, easy in his skin.

"Y'all look happy. Makes me proud." Momma nodded, patted his hand. "Makes it right."

"Thank you, Momma," Dick said quietly.

Rock grunted, nodded.

He hugged her tight. "I'm so glad you came, Momma. The party was perfect."

"Yeah, we couldn't have done it without you," Rock told her.

Dick laughed. "Without Momma it would have been beer and chips at the pool hall."

"Maybe not even chips..." Rig chuckled and winked at Momma.

"Oh, I'd have made sure there was chips, Rig."

"And I'd have given the kid enough money for dip."

Momma's laugh filled the kitchen. "Oh! Oh, good lord and butter I do love you boys!"

"Of course you do -- what's not to love?"

Dick chuckled at Rock. "Still nothing wrong with that ego."

"No. It would take more than retirement to screw with that." Rig shook his head. "It would take... nuclear-type explosions."

"Well, we're all agreed I'm a stud and everyone loves me."

"Yes, Rock. You're a stud and everyone loves you. Go take

your shower so you can be ready for lunch." Rig gathered up the cups and turned off the coffeepot. "We'll have to stop and buy some packing boxes on our way home." He stopped short, realizing he was already acting like Momma was gone. "Sorry, Momma. I'm just..."

She grinned at him. "Living your life? I noticed."

Rig grinned. "Yeah. Yeah. Just living my life."

"It's a good life, Rabbit," Rock said softly, kissing him on the top of his head before heading down the hall.

He nodded. Yeah. Yeah. It was a good life. Dick grabbed a piece of paper and a pen and they worked on a list of things they needed, Momma chiming in now and again to help.

Chapter Forty Seven

He moved the last of the book boxes into the back of the garage, setting things up for the marin... for his men to start loading when they got back with the U-Haul, then went to unplug the washing machine.

They were going to California.

Really.

They'd closed on the house last week, his place at the clinic was waiting. The sweet young couple who bought this house were ready to move in on Monday. Rig shook his head. They were going. Really. Rock and Dick were getting the truck and they were leaving. He thought he might just be sick.

By the time the guys pulled into the driveway, though, he'd managed to cover his nerves with energy and had moved the washer and dryer and recliner out and was struggling to move the couch out the front door.

"You take one more step and I'll break your back myself."

Dick chuckled as Rock came up the stairs, glaring at him. "You let me and Dick take the heavy stuff."

"Neanderthal! I'm managing just fine. I got the fridge as far as the front room before I got stuck."

"The fridge!" Rock looked like he was going to have apoplexy and Dick's chuckles turned to laughter.

His Pretty came up and gave him a kiss. "Just let Rock do his macho shit thing, Rig, and we'll all make it through this move happier."

"But..." Rig opened up his mouth, then shut it again. "Yeah. Sorry. Got a little wigged out while y'all were gone."

Dick gave him another kiss and whispered in his ear. "Why do you think Rock needs to be the macho jerk of us?"

"Natural inclination?" He grinned, nestled close for a second. "You okay, Pretty? Happy?"

"A bit jittery. Just want to get going, you know?"

"You two gonna keep nattering like old women or are we

gonna get moving?"

Dick grinned and winked, taking another quick kiss before hoisting one end of the couch. Rig shook his head and grabbed a coffee table, following behind. "Are we leaving tonight, Rock? Or spending one more night here?"

"This is your show, Rig. You tell us."

"My show? Oh, no, jackass. This is our show." Rig put the table on the ground and headed in for the other one.

Rock followed him, with Dick bringing up the rear. "Fine, it's our show -- but you're running it. You want to stay another night, we'll stay. You want to go, we'll go."

"I..." He looked around at Rock and shrugged. "Part of me wants to stay one more night, part of me wants to just go, get this behind us. We've been here a long time, you know?"

"Yeah," said Rock. "We have."

Dick looked around and then nodded. "How about we pack everything but the bed, have one more for the road and then head out and get started with our new life?"

"Yeah. I like that. One more for the road." He grinned. "We hurry, we can pack, fuck and then spend the night in a hotel and mess up perfectly clean sheets."

Rock nodded. "A reason to get the truck packed up quick. I like it."

Dick grinned. "All right. Let's get to work."

They worked together well, barring the minor altercations over him digging up the rosebushes on the side of the house, whether they were going to tow one of the trucks or the jeep, where the maps got hid, and where the dogs were going to ride.

Finally their lives were packed away, barring three suitcases, the mattress and the pups.

"Wow."

"This is the only place I've been that ever felt like home," Dick said quietly, looking around the barren living room.

"Home is where you hang up your hat, kid." Rock winked and leered, making it quite clear he wasn't actually talking about hats.

Rig grinned at his Blue. Man had his priorities right. "Come on, y'all. Let's get showered and get off and get gone."

"Off, showered, then gone," grumbled Rock. "I like the way you both smell when you've been working."

Rig's prick went from semi-awake to ready in a single

fucking heartbeat and he reached for Rock's wife-beater, needing skin. "Yeah. Now."

Dick was right there, helping him get everyone naked and Rock hustled them into the bedroom. They went down on the mattress in a heap, hands and mouths all reaching and tasting, a little desperate, a little worried, a lot excited. He wound up with Rock's prick in his mouth and Rock's mouth around his own cock, the kid's fingers buried in his ass as Dick licked at his neck.

Rig pulled hard, needing the taste and smell of his men inside him, all around him, easing his nerves. Rock groaned around his prick, hips filling his mouth. Dick continued to nuzzle his neck as the long fingers slid away to be replaced the head of Dick's sweet cock.

He cried out and shifted, shuddered, taking both cocks down to the root. One groan vibrated around his cock, the other one along his neck. Dick drove their rhythm, pushing into him slow and deep, over and over. He floated and rocked, fucking lost in the sensations and tastes and smells. Made for them. Fucking made for this.

Dick came first, pushing hard against his ass, his cry echoing strangely in the near empty room. Rig pulled Rock in tight, sobbing as his pushed into the tight heat, swallowing around the head of that fat cock. Rock roared around his cock, pushing deep and coming down his throat, even as Dick continued to push gently into him, nudging his gland. He drank Rock down, his own balls shooting, electricity filling him.

They lay curled around each other, catching their breath. Dick's hand slid over his side, touched Rock and then settled.

"It's been a good home," Dick murmured softly, kissing his neck again.

"It's been a hell of a beginning, Pretty." Rig grinned, kissed Rock's balls. "It's time to start us all off on the same foot. Come on, Rock, Dick. Let's go shower and get Grim and Lucy. It's time to go home."

end

Breinigsville, PA USA
31 May 2010
238970BV00001B/111/A

9 781933 389424